ZER⊗SCAPE

ZEROSCAPE

Dear Forrest,
Hope you enjoy this
flight of fancy —
Thanks for everything!

MICHAEL T. GAMBLE

M. Gamble
Jany 2011

aka Micky G.

MTG
PUBLISHING
Santa Fe, New Mexico

This book is a work of fiction. Names, characters, places, and incidents either are products of the author's imagination or are used fictitiously. Any resemblance to actual events or persons, living or dead, is entirely coincidental.

Visit our website at www.zeroscape-thebook.com

Manufactured in the United States of America
First Edition: November 2010

10 9 8 7 6 5 4 3 2 1

Library of Congress Control Number: 2010916783
ISBN 978-0-578-07267-8

Book design by 1106Design, LLC

To my loving wife Chérie

ACKNOWLEDGEMENTS

The author is deeply indebted and grateful to many colleagues and friends who provided both professional and moral support during the development of this book. Our candid conversations, often regarding sensitive topics, were invaluable. You are all so dear to me. And you know who you are.

PART A
Mentorship

Mentor: Someone whose hindsight can become your foresight.

—A<small>NONYMOUS</small>

CHAPTER 1

THE MAN crouched low against the wall, his eyes adjusting to near darkness. Harbor lights winked in the distance. But only the dull, fog-induced halo of a street lamp, two floors below, illuminated the clutter. The room seemed a life-size jigsaw puzzle, now silent. The Powell Street cable cars no longer clanked by. They had retired for the evening, along with their riders: hordes of tourists and locals, such as Dr. Yamamoto, a resident and laser physics researcher at Sandia National Lab, who lay sleeping two meters away. The gentle, yet deadly arc of his *katana* shone by the bedside. A sword at hand, probably razor sharp, was not surprising for a *Kendo* Master. He identified with his ancestors' warrior past and practiced their Samurai discipline and rituals. It hadn't taken much investigation to recognize that Dr. Yamamoto was a man, who rather than forsake *bushido* and live without honor, would prefer to die honorably. So be it—

Unlikely dwelling for an eminent scientist, he thought, detecting the odor of moldy clapboard about 100 years old. Cardboard boxes stacked in the corners and against the walls. The man understood that Yamamoto was packed and ready to go. Even so, this house was not at all like those of some of the prima donna researchers at the Los Alamos National Lab in New Mexico. Their lust for splendid homes and performance cars made them easy prey for an enterprise offering handsome overtime pay. And the addiction to sex and expensive drugs, the foibles of the *Feynman friends* and their soon-to-be newest recruit, just made it that much easier.

A half-open window admitted the night's chill and the scent of salt air. The man accessed the front pocket of his black vest and slid his gloved hand into an oversize, prophylactic-thin latex glove. He carefully withdrew from a plastic baggie a lubricated swab, which he extended toward the window's decaying side jamb, swiping quickly down its length. Likewise, he greased the opposing jamb. Stashing the outer glove and swab, he exhaled softly and focused before grasping the lower sash, pulling it downward. A nearly indiscernible groan . . . and the sash descended quietly. The seal, snug. Crisp sea air continued to shroud the small space, helping him to regulate his respiration and heartbeat, and to minimize the coming rush. A pregnant moment. He reflected on the Academy. *Bushido*, even use of the word, was forbidden. It was considered a dangerous impediment to the accomplishment of critical missions. He eyed the sleeping man—*Too bad it had to be this way. You might have been a worthy adversary*— Dr. Yamamoto lay perfectly still. The man's intention was to perpetuate that . . . lengthily . . . eternally.

The man cut his gaze to a nearby wall heater, and bent low. Canary-yellow, ribbed flex piping disappeared under its rusty lower margin where it mated with the gas regulator. No wrench required. Only an instant of concentration and torque, applied by fingers gloved in nubby leather. The fitting broke free, emitting a hushed shhhh. His adrenaline spiked just hearing it. One whiff of the mercaptan additive and perspiration developed on his palms and upper lip. He licked away a salty drop, lest his DNA betray him. His pulse beat forcefully in his temples as he took an instant to focus on the faint hiss, the deadly hiss.

One last glance at the bed. Yamamoto seemed to sleep so placidly; as if he embraced his death. The man turned toward the door. He took one small, silent step. What was that? A rustle? The room went black. And then came the pain. A coat? A blanket? He was enveloped in a confining cloth, fighting his way out and experiencing the trauma of the initial assault on his stomach. And then the blows to his arms. They ached the most, before the near-crippling thrust to the thigh.

The man marshaled his mental and physical resources. He leapt into the air, completing an aerial cartwheel and dispelling the bathrobe. He landed upright with his feet shoulder-width apart; arms akimbo. Quickly he shifted weight to his out-turned back foot and raised the forward foot slightly. His hands at chest level, nearly limp, awaited the instant for a fatal strike.

Yamamoto registered the faintest expression, seeing *neko ashi dachi*, the cat stance, used against him. He grunted and assumed a classic Samurai battle stance, *jodan no kamae*. His feet were well apart and turned outward; knees flexed; his elbows spread wide and his hands high above his head; the sword, transverse. The man understood that foreplay was finished and the mercy of *bushido* past. Dr. Yamamoto perceived him an adversary worthy of execution.

A circular dance ensued. Lethal tango on the scuffed oak floor. The man was rapt; Yamamoto, too. Each awaited an infinitesimal lapse, a single neurological misfire, defining the opportunity to kill. The man's shoe caught the protruding edge of a box. Yamamoto seized the instant. His *katana* cleaved the palpable salt air, seeking the man's skull. He ducked. The pole of a floor lamp was sheared clean. The glint from the blade striking metal sent a shiver up the man's spine. He could almost hear the shhhh of gas. The room would soon be a bomb. He must accomplish his objective and escape.

When the man refocused on his adversary, it was too late. Yamamoto's *kiai* was paralyzingly shrill. A harrowing scream accompanied by firing his sword toward the man's abdomen. Near its blood-rich target—and just shy of deadly penetration—the man's outstretched arm swept upward deflecting the blade into a cardboard box.

His slashed forearm burned like a firebrand as the man began the onslaught on Yamamoto. Abdominal knee thrusts, moving upward toward the chest, rendering him double. Repeated shocks of bone and muscle culminating in the violent cracking release of Yamamoto's left shoulder, which swung freely from his torso in a grisly arc. With his right hand, Yamamoto made a swipe at the sword's hilt. But before his fingers closed, the man yanked the blade from the box, gashing Yamamoto's hand and sounding an ominous ring. The blade continued to resonate until the man drove it deep into Yamamoto's belly. Buried to its *tsuba*, the sword's tip exited his back, marred by gore and sinew. He heaved

Yamamoto toward the heater. As Yamamoto slumped against its rusty grill, his contorted facial expression seemed to question why.

The man grabbed a shirt from a nearby chair, which he managed to wrap as a stricture against his dripping DNA. He exited the bedroom door and darted across the living room to the unsecured window. Outside, standing on a corroded platform, he cleared his head and produced plan beta. It appeared to be a small plastic cigarette lighter topped by a little digital clock, set to 30 seconds. He released a latch. The clock read 29 when he tossed it toward the open bedroom door.

A rapid, almost cat-like descent of the pockmarked fire escape to the ground. The man did not slow, but moved briskly through brackish fog down the seedy alley. He ignored the sear of his wound, the ache of cold, penetrating his battered joints, as well as the hale of glass shards at the explosion's concussion. Although he could not feel the heat of the inferno, he basked in the warmth of success. When the time came to eliminate Yamamoto's replacement—the New England renegade—it would be an easier job. And potentially, a greater pleasure.

CHAPTER 2

RICK ADAMS stole a last glimpse of the distant Sangre de Cristo Mountain Range. Beneath cotton-candy clouds, snow-covered summits towered. The Truchas Peaks, as he had recently learned, stood majestically in excess of 13k feet. Big *trout*, he mused, recognizing afresh that Boston and his running route across the old Longfellow Bridge down along the Charles River were a world away.

"Hey, you coming?"

A change of focus—distance to foreground—to watch Fred Larson add another ten meters to his lead. Fred's waffle-soled running shoes kicked up tiny dust devils on the canyon floor's unpaved vehicle access route. "With a vengeance," Rick murmured. He launched down the trail traversing the technical area 38 mesa, just behind his new office at the Los Alamos National Laboratory. "I'm with you," he said, pulling alongside his new friend and mentor. Rick pushed himself to gain a nose.

"So my point is, don't use your badge as ID in town," Fred said, continuing his security lecture and effortlessly regaining the lead. "Keep it in your vehicle's glove box."

"Gotcha," Rick replied, thinking this man must have hidden gills, because he sure didn't seem to need to breathe. "And don't use ye trusty olde badge as an ice scraper," Rick gulped an extra mouthful of air before adding, "although the security catechist said in the bad old days he used his on his truck's windshield every icy morning."

Gaining a few more feet, Fred said, "And the new buzz phrase is *Zero Tolerance Security*." He glanced back at Rick from over his shoulder. "Was the only way the NNSA watchdogs let us get back to work, after the last security fiasco."

Rick slowed and snuck an extra deep breath. Good ol' ZTS he thought, squinting down at the badges clapping together against his chest. Standard issue stuff: photo badge, radiation dosimeter, personnel safety contact list. They hung, suspended on a thin plastic cord, around his neck—like a noose.

"Consider that if the small stuff is kept straight, a big slip-up might go unnoticed."

Rick mulled the possibility. Employed at the Lab for less than a week, he really needed mentorship. But even more vital at the moment, he needed an oxygen tank, preferably tracking him on a motorized cart.

"Pretty quiet over there," Fred observed, "excepting your locomotive breath."

"Ah, a Tull fan. I thought Mozart was more your style."

"Jenna helped round off my rough edges."

Rick liked edgy. Practiced it as high art in his personal and professional lives. Right now, all he wanted was to minimize his wheezing; get a decent breath of air. Could he be in for his first asthma attack in decades? The helplessness of nearly suffocating during athletics was something Rick knew well from childhood. Now the trail seemed to constrict him with each step. The canopy created over the path by towering pines obscured the sunlight. Ahead the route converged to a line. Razor thin. Black. His lungs spasmed. Rick refocused on the conversation, seducing himself subliminally. "Can we discuss you know which project out here in the wide-open spaces?"

"This isn't a TEMPEST-secure area."

Rick eyed tall, dry yellow grass and the late-blooming spring flowers mottling the landscape. For sure the route wasn't encased in three-foot-thick concrete. "The Lab owns land for miles in every direction, right?"

"We're on the periphery of Indian land." Fred spoke so easily he might have been lounging poolside. "There's elk, deer, mountain blue birds. Don't see that stuff here."

"There an electric fence? Surveillance gear?"

"No, but there're good reasons to stay off their land." Fred hardly hesitated getting back on message. "We're talking about interceptable communications."

Today, information control; tomorrow, mind control, Rick thought. "Maybe we could carry a copper cage. And discuss top secret details . . . like the project's name."

"A cage wouldn't inhibit audible emissions. And there's electromagnetics. TEMPEST-secure areas have their RFI, EMI, and even optical emissions controlled."

"The shutters over my office windows I can handle," Rick said. "Guards with automatic weapons in towers by the cafeteria, that's a bit much."

"You mean the CMR building. You'll probably do some research there."

Rick rolled his eyes, continuing to lumber down the trail. He clutched the appendages hung about his neck and said, "They're drivin' me nuts."

"Think ZTS: One strike and you're out."

The run was getting long for Rick. Los Alamos's 7,500-foot elevation was wearing him down. Even a body as fit as his required a couple of weeks of acclimation. The searing sun, which scorched the periwinkle sky, radiated down onto the back of his neck. Rounding a bend, he spied a path lined by statuesque pines. A blanket of shadow spread on supple ground, a natural picnic. Rick swerved.

"There's nothing to see," Fred said. "That's Indian land."

Rick pushed ahead past a NO TRESPASSING sign, then slowed. Fred caught up and they panned for game. Leaves rustled just ahead.

They bent low. Continued forward more quickly, securing their jangling badges.

It was big. Rick's heart thumped. He moistened his lips in anticipation. The two men crept closer. Paces away now. Rick wondered: what if the damn thing got spooked and gored one of them? Him! Another step forward. Rick's foot hooked under a fallen branch. He stumbled, falling sideways into Fred, who tumbled. Both went down. Rick recovered first. Standing, he gazed in a frisson of disbelief. The vision, with its fiery eyes, hurled a stone, striking Rick on the chest, before disappearing.

They trudged upward from the canyon vehicle path toward the TA38 mesa. Rick said, "Look Fred, he was a foot taller than me and 50 pounds heavier. His head was as big as a . . . a basketball."

"And the bewitching eyes. I heard you, the first five times. Rick, you're over six feet and 180, at least. So there was a giant there and I couldn't see it—or him—at all?"

"Saw blood, didn't you?"

"Could be deer blood, rabbit blood," Fred said, exasperated. "There's no way we were that close and he just vanished. And we scouted the area afterwards; nothing."

"Something made size 18 footprints. And that rock barely missed my head."

"Rick, just stay off Indian—"

"What's with that land?" Rick stopped dead in his tracks.

"According to the Natives, there are powerful natural gods . . . Spirits."

"I'm listening."

"The Apache claim Spirits called Ga'an are angry at the Lab for polluting the Jemez Mountains, a sacred site for their ancestors. They believe one day the Ga'an will destroy the Lab."

Rick's head cocked, asking, "You believe that?"

"Of course not."

Later, in the locker room, Rick reflected on the incident. Could Fred be right? Had he really seen a giant Indian-like creature? Rick worked his shoulder joint, admiring the reddish bruise underneath his neck. And wiping his hand on his shorts, he thought, "Whatever it was, I've still got its blood on my fingers."

CHAPTER 3

Freshly showered, Rick walked the lackluster cinderblock corridor toward his office in Building Two. Indian Spirits destroying the Lab? Great, I just got here, he thought. But that was no Spirit. It had flesh. Pale as a ghost, but flesh. And it bled. Just like a man.

His weighty office door closed with a clunk, exciting a low frequency rumble that rippled through the small, dark room. It was kind of like closing a crypt. Solitary confinement, maybe. Flipping the light switch, Rick's eyes blinked rapidly at the assault of the fluorescent lighting's cold blue spectrum, which glinted in specular jabs off of the metal shutters cloaking the windows. His former office had overlooked MIT's lush campus. He could see Memorial Drive and the Charles River below. Sculling teams plied the smooth waters. He used to admire passing crews: taut, disciplined, inspiring.

His eyes adjusted quickly from the visual attack as Rick approached his desk and sat. The hum of power supplies feeding his computers comforted. His musician's fingers spread over a keyboard. No use. His thoughts returned to the lunchtime run. Not just the eerie apparition and its gory footprints, but what did it really mean? If it was an omen, he wasn't heeding it. This was his last shot, and he was taking it.

His eyes roved—tired cinderblock walls, vintage '60s brown floor tiles with grey flecks, and dingy strips of yellowed fabric, securing useless window shades. The requirement that the exterior metal louvers always be closed, obscuring the brilliant afternoon sun, was cruel if not unusual punishment. His heart panged for Cambridge. This, not Cambridge, is *home* now, Rick reminded himself.

Willing himself to his work, Rick examined the trio of large, expensive, plasma monitors confronting him. He nodded approvingly. The money goes here. Equipment and science, not aesthetics. He admired the separate screens with independent power sources as well as differing degrees of communications shielding and user authorization. One workstation was dedicated to classified computing and communications, another for those same activities that were unclassified. The third workstation was used for local analysis. Rick focused on his unclassified computing account until his concentration was interrupted by a rap on the door.

Glancing around to ensure that all of his classified materials were either stowed or covered, Rick called out, "Come in."

"Hey, man, how's it going?"

"Bruno, I wondered if I'd see you before the big meeting."

"Big, schmig. Routine safety meeting." Bruno scanned the space. "Well, uh, all your big-time secret documents are either in the safe or under that cloth, there on the work table. Annnnd lemeee seeee. Uh huh, you checking unclassified e-mail while my roaming eyeballs are nearby. Good boy."

Rick placed both hands around his neck, tightening the grip as his head tilted sideward. His tongue slipped to the corner of his mouth.

"You'll get used to it," Bruno said, squeezing Rick's sagging shoulder. "Gotta quickie with Arthur. Save me a seat." He added, "And don't forget dinner tonight. Mary's dying to see you."

Rick's mind wandered back to when he and Louie Brunello were best buddies at MIT. Because the topics of safety meetings were often drawn from Rick's unorthodox laboratory techniques and their sometimes unfortunate results, Rick seldom attended.

A half hour later, Rick was seated in the minimally-furnished conference room. The meeting was unclassified, yet the metal window shutters were closed tight. Harsh fluorescent light caromed off the chairs' steel frames, illuminating their too colorful molded plastic seats. The nearly psychedelic scene teemed with discussion, dissention. Rick seated himself among the scowling members of XP-12's scientific staff. Of the forty-something group members present, he'd been introduced to few. He took particular notice of a nearby colleague he'd met, a thin thermodynamicist whose slate-blue eyes jittered behind thick lenses. "You know it's impossible, macroscopically," the man said. "I demonstrated that using the Second Law. Bowman agreed with me. That's why he moved on."

His colleague replied, "But Boltzmann's equation supports non-equilibrium distributions of lasing gammas in gaseous media."

"Gammas lasing in a gaseous medium, indeed," the man said. "Sooner will New York City be powered by cold fusion in a Harlem bathtub than you'll get kill intensity from isolated pockets of lasing gammas."

Rick understood the thermodynamicist's comments as a not-so-subtle denunciation of the Laboratory's biggest program since the Manhattan Project, a super-powerful gamma ray laser, code name: GRIT.

Bruno sauntered in and plunked down next to Rick. "These guys are out for blood," Rick whispered, adding, "you know, Bowman could be right? I've read his work. Using the Mossbaur effect in metals may be the way to go." He scanned the room. "Is he going to be here?"

"Bowman, that naysayer. He's off the project. Hasn't proven a thing."

"What? He happens to hold a U.S. patent related to graser design and works at this Lab. Is he really off the project?" Rick's stomach churned.

"Patent schmatent. We got more than a hunch this shit'll work."

"But Bruno, no one's ever stimulated gamma ray emissions in a gas."

"Terrestrially."

"Well, yeah," Rick replied. "We would build this thing on earth, yes?"

"But you agree that neutron stars with their strong gravitational fields routinely emit jets of lasing gammas."

"Astrophysicists say so. But that's millions of light years away in a vacuum."

"Lemme tell you a secret." Bruno's tone grew lower and quieter, nearly sinister. "Our spooks got humint on this."

"Our who, got what?"

"Human intelligence. The Lab's spies, man." Bruno's eyes flashed.

"From where? How?" Rick paused. "Are you supposed to know that?"

"A Russian contractor. Well, former Soviet Union, if you know what I mean."

"Oh."

"There's plenty of secrets that fall through the security sieve." Bruno leaned toward Rick. Shoulder to shoulder, now. "The plans you saw ain't no tabletop contraption. GRIT, my friend, is the ultimate nuclear counterweapon. An enemy with that technology and our nukes . . . ." Bruno extended an index finger. His facial expression darkened as the finger drooped.

Rick shuddered. He needed a moment to refocus and gather his thoughts. "You mean the usefulness of America's nuclear arsenal could depend on this program?"

Bruno leered and interrupted Rick's dread, saying, "Take it easy. If it don't work out, nobody's gonna whack ya." He poked a finger in Rick's ribs. "Hopefully."

CHAPTER 4

Labored breath, aching muscles. The passion and resolve that burned within Big John Thunderbird far outweighed the pain of his injury. He sensed that they were just up there, north of Los Alamos in the Jemez Mountains. Sacred. Divine.

Carefully avoiding New Mexico Highway 84 on his journey south from his home, he had bounded and slunk through the high desert pinion and juniper forests. Even his glancing encounter with the white man earlier in the day was disagreeable. Big John avoided them whenever possible.

The lacerated thigh burned hot. The broken juniper limb that had pierced his thigh-high moccasin had bored a hole in his quadricep. From blood loss, his reddish skin was as pallid as a warrior ghost. He shut out the pain and continued.

High in the Jemez Mountains the air was cooler. But his smooth flesh remained soaked with sweat. Long coal-black hair lay wet and tousled across his soiled elk hide pack. The doeskin pants and overhanging hand-beaded top he wore, both patinated with the sacred earth of many hallowed places, were smeared with blood. This time, would redemption be his? He forged ahead with the resolve of an Apache warrior and a decades-long spiritual supplicant. He would not be denied in his quest for redemption and in his demand for the destruction of the Los Alamos National Laboratory.

Just then, an ecstatic flood bathed him. Divine refreshment. He quickened his pace, slipped on a moist rock. His leg fell hard against the earth; the wound gushed. Transcending pain, he pressed on. The Ga'ans' sweet fragrance enveloped him; led him to the source of the euphoric breeze. Exhausted, yet exhilarated, he lay prostrate and closed his eyes. Big John Thunderbird was on holy ground.

CHAPTER 5

Rick extricated himself from the pack of well-meaning scientific zealots after the meeting and raced to his office. He imagined rolling a massive stone across the entry, before hunkering into his desk chair. The safety meeting had morphed into an intense debate regarding how he would maximize the gamma lasing cross-section within GRIT's gas-filled grasing cavity. In short, how was he going to prove the viability of the "ultimate nuclear counterweapon," pronto?

Obviously, the grasing cavity had to be designed to make maximum use of gammas emitted by stimulated nuclei. These *stimulated emission* gamma rays would bounce back and forth inside the cavity along its axis and multiply in number in the process. No biggie, in theory. But it was *the* question in practice, a question Rick was unprepared to address after less than a week on the job. More disturbing, it was a question that some great minds had never been able to answer.

A sharp knock on the door jolted Rick from his work-trance. "Come in," he said.

The door opened slowly and Fred poked in his head. "Pretty rough going in the meeting. But, well done." He stepped inside and closed the door.

Rick gestured toward the lone empty chair, a generic swivel base job with a faded seat. "Yeah, why me?"

"Because you're special." Fred grinned. "So special that you get a peek at something no one else in that room has seen. Sure to get your creative juices flowing."

"Uh huh."

"Most don't even know it exists." Fred's smile turned grave, saying, "And needless to say, officially, neither will you."

Soon Rick and Fred were proceeding down a winding two lane road in a nondescript laboratory van. A lengthy stretch of pristine land bordered the pavement. Lots of alpine trees, few road signs, and no billboards. Had he not known their general location—and enjoyed the cool, dry air from Fred's open window—Rick might have guessed himself on Maine's border with New Hampshire. He tried his window switch again, to no avail, and continued to admire the scenery through dirty glass.

When Fred slowed and turned onto a strip of pavement that disappeared into a forest, Rick's heart rate elevated. When out of nowhere they approached a gate manned by armed guards it skipped a beat. The entry procedure was simple. The guard touched the badge while visually verifying its holder. The guard must physically touch each badge. They drove in silence for a couple of hundred meters, past a sign indicating the turnoff for DARHT, the dual axis radiographic hydro-test facility. Rick had read about the high explosive-related tests conducted there. Must be a kick to blow stuff up legally, he thought. Bernard Barish's face flashed into his brain.

Approaching a second, heavily fortified portal, Rick tried to ignore a wave of dread. But there was something about automatic weapons that he didn't particularly like; especially when almost everyone excluding him had one.

A guard approached Fred's open window. Rick extended his photo-badge toward Fred to pass along to the guard. Rick also thrust his face toward Fred's window, for verification. Fred nodded, refusing the badge. Rick was confused. Thump! Thump! Rick flinched and jerked his head toward his closed window. A guard imperiously rapped with his knuckles.

Nervous, Rick shoved open the door to present his badge. The door slammed into the guard's machine gun. He stood back and leveled his weapon on Rick, a menacing glare filling his face. Rick's hands shot into the air. His badge hit the ground.

"Easy does it," Fred said, his hands chest high, fingers fully extended.

"My, uh, window doesn't work," Rick croaked. The guard lowered his weapon. He eyed Rick suspiciously while picking up the badge and sliding it through what appeared to be a small credit card reader with a diving mask on top. Rick's heart rate continued to race, and he nearly dropped the reader when instructed to peer into it and stare at the flashing red light. The light turned green, indicating the biometric validation was complete. Rick handed the reader back to the guard and gingerly closed his door.

Dense forest gave way to a clearing, bearing a large greenish-brown covered parking lot and an enormous structure resembling a jumbo jet hanger, painted in camo. Exiting the vehicle, Rick spotted disguised towers. He looked closely at one and resolved guards and bulbous search lights, all partially obscured behind fake foliage. It was a pillbox camouflaged as a tree house! He stopped dead and glared.

"Ready?" Fred asked.

"For what?" Rick shot him a look.

"GRIT!"

CHAPTER 6

The scale and sophistication of GRIT's experimental facility dwarfed every experiment Rick had ever seen or read about, even in novels. High intensity ion-discharge lamps, from fifty feet above, illuminated the workspace brighter than daylight. He squinted at the glint on an enormous U-shape aluminum tube with a rectangular cross-section. Must be a housing for one of GRIT's high temperature superconducting magnets, he thought. Dr. Gregory Hazelius could have appeared any minute—

"Use these," Fred said, handing Rick a pair of tinted, wraparound safety glasses.

Rick recognized the glasses from photos in a chemical supply mag. On his puny budget at MIT, he could never afford anti-ballistic safety glasses with lenses coated to block electromagnetic radiations like visible and non-visible laser light. He stared directly at the housing, suspended on thick, wide, Kevlar-reinforced straps connected to hefty steel cables that shot upward almost three stories to an overhead crane's massive motors. Rick engaged with their hum as they progressed slowly down the crane's race. He needed this. The low frequency, inexorable drone of experimentation. This was the closest he'd ever get to meditation. But it was close enough.

Fred said, "Cough up a nickel if you want the tour."

Rick stiffened and panned the immediate vicinity. "Let's see," he said, "this appears to be the equipment staging area." He saw a stack of thick metal plates, perfectly cut to size. He listened. No whir of a traditional cutting tool. Then he noted large placards screaming, 'CLASS IV LASER DEVICE' and 'EXPOSED HIGH VOLTAGE'. He said, "I'm guessing behind that panel there's a neodymium-YAG laser cutting tool."

Fred smiled. "Check."

Rick looked down the gallery; stared at an opaque curtain. Brilliant arcs of blue lightning sputtered and flared, illuminating the metallic wall behind. Even though his shirt flapped like a flag in the high-bay's gusty airflow, intended to expunge the virulent fumes of shop work, Rick inhaled deeply and crinkled his nose. "You smell that?"

"What?"

"Brazing flux, son," he said in a drawl. "Nothing else in the world smells like that."

Fred threw up his hands.

"Smells like joining dissimilar metals," Rick continued. "Maybe super-invar optical mounts being brazed to silicon substrates?"

"Check, you sandbagger. I suppose we can forget about that nickel."

"Understanding the fabrication of components for a graser is a lot different from designing one," Rick said, proceeding along the staging area's safety corridor, adjacent to the wall. He stopped abruptly; stared across the floor. A man wearing what looked like a space suit, complete with two large air packs and a bubble helmet, leaned against the closed door of a sealed work space. He rested beneath an array of prominent placards:

DANGER
Beryllium Exposure Area

DANGER
Severe Inhalation Hazard

DANGER
Possible Beryllium Contamination

"Now that's scary. You know the National Defense Stockpile controls the raw material." Rick's eyes darted around. "There an actinide fabrication shop here, too?"

"Oh, they can handle plutonium in there," Fred replied.

"Lovely."

"Don't worry. GRIT has no need for a plutonium-based radioisotopic thermoelectric generator. The gigajoule capacitor banks out back are much juicer."

"But, I guess GRIT'll have ultra-lightweight, coated beryllium mirrors."

"Check."

"And beryllium aluminate crystals doped with chromium or titanium ions to spice up the resonator?" Rick asked, his brow furrowing.

"That's your baby. You want 'em, you got 'em."

Rick's shirt seemed to billow in slow motion. The room became eerily quiet. His bead on the ominous warnings faded. Lightheaded, almost nauseous, he realized this program was a monster. Any material on earth, any extraordinary process, every technology developed by man, could be marshaled for its benefit. That instant, Rick recognized that the parameter space available in his design of the grasing cavity was infinite. How could he possibly converge on a unique solution to optimize GRIT's performance?

He blinked twice and refocused down the floor. Rick ignored the world-class 6-axis Biglia computer controlled milling machine, apparently fabricating a helical spring for heaven only knew what aspect of the gadget. His eyes fixed on the area where a finished superconducting magnet was being fitted into place on GRIT—the *beast*, as he was beginning to think of it. Unable to help himself, he launched into a jog.

At the GRIT assembly area, Rick stood motionless. Labored breath. He looked in awe at the device meant to disrupt the international balance of power that nuclear arsenals had ensured for decades. The array of superconducting magnets that already had been installed soared upward at regular intervals down the device's 10 meter length. An anthill of scientists, engineers, and technicians. They secured and tested massive gold-plated electrical power conductors, installed and checked the flow characteristics of cryogenic fluids for cooling the powerful magnets, installed and aligned optical benches for directing GRIT's devastatingly powerful output beam.

Nearby, a carbon-fiber reinforced cylindrical vessel, several meters long and at least two in diameter, was lashed to the wall. From Rick's brief examination of four pages of GRIT's specifications—all he was cleared to see—he recognized it was the shroud that would contain GRIT's resonator, the grasing cavity . . . his baby. He noticed a cobweb near the top and swallowed hard.

Typically, the shroud would encompass a gas-filled Fabry-Perot cavity, used to bounce photons back and forth between flat mirrors on either end. But for GRIT, for any gas-based gamma ray laser, the cavity would need to be much more ingenious. Rick worried his thumbs against his sweaty palms. He glanced alternatively at the empty shell of a resonator and at the experiment itself. Without the grasing cavity filling out the interior—the guts of this beast—GRIT looked more like a useless carcass. Rick came seeking inspiration, but found desperation. He trembled, thinking that the fate of the free world hinged upon what appeared to be a giant mastodon's skeleton on display for archeological inspection. Even more frightening was the fact that he was responsible for animating it. Making it a bona fide nuke killer.

CHAPTER 7

THE SCENERY on the drive back to TA-35 wasn't nearly so engaging. Rick's thoughts darted and dodged among GRIT's inherent intimidation. He obsessed over how he could possibly do his job, why he was here in the first place—guards with guns everywhere—and his next step. He flicked the inoperative window switch absentmindedly.

Fred said, "That's broken, remember."

Rick cut his eyes.

"Come on. You must be used to small, annoying automotive malfunctions, given that beater you drove out here. Ready to test-drive your new ride?"

"What?"

"I recall you said you wanted a Bimmer SUV. Turns out, Gerry, the German car guru I told you about, got a one-owner X5." Fred continued, "Says it's cherry."

"Uh huh."

"Anti-lock brakes are a must for icy mountain roads. And your All-Trac doesn't even have air bags. Now that's dangerous." He paused. "Think about Desiree."

"Yeah, but I hardly drove in Boston. Took the 'T'."

"When's the soon-to-be Missus Adams coming out?"

"Soon, real soon." Rick kept his expression neutral, while lying through his teeth.

"I hope so. She and Jenna'll be best friends in no time."

Rick found the comment ingratiating.

"I told Gerry I'd bring you out tomorrow, to meet him and see the suv. It's from Arizona. Nice dry climate."

Rick couldn't help the pang in his heart, recalling Boston's luxuriant moisture. "That was for later. I mean . . . the new house and all."

"Doesn't cost a thing to look. And it's Saturday. I'll drive," Fred said. His hand rose when he added, "Sure can't beat his pricing."

"Okay." Rick shrugged. "Just for a look."

"Think of Gerry as another mentor. I'll meet you at Downtown Subscription coffee shop. The place we went when you came for your interview."

"Off the Paseo?"

"Yeah. About eleven." Fred beamed.

Rick's expression darkened. He blurted out, "Is this security stuff well proven?"

Fred straightened his face.

"I can understand limiting an individual's information on a highly secretive project to only what the person needs to accomplish his work," Rick said. "That kind of *need to know*, or compartmentalization they called it in National Security 101, places limitations on how much damage one person could do in the event of a security breach."

"Right."

With a sigh, Rick flicked the window switch again. "But how about a coordinated team? Is there any evidence that compartmentalization really works?"

"It worked during World War ii. Of course, it was taken to extremes." Fred squirmed. "The nuclear fuel enrichment facility in Oak Ridge, Tennessee didn't know where the weapon was being designed or assembled. Los Alamos was called Project Y. That's it."

"And everyone's address was P.O. Box 1663." Rick shook his head. "Maybe zts is not such a crazy idea."

"Consider that playing along with the security people is like keeping your enemies close."

Rick brushed aside the question of whether they were really his enemies. His thoughts flashed back to Cambridge. He said, "I know all about living with the enemy."

"How's that?" Fred asked.

"Academic freedom fanatics at the Institute," Rick said, rolling his eyes.

"Who was your mentor?"

"McCleary was my dissertation mentor; occasionally was there a 'tor' on the front, too." They shared a knowing glance. "McCleary was cool. But I refused to tolerate abuse of academic freedom by some other profs. Cost me political capital."

"Wasn't bad at Stanford. They had strict guidelines against stealing research."

"They never cracked down. Even on repeat offenders like that scumbag Barish. But now he's tenured and I'm exit stage west." Rick's heart seized at the thought of Barish with Desiree. He couldn't bring himself to dignify those rumors with consideration. And if she had strayed, he could win her back.

"Stage Southwest," Fred said. "At least you're done back there."

"Hallelujah! Except a doctoral defense fall term. I'm no longer on faculty, so I can be an external member of Rashid's doctoral committee."

"Must feel good," Fred said as he pulled alongside the curb near the TA-38 guard gate. "Go get 'em, man."

Rick exited the van, but before closing the door he turned and asked, "How'd you know about what we just saw?"

"I'm special, too."

Rick half smiled, thinking, maybe everything at this place is special. His predicament certainly was.

A BIG, BLACK SUV entered the TA-38 parking lot and turned down the first row, parking at its far end. As the engine idled, the passenger scribbled: "4:47 PM: LANLI and LANL4 return to TA-38 in white van." A moment later, driver and passenger in the SUV watched as the van looped the lot and proceeded toward them. The men in the SUV crowded together, sticking their heads into an open map. Seconds later, they re-emerged. The driver shifted the vehicle from park to drive and the passenger wrote: "LANLI exits TA-38 solo in white van. Continuing surveillance."

CHAPTER 8

Gerry lay on a sterile articulatable surgical chair. The array of electronic equipment surrounding him included a suite of medical diagnostics, which added to the space's high tech ambience. A surgical quality overhead lamp indirectly illuminated his head and smooth bare chest, both dotted with rubber sensors powered by colorful electrical leads. His clear blue eyes, a shade lighter than robins' eggs, were closed. Powerful, slightly weathered hands rested open, relaxing the musculature of his forearms, one of which bore a pale crescent of a scar transverse to the arm's axis. The blemish was so thin as to have been wrought by a razor. Perfectly differentiated quadriceps—a ballerino's quads—massive, yet supple. His own blood dripped from an IV into a groin catheter. It had been previously extracted and maintained in clinical conditions in the stainless steel freezer across the room. Gerry believed he could sense the oxygenating effect of a single drop.

A nearby computer stored Gerry's vital statistics: heart rate, 55 bpm; respiration, 9 bpm; subnormal temperature, 97.8°F; and slightly elevated resting blood pressure, 140/90. Admitting a second pint tonight was the key to the performance he demanded of himself during the race tomorrow. Briefly flexing his biceps, which bulged against the flared pectorals on either side of his chest, caused the heart rate monitor to respond. Gerry relaxed. Focused on his respiration. He was his breath.

His surroundings suited Gerry perfectly. Pristine. Antiseptic. Brushed stainless steel storage cabinets with tempered smoked glass doors—without smudges—contained glassware and plastic supplies. Sophisticated chemical equipment and associated reagents for quantitative analysis were stored under a gleaming fume hood. Hardly a typical stand-alone workshop, as the structure located just paces behind Gerry's main house appeared to be when viewed from its simple exterior.

His mind was calm. Gerry had mobilized an underling, who although dissatisfied with their working relationship would be zealous in accomplishing his final objective. Gerry understood the man was motivated by self-interest. An egocentric American, like the rest of Los Alamos Lab's elite. Gerry assessed his mission's progress. Things were going well in spite of the facts that the preparations had been long and painstaking and his *staffmembers* were all cut from similar, selfish cloth. Of course, he, too, was paid. And handsomely. But there was more. Professionalism. Integrity. Honor. He was a consummate professional, directing amateurs. Soon enough, one less amateur. But another with plenty of vices was coming to take his place. To help render Los Alamos National Lab an apple rotten at the core with an exterior hardly tarnished.

Believing himself superlucid from hyperoxygenation, Gerry exhaled deeply. An image of himself being hailed a Hero by the State and being embraced by his formerly humiliated family dominated his thoughts. The doping complete, he prepared for a healthful natural cocktail: 15 ccs—a typical specimen for him—of precollected bodily fluid spun into 10 gms. of colloidal silver carrier, to intensify the potency and kill the salty aftertaste.

CHAPTER 9

Rick stepped out of the Taj Majal restaurant into a temperate Santa Fe eve-
ning. It felt good to have his first week on the new job behind him. He took a
deep breath and cast a wistful glance into the cloudless sky. A peaceful evening,
featuring billions of stars in a not-so-far-away sky. He lagged behind the love
birds. Bruno and Mary held hands and whispered, ambling across the parking
lot. He secretly admired their relationship. Desperately wanted someone to love.
A fiancée in heart, not just in name.

Rick tugged at his blazer, asking, "Should I unload this? Where's the club?"

"It's not a club," Mary giggled. "More like a beer joint."

"Remember, Mary's cousin Diego owns the place. A real bidness man. Buys
corrupted batches of microbrew in Albuquerque and bottles it as his house signature beer. Also drums for the band. Tries to, anyway."

Rick watched them throw their heads back and laugh. That's all he wanted:
a simple life with love and laughter. He believed this out-of-the-way, turquoise-
trading town was just the place to recapture what Desiree and he had had.

"Mary's other cousin, Carmen, waits tables and sings with the band. Very
hot."

"Not interested," Rick said.

"Don't be too hasty," Mary interjected. "Carmen's got a good heart. Smart, too. Graduated from St. John's College. Full scholarship."

Bruno eyed Rick. "The girl's no bookworm. Samples and devours Angel's patrons like a chocoholic working in a fudge factory."

"Cutitout," Mary said, giving him an elbow to the ribs.

"Honey, she has no clue what some of the stuff she can say about physics means."

Carmen might be an interesting person. But Rick was unavailable; emotionally, at least. What he really needed was a pet. Maybe a cat like his mom had years ago. Just something to be there when he got home from work. Maybe a dog that would love him unconditionally.

His musing gave way to the low frequency rumble of amplified bass guitar. Soon they stood at the saloon doors of Angel's. Rick followed Bruno and Mary inside. He lagged, taking in the scene, radically different from that of Boston bars. But the band was hot. He thought, this is going to be okay. And the pleasant walk over was much better than a menacing late night stroll along thug-ridden Lansdown Street by Fenway Park.

The music was loud, but the fidelity surprisingly good, especially considering the bar's small scale and low ceiling. Rick recognized the song as Clapton's *Crossroads*. The big guy on guitar did it justice. His Stratocaster shrieked stiletto shards nearly identical to the recording on the virtuosic second lead. It was one of Rick's dino-rock favs.

The band's vibe was engaging and the sound level was no problem. Rick believed that for some things in life, like an irritating, constant inner dialogue, screaming that you've been set up for failure, yet again, external high volume was a good solution.

"See, not too shabby, the band," Bruno shouted. "Lead guitarist is T'Bird."

"He's good." Rick's toes kept time inside his shoes. "What're they called?"

"Taos T'birds."

T'bird stepped into the spotlight and wrung out the introductory notes of a blues number. Rick didn't recognize it, but he was hooked. As billed, the drummer was the weak link. The dead crash cymbal sounded familiar to Rick. And the bass drum could have been half-full of mud. But an instant later the organ made an elegant, emotional entry. It sent a chill up Rick's spine and a pang to his heart, like when he was 16 and onstage for the first time.

A chubby old guy with a disheveled nest of wiry gray hair and a great mossy beard sat behind a mammoth console that consumed almost a third of the dinky stage. His pose—head thrust back with a heavenward gaze—projected a messianic quality at odds with his crazed eyes and the cigarette dangling from the side of his drawn meth mouth.

The song's end was an emotional relief for Rick, who applauded loudly when T'bird acknowledged 'Doc', the keyboardist. T'Bird identified the song as Stevie Ray's *Riviera Paradise* and cast his eyes upward.

Boom-che, boom-boom-che; boom-che, boom-boom-che . . . began the drummer's up-tempo groove.

"Santa Fe's own Carmen Cdebaca," T'bird said without the mike, breaking into a scorching three-cord progression.

"Gimme some love, Santa Fe," Carmen shouted, charging onto the stage, clapping her hands high above her head, inciting audience imitation.

Rick focused on Carmen. She wiggled and jiggled her prized assets in perfect time with the rhythm, strutting across the tiny stage. Just a girl acting out, he wondered? A woman-child, maybe? She blew kisses with one hand while pounding her heart with a clenched fist. Carmen radiated love to the crowd. Rick felt it.

"¡Que guapa! Look at that outfit," Rick heard Mary say to Carmen during the music break. Carmen stood tableside, flanked by T'Bird.

"I modeled this for Wild West Origins," Carmen said, impishly placing one hand on her hip and the other upturned palm behind her head. "So they had to give it to me."

Rick held his tongue when Mary told him, "That's the most outrageously expensive clothing store on the plaza."

"Costs alotta money to look this cheap," Carmen said in an affected twang.

"Must not charge per square inch," Rick blurted, grinning to Bruno.

"I think they'd make out better selling stuff to me in that case," T'bird said.

"Oh, that's a good one," Mary laughed. "This is Lou's friend, Rick Adams. A former professor at MIT. Rick calls Lou, Bruno, but I told you that yesterday."

Carmen appeared not to register the comment.

Mary turned to Rick and said, "This is my cousin Carmen Cdebaca. And the amazing guitarist Tommy Thunderbird. We call him T'bird."

Rick plastered a pleasant expression on his face and glanced back and forth between Carmen and T'bird, finding nary a smile.

"Professor Adams . . ." Carmen said, "or is doctor sufficiently formal?"

"Rick'll do fine." He spoke to T'bird, hoping to atone for his crack about Carmen's skimpy outfit, "I'm familiar with Vaughn's music, but didn't know *Rivera Paradise*." Then he said to Carmen, "I confess that I didn't know the final tune, either."

"*I Got a Line on You* was by the 60's R&B band, Spirit. Randy California picking the guitar and Clit McTorious fingering the bass." She paused. "They were California phenoms. Maybe not much of a following on the East Coast, Richard."

"Please call me Rick." He smiled narrowly, weary of way-out-West arrogance.

"If you're called Rick, back East, in the country shouldn't we call you Dick?"

Rick was struck by the curve of Carmen's high cheek bones and her startling ebony eyes, as she assessed him steadily. "Ahhh, you're wily or should I say, Wildely."

T'bird snickered.

Blood rushed to Rick's head. The charge that accompanied a desperate need to defend himself was always the same, enlivening, yet irritating. The more inappropriate his response, the better to relieve the anxiety-provoking pressure. The behavior had begun long ago. Unfortunately, it continued through MIT where it was triggered by the dishonesty of his colleagues and the pressure to kowtow to authority.

Bruno said, "Hey Rickster, you're about out of gas there. Let's go get more beer."

"That's it for me," Rick replied, standing. "Packing it in." He nodded his regards.

"Drive carefully. Give us a call," Rick heard Mary say, after he'd turned away. He turned back for a quick wave goodbye.

Carmen flicked a wrist. With a lip-smacking smile, she said, "Goodnight, Dick."

Rick made his way to the doors, trying not to think of the social face plant he'd left in his wake. Did someone call his name? He refused to turn around. Outside, crisp night air relaxed his bronchia until he twitched at a tap on his shoulder.

"Where's the fire?" Fred chuckled.

"In my belly. I'm fleeing before I run afoul of Carmen and T'Bird." Rick's eyes darted, asking, "Your wife with you?"

"She wanted to come, but couldn't. Jen's really excited about tomorrow afternoon, though." Fred demonstrated a topspin tennis forehand.

"Oh, I forgot. The oddball, Walter, called and said a mixer was all setup before asking if I could come. And what a voice. How'd you know, anyway?"

"It's tradition. Besides, Walter left a message for us. Definitely a character." Fred shook his head and smiled good-naturedly, before turning toward the saloon doors.

Rick watched Fred enter Angel's, thinking, although a bit pushy, he seemed a good guy. Rick just hoped there were no strings, much less heavy cables, attached.

CHAPTER 10

RADIANT morning sunlight bathed Rick's room and, seemingly, his heart. He sprang up and stretched before pulling on jeans and a Muddy Charles tee. Headed early to the coffee shop where he would meet Fred. Brushing up on the subtleties of gas lasing schemes was on his mind. For fear of violating ZTS, Rick dared not study a graser research paper, even an unclassified one. His newly acquired, although classic, text by A. E. Siegman, *Lasers*, was perfect, gas lasers and gas grasers having much in common.

At an out-of-the-way table, Rick gently set down his coffee and toasted poppy seed bagel, slathered with traditional Philly cream cheese—no green chili, thank you very much. He plunked down the book and sat. The colorful abstract paintings that had been hung throughout the shop by no estimation were masterpieces. They were, however, vast improvements over the burlap coffee bags that adorned the walls last time he was there. Rick eyed a female nude. The voluptuousness of which harked back to the previous night's erotic nightmare of Carmen suffocating him with her bare breasts. A big slug of coffee downed, he split the book's covers, ending the treacherous thoughts.

Engrossed in Siegman, Rick heard a vaguely familiar voice, asking, "Isn't that a bit much for breakfast?" He looked down at his mostly-eaten bagel and then up over the book's margin to see a heavenly figure, clad in knee-length hiking shorts and a snug tie-dyed tank top. His gaze continued upward to Carmen's mischievous smile. Coffee steamed lazily across her face from her to-go cup, which she held at breast level. Rick swallowed hard, wondering if he'd ever really awakened. He said, "Isn't it a bit early for you to be out, looking so . . . *sportif?*"

"Going hiking," Carmen replied, kicking up a jaunty lightweight boot. "Hardly recognized you, hiding in the corner, *sans cravat.*"

"I didn't have a tie on last night."

"Well, you know." She grinned devilishly. "I'm walking a dog, actually. But all the way up Sun Mountain."

Steam continued to waft up Carmen's forehead. It drew Rick's eyes up past hers, toward her shiny hair, pulled back from her face and fastened with clips. She looked at him over the rim of her cup. He felt her black eyes probing him. Transfixed, he reached for his cup, nearly toppling it. "Oh, you have a dog. What kind?"

"It's a friend's German shepherd," she said.

Something clicked and Rick asked, "Is your friend German?"

"Maybe. Why do you ask?" She batted her lashes, before tapping his book. "So, you a hiker or just a laser jock?"

"A gas dynamicist. More like an engineer than anything."

Carmen nodded lazily.

"Don't be underwhelmed. I have a degree in physics. Two, actually."

"Then you're an applied physicist. I have a friend in the Lab's theory division, researching quantum computing. His motto is: I think, therefore I'm paid."

Rick laughed.

Carmen asked, "Why the laser tomb?"

"Gas lasers have some very critical gas dynamics considerations."

"Tell me about the gas dynamics of gas lasers, Dr. Dick."

To Rick's surprise, Carmen seated herself. Stared expectantly at him. She said, "I took a modern physics survey course at St. John's. A modern physics *intensive.*"

"Just how intense was this *intensive?*" Rick asked, mimicking her inflection.

Carmen's eyes held his. "I could've handled something much more *intense.*"

Goosebumps rose on his forearms. Rick's gut tingled. "In that case, you may know that lasing is a chemical phenomenon. It's caused by electrons emitting a special kind of light when they de-excite amid certain conditions."

"And gas lasers . . . ."

"As the name suggests," Rick continued, "gas lasers use a gas or a combination of gases as the gain media. Other kinds of lasers can use materials in the solid state, say, a diode made of semiconductor or a synthetic precious stone."

"Like a small rod made of ruby," Carmen said, batting her eyelashes again.

"That was the basis of the very first laser. It produced a 694 nanometer, red lasing line. Kinda like your ruby lips." Rick took the opportunity to stare at them.

"Appropriate since *ruber*, the word from which ruby is derived, is Latin for red."

Rick beamed. Carmen grinned wickedly. This was getting fun. "Gain," he said, "is the amplification of the desired frequency of the special light." He eyed Carmen. "You contain the gas in a cavity with mirrors on each end. It's called a lasing cavity. The special light bounces back and forth between the mirrors creating more and more special light. One of the mirrors is somewhat transparent, maybe, one percent, meaning it emits that fraction of the amplified beam for use." Rick crossed his arms and sat quiet.

Carmen rested her hands on the table and leaned forward. She appeared to admire her slender, tapered fingers. Blue-red nails. Rick felt himself slipping into the soft abyss of her cleavage. Struggling not to ogle, he told himself the heavenly contours of Carmen's chest were just a couple of asymmetric paraboloids. It backfired, providing him a mathematical excuse to stare. Her eyes flicked up. Busted— Rick moved his hands as though juggling, asking, "Um, does that kinda make sense?"

Carmen ignored his fixation. "Special light? Pretty top-level, Dr. Dick. What about microwave lasers? Not exactly light, is it?"

"Ookaay." That course must have been more intense than I thought, Rick mused. "I mean not just visible light, but light in the broader sense, including everything from slowly rolling radio waves to penetrating gamma-rays." His stomach flipped, thinking, maybe I shouldn't say that word outside the fence? "They're all electromagnetic radiations. And the microwave laser was actually called a maser."

"An acronym for microwave amplification of stimulation—"

"That's stimulated," Rick interrupted. "A word near and dear to the hearts of laser physicists. Mine, too. Laser is light amplification by stimulated emission of radiation."

"And for maser, replace light by microwave," Carmen said, exposing gleaming white teeth.

"Exacto. Now, about the special light. Consider a small space heater. You plug it in, the little coils glow, and heat energy radiates out onto your chilly feet," Rick said, leaning back in his chair, sipping coffee. "The heater's a source of radiant emissions. All of these radiations—lasers, infrared heat, ultraviolet light, even the visible spectrum of light and microwaves for that matter—are similar."

"What's the difference?"

"While infrared, visible, and ultraviolet radiations are from the same family, except for the laser, these emissions are diffuse and disoriented. Their waves have no special relationships linking them more closely, coordinating them." Rick lowered his chair to the floor and hunched forward. He counted on his fingers: "They're not monochromatic, well collimated, or coherent."

"Okay."

"Well, those three properties make laser light unique and very penetrating."

"I like this," Carmen said, her eyes shining like a little girl's, one who wants more candy.

"Let's agree that radiations, whether you can see them like red or green light or not, like penetrating ultraviolet rays from the sun, are just forms of energy. Then lasers are radiant energy generators." He put down his cup; fell silent.

Carmen jiggled her fine fingers at him. "So, tell me more."

Rick admired the flesh of Carmen's perfectly formed palms. Pillowy soft, he imagined. When she smoothed back her hair, he nearly moaned. Refocusing, he said, "Uh-hum, when an atom is hanging out in the ground state, its electrons are closest to the nucleus. Consider a noble gas-filled container. Full of argon, say. Hit it with a burst of electrical energy. The energy stimulates the atoms, causing electrons to jump up to higher energy so-called excited states. When one of these electrons de-excites down to its ground state, energy—in the form of a photon or particle of light—that is exactly equal to the energy differential of the excited and ground state is emitted."

Carmen said, "Ah, the quantization of energy. In Latin, *quantum* means how much. But, how do you make the light behave?"

"You stimulate the emission of the special light. Just like the name suggests." Rick took an instant to gather his thoughts. "Listen up, stimulated emission is when a photon whose energy is identical to the differential energy of the excited and ground state smacks into an excited atom and induces it to de-excite by emitting two identical photons with the exact same energy as the incident photon."

"How easy is that?" Carmen's head and eyes darted erratically She said, "Don't photons fly around randomly? And aren't there an infinite number of excited states?"

"Good points. That's where the mirrors on either end of the resonator, uh, lasing cavity, come into play. They bounce the stimulated emission photons back and forth along the cavity's length, multiplying them. The other photons quickly get scattered into the cavity walls or absorbed by other atoms which radiate randomly, like the heating element, diffuse and incoherent. In a well designed resonator, a growing beam of stimulated emission photons are amplified along the lasing cavity's axis." Rick considered his grasing cavity design turned on exactly the same circumstances. Now how coincidental is this, he wondered, feeling his gut wrench just a little.

"So all the stimulated emission photons have identical energy—that exact energy needed to produce more stimulated emissions. And because the beam is formed along the cavity's axis, it's convenient to extract it from one of the end mirrors."

Rick fidgeted. "You got it," he said, finding his eyes scouring the little room, for what or whom, he didn't know.

"I think so. But how can you—"

Fierce barking erupted outside. It sounded as though a litter of Chihuahuas was opposing a Great Dane. Carmen hopped up, comically arched an eyebrow, and raised a finger. "I know that bark. Gotta run." Turning to go, she raised her hand and twiddled her fingers. "To be continued . . . Dr. Dick."

An instant later, he sat alone at the small table. Flopped Siegman shut, almost wondering if he'd imagined the whole thing. But her lipstick-stained coffee cup bore witness to the fact that this time Rick was not just dreaming about Carmen. Whether that was a good thing, only time would tell.

PART B
Setup

"See how cruel the whites look. Their lips are thin, their noses sharp, their faces furrowed and distorted by folds. Their eyes have a staring expression: they are always seeking something. What are they seeking?"

—Taos Pueblo Chief Ochwiay Biano (Mountain Lake)
Carl G. Jung
Memories, Dreams, Reflections

CHAPTER 11

THE GUARDS RED Carrera 4S devoured the Old Santa Fe Trail. Rick watched the landscape whiz by from the kidskin-soft, ventilated black leather passenger's seat. Fred said that he'd purchased this car from Gerry for a song. Rick sunk in deeper, wishing he knew the tune. A moment later, he was back to replaying his morning interaction with Carmen. There was chemistry. Could she have felt it, too?

Fred motored south out of the Santa Fe city limits before goosing the throttle on a tortuous route through wind-swept land. Rick admired southwestern vistas, adorned with prominent peaks and endless azure sky. To the east, hacienda-style mansions were set well back from the road. Massive adobe brick walls. Mud-color. Earthy. Some were embedded into hillsides and interspersed into the hilly topography's saddle regions. Others perched, to Rick's dismay, upon prominent peaks.

They turned off Highway 285 onto Old Spur Road, quickly arriving at Gerry's gate, which impressed Rick as a tollbooth in the middle of the desert. The gate opened magically and they drove up a winding gravel trail to a small cluster of squat, dirt-color buildings. Desolate grounds. Barren earth. The epitome of xeriscape, a new term for Rick. An even newer one popped into his head:

zeroscape could be the solution space his computer code would calculate using GRIT's grasing cavity design parameters. A meaningless null solution: long, wide, deep matrices of bagels!

Rick's dread transformed into curiosity when he saw a tall, broad shouldered man, wearing oversize, heavy plastic frame sunglasses, standing at the circle drive's apex. If not for Fred's description, Rick would have thought him a Hollywood action hero. His hair was wet and combed straight back, affording a view of his tanned, chiseled face. Perfectly distressed low-rise jeans with taut thighs were secured with a belt buckle bearing an enormous 'H'. It gleamed in the sunlight. His multi-color, vertically striped shirt was unbuttoned to mid-chest. And instead of ubiquitous cowboy boots, the man wore hush puppy-like slip-ons. For Rick, the look was more 90210 than P.O. Box 1663. He felt the slightest rustle in his gut.

"Now you meet *der Gerrymeister, Ja*," Fred said, switching off the ignition.

"Hello, Fred," Gerry said in a thick European accent. "And you are Rick, *Ja*."

"Rick Adams," he said, sucking in what suddenly felt like a paunch. "Pleasure."

"Gerry Mueller. Welcome."

Rick entered the foyer and peered into the immaculate living room. "You have a hell of a housekeeper or maybe a live-in girlfriend who's a neat-freak."

"The place stays clean in spite of my girlfriend."

Fred said, "Gerry only sleeps here. He lives in his workshop."

Hard to believe, given those buffed nails, Rick thought to himself.

"*Ja, der* shop's out back," Gerry said, leading the way.

The home was sparsely furnished with Scandinavian design furniture made of polished wood with firm-looking, tailored cushions, upholstered in textured cream-color fabric. A lightly stained cheery wood floor proudly demonstrated its beautiful grain while myriad discrete halogen lights were strung high overhead, some optimally adjusted to illuminate large modern art canvases, glorifying the human form in movement. Rick wondered, abstract ballet poses? Surely not.

Above a generous fireplace hung what Rick assumed was the *pièce de résistance*: an entwined couple dancing in the throes of passion. Their bodies melded together organically becoming one from the torso downward, but their heads appeared to strain away in a struggle to be free. Rick considered that dichotomies and heads versing hearts were universal themes. Maybe there was more to it than that for Gerry?

All three concurred that the BMW x-5's previous owner had taken exemplary care of his toy. The titanium silver metallic paint glistened; the distinctive fragrance of new leather filled its interior; and its generous tires, mounted on 10-inch-wide, 19-inch-diameter polished aluminum alloy spoke wheels, hugged the earth.

"The 4.4 liter is the fuel injected V8?" Rick asked.

"*Ja, ist schnell, mit fahvegnugan.*" Gerry answered grinning; exposing a mouthful of extra-wide white teeth and a cavernous dimple in his chin.

"The V-8 goes like hell and the handling's great." Fred interpreted. "Go for a test drive. See for yourself."

Rick drove and Gerry took the passenger's seat, relegating Fred to the back. Two minutes behind the wheel and Rick was in love with the handling. The vehicle's excellent safety rating was a plus.

Approaching the entry to Gerry's property, Rick observed that the heavy iron gate that had opened magically earlier remained closed. "Wha'do I do?" he asked.

Gerry reached over from the passenger's seat and depressed one of several buttons on the keyhead. The gate opened.

"That standard?" Rick asked.

"I reprogrammed the rear portal release functionality."

"What else can the key do?" Rick asked, noting Gerry's wry smile.

The deal-making was effortless. Gerry's price was nearly ten-percent less than the low range suggested by the websites Rick had consulted. And maintenance was included. Gerry insisted on it— After Gerry reset the trunk release mode of the SUV's clever key, Rick was primed to drive his new baby home. He motored alongside Fred and Gerry, who headed toward the main house, and called out, "Fred, I'll see you later at the tennis club. And Gerry, don't worry. I'll wire the money Monday."

Gerry said, grinning, dimpling, "I'm not worried. I can find you."

Rick drove away thinking he hadn't paid a cent. Not even a post-dated check. Odd. And while Gerry was obviously German, he wasn't like any other

German he'd ever met. He was hard, but polished. Just like a diamond. Thinking of diamonds, Rick was pretty sure the Hope could be mounted in Gerry's chin.

FRED PACED the living room floor. Shuffled in vain for a gritty spot to grind out his frustration. He wanted to tarnish this place before leaving for the last time. What he really wanted was to scream how fake it all was, and how sinister. But he would take his pay, which he desperately needed, and keep his mouth shut. He looked at Gerry, whose placid composure irked him. Fred said, "That's it for me. Now, take my car into your little shop of horrors and get the spy shit out."

"You trying to be funny. Too bad you couldn't just do your job." Gerry drilled Fred with his gaze. "Would have made things much easier."

"I provided my replacement."

"No! I provided your replacement. Without me, some straight-lace, Bay-area nerd would be here instead of Adams."

"Whatever. I guess you are Gerry the Gruesome German." Fred returned the glare. "And I want my money, today. I need to get back to Los Alamos."

"To your drunk wife."

"Kiss my ass," Fred said, balling his fist.

Gerry's hands fell to his sides. His eyes narrowed.

A chill shot up Fred's spine. His hand relaxed. "Just rip the spyware out."

"Take my Turbo, and get the hell out of here. You get the money tonight, by drop." Gerry extended his hand and opened it.

Fred saw the Porsche's keyhead in Gerry's palm. What he couldn't see, but understood, was that the steel shank protruded from between his index and middle fingers. Even a key was a lethal weapon in Gerry's hand.

CHAPTER 12

THE LOS ALAMOS Tennis Club over-looked an array of mesas that fanned westward, seeking or at least gesturing toward the glowing afternoon sun. Rick's tennis togs were typical of Cambridge, a colorful polo shirt, not ironed but not wrinked, and elongated white shorts, cut just above the knee. A BoSox ball cap topped his head.

Rick peeked over the manicured hedge that separated the courts from the walkway leading to the clubhouse. He admired a lean, leggy woman. She stood with one hand on her hip, shaking her racquet at Fred, who twirled his racquet like a pistol, blew imaginary smoke from its butt, and shoved it into a make-believe holster. Rick laughed.

Fred turned and said, "Rick, you a tennis player or tennis voyeur?"

"Hopefully not the latter. That's *my* job," said a wrinkled, stump of a man in a grating, gravelly voice. He wore a threadbare yellowed tee and wrinkled, ill-fitting shorts.

"Walter Bowers, live and in person," Rick cracked to himself.

"Renée, come meet Rick," Walter croaked from across the net.

She trotted closer. Her pale blue polo shirt and navy fitted shorts came into focus. Renée smiled sweetly from under a HEAD ball cap.

"Renée Roxbury," said Walter, "Rick Adams."

She removed her wayfarer sunglasses and their eyes met, for what Rick judged to be the slightest instant too long.

"Wicked lefty serve, that one," Walter cautioned.

Rick was reluctant to alter his gaze toward the irritating talking stump.

"Today we'll play a six game round robin," Walter continued. "You know, every man plays with every woman." Cocking his head, he added, "Neither the women nor the men will get bored."

Renée rolled her hazel eyes, while arching an eyebrow.

"Well then, why don't you two warm Rick up. I'll attend the tender elk tenderloin," Walter joked, turning toward the clubhouse.

"Ignore 'im," Fred said. "Quirky, but benign. A double E."

Rick disregarded the engineering slight. He knew Los Alamos was a physics lab.

"Ah, there goes my better half," Fred said, smiling.

Rick saw Jenna Larson heading toward a far court. She brushed back baby-fine blonde hair from her face as she strode, obviously enjoying, but not acknowledging, the attention of her husband and friends.

Fred said, "I'll introduce them later." He added, "Renée, stay with Rick. I love the challenge of two on one."

"The challenge or the concept?" she asked, wrinkling her nose.

Rick sailed the first couple of balls long. He frowned.

"Don't worry," Renée said, spreading her arms wide. "This is the only place in Los Alamos where you can throw caution to the wind."

After the tennis, which Rick and Renée won; after the dinner, which Walter had prepared to perfection; after the drinks, including wine, cognac, single malt; after the suggestive film, *Doña Flora et su dous Marriages,* Rick wondered if this were really possible? Right here in the closest thing to a police state in the free world! Even the delicious home-baked cookies were an enigma. Semisweet chocolate morsels set off by bitter blue and white flecks. Rick felt flush just eating them. In the low light, he glanced at his watch. Nearly eleven.

"Don't even think about getting back on the road, Rick," Walter cautioned.

"Why not?" Rick asked. "Think I'm going to get busted?" A hush, a pall dampened the room, whose air tangibly seemed to thicken. What did they have to worry about, he wondered? I'm the new hire with six-months probation—

The lights went way up, bright, startling. The group quickly rearranged itself with all the convincing effect of a schoolgirl smoothing down her dress when unexpectedly she and a date are discovered by her mother.

A voice with a thick German accent said, "Rick, loosen up. Stay awhile. Have another drink."

It was Gerry.

"The Feynman friends here will show you a real good time," He added.

Rick snapped his head to the rear of the room where Gerry stood, towering. He peered down, looking more imposing than ever. Cut abs rippled his snug black tee and paramilitary pants accentuated his lean waist. His clothing and posture looked as though he might produce an RPG and at any moment blow away the entire room of well lubricated, very cozy Labmates. His facial expression suggested he might enjoy doing so.

"Look at Fred," Gerry said, matter-of-factly. "He's in no hurry to leave. Renée, you're not going anywhere, are you?"

Rick turned to her and whispered, "Who are the Feynman friends? Is Gerry a member here?"

She nodded.

"He in the film club?"

"Oh, he's been known to show up," she said, her hands fanning.

Rick refocused on the rear of the room where Walter extended a goody tray toward Gerry, who scowled. Rick's palms began to perspire. He wanted to disappear.

Gerry said, "Fred, looks like I've disturbed the party. I'm here to deliver your car." He raised a key. Fred jumped up from the sofa he shared with two women. *"Auf Wiedersehen,"* Gerry said, bowing his head and disappearing into the shadows. Fred followed closely behind.

Deathly quiet.

Rick stood and bid everyone good night, not looking directly at anyone. At once he felt like a peeping Tom and an extra in a David Lynch film. Maybe this is what Bruno meant when he said that national labs were a perfect synthesis of prosperous corporations and top-tier universities. This was like a ritzy, albeit bizarre, frat party.

Traversing the walkway to the parking lot, Rick's head was dizzy as though he'd been drugged. A gust of fresh air slapped his face. He shivered and noted Fred's Carrera's taillights cresting the lot's exit, fishtailing. Must be in a hurry, Rick thought.

"Wait up," Renée called out. An instant later, she laced her arm through his. They strolled woozily. "Big day tomorrow?"

"Whole lotta work."

"Take it easy. You don't want to burn out." They reached her dusty Volvo wagon. She turned to Rick and said, "This has been fun. I look forward to next time."

She gave him a kiss on the cheek; lingered near his face.

Rick wanted to press his mouth to hers. Their eyes locked. Lips followed. Renée leaned into him. Crazy with lust. Rick fought himself. His sexual desire for a colleague pitted against his will to be principled. And Desiree? He pushed Renée away. "I'm sorry," he said. "Don't know what came over me."

"That's okay. See you soon."

FLAWLESS PHOTOS. Not grainy ghosts produced by previous generation night vision goggles. He worked the fine focus, striving for even more clarity—a matter of nature, not necessity. One final shot of Rick betraying his *love*. Renée was perfect for this part. But it was insufficient. The Eurasians knew well before Machiavelli that it's more certain to rule by fear than by love. People betray their love so easily. Besides, Adams was as strong headed as a bull. A little thwack on his hard head would get his attention. But it would take much more than that to ensure his loyalty.

CHAPTER 13

Gerry exited Route 4 into a White Rock gas station. He topped off his Turbo and purchased a cola, loitering near the cash register, chatting up the attendant while facing the security camera. He returned to his vehicle, pulled behind the station, and killed the engine and lights. His sleek PDA glowed in the passenger's seat. It demonstrated a map of Pajarito Mountain and a blinking red dot progressing upward toward the Los Alamos ski area. He couldn't help but smile, considering he was about to give a new meaning to the old term 'dead drop.'

The dot was stationary near the hill's crest. Gerry imagined the expression on Fred's face when he sloshed around in the muddy equipment shack only to find nothing. Gerry waited patiently. The dot began to descend the treacherous route. He zoomed in, to identify the longest downhill straight. It led to a hard left turn opposite a thousand foot plunge. Almost there. A slowish jog to the right. Now, straitening out. The satellite relay that Gerry had embedded up among the aspen trees had a few seconds delay. He pressed the send button and a small nitro canister that he had installed earlier began to empty its contents into the fuel distributor of Fred's car.

SPEED: 27 MPH. Turn after turn, Fred had carefully negotiated the winding mountain road. Gnawed by angst. Slowly, he proceeded down a particularly steep pitch. Xenon discharge headlights illuminated the pavement far ahead. Black. Lonely. Caution signs dotted the roadside. Fred caressed the center striping: solid line, his side, dotted, the other. The Carrerra's engine sputtered. My God, he thought, what will this cost. His next sensation was disbelief. It was as though the world suddenly sped up. White dashed lines came at him like bullets . . . then machine gun fire . . . nanosecond laser pulses. He jolted in response. Tried to shake his head, to clear it, but the force pinned him to the seat. His body crushed the glove-soft leather. The Carrera accelerated.

Speed: 79 mph. Confused, Fred smashed the brakes. Useless. The engine howled a menacing mechanical roar. He saw the towering Aspen trees on the passenger's side come alive. Leafy, green. Brutal jags of mountain stone flew by on his side. Every protrusion visible. In the rearview, the scene was bright as day. Fred's mouth gaped as he witnessed fire jetting 10 feet from the stubby exhaust pipes. The Carrera accelerated.

Speed: 104 mph. Approaching a left turn, Fred fought panic. Instinctively, he grasped the handbrake. Yanked upward. Rear tires stopped rotating. He saw black smoke boiling up into his infernal wake. Train tracks of rubber. Railing looming, the car bulleted through. It's firey exhaust illuminated everything as clearly as daylight. As though in a quarter-speed world or weightless in outer space, Fred watched the tree tops slowly turn upside down. Surreal. And then . . . the Carrera smashed into the mountainside. The car tumbled to rest, upside-down and ablaze. Fred struggled to open the lodged door. Seatbelt constricted. His back scorched from the flaming rear engine. Suffocating, Fred exerted a super-human push. The door latch freed— But behind his seat, the fire extinguisher in which Gerry had placed nitro, exploded holocaustically. Shrapnel from the tank gashed Fred's back as fire engulfed the cabin and the Carrera imploded into an incendiary heap.

CHAPTER 14

Early Monday morning, Rick parked his vehicle, removed his badge from the glove box, and entered the unmanned guard gate. The procedure for entering the access controlled technical area was sometimes cumbersome between midnight and 6:30 a.m., when guards were not present continuously. Rick had to admit that he wasn't comfortable with their probing eyes and grimacing faces—either real or imaginary. And their touching his badge, staring him in the eyes, and ushering him through the small portals.

Inside XP-12's automated-entry turnstile, Rick imagined the circular steel cage impaling him if his access to the controlled area were denied. He swiped his badge and carefully placed his right palm on the reader. Looked up from under his BoSox ball cap at a security camera, protected by grayish bulletproof glass. The flashing beacon changed from red to green, indicating the Lab's central security computer had authenticated his fingerprints. He recalled almost being shot at the security gate when Fred and he visited GRIT's experimental facility. The turnstile unlocked with a loud clank.

Building Two was only a 100 meter shot from the gate. Once inside, Rick made his way to B-wing's dual set of entry doors. He swiped his badge again. Placed his forehead on the boss of a small black plastic enclosure that protruded from the cinderblock wall. He stared forward until the central security computer authenticated his retinas. The fortified door unlatched with a low frequency buzz.

Finally inside his office, and having hefted a healthy stack of secret documents from the safe onto a worktable, Rick tossed back the opaque cloth covering his marker board, bearing a flow chart of GRIT's grasing cavity computer model. He plopped into his chair and snugged up to his desk. After a brief sigh, he entered his six-digit Lab ID number, his 'Z' number, and his seventeen-digit alphanumeric password to access the classified computing partition. Fred had advised him to memorize the gibberish password upon viewing it on a small CRT at the Operations Security HQ to avoid double-wrapping it with security badging on the inside and a plain envelope over that. It would have to be logged as a classified document in your group office and required continuous storage in an approved document repository. He'd said that although there was no shame in not being confident about instantly memorizing umpteen digits of nonsense, it was not the ideal way to begin a distinguished Laboratory career.

By 8:45, Rick had anxiously scrolled through code runs executed over the weekend. Randomness. Nothingness. The solution algorithms had not converged. Only big fat zero solution vectors. He decided to check e-mail. On the classified partition, a curious message of Subject: Security Meeting had been sent via a shielded, high security server. No originator information was available. Rick double-clicked it.

***

**From the Office of the Associate Director,
Operations Security and Computing Resources
for the Los Alamos National Laboratory**

Dear Dr. Adams:
Please call internal extension 7842 at your earliest opportunity to establish an appointment with Associate Director Gavin Burton.
This call may be placed using an unsecure line.

Kindest regards,
Connie Sanders
Administrative Assistant

CHAPTER 15

T HE MASSIVE double doors of Building Two clanked shut behind Rick, who made for the XP-12 guard station. He felt like a schoolboy, summoned to the principal's office. Who is associate director Burton anyway? Ms. Sanders's voice resounded in his head, "He can see you in half an hour. That should provide sufficient time for you to drive to TA-3 and park in the visitors' lot of the Otowi Building, the Lab's administration headquarters. Proceed through the main guard gate. Take the elevator to the fourth floor and follow the signs to the administrative offices." She'd hung up so fast he'd had no time to protest.

Dead ahead Rick saw his group leader, Arthur, speaking animatedly to an elderly man with such crooked posture that he had to lift his chin to keep from staring at his feet. The man's heavy tan corduroy trousers and professorial-looking olive woolen waistcoat imbued him with the sensibility of an elder statesman of science. One who carried its burdens on his own back. For an instant, Rick could've sworn he glimpsed a sack load of troubles weighing the man down. *Compañero.*

Arthur corralled Rick with a wave. "Richard, I've someone for you to meet. Sam Smith. This gentleman is as capable a physicist as you'll find."

Sam is modeled after? MURRAY GELMAN?

"Hello, Sam. Rick Adams." Rick studied Sam's face, finding its peaceful demeanor comforting. He was not so old, but his fragile bearing appeared to belie his age. And his rugged features, perhaps Eastern European, were no match for a good ol' boy name.

"Pleasure to make your acquaintance," Sam said, extending his dry, bony hand and lightly grasping Rick's.

Sam's wide-eyed gaze impressed Rick as genuinely warm. Not a quality Rick was taking for granted, given his experiences with the scientific elite.

"Sam's a Senior Fellow," Arthur said. "A member of the scientific aristocracy here on the Hill. Only problem is he listens more than he speaks." Arthur grinned at Sam, continuing his praise.

Throughout the encomium, it seemed to Rick that Sam stood by humbly. He often waved a hand in dissent or dismissal, completely different from that of 99% of the recognized scientists Rick had met. Not rocket, but rock star scientists— Typically it was clear they, too, were convinced of their star status.

"Richard ran a hydro lab at MIT," Arthur continued. "You know he's heading up the gas dynamics work on a certain gadget that we can discuss in my office."

"I'm modestly familiar with Dr. Adam's selection for that post," Sam said. "I must say it's not often that you meet a man who can advance the theory of a project that might not even be his, run the design codes to define the machine to test it, and then weld it together and use it." Sam clapped Rick's shoulder.

"That sounds like a wild aggrandizement of my career," Rick said, blushing. "But I should be on a first name basis with someone who has bothered to understand my intentions that clearly."

"Welcome aboard, Rick," Sam said. "You might be interested in what I have to say to my friend here. I'm doing some trouble-shooting on a certain project and would value your feedback."

"I'd like to join you, but I've been called for a security meeting."

"Persevere, it gets better," Sam said.

Rick tried to make good his escape.

Arthur intervened. "What kind of meeting?"

"Some guy named Burton called. Well, his office called." It occurred to Rick too late that perhaps even the mention of the meeting was a security transgression. He sighed, already weary of the Lab's cloak-and-dagger games.

"Associate director Burton?" Arthur asked.

"Is that a big deal?"

"He's master of the Lab's Operations Security and Computing Divisions," Arthur said. "I've never been to his office. How about you, Sam?"

"No. Uh, never."

"Just my luck," Rick said, extending his hand toward Sam. "Pleasure meeting you. Hope to see you again soon."

"Certainly you will."

ONCE BEHIND Arthur's closed office door, Sam took a seat at a round conference table. He watched Arthur, pacing, railing, "Damn ADs! Next they'll want to micromanage my staff meetings. If they could just keep the money flowing in and the top secret data from flowing out like water from a weather-beaten garden hose, this place would be just fine."

"Oh, yes," Sam agreed halfheartedly. His thoughts remained with Rick and his curious meeting with the Lab's Security Czar.

Arthur dropped into a swivel chair at the small table. He exhaled forcefully.

Sam said, "Rick seems like a solid contributor. But the selection committee was unimpressed by his credentials in comparison to the Sandia Lab's man."

"Right, Sandia in California," Arthur said. "Yakimoto, was it?"

"Yamamoto, I think," Sam replied. "I saw his vitae. Thought he was hired, but then he just vanished from consideration."

"I blocked it out." Arthur shook his head solemnly. "A case of bad luck and bad timing, too. Only 34 years old."

"Oh?"

"He apparently lived in a Nob Hill hovel." Arthur's hand sprung up, adding, "The gangs and druggies . . . . One of them tried to rob him or something." He sighed. "Somehow Moto's sword got in the way. He fell against an old wall-standing gas heater and blew the place to bits."

"I'd no idea." Sam sunk deeper into his chair. "I recall he was a master swordsman or something like that." He fidgeted. "It was odd, but impressive, just like his laser cavity design experience. And his graser research."

"I know that Richard was not overwhelmingly preferred for the job." Arthur folded his arms and leaned back. "He was really the only one left, willing to come out here at the drop of a hat and work his tail off. But the Review Committee really wanted a man with graser experience."

Sam rubbed his wrinkled forehead, well-exposed by a thin, receding hairline. "Well, as the MRC's name suggests, it is a multidisciplinary committee, but not an omniscient one."

"That's for certain."

"And he's an arguable genius in the lab," Sam nodded emphatically. "But Rick has no experience designing lasing resonators much less grasing resonators."

"Fred wanted him. Of course, Bruno thinks he walks on water."

Sam hesitated. "I must say that I . . . I was in agreement with the MRC that time."

"Well, he's here and Moto's clacking swords with his ancestors, I suppose."

"And the perpetrator is facing his just deserts?" Sam set his jaw.

"Funny thing." Arthur tapped the table. "He, uh, the perp got away clean."

"That is unbelievably bad luck."

"No trace of evidence. The entire house burned to the ground." Arthur leaned in, adding, "Scuttlebutt had it there was pressure to rule it a suicide. To close the case."

Sam felt a charge of outrage course from his disbelieving brain through his entire body. He wanted to bolt up, raise his fists to the ceiling to denigrate the slack, apathetic attitudes of some law enforcers. He knew the personal price to be paid for looking the other way, leaving a quarry full of stones unturned in an investigation, and shrinking away in fear from one's duty. He diverted himself, asking, "And the bad timing?"

"He was supposed to already be here working. The poor fellow had sold his house and was ready to leave when our security hawks decided to investigate his finances a bit more. Turn's out, the guy was a gem. He sent most of his money back to Japan to develop rural schools."

Sam's eyes narrowed. He remained silent.

"And then Richard, with all of his, uh, *issues*, comes on board in record time."

The desire to explode into rage was stronger than ever as Sam considered the role of the Lab's security department in Yamamoto's ostensible bad luck. But he controlled his emotions. The way he always had. Especially since that frigid night on the banks of the Charles River, decades ago. An image of a body disappearing face-first into the black depths flashed into his mind. Sam's heart wrenched him back to the present where he gasped, recognizing that Rick was already over his head in treacherous water. Would he be the next to have the *misfortune* of descending into blackness?

CHAPTER 16

DR. GAVIN BURTON eased back in his faux leather executive chair. He held a dossier labeled "Richard 'Rick' Adams: Experimental Physics-12." His reading glasses rested precariously on the ball of his narrow, pitted nose as he perused the six-inch stack of documents and photographs. A corner of his mouth was drawn up sharply, wrinkling his deeply-pock-marked face into a sneer. The dossier had been distilled onto a single, high-capacity flash drive, which was attached in a plastic bag stamped "PERSONNEL SENSITIVE" in red type. Gavin preferred hardcopies. He squinted in the low-light at a glossy 8x10 of Rick's family home, a frame and stucco, zero lot line job. The son of a travelling salesman. Apparently, dad travelled too far to find his way back home, leaving Rick and his mother to tough it out together.

The record was complete; typical when it came to background investigations of candidates for high-level security clearances. Rick's life history was detailed, including successes and failures, especially the failures and how they were handled. Contributors included family, friends, neighbors, professors, romantic interests, admirers, enemies, frienemies, and just about anyone else who could be cajoled or intimidated into spilling their guts to an imposing FBI agent carrying a shiny badge. Co-conspirators and comrades in crime were consulted and often ratted out a confidant with little inducement. Rick's Boston buddy, Joel, was among the chorus. And Desiree, his erstwhile fiancée, who'd dumped him for an MIT colleague after Rick's dismissal, had chimed in, too.

Judging by the dozens of pages of facts gleaned from credit reports, driving records, tax filings, academic transcripts, adult and juvenile court proceedings, and other records, along with the hundreds of pages of sworn statements by individuals, Richard Adams was an interesting man who had been an interesting adolescent. So much so that the FBI had recommended not clearing him. They cited myriad details in their formal findings document, even noting that Rick sometimes talked in his sleep, a security no-no.

In fact, Burton, himself, had found Rick too interesting for most high-security-related endeavors, but just right for others.

Before placing the entire stack in a large folder, Burton eyed a copy of an old photo. Good-looking kid, he thought. Too tall. A bit skinny. So much curly hair. He smoothed his stringy gray comb-over, trading the photo for a document. Rick's terse resignation letter to his department head at MIT. It was stapled to a previous letter addressed to his department chairman accusing him of myopia regarding purloined research. In Burton's stack, Rick's letters were immediately atop MIT's letter informing him that his rolling tenure appointment as assistant professor of physics, which was renewable annually, would not be renewed for the following academic year. And that was the main reason former professor Adams was here.

Burton rose and donned his slightly wrinkled navy blue, polyester blazer. He slid the folder into an open file cabinet drawer, closed it, and spun the large safe dial on the front, per security procedures. He glanced lovingly at the photo of Kelly, the single personal artifact on display. Silky, dark red hair. The world's most precious Irish setter.

RICK STARED at kitschy WWII security posters in Burton's anteroom. Horrific battle scenes with cautionary slogans like "Loose Lips Sink Ships" and surreptitious scenes asking, "Need to Know?" He assumed Rosie the Riveter was on lunch break. It all seemed so . . . so passé. It's been what, 50 years or more since the Rosenbergs' execution. Rick believed the modern world was different. It'd never happen again.

Ms. Sanders, Rick's new favorite administrative assistant, interrupted his thoughts to escort him into Burton's dimly lighted office. The AD stood at the head of a vast oak veneer conference table, wearing a buttoned coat and tie. Burton thrust out his hand. "Thank you for coming over on short notice, Richard."

"No problem."

"They do call you Richard?"

"Rick, actually."

"Rick, do you care for something to drink . . . coffee, tea?"

"No, thank you."

"Please take a seat," Burton said, gesturing toward a chair at the conference table adjacent to the head, where he seated himself.

Rick noted that the cinderblock walls of Burton's work space were covered by *faux* mahogany paneling. Light absorbing surfaces designed to endow the generous office with bureaucratic gravitas, he surmised. Burton's metal window shutters were cloaked in curtains. Vintage Herman Miller chairs with five wheels. OSHA standard. Their earthy fabric coordinated with the dolorous draperies and the chocolate brown fabric used to upholster dozens of closed, wall-mounted storage cabinets. Pools of light from recessed overhead incandescent bulbs barely illuminated the drab space. Rick assessed the anteroom cheerful by comparison.

"So, Rick, how do you find Los Alamos? Not exactly Cambridge, eh?"

"Few places are. But I'm sure I'm going to like it here."

"I certainly hope so." Burton paused to flatten his palms together near chin level. "You know, Rick, the Lab is more like a small town than a small town. Remember Titusville, Iowa, where you grew up. You're aware that your challenges there are documented in your security file."

"I considered pot smoking medicinal. Trying to maintain my sanity."

"It's the pot smoking at 35 that's tough to gloss over," Burton continued. "What I mean to say is, you should be extremely careful not to cast the wrong impression here."

"I've been instructed in minute detail by the Lab's security staff, regarding what *not* to do." Rick crossed his arms and squinted at a bushy ficus plant in the corner. Must be rubber, he thought, because there wasn't sufficient light in the place to grow a weed.

"I understand you perfectly. And let me say that your forthrightness regarding your continued use of marijuana while in Cambridge was impressive. Some try to hide unlawful abuses." Burton cleared his throat. "You did not admit to using other controlled substances—cocaine, for example?"

"No."

"A place like Santa Fe has ready access to the world's wiles. Yet I realize that you have forsworn those abuses to which you admitted."

It dawned on Rick that he might have moved over 2,000 miles—from one Orwellian enclave to another—only to have this tightass accuse him of doing coke. Why give him a high-level security clearance in record time if he were destined to be Los Alamos Enemy #1? Rick said, "Excuse me, but I'm not following your logic."

"You are working on the most crucial program administered by this Laboratory in decades, perhaps since its inception. Devastating security leaks and management scandals have weakened our credibility. This undertaking must be scientifically flawless and security-wise hermetic."

Rick nodded.

Burton leaned forward, continuing, "Each program involving highly secretive information has principal security custodians. These security officers possess direct charge and authority to maintain overall security, including establishing and enforcing particular security domains." Burton extended his hands as though compressing a foot-long baguette along its length. "We call them compartments."

Burton dropped the imaginary baguette and clasped his hands. "These officers have assistants called derivative classifiers. They are more readily available to answer straightforward security-related questions and interpret compartment boundaries. I have established very narrow boundaries for GRIT. Not only is the left hand ignorant of the right's activities, but the pinky and ring fingers are also completely separated."

Rick's eyes were glazing, but he thought he heard Burton say the unthinkable, "… you to act as a covert security asset within GRIT."

"Wha?" Rick sat erect.

"Seldom is a new hire chosen. No one will suspect you. You'll report directly to me. And as an added benefit, you'll have access to a wider array of intelligence."

Rick tried to hide his shock and dismay. He was supposed to be an informant on top of having the most demanding technical job on the project. This is crazy, he thought.

"I believe you've already benefited from your selection to this post," Burton said.

Rick's head skewed.

"What did you think of GRIT? Impressive, yes? Why do you think you were allowed in?"

Rick's mind changed gears. Now, this was getting interesting. "It's a behemoth; a beast," he said. "It'll still take a miracle to make it work."

"The Russians have a grasing cavity design. Now they're integrating their system." Drilling his grey eyes into Rick, he said, "We're playing a deadly game of catch-up."

"But I'm not so sure that we or they could possibly blow a warhead out of the sky with a ground-based weapon. Assuming warheads are launched from a delivery vehicle in low earth orbit, maybe 200 miles up, atmospheric attenuation of the beam—"

"Rick, I have another highly classified tidbit for you. I can only share this because of your new assignment. GRIT doesn't need to achieve warhead kill intensity."

"But a staff member even said so."

"No one that you know understands how GRIT will marginalize nuclear warheads. They just think they know." Burton poked his chest. "I know." Hands wide, palms up, he said, "How much energy is required to fry sensitive electronics?"

"Not much."

"Shall we say, 50 or 60 kilojoules? About what it takes to boil over your coffee in a typical microwave oven."

"Yeah, but it takes the oven a minute to deliver that much energy. That's like infinite in comparison to the time we have for shooting down dozens of warheads."

"Duration is not a problem for us or the Russians. We have access to NASA's acquisition, tracking, and pointing algorithms. We can train a powerful beam on a speck of space dust for as long as we want. So can they. And we had terawatt chemical lasers decades ago. A gamma ray laser is a thousand times more penetrating."

Rick's head was shaking yes.

"The threat is genuine, Rick. Dispel your doubts and get cracking."

Reality set in once more. Rick stammered, "I, uh . . . don't know what to say."

"Perhaps, *thank you*, for having invested my trust in you."

"But, Mr. Burton, I've got more than enough to do." Rick squirmed, wishing he could screw himself right through the bottom of his seat, through the floor, down into whatever lay beneath, tuff . . . China.

"This will require little cognitive effort on your part."

"What will I do . . . exactly?"

"No need to snoop," Burton said. "Just prick up your ears."

Rick's head shook no.

Burton eased back in his chair. He spoke softly, deliberately, using his lower vocal register. "Rick, did you know that even a white lie to the FBI is a punishable offense? Odd as it may sound, Martha Stewart went to prison for lying to the government, nothing else. And perjury on a Laboratory security affidavit is grounds for immediate dismissal. Have you formally terminated your affiliation with MIT?"

Rick stared at Burton. He held all the face cards. Rick was being forced to play high-stakes poker with his dog-eared deck. He considered folding his hand right then. The rush of blood to his head was almost dizzying. An instant passed, then another. His stomach churned and fire raced up his spine to his shoulders. Was his fresh start slipping away so soon? How would he like teaching freshman physics at Podunk U? What about Desiree? The limbic brain moderated and Rick relaxed his shoulders. He etched a thin grin on his face and kept his mouth shut.

Burton continued, "Now, it is imperative that you speak of this to no one."

Oh, you won't have to worry about that, Rick thought. A shiver shot up his spine, as though a sewer rat had traversed his grave. A rat, exactly!

"Regarding your fiancée—"

"She doesn't work here."

"I was hoping she might consider it. There are many positions available for a woman of her capabilities."

Rick wasn't certain how to interpret Burton's smirk.

"It turns out," Burton said, standing, signifying the session was finished, "I know a thing or two about hydrodynamics. Spent a little time at 77 Mass Ave., myself. You are the man to crack this tough nut," Burton said, extending his hand.

Rick's hand was as limp as an overcooked turnip. He just hoped his ignominy wouldn't similarly affect the remainder of his anatomy.

LESS THAN A MINUTE after Rick's departure, Burton typed furiously on his classified machine. He believed that there were multiple ways to skin a cat of Rick's stripes, but the most brutal means were not going to be necessary. He'd been reassured by Rick's restraint when needled. And Rick had jumped at the mention of Desiree's name. He deemed it pure genius, constraining Rick using job security and his semi-fixation with her. Burton had insisted on it. Even at the intense objections of others, who preferred using more stringent measures to manipulate Rick. Measures sure to fill multiple body bags which Burton, himself, would have to explain away.

CHAPTER 17

The OFFICE door clunked closed. The room continued to reverberate as Rick dived into his work, barely taking his eyes off of one display before peering soulfully into another. The Computer, answer to all life's quandaries. Of course not, but hopefully, this one was going to be the answer to generating a more successful model of GRIT's grasing cavity. The results from his first-order mock-up were disastrous. If he rushed, maybe, just maybe he could generate something worth showing to the MRC at their Thursday meeting. He would use the model to test his initial ideas for a reasonable—still suboptimal, but tractable—design.

The algorithm Rick was developing would discretize the cavity's volume into small spatial elements, millions of one centimeter cubes. The grasing energy developed inside each cube would yield an estimate of the volumetric power produced inside the cavity. Summing all of the discretized elements would indicate the total power producible by a particular design.

GRIT's volumetric output power would be stored as a three-dimensional matrix, demonstrating each cube's power contribution. In graphical form, such a three-dimensional plot typically looked like a landscape with mountains, hills, mesas, plains, and valleys, representing areas of high to low power production, respectively. Rick's earnest hope was not to produce a plot of Gerry's backyard: xeriscape, the null solution. If the mathematical solvers failed to converge on a reasonable solution for the power generated by each cube in the three dimensional array, then zeros were yielded as the solution. The resulting plot was a desert with nary a hill or topographical bump: a perfect zeroscape.

Lost in a world of numbers, Rick wanted to ignore the knock on his door. "Come in," he said, slowly.

Bruno stood in the darkened doorway. Stone-faced.

Rick turned and asked, "Whoa, man, what train ran over you?"

"I thought you might not know," he murmured.

"I've been at it constantly today." Rick stretched his arms wide and rolled his head around his shoulders.

"There was an accident."

Rick sat up.

"Fred . . . crashed his car."

"Fred Larson?"

"He's dead."

Rick sprang up, but couldn't stand on wobbly legs. Bracing himself on his desk, he sat heavily on the edge. "What happened? Fred was an excellent driver."

"Ran off the Los Alamos ski hill road Saturday night. Positively IDed his body this morning."

"What was he doing up there?"

"Nobody knows. He was alone."

"Jeeze, I can't believe it." Rick stood unsteadily before plopping down into his chair. "Such a good guy." He hesitated. "Was it bad?"

"Burned beyond recognition," Bruno caught his breath. Stammered, "Had to use dental records to, uh, identify him."

Rick shook his head. Tried to relax and oxygenate his tightening lungs.

"Service is tomorrow afternoon at two."

"And where's he going to be . . . ."

"Jenna's taking him home to Oregon."

"What can I do? Is there anything—"

"I don't think so. She asked no flowers be sent."

Rick's mind blanked and he ignored Bruno's exit. Vines seemed to cord his windpipe; the bronchia cinched like a knot of constricting snakes. His heart ached with every beat. Why did terrible things happen to good people? Why bother? His demons came out to play.

The one saving grace that had never let him down completely was available. Rick turned to his classified monitor. He fixated on developing another input file. Forced all thoughts other than work from his mind. Life was too strange to understand. He would strive to understand just one thing: GRIT's prospects for destroying a live nuclear warhead that was hurtling through space.

CHAPTER 18

Late that evening, in his home office,
Sam sunk into a leather desk chair.
Dug in deep, teacup and saucer in hand. His sleep was disturbed by the warmth
in his unairconditioned home. Surely, his previous thoughts of Rick Adams were
uninvolved. A book lay open on the desk, the feeble light of his desk lamp barely
illuminating its glossy pages. His re-examination of Wallenberg's WWII heroics
had not lifted Sam's spirits. They had been dampened by considerations of Rick's
portentous meeting with Herr Burton. An ill omen. Oh, Burton wasn't personally
to be feared. Fancied himself an intellectual. A man of the higher mind. Sam
knew it was a mind without scruples or conscience. But Burton's *associates* . . . .
Sam's life bore a gash—one that refused to heal—from their wickedness.

The teacup jiggled; Sam's chest tightened. Nothing, really. A little cardiac
arrhythmia. Doctors are often wrong. Sam would have noticed a heart attack.
Besides, he felt fine most of the time. The doctor was probably angling for more
tests, return visits, a medication regimen. Working his *schtick*. Another pang;
another denial.

Sam wondered how his Uncle George had slept. He'd been an isolated man who didn't even identify with other survivors. Closing his eyes for a moment, a scene from a Hanukkah long-past commanded Sam's mind. Bitter cold. His mother's steaming matzo ball soup, served at his parents', the Goldschmidts', drafty tenement in Brooklyn. Uncle George fasted. Sat mute, wearing short shirt sleeves, exposing the scrawled bluish tattoo on his left forearm. Sam's father, Ben, who'd been spared incarceration, ate in silence.

Sam had been schooled well in tragic family lore. Levi, George and Ben's father and Sam's grandfather, had been confined with George in Auschwitz. Levi, an old man when incarcerated, died quickly from a work-related injury. Many of George's torments there were known to all. Sam suspected that some abuses went unshared.

Sam shouldered an incomparable load of guilt, no small portion of which was inherited from his parents. They escaped death, even incarceration, unlike their parents and some siblings. Sam believed his parents' initial attraction was feeling unworthy and shameful for having escaped imprisonment. Although unscathed physically, the shame of their fathers lived on hauntingly in them.

Sam believed that George's Auschwitz nightmare was not what had made him perpetually angry. Other grief-stricken, traumatized survivors lived normally, cherishing their families and enjoying their lives. Some even found the courage to spread a message of hope and healing. Sam imagined that George was continually sullen because his *beshert* did not survive. Rachael had been raped while incarcerated in a labor camp. She slashed her wrists with a rusty razor blade hidden in a fetid straw mattress. Her shame was passed along faithfully to younger sister Esther, who, safe and chaste, escaped abroad to New York City where later she married Ben.

Ben's most intensive efforts to reconnect with George were futile. Ben paid for the room, board, and education of his brilliant brother, now an esteemed professor of physics in Chicago. But George lambasted Ben constantly, especially for accepting a blasphemous Anglicization of his surname. Sadness fell like a wet cloak over Ben's casket. George was absent for his only brother's funeral. The doctor said it was a heart attack. Ester said he died of a broken heart.

Distraught and only marginally more accepted by the family than her late husband, Esther had no choice but to yield her bright son to live with his stern uncle. As an undergraduate at the University of Chicago, Sam thrived academically under Uncle George's harsh hand. Later, Sam was accepted for postgraduate study at MIT's Department of Physics. Sam's move to Cambridge was both a beginning and an end. George never spoke to him again, a result of his disdain for what he called "the pinnacle of pretentiousness in American post-secondary education. And the BU School of Revisionist History."

Sam's thoughts eddied into the present. He was no Wallenberg. If he were, he couldn't undertake such exploits. Even self-disclosure was too great a risk, Reba had always said. Sam had seen things; he knew too much. Retaliation and misery for his entire family were at stake. He loved his wife and his offspring too much to let an impulse to be a savior or even a good Samaritan jeopardize them.

He turned the page in hopes of refocusing attention on his hero, to expiate his own impotence. Sam found an innocent face staring back at him. Innocents are everywhere, he considered. They come in all shapes and sizes. Rick Adams, for example: an innocent, probably; a sheep, probably not; beset by wolves, definitely.

CHAPTER 19

THE CHILLING breeze that swept in from the nearby Bandelier National Park enshrouded the Jemez Mountains above Los Alamos. Cold infiltrated Big John Thunderbird's hip and knee joints, stiffening them like rust in an old machine. His head drooped, his chin indenting wet buckskin.

Two fevered days and nights, he'd supplicated continuously. His injured leg had swollen to twice its normal size. Yet Big John practiced his ritual without ceasing. His barrel chest heaved and dripped sweat as he wailed, crying out to his Ancestors and the Mountain Spirits for forgiveness, for the restoration of his family, and for the destruction of Los Alamos National Laboratory.

Silence. Nothing.

Tight cuff bracelets corded Big John's muscular biceps. They shone in firelight as he waved a newly blessed eagle's wing feather. Both ankles were dressed with sacred, bead-laden horsehair loops. One leg ached; the other burned. A paste of healing herbs was lashed with wet leather cord to his wounded thigh. His stealthy, animal-like movements as he circled the sacred fire had degraded long ago into a flatfooted trudge. Faint, Big John collapsed to the ground.

Thoughts of the Los Alamos National Laboratory spoiling his ancestors' home tortured him. The Lab occupied and defiled this consecrated land still. Big

John dragged to his knees. He raised his face and thrust clenched fists skyward. Trembling, he stood and screamed at the top of his lungs for a sign . . . any sign. And for the aid of his natural gods to destroy the ravagers of this land.

Silence. Nothing.

A thin crescent of a moon lingered overhead. It shed precious little light upon the towering ponderosa pine tops and even less upon the ground, hundreds of feet below where Big John bewailed in ecstasy and agony, encircling the sacred fire. Suddenly, he perceived an answer to prayer. A lone birdcall in the highest reaches of darkness, the top of the most majestic pine. The cry was accompanied by a rustling of branches and a quiet trickle that stopped overhead. A sign. Eyes wide-open, expectant, Big John carefully combed the dry earth beneath the tree, using a glowing orange-red ember. A test. He must find the symbol that the Ga'an, the ancient and most sacred of Apache Mountain Spirits, had used to reveal themselves. Finally, his petitions had been acknowledged.

Heart beating wildly—pulse banging in his temples—Big John scoured the earth. Moving his head in minute saccades, he examined everything and nothing with eagle eyes. Was his life restored? Was the extraordinary birthright of his son returned? Had the decades of remorse, years of penance, nights and days of unending grief yielded fruit? A brisk breeze rustled the trees. He stopped dead. A trickle directly overhead. He froze with exultation and dread, awaiting his fate, which fell upon his shoulders as a bolder crushing an ant, although it nearly floated like a feather to earth. A sliver of moonlight scattered through the tall trees, illuminating it. Not a sacred gift from the Ga'an, but a mere pine cone. Silence. Nothing.

CHAPTER 20

Angels and demons, deliverance and damnation rocked Rick's sleep. He woke choking, pulse racing. He sat up on the bedside and massaged his temples before stumbling toward the bathroom to slake his scorching thirst. The dream sequences had been real—based on actual events—yet surreal. The big faded tent, held together by patches and prayer; the Happy Munnys whipping up the congregation; and Rick, himself, keeping a choppy beat on a battered trap set.

Rick guzzled tap water, thinking the scene he'd recalled in his sleep seemed a tough gig at the time. How could his mom have gone for it? Sure, after his dad's *unexpected departure* from their lives, Rick and his mom were down, scared. But when Reverend Munny showed up at church one Sunday morning, seeking recruits for his band's summer tour, she made Rick talk to the guy. Munny was a charmer with tales of life on the open road. And the allure of thousands of hell-bound sinners being saved, each one a star in the band members' heavenly crowns . . . . Rick splashed his face in the elegant basin, but the scent of his perspiration threw him back in time: thrashing away on the drums in a smelly shirt, wringing wet, at some backwater tent revival.

The Reverend Munny, a former juvenile delinquent, himself, kept Rick on a short leash. Taught him a few riffs on a yellowed, white-pearl Slingerland trap kit. Three pitiful pieces. The little bass drum was deadened with Rick's pillow, the rattley snare drum sounded like it contained marbles, and the bent ride/crash cymbal, when struck forcefully, resembled striking a twelve-inch skillet on a human skull.

But Rick had been a good boy. Hadn't caused trouble and hadn't ratted out the members who did. That was one reason Burton's directive to him seemed so wrong. Rick had been respected, even in childhood, for his rigorous personal code. Would he betray it now? For an impossible job at a wacked-out weapons Lab? But this was his last shot. The tap splashed cool water into his face. Rick's mind relaxed. So what happens when GRIT collapses? The thought jolted him to the core. He was already going to be a snitch. No real fear of further personal abasement. But should he fail to perfect GRIT's grasing cavity, it may be back to the Stone Age for the whole country . . . yaba daba doo—

And then the thought, 'Fred is dead' captivated his mind. I'm obsessing over trivia and Fred's beautiful life is over. Rick's guts tossed as rage and revulsion overtook him. He cranked the tap and thrust his entire head underneath. Held his breath. You selfish bastard, he thought. Your mentor is dead and you're whining about a bad summer job and being elevated in importance at your current job within the first week! Get over it and get some sleep. Tomorrow's going to be a tough one.

Rick was surprised at the generous scale of the sanctuary at the Los Alamos Methodist Church. And it was nearly filled. This was a community that closed ranks when it was time to shield one of their own or to mourn. The service was low-key and brief. Afterwards, Rick saw Jenna standing at the rear of the chapel, flanked by a woman who looked to be an elder sister and Arthur Purcell, Fred's group leader. They lightly shook the hands of attendees as they filed past, some stopping to express condolences.

It was no surprise for Rick to see Walter standing near the back, wearing a rumpled red tee and green jeans. Rick kept his distance, but when he saw Gerry, he maneuvered toward him.

"Hello, Rick," Gerry said. "Too bad about Fred."

"He was a great guy," Rick said. "I heard his car went off the ski hill road. You sold him that car, right?"

"It was cherry," Gerry enthused. "I just serviced it myself."

Did he say, "just serviced?" Rick wondered if he should find a new mechanic.

"Maybe he got distracted?" Gerry intoned. "And Fred drove a bit too fast sometimes." His harsh, chiseled features morphed into a pleasant expression.

Rick found Gerry's demeanor to be at odds with the caring words. He studied Gerry's face more carefully. It was a goddamn repulsive smirk. He was smirking about Fred's death. Rick began to get that irritable feeling. His head buzzed; his ears rang. His fist was balling, involuntarily. Was he going to punch Gerry? Forget the consequences. It would not bring Fred back. Fred was dead. Period. He held Gerry's gaze an instant longer—too long already—and then he turned his back and walked away.

SAM SAT QUIETLY in a back corner of the sanctuary. He would wait to speak to Jenna, although he realized there was nothing he could say that would help. She wouldn't appreciate his resonance with the pain of her unanticipated loss. He waited patiently, frequently sticking his face into a hymnal, avoiding Gavin Burton's surreptitious survey.

And then Sam's eyes burned with disbelief. He shook his head, blinked rapidly to dispel the vision. Those eyes; that chin; the evil grin. He shifted his weight on the pew while being catapulted back through time. His insides churned. He rose and almost stumbled making his way to the side doors. He was hyperventilating, starving for fresh air. Sam tried to breathe deeply, to calm himself. No use. He felt sicker. Clenching the shrubbery, he bent over and wretched into a manicured flowerbed. The scene whirled rapidly, before he descended into darkness.

"Are you okay?" asked a brawny man dressed in a dark suit, who stood over him.

"What happened?" Sam asked.

"You fainted," replied a tall, skinny fellow, similarly dressed and holding a small note pad and pen. "Are you ill? Particularly upset about anything?"

"No," Sam said. "Shouldn't have skipped lunch." Noting a furtive glance by his inquisitor, Sam smiled disarmingly. "Are you gentlemen with the mortuary?"

"No sir. We're, uh, friends of the family," the brawny man replied.

"What's your name, sir?" inquired the scribe.

"I'm Sam Smith. I used to work with Fred." Sam stood to his feet. He brushed grass from his trousers and straightened his knit tie. "Where will he be laid to rest?"

Another glance. The brawny man said, "California." OREGON

"Well, I wish you gentlemen a safe trip. Thanks much for your help." Sam excused himself politely, saying, "I'd better see about getting some food."

Sam rounded the corner. Peeked through the shrubbery at the duo, who studied Walter. When Walter approached, they huddled and chatted animatedly, until he passed. Sam limped away, realizing their story of being family friends was a bunch of *chazari*. And he would bet his balls that Fred's demise was no accident. Satan had returned.

CHAPTER 21

THE STRAIN that his harsh office lights would inflict on his eyes was simply unacceptable, so Rick sat in near darkness considering the graphic's meaning. His classified workstation's high resolution display glowed with the results of the latest run. His emotions were exhausted. And his pitiful attempt at sleeping the previous night had drained his analytical acumen. Still, he'd work day and night for a month to produce something better than the dull gray-black plot with a few orange-red splotches he observed on the screen. The new and improved model indicated an anemic grasing cavity where small pockets of lasing gammas produced paltry output power. The thermodynamicist's sardonic joke about the Harlem bathtub resounded in his ears.

When the phone rang, Rick hesitated. And when Walter Bowers croaked, "Hello there, Rick. How are you holding up?" Rick was certain that he shouldn't have answered. But he replied kindly, "Not too bad. How about you?"

"Damn shame. Fred was a terrific person and an excellent physicist."

Silence.

"I didn't know him as well as you, but he took me under his wing." Rick caught his breath. "I'll, uh, miss him."

"He liked you, too. And I've got something to tell you. You live in Santa Fe?"

"Yeah."

"Can we have a chat? Maybe a little drink tonight? It's important."

Rick's pulse quickened. His breath shallowed. "I suppose so."

"How about Angel's bar. Say, eight?"

"See you there."

Rick could hardly wait. At ten till eight, he entered the smoky din through the back door. Scanned Angel's crowd, before heading upstream toward the bar, craning his neck around ten-gallon hats. He even had to dodge a pair of protruding spurs.

"Rick, over here!"

He spotted Walter sitting in the back, waving his arms.

Barging through the mêlée to a small table, Rick shouted, "Happening place."

"Let's listen. Almost break time."

The lights went down. Diego's driving beat gave way to a slow rhythmic concentration on the high-hat cymbals. But it was the B3's sinewy entrance that transformed the feel of the fray. And then, a single, white spotlight illuminated Carmen. She posed with her hip thrust against the massive keyboard. In a breathy voice, she sang, "I'm a black magic woman . . . ."

Carmen worked her magic, sucking the helpless crowd's attention. And like supergravity, she imbibed their energy, too. The shimmering black satin dress was a black hole. It's slit, jutting up her thigh, an event horizon. But she exceeded black holes in that her presence encompassed not only light and energy, but also beauty.

The music faded and the lights dimmed to wild applause.

"She's great," Rick said. Focusing on Walter, he asked, "Everything okay?"

"Just wanted to tell you about something Fred mentioned to me, regarding you."

Rick edged closer.

"He thought you should attend a gas dynamics seminar in San Diego. Given the state of your task, he, uh, thought some fresh ideas might help."

Rick crossed his arms. "I know everything there is to know about gas dynamics." He trained his eyes on T'Bird fussing quietly with his strat's tuning keys.

"They're some of the best computational physicists in the country. Can't hurt. I believe he took the liberty of having Jacqueline, remember her, from the round robin?"

Rick recalled her haughtiness when they were introduced at the tennis courts. She never warmed up to him, like she did to Fred . . . and Dorothy.

"She runs a group in the travel department. I believe she's already booked your trip." His thumb shot up, adding, "Real efficient."

"What? When?"

"Next week. Tuesday through Friday."

"Short notice, especially for them. Isn't it?"

"You're coming from Los Alamos National Lab. They'll probably froth at the mouth to have you attend." Walter raised his beer to Rick and slurped a slug.

"I don't know what to say."

"Thanks?" Walter replied. "Hey, there's Gerry."

Rick observed that Gerry's approach was nothing like his own. No jostling. No jolting. Bikers, bankers, bull riders stepped out of his way, like the Red Sea parting.

"Hello, Rick, Walter," Gerry said. "Good that you two are talking it out."

"Just got to keep on keeping on," Walter said, glancing from Gerry to Rick.

"Oh *Ja*, that's true." Gerry asked Rick, "So, how's the new vehicle?"

"Fine."

"Your new X5?" Walter asked. "Probably a case of the right vehicle finding the right owner."

"There are lots of right owners for that one. I have one, too," Gerry said. "And Rick, can you bring it over this weekend for me to repair that bent heat shield on the underside. Won't take long."

This was getting to be a bit much for Rick, who felt like his life wasn't even his own. He said, "Don't think I'll have time."

"No good. It's a fire hazard. Very dry climate here, you know. Oh, *Ja*."

"Maybe while you're in San Diego, you can leave it with Gerry," Walter said.

"Good idea," Gerry replied. "You can take my Porsche to the airport."

Nice gesture from a guy with a granite jaw and pale-blue raptor eyes, who smirks at his friends' death, Rick thought. Feeling like he needed a momentary break from present company, Rick asked, "How about a drink." Both men declined. On his way to buy a beer for himself, Rick made a pit stop. Although Angel's outdoor facilities were adjacent to the parking lot, the air was refreshing. Rick stood in line, admiring his shiny new suv, amid a desert of dirt. Thought he recognized a burly, bearded man, who exited the driver's side of a filthy Datsun pickup, fiddling with his pants' zipper. A woman wearing a ball cap exited the passenger's side and disappeared.

In the distance, the man's wild hair and poor posture resembled Doc's, the Thunderbird's keyboardist. As he approached, Rick half averted his gaze. But from the corner of his eye, confirmed it was Doc. He passed and Rick observed a white puff lightening Doc's dark mustache, above the graying morass of beard. What a waste, thought Rick. But even he had condoned the use of coke by someone close to him. Had supplied it to someone so close he thought it would have killed him to see her leave.

CHAPTER 22

SAM EYED a photo of a real *mensch*. His anti-self, he thought, trying to squelch his fear, self-loathing. They were the same emotions that always accompanied these moments. Perhaps that was why he hadn't examined the heroics of Raoul Wallenberg for quite a while. Even an esteemed Senior Fellow at Los Alamos National Lab was not an analytical genius all of the time. Sam was human. All too human, and he knew it. His stomach felt queasy again, just like in the afternoon, considering who had appeared on the scene. Fearsome, gruesome, the very essence of evil.

From a dainty ceramic cup, he sipped steaming tea while peering out of the open window of his White Rock home office. Down past the rugged landscape, hundreds of feet below, lay the Rio Grande River. He caressed the teacup and closed his eyes, focusing on his wife's voice, clearly audible from across the house. A sweet soprano that broke his heart every time. A beautiful song from a bird in a cage of her own making— The piece she sang was typical for her, a melancholy classic. Neither Sam nor Reba cared for the rapture of romantic music or the drama of modern music. They were beyond that, had been for decades, their entire lives, seemingly. Too much emotion was dangerous.

Glancing back at the photograph of Wallenberg just once more, for maybe the dozenth time, Sam was awestruck. Wallenberg had faced pure evil nose to nose without so much as flinching. A real superhero. Handsome, aristocratic, yet self-effacing. An unusual combination. Sam considered what Wallenberg had done during WWII for so many Jewish peasants whom he didn't even know. Risked his own life. The knot began to re-form in Sam's stomach. Why couldn't he bring himself to do anything to help anybody, other than his miserable self? Rick Adams had played on his mind all evening. Yes, he was the provocation for tonight's recapitulation of the Wallenberg saga. What intrigues lay before the young man? And why couldn't Sam generate the resolve to at least offer Rick a warning?

Hot tea scalded Sam's quaking hand. Grimacing, he placed the empty cup on its saucer. Sidetracked himself by refocusing on the tranquil waxing moon, casting its ashen light on mountain tops, mesas. In the near-ground, the land sloped downward toward the river. Chamisa, or rabbitbush as he liked to call it, cholla and prickly pear cactuses, and scrawny pinon seedlings struggled up from crags in the fractured tuff. Gazing around his office, Sam admired photographs he'd taken of the scene. Color, black and white, even high resolution infrared night photography. He'd pioneered the technology decades earlier. In all, he'd photographed the rugged landscape leading from his property toward the muddy Rio Grande hundreds of times. These photographs were his haystacks.

The camera lens recorded objective statements of fact. Reality. Sam asked himself why he should endeavor clumsily and in vain to describe the ineffable when a single 4x5 plate could speak volumes eloquently. A sunset, a bridge, an old woman's patchwork dress, her husband's leathern face. Unlike humans, the camera could be trusted to speak the truth. Sam began to feel that he should be toying with his table-top, holographic photography setup now. It might benefit mankind in ways he couldn't predict. He hadn't so much as taken the cover off of it in months, although it was in the shop just outside.

Reba also appreciated the certainty of photographic art. Sam realized not everyone did. Then few shared Sam's and Reba's burdens from the past. Their kinsmen's pasts, to be accurate. The survivors' stories were ingrained in them in lurid detail. Every Passover, Yom Kippur, and almost every Sabbath they had instructed the young and everyone else within earshot, exhorting them never to forget, never ever. Sam and Reba had obeyed rigorously. Sam desperately wished he could forget that long-ago Cambridge night. Lay it to rest, as he had Hannah. Yet it was as vivid as though he witnessed it yesterday. Didn't the survivors know the mind is wired to forget what you want to recall and never to forget what you wish you could?

Pain shot the length of his left arm. His chest heaved. As the room spun about him, Sam stabilized himself on his desk. Sam's final thought was that should he be granted the Grace to continue his life, his one wish was for the strength to confront iniquity. Mustering sufficient courage to whisper a word of warning to Rick Adams would be a fine start. He was incapable of uttering the blackness of the whole truth to Rick; he could barely acknowledge it himself.

CHAPTER 23

Rick arrived back at the tiny table in the corner of Angel's and found Renée chatting with Gerry and Walter. She sported her easy smile that contrasted her disheveled appearance, and severe hat hair.

"Good to see you," Rick said, embracing her. "You alone?"

"Not here."

Rick noticed that Walter and Gerry smiled amiably at Renée. But Gerry's eyes were narrow as though harshly appraising her.

"I was out and stopped by for a nightcap," she said. "My daughter's with her grandparents this weekend." Her lips curled, adding, "No hurry to be home . . . alone."

A proposition? Rick considered it and its consequences, hardly noticing the men's departures. He was jolted back into the moment by Carmen's arrival.

"Dr. Dick! My personal physics professor. Oh, hi, Renée."

Renée shifted in her seat; mussed up her hair; fished lipstick from her bag.

Carmen leaned across the table and smacked Rick's cheek. "That's for Saturday."

Renée's eyes widened.

Rick's reply was drowned out by a majestic chord from the B-3, followed by a smattering of the fugue from Bach's *Great Organ Mass*. Oceanic depths and stratospheric heights howled from the Leslie amplifier, transforming Angel's into a Boston Cathedral at High Mass. For a finale, Doc maxed the volume and jostled the organ's reverberation banks into spasm. An Armageddon of sound.

"Showtime," Carmen mouthed, pointing to the stage.

Rick said, "Sounded like a call to the cross, not the stage."

"Doc's full of surprises, isn't he?" Carmen said to Renée, who dove for her drink.

As the Thunderbirds rocked, Rick stole glimpses of Renée. Definitely preoccupied. By the music? He didn't think so. At a song's conclusion, he said, "A penny for your thoughts." He covered his mouth quickly; opened his eyes wide. "Oh, my low-brow upbringing's showing. They should bring at least a couple of bucks."

"I've heard this set before."

Showing off his newly acquired Spanish vocabulary, Rick said, "*Vamos.*"

Approaching the back of the lot, the band's rumble faded. Rick took the key to Renée's Volvo and opened the door.

She stood close to him. "Want to come over for a nightcap?"

"Tomorrow's another busy day."

"Sure." Her head sunk.

Rick felt his throat tighten. He didn't want to be a heel. And Renée seemed like a nice person, but this could be trouble, he told himself. A star-filled sky. Does the galaxy feel pain? Are raindrops cosmic tears? Rick understood all too well that humans hurt. That Renée was hurting was clear. He could feel it. It highlighted his pain, frustration. My God, he thought, could she ache as much as I sometimes do? Rick's contemplative expression gave way to a smile. "One drink won't hurt, I suppose," he said. "I've been good this week." And, yes, he was being nice now. He intended to be nice later, too. One drink was going to be it.

CHAPTER 24

Rick and Renée drove in tandem up Canyon Road until she turned onto a snaking dirt lane. He'd learned last week that dust and ruts signified Santa Fe chic. By that reckoning, this was a ritzy neighborhood and Angel's parking lot must be priceless.

Renée's place was eclectic and inviting. "Make yourself at home," she said, disappearing behind a beaded Moroccan curtain, separating living and dining rooms.

Rick absorbed the ambience: colorful art; curious African carvings, interesting stones. A boulder supported a lustrous mahogany occasional table, bearing an inlaid chess board, its pieces carved to perfection. Cool stuff everywhere. Rick realized his place was Spartan and dull by comparison. And then he observed the stereo. "Wow," he said. "I didn't know you're an audiophile."

"My ex-husband. His new setup is mega. So, I kept this one."

"Great music, too."

"Put some on."

Rick passed over Big Head Todd and his Monsters for a Grover Washington classic, *Limelight*. He saw cushy wireless headphones hooked on one of the entertainment center's section dividers. Slid them over his ears and depressed "play" on the CD unit. Anechoic silence. Removing them, he heard mellow tenor sax through the large-scale Magnaplanar speakers. A tiny digital video camera charged on a small stand. Rick fingered it. Felt good in his hands. Carl Zeiss optics. Quality. He observed the room through the viewfinder. A squashed, psychedelic image. He wondered if *Rick the Rat* should steal it and use it to capture the after-hours shenanigans at the tennis club, to prove his value? He cringed and replaced it haphazardly when Renée entered, bringing a bottle of red wine and glasses.

Rick poured while Renée disappeared again. She returned with a small baggie, which she placed inconspicuously on a side table.

Half the bottle consumed, she asked, "Want to get high?" Under soft lighting, her gray-blue eyes were sedate and miles deep.

"Are you serious?"

"Smell this," she said, producing the baggie, spreading it open.

"I can't even remember the last time I smoked," Rick said. "And, uh, I got a full day tomorrow."

Renée fixed him with her gaze, extending her torso and the baggie toward him.

He inhaled. "So aromatic."

"It's Columbian. You're gonna love it."

"I really shouldn't."

She nodded and closed the baggie. "I understand. It's just smoking by myself feels a little lonely sometimes."

Silence.

"I hoped we could be, you know, real friends," she said. "That's all."

Rick's thoughts ping-ponged. He'd been here before. Too many times with Desiree. But if Renée wanted to smoke, who was he to stop her or to judge her? "You go ahead."

Renée torched a fat reefer and toked. It was gone in a minute. Rick had to admit it was fragrant stuff. She lit another and handed it to him. Hungrily he inhaled once, and then again. Soon they were giggling and pawing. Renée covered his mouth with hers. When he cupped her breasts, she attacked. Rigid and ready, Rick swooned at her moves. Breathless, he tore her mouth away. She dove down on him again.

"Wait," he said, gasping.

"Just let go."

Rick didn't like it. She didn't even know him. How needy is she, he wondered. Rick looked down at Renée. That face . . . nice, kind. Its plaintive expression. He asked, "There a bed in this place?"

"I like it here," Renée said, quickly slipping off her panties. She straddled him awkwardly and began an insistent rhythm.

Rick reached around and unfastened her bra. He stroked her nipples with the back of his hand. Kneaded them between his fingers. Soft, delicate flesh. He looked up to admire her fine jaw line. Renée's head was thrown back. She moaned, riding him harder.

Rick hoped her climax was near, because his certainly was. He whispered, "Keep on 'til you explode."

"I can't," she murmured, lifting herself off him and heading south.

"Oh, yes, you can."

Vaulting on top, Rick took Renée masterfully, stimulating her manually while thrusting. He delayed his pleasure to satisfy her.

"Rick, just let go," she said anxiously.

His climax was a torrid release of pent-up sexual energy, romantic frustration, and escapism. Rick convulsed and fell atop Renée.

She led him to her bedroom. Snug in Renée's bed, Rick lay quiet. He just wanted to hold her for a while, but she exited the room. When she returned, Renée eased into bed and draped herself across Rick's chest. Her breath, a continual sigh. He stroked her lean body through a slick silken robe, ran his fingers through her yellow hair, and kissed it. A pungent smoky odor, harsher than sweet Columbian pot, shocked him.

Renée turned and stared. Her glassy eyes sunk into her head. She looked sick.

Rick collapsed into fitful sleep. A maniacal Burton, demanding damning evidence on everybody at the Lab, threatened to fire Rick, to prosecute him for lying on his security affidavit. A black night. Rick awoke and looked at Renée. No hint of lengthy legs or svelte torso. Her body was contorted into a little ball. Fetal. Scared. Her pretty face drawn and hollow. What emptiness was she trying to fill? Where was his will to play it straight? He dressed, jotted a sweet note on a writing pad, and turned off the bedside light, before walking carefully through the house. A burden of dread lifted once he'd shut the door behind him.

Renée awoke just after dawn. She limped to the bathroom and gulped water from the faucet. Avoiding the mirror, she returned to bed. Her eyes burned, reading Rick's note. She crushed it, sobbing. Threw it to the floor. Time passed slowly, because she filled every minute despising herself. Hours and a pot of coffee later, Renée shuffled into the living room where she grasped the fancy digital video camera. Squeezed it in her hand. Wished to smash it. But didn't. She stood, staring into space, before stuffing it into a gym bag. Her knees weakened and she fell on the sofa. Clutching her purse, she found her wallet and flung it open. Renée's raccoon eyes met the crystal clear eyes and smiley face of a little girl. She peered out from under too-long blonde bangs. Renée pressed the photo to her breast.

Emily was her only love, now. She'd loved sex. Maybe too much. Drugs, hard not to love . . . for a while. Her loss of orgasm meant nothing. The ecstacy/viagra cocktails at the club were useful for stimulation. And so what if she were slipping back into an 'H' addiction. Her life was worthless without the love of her perfect little child. Emily was all she needed.

Renée wound herself into a tight ball. She quaked, contracting her muscles even more. The judge had been right. She'd been an unfit mother. But that decision must be reversed. And Walter was the answer. Connections, he had high ones, he'd said. She would do anything to get her daughter back. Screw the devil and all his demons. Smoke crack by the pound. Trash the lives of everyone she met; even those she might want to care for. She pictured Rick's face, the tender way he'd looked at her last night. How he wanted so much to please her. Renée blinked away the image and focused on the photo in her trembling hand. She would destroy everything and everybody to be with her daughter. By God she would.

CHAPTER 25

G ERRY'S compound seemed more desolate in early morning light. Rick arrived feeling better about the errand, having taken the time to verify that indeed there was a bent heat shield on the underside of his vehicle. The X5 purred as magically the heavy gate opened. Crunching his way up the gravel path, Rick saw Gerry standing at the driveway's crest, sporting a toothy grin on his hard face. An early model Porsche Turbo was parked by his side, its lustrous black paint gleaming. Rick disembarked and approached, saying, "I really appreciate this."

"It's nothing. Just don't forget to give my key to the attendant at the airport parking lot. I'll trade out your SUV for my car while you're away."

Gerry shoved the key toward Rick. "Beware of the turbo lag if you get aggressive. This engine has one big blower. Lots of mechanical and combustion inertia. When the intake air box is fully pressurized and the cams catch up to optimize the fuel-oxygen mixture, you gonna go like a rocket."

"That's an impressive take on combustion dynamics," Rick said.

"Every German truck driver knows Bernoulli's Principle is just a restatement of the conservation of energy." Gerry grinned. "Oh, Rick. You have a second to help me?"

Rick waved the car key. "It's the least I could do." He followed Gerry inside the workshop's anteroom, where an ordinary looking pane of glass rested on a squat metal table. Rick examined the workspace. Natural lighting, well constructed. An immaculate floor. He noticed a corner cube embedded in the joint of two nearby walls. It seemed odd to have an optical component used to bend a light beam in a workshop. With his eyes, Rick traced the incident and reflecting paths from the cube. They led to other optical elements across the room in two, orthogonal directions. He traced each pass of the beam, which formed a light truss crisscrossing the floor about a foot off the ground. Incredulous, Rick asked, "Hey man, what's—"

"Excuse me. Can you give me a hand now?" Gerry asked. "I need your muscle; not your big Los Alamos brain. Hold down the glass while I etch it for a clean break."

Rick frowned. "My hands are sweaty from driving."

"It's okay. Press them flat down. And put some weight on it, so it doesn't move."

Gerry ran a glasscutter across the opposing end. "I've never seen a scientist do a technician's job so expertly."

"Sometimes I think I was born to be a technician. The scientist thing is a mistake."

"Speaking of technology," Gerry said. "Look at this."

"What have we here?" Rick asked, inspecting a pair of hefty binoculars.

"Let me turn off the lights. It's just a prototype."

Rick panned the small space. "Ah, man, perfect night vision. You could spy on anyone with these."

"Never thought of that," Gerry said. "Hold them very still and gently press the button on top."

"Ouch!" Rick said, yanking away the glasses. He was temporarily blinded by a bright flash. "What was that?"

"Oh, I'm sorry," Gerry said, flipping on the light. "*Ja*, rough transition between night and day modes. The technology will debut on the next-generation Porsche supercar. A night driving aid." Gerry asked, "You okay? Want to go inside the house?"

"No, thanks. I better get going," Rick said, still blinking and squinting.

"Thanks for your help. I'll take good care of your baby."

Rick headed for Albuquerque, thinking that Fred was right. Gerry was an exceptional guy. But he was too smart, and too knowledgeable, and too something else that Rick couldn't define . . . yet. No used car salesman understood the particulars of combustion dynamics. And no truck driver—from any country—appreciated Bernoulli's Principle as a restatement of the conservation of energy. Rick cranked up the volume on the powerful stereo, to drown out the inconvenient chatter in his head.

GERRY LOCKED the workshop door before taking the binoculars and glass pane into his inner sanctum. He accessed a magnetic strip analyzer he'd used last week. While Rick lived it up with Renée in Angel's, Gerry had accessed the glove box of Rick's vehicle and read the data on Rick's Laboratory-issued ID badge. Now, he was ready to concentrate on the glass and binoculars.

The finger and palm prints were lifted from the glass with the skill of a forensics pro. Gerry meticulously transferred them to a slick white board. Passed a digitizing head over them and stored the digital file in a computer. Next, he downloaded the retinal scan performed by the high tech *binoculars*. Rick's retinal minutiae were digitized into a massive graphics file. Gerry's computer compressed the file into a manageable size and stored it. He encrypted both files and e-mailed them to a lab in Wu Han, China.

Afterward, Gerry prepared to pierce the Los Alamos Lab's firewall, using Rick's classified e-mail account as an alias. Gerry thought that although he was leading a momentous mission, he should be able to have some fun. And he believed of all people, Rick Adams, aka Rickster, would agree. But first, there was a little research to do. Gerry googled 'GRIT'. Once his research was finished, Gerry typed a message that he would send via the Lab's secure computing system. For him, the WEB was a powerful resource. He exploited it proficiently, using dozens of free, untraceable accounts originating in Eastern Europe and Scandinavia, most linked through Asia. They enabled him to acquire anything he needed. The best part was that he could blow right through Los Alamos National Lab's firewall and communicate with anyone he pleased, emulating any originating address the system recognized.

He'd needed some help from within the Lab, but it had been managed with relative ease by a Feynman friend. Gerry believed that Americans were lazy and greedy. His view was reinforced by his experience with team members wanting to renege on their promises and commitments to him. But given the proper motivation—money, drugs, sex, blackmail, all of the above—he was impressed by what he could command from his underlings. As for Gerry, he was in the States for one reason: to undermine the entire façade, to rip it into a billion pieces, beginning with Los Alamos National Laboratory.

CHAPTER 26

GAVIN BURTON plodded through dozens of new unclassified e-mail messages. He handled most of them with dispatch before opening one from Richard Adams, denoted IMPORTANT. He grimaced at the quiz's conclusion. A sharp jab, to be sure. But the import of the message was that a sticky web of governmental property abuse and security infractions was being spun about Dr. Adams.

Switching over to the classified partition, Burton found a message of Subject: Nuclear Materials. Ostensibly it had been sent from the weapons physics division leader. The message was actually sent by Gerry, using a military megabyte encryption algorithm. It was the only way he communicated instructions to Burton. Because Gerry and Burton had not met in New Mexico, and never planned to.

The message directed Burton to convey elements of secure media containing highly classified information *unrelated to GRIT* to the dead drop site near the Santa Fe plaza by 10 p.m. Burton chose stashed-away nuclear chemistry materials, provided compliments of a conscripted nuclear materials specialist and ardent Feynman friend.

The dead drop site was a neglected SANTA FE REPORTER magazine holder located in an alley beside the El Meson restaurant. Gerry would arrive early and open the door of the holder as though he wanted a paper. He would leave the door raised when he left. Burton would carry the drop in a folded newspaper. He would proceed to the REPORTER holder and pretend to take an issue, letting the package, wrapped in a second newspaper, drop inside. He would then close the door and leave.

CHAPTER 27

Santa fe's San Francisco Street borders the Plaza and leads directly to the entrance of the city's premier landmark, the St. Francis Cathedral, to the east. Carmen strode San Francisco Street, shielding her eyes against the brilliance of the afternoon sun. It was a temperate afternoon, but she was worried. T'Bird hadn't shown up for coffee. He'd neither called nor answered her calls. Maybe no big deal, but under the circumstances she needed to know for sure that he was safe.

She climbed the finely polished wood stairs leading to his second floor apartment, humming a *tejano* melody that she and T'Bird had devised. A heart-rending ballad of lost love. She rapped the door and was relieved, for an instant, when T'Bird answered. He stood barefoot, eyes filled with spider webs of scleral capillaries. They peeped from under a mussed mane of black hair, which reached down to his bare brown chest, resembling a sooty mop.

"You okay?" She asked.

"Yeah. Come on in."

She ignored the apartment's disarray. Focused anxiously on T'Bird and on the stench permeating everything. She marched over and cranked open a window before pointing at paraphernalia on an oversize coffee table, once a Thai bed. "Good shit?"

"Pretty good," he said, turning away. "Wanna drink."

"Water, maybe. We gotta do a show. One of us ought not be totally stoned."

"Thanks, mom. I'm having grapefruit juice. That too strong for you before a gig?"

Carmen sat on the softback leather sofa and glared at a stubby glass pipe whose charred bowl rested in an ashtray. A crinkled bar napkin with loopy blue scribbles lay on the floor beside a blank page of writing paper. A mechanical pencil, broken into two pieces, screamed at her. She snatched up the napkin, crushed it into a smallish wad, and thrust it into her pocket. She felt like crying.

John Irving's *A Widow for One Year* was partially hidden by a bicycle racing magazine. She remembered the day she gave the book to T'Bird, hoping to rekindle his interest in reading. They'd both read insatiably when he first moved from the reservation in Dulce to Santa Fe. Now, almost 10 years later, things had changed. Carmen wondered what lay ahead for them.

"Here you go," he said, handing her a glass.

She glanced toward the coffee table and then drew a bead on his flushing face. T'Bird slung back his mop of hair, disrupting their eye contact. She asked, "Productive afternoon writing? Or did smoking overcome the creative impulse?"

"Very creative day, starting with a bike crash."

"Sounds to me like you have more trouble than that. Chico was half drunk in the bar last night. Said you still owe him. You told me you paid."

"Diego didn't pay his half."

"Damn Diego. I told you not to go in with him." Carmen had always wondered how her mother's sweet sister could spawn life that low. "Chico's after you," she said. "Maybe you have to go to the police? He killed Poncho. I'm sure of it."

"That was a south of the border thing. Chico was just the local taxi driver."

"Seems *the border* gets further north every year," she said, biting a cuticle. "Why not ask your mom."

"You know the story: no college; no money. Maybe I'll trade my bike."

That was a tough one. But Carmen knew T'Bird's mom, Sunflower, was no dummy. In fact, she was a powerful Jicarilla Apache medicine woman. His dad was the mystery. Although T'Bird had seldom spoken of him, Sunflower had told Carmen his apocryphal story.

"I can stall Chico a little longer. But there's more bad news," he said. "I didn't write the melody for your lyrics."

"That's okay. But you should've called me. I was worried about you."

Limping toward the door, he said, "If your sermon's finished, I gotta get ready."

"What's wrong with your leg?"

T'Bird hobbled over and drew up his right leg and flexed his quad, expanding an embroidery-stitched American flag on the front of his faded jeans. She patted the cushion beside her. "What happened?" she asked, running her fingers the length of his thick thigh.

"Training. It was wet. My bike slid into a ravine."

"You afraid that Sour Kraut will beat you, again?"

T'Bird smiled at Carmen's nickname for Gerry.

"I don't know exactly what to think of him," she continued. "But he's a creep and nothing compared to you."

T'Bird's face fell. Carmen stroked his cheek, sensing his heart melting. "You're still in the game, Big Man. And it's rigged, no doubt about it. But you can't win if you don't keep playing." Carmen pecked his forehead. "I'm going over to the Das and get a smoothie. I'll treat you!"

"Thanks. Gonna shower. Have an espresso here."

"Good idea," she said, ignoring a pounding heartache.

CHAPTER 28

G ERRY glanced at his watch and set the timer before mounting a commercial grade treadmill kept in the nerve center of the air-conditioned workshop. His den was illuminated by soothing indirect lighting. He alternated his pace between jog and sprint, frequently appraising himself in the mirrored glass wall opposite the exercise equipment. His form a model of élan. The alarm sounded after an hour and Gerry dismounted, took a crisp white towel from a gleaming metal bin, and dabbed his face.

He dropped the towel on a weight bench and struck his favorite marshal arts pose, *neko ashi dachi*. Yamamoto's gory corpse flashed into his mind. The guy had a chance, in the end. He shook off the disquieting memory by glancing down at the fine white stripe across his forearm. He must have that pigmented or surgically removed, after completing this assignment. Gerry sighed and gazed into the mirror before him. For an instant, he saw a skinny teenager staring out. A poised ballet dancer. Someone from a dream? The boy stared tentatively. And then he softened his demeanor to a smile so full of promise. His chin dimpled deeply with the delight of being alive.

Snapping his head from side to side, Gerry clamped together his eyelids. Flashing his eyes open, he glared at the killer in the mirror. Gerry rushed into martial arts kadas, his image swept across the glass panels. Powerful. Angry. Lethal. The ancient maneuvers had been altered by the addition of fatal final flourishes. At the Academy, spine-rupturing lunges, neck-cracking torques, and skull-smashing blows were integrated into the beautiful movements. Gerry grimaced at himself, enacting a shoulder-snapping wrench, the one he'd used on Yamamoto. This is who he was. Surely, who he'd always been.

Aerobic exercises completed, Gerry decided that tomorrow he would use heavy weights to work out his upper body and arms. A complete body workout in three days, some rest, and then a weekend bike ride. Efficacious. His life had always been regimented. At first, by his father; later, by the State. Gerry's father had used his brains, athleticism, and regimentation profitably. He'd been honored and special privileges had been granted for his family, including Gerry, who'd excelled at everything he tried. He didn't believe it was his fault that his father was unjustly sentenced to 25 years at a special labor camp. Special denoting especially inhumane. Others had declined an *invitation* to attend the regular military academy without disaster. But, then again, Gerry's reason had been different.

Gerry splashed his face with water, drank, spit. Toweled off, once more. Again, he faced the mirrors. Focus, he reminded himself, is the key. His plan was progressing well, in spite of his conscripts' peccadillos. A Calibanesque crew. He, himself, must exclude every distraction. Gerry was capable of a spartan life. Could live like a monk; had done it. Celibacy was nothing. Besides, he saved his life-generating fluid for personal regeneration. In that regard, from a metal cabinet he withdrew a small sterile, amber glass bottle; applied a blank white label; dated it in indelible black pen; and then stripped completely. He popped the fingers of prophylactic-thin, surgical-grade latex gloves, snugging them on his powerful hands. He commenced martial arts kadas, savoring his power and elegance. Moments later, the sample was collected unceremoniously.

Afterwards, Gerry carefully tapped out the electronic lock's combination on a tall freezer. Before opening the door, he reached around toward the equipment's back grill and locating a toggle switch, pulled it down forcibly. It would be a shame to detonate a freezer full of such wonderful health aids. Including his personal specimens, Gerry had stockpiled Chinese black bear gallbladders and African embryonic stem cells. Sample stored, he closed the door and rearmed the charge. He secured the workshop's massive door and swaggered across the flagstone path into the main house. Once inside, he activated the workshop's internal and external laser intrusion systems, thus arming the massive charge located underneath it. Time to get ready for work.

CHAPTER 29

CARMEN entered Angel's back door and grabbed an iced tea. She eyed the nearly-empty bar and heard Diego obsess, "Where's them Los Alamos bullet heads? Workin' late, trying to blow the world up?"

"In the parking lot, scoring sex and drugs," she replied, before rounding the corner. She saw Diego bent over a giant trash bin, a late afternoon ritual.

Finding only empty Mexican import bottles, he cursed, "Stupid-ass buncha touristas. Don't these people read." He glanced up at a printed come-on for happy hour: ¡DSB! Buy 1 get 2 free! Diego kicked the smelly bin back under the bar and bellowed to no one in particular, "Where's José Maria? Why ain't there no music playin'?"

Carmen saw the sallow, young Mexican import grab a plastic cup and spill half its contents, racing toward the stage. "I didn't take my first break, Diego. I swear it."

"Just play. And it's Flamenco Happy Hour," Diego fumed. "Enough of that *penitente* shit. We want people happy. What'd ya think this is, a cave in Andalusia?"

José Maria broke the ensuing silence with a dark cord—*muy profundo*—beginning another heartbreaking southern Spanish melody. Carmen watched as he sustained the notes, bending the strings slightly, lending vibrato. A musical drill, worming its way to the soul. She felt his self exposure in its heavy resonance. He raised his eyes to meet hers. She believed that he could feel her longing and frustration as powerfully as she felt his shame and sorrow. Carmen knew that she would be able to wait for satisfaction. She hoped that José Maria would be equally patient.

Carmen was glad that the Labites seemed to be taking the night off. Just wasn't the same without Fred. She exhaled heavily, noticing Chico and his posse at the far end of the bar. Chico leaned on a chunky crew member. Sloshed already, she thought.

In an instant T'Bird entered the saloon doors, carrying his guitar case. Chico spit a string of gutter slurs to him. Before Carmen could move, Eddie had dropped the case and stemmed the tirade using a powerful right hook to Chico's jaw, felling him. Carmen flew toward them, but Chico had scrambled up, brandishing a scarred shiv.

"*Joto,* I kill you," Chico screamed.

"Fight! Fight!" the room resounded.

Carmen wedged herself between them. "Chico, T'Bird, stop it!"

"Lemme to you *caballero.*" Chico demanded, thrusting to her face the knife, gripped in grimy fingers. "This for him."

Carmen stepped back from the blade, displacing T'Bird. She held Chico in her gaze, saying, "Chico, settle your tab and get going, before I call the cops."

"I don' pay, 'til he pay," Chico said, nodding to his posse.

Carmen whispered, "He paid you."

Chico ignored her and stormed toward the exit.

Carmen's pulse stabilized and the melon that had plugged her throat vanished as the doors loudly clacked together. She said to T'Bird, "Cool off. Get some dinner."

"The little punk," he spewed.

"He's a dangerous little punk."

CHAPTER 30

Sᴀɴ ᴅɪᴇɢᴏ's Town and Country Hotel sprawled. Conference rooms and ball-rooms as large as football fields populated the property. The Nonequilibrium Gas Dynamics Conference was small and relegated to the least attractive meeting rooms. Rick couldn't have cared less. He wanted to idly, yet purposefully, chat-up world-class nonequilibrium reactions researchers. His questions must be sufficiently vague not to compromise GRIT, yet elicit prescient responses regarding how to resolve his computational dilemma.

During dinner, Rick got an idea for estimating an upper bound for GRIT's effectiveness. The insight would enable him to ballpark the gamma ray laser's peak performance; its kill potential.

In high spirits, Rick called Desiree. Just because the engagement was off didn't mean they were enemies. No answer. He rang Renée, who sounded groggy. After a brief chat, Rick determined to return to the Lab the following evening. He was the man to crack GRIT, the tough nut. Burton's face hovered above him, as he thought: And I'm going to do it with a feather, not a sledge hammer.

Aᴛ ᴏɴᴇ ꜰɪꜰᴛʏ ᴀ.ᴍ., Gerry parked his SUV in the back lot of the Los Alamos Tennis Club. Removed his bicycle and hoisted on a black nylon backpack. Soon he was cycling toward TA-38. A twenty-five caliber pistol in an ankle holster barely bulged his lycra cycling suit. An invigorating breeze. He arrived and stashed his bike behind some trailers, removed his half-finger cycling gloves, and accessed the pack. He pulled on a change of clothes, baggy khakis and oversize oxford cloth shirt. He stuffed a Sig handgun in the back of his pants; pulled out the shirttail a bit to cover the grip. Around his neck he hung a badge, suspended from a Viton o-ring, the type of badge cord preferred by the Lab's experimental staff, including Rick. Tucked it neatly in his shirt pocket. Added a pen and pencil before donning a pair of ultra thin, flesh color latex gloves, bearing intricately contoured finger pads and palms. Gerry slid a stiletto switchblade down the side of his pants; tightened his belt a notch. He pulled down the bill of a Red Sox cap and headed toward the unmanned security checkpoint.

It was a quarter past three when Gerry neared the turnstile, carrying a small, gray Los Alamos National Lab nylon tote. Suddenly, a bright light illuminated his face, partially blinding him. A camouflaged Hummer occupied a narrow vehicle access trail. Shielding his eyes, Gerry discerned that the bulky body filled the entire trail. Its spot lights were irritatingly radiant. When its engine fired, Gerry's heart rate spiked.

Gerry yanked out his bogus badge. Regulated his breath. Panned the area. He saw that the entire perimeter was sealed off with razor wire-topped 14 ft. fencing. Nowhere to run, except back between the trailers, a good 50 meters. The pistol . . . but the Hummer undoubtedly was armoured. Now was the time to be cool. Gerry watched as the vehicle slowly pulled to the curb.

"Everthang all right?" The driver asked through an onboard PA system.

"Yeah, partner. Thanks for checkin'." Gerry said, thrusting up his hand.

The driver's bullet-proof window creaked down.

A clean shot, Gerry thought. His hand twitched.

"Turnstyle's been sticky," the man said. "Go on ahead in. I'll wait."

Gerry paused. The guard turned to speak to his partner. Two targets. Gerry turned and proceeded toward the turnstile, giving them his back. The Sig worried his backbone as he walked. Had it worked out from the fold of his shirttail? Was it going to fall? He told himself to just keep walking. Arriving at the cylindrical enclosure, fabricated of a meshwork of tubular steel, Gerry hesitated. A cage. And if his biometric data were not accepted, he would be trapped more securely than any rat. The Hummer's engine droned. The high intensity halogen lighting at the checkpoint irritated his eyes while illuminating him like a target. Gerry could feel his heartbeat pounding in his temples. If he ran now, the mission could still be saved.

He took a deep breath and ducked into the claustrophobic turnstile. Swiped the badge and placed his right hand on the palm reader, while facing his cap's bill toward the security camera. The light glowed red; Gerry's pulse jarred his temples. A bead of perspiration developed on his nose. It dripped. He caught it with his tongue. Still red. The computer wasn't authenticating. Was that the driver's door unlatching? Slowly he slid his hand toward the Sig. He glanced at the light. The goddamn light was still . . . green. He exhaled when the gate jangled loose.

Gerry looked back and waved. The driver nodded and stepped on the throttle of his massive vehicle, which groaned, lurching toward Pajarito road.

The main entry of Building Two was a straight shot. Gerry walked quickly. Once inside, he proceeded directly to B wing. Before entering the double doors, he stopped briefly in a darkened corner to remove his intricate gloves. From a plastic contact lenses case, he withdrew a pair of nearly opaque polycarbonate lenses and inserted them over his eyes. Stuck a piece of wide, flesh-color athletic tape across his forehead and replaced the gloves. Almost blind, he carefully made his way inside the outer doors. Gerry swiped his badge and placed his forehead against a boss at the top of a biometric mask that protruded from an embedded enclosure. He stared forward. The central security computer authenticated Rick's retinal minutiae. The heavy door unlatched with a rumble.

Gerry paused, once inside B wing, to remove the gloves, pop out the contacts and store them, before replacing the gloves and setting off for Rick's office. Having memorized the building's floor plan, he located the office quickly and picked the door lock in seconds. Gerry cracked Rick's safe easily, using a flyweight accelerometer coupled with a hand-held digital signal processor to mark the slightest movement of the safe's tumblers. He removed a manila envelope from his bag. Contents: a stick of flash memory in a plastic baggie; a somewhat larger, removable computer data storage disk, a ZIP disk; and a thin paper document, all numbered and labeled TOP SECRET. Gerry approached Rick's computer keyboard and ran the finger pads of both gloves across the oily keys several times.

Using the gloves, Gerry smeared *Rick's* fingerprints and DNA across the objects, just clearly enough to identify them when analyzed. He stuffed the items in the back of the safe and secured it.

CHAPTER 31

THE KIVA fireplace glowed red-orange. Flickering flames painted the old woman's weathered face with light and shadow. She huddled near the tiny hearth, stirring a small cast-iron kettle suspended over the fire by a swiveling wrought iron hook. Firelight danced in her small, black eyes. An oil-burning lamp sputtered across the room, casting irregular shadows, creating an eerie ambience. Licks of illumination highlighted antique photographs of ancestors and her son T'Bird.

Earlier, in her favorite rocker, Sunflower had rhythmically stroked the oxblood-cured dirt floor using a single, moccasin-clad foot. Her body had rested peacefully while her spirit had soared above the walls and roof of the cabin; beyond the confines of the reservation; up past the aspens at the New Mexico and Colorado border; into the vastness of space, where she communed with the ancients.

Now, the smell of a sacred medicine stew pervaded the air. A bubbling foundation of mistletoe and aged juniper berries, cholla cactus root, and chamisa leaves. Large prickly pear cactus pockets were drying on the mantle. They would contain the reduced medicine paste, now at a rolling boil in the kettle.

She carefully added a few drops of high potency scorpion venom. She smiled, knowing that her preparations were nearly complete. Sunflower thanked her ancestors once again for their warning.

CHAPTER 32

THE CLOCK radio ramped to life at five on Thursday morning. Rick had gotten in from California late the previous evening, but it was a short work week and he meant to make the most of it. He mastered the twisting roadway from Santa Fe down into the Pojoaque valley, setting a personal record. Ignored the remnants of road construction and the 35 mph speed limit, until noticing colored lights in his rear view mirror. He hit the brakes and pulled onto the roadway's ragged shoulder.

"Driver's license, vehicle registration, and proof of insurance, please," the man said in a gruff baritone with a hint of sing-song elocution.

"Yes sir, officer . . . Gonzales."

"I see that your vehicle is registered in New Mexico, but you have a Massachusetts driver's license." Gonzales frowned. "I also need to see proof of insurance, sir."

"Yes, officer. As you can see, I've just bought this vehicle and haven't received my insurance card for it in the mail yet. Also, I just moved—"

"Thank you, Mr. Adams."

Gonzales disappeared into his unmarked Camaro, still blinking like a vintage General Motors Christmas tree. He returned with a ticket for exceeding the posted speed limit by more than 15 mph, inaccurate vehicle registration, and failure to produce proof of insurance. The tally, $520, accounted for the construction zone's Double Fine posting.

"I'm not paying this. I'd like to present my case in court."

"Your mandatory court appearance is a month from Tuesday at seven p.m."

Rick scribbled across the bottom line, retrieved his licenses and registration, and thrust the clipboard at officer Gonzales. He stashed the citation in the center console.

"Drive carefully, Mr. Adams. And have a nice day."

At work, finally, Rick thought, slumped into his chair. When he dived into the morass of unread e-mail, his secret documents were still stowed and the marker board covered. Soon thereafter, he heard a knock on his door that he answered reluctantly.

"Good morning, Rick," Margie chirped. "Saw your light. Are you back early? How was your trip?"

"Ah ha! I see you're here to get the goods on me right away. Go on, take a look. Everything's shipshape." He stretched his arms high above high head, yawning.

"Sorry to bother you, but I'm conducting a classified materials audit."

"Can it wait? I'm in the middle of something really important."

"You're the only one here and I've got to do the whole group ASAP. A rush from on high."

Seeing her pen pointed skyward, he wondered, *Il Papa*? Maybe the authority was even Higher—

"A security situation arose while you were away, Rick. It's aggravated by the fact that the director is hanging by a thread after the last security scandal."

He nodded. "Guess it's understandable he demanded an audit."

"Actually, the order came from the security division leader, Dr. Burton."

"That unusual?" Rick asked, fidgeting. Perfectly Pavlovian.

"Sort of," Margie said, approaching the cabinet containing Rick's safe. "Now, let's get this over with. You have a new combination, correct."

"You know me. By the book, Adams." He neared the safe; she turned away. Fingering the dial Rick's thoughts raced: A demand for an audit from on high and he's the only guy around. Were a sacrificial lamb needed, he prayed it'd be under his desk.

Margie compared Rick's document's numbers to entries on her computer printout. "Looks like it's all here. Nothing else in there?" She craned her neck. "What's that?" She poked her pen toward the cavity's dark reaches. "Do you have secret data on removable media?" She double checked her printout.

"No." Rick moved his head closer. "Damn, I never noticed that." He drew out the ZIP disk, flash memory, and papers, all marked TOP SECRET.

Margie balked. She observed that the paper bore a nuclear technology document number, exactly the kind of material putting the Lab in a full-fledged frenzy.

"Rick, are these items assigned to you?"

"No. Uh, I mean, absolutely not."

"Right here it shows you signed that the safe was empty when you took possession of it."

Rick peered into the black depths of the safe, dreading what else he might find. It was like staring down the bore of loaded cannon.

"Per security procedures, you changed the combination before receiving classified materials. Is that correct?"

Bewildered, Rick replied, "Sure, I did." He turned to face her.

"Do you have any explanation regarding how these materials came to be here?"

"Maybe, the previous guy left it." He shrugged. "I just didn't notice."

"Jon Christensen had this safe before you. He didn't do nuclear technology work. No one in this building does nuclear technology work. But don't worry," Margie said, opening an envelope and presenting it. "Just put those materials in here. I'll secure it. We'll both sign across the seal. Everything'll be sorted out later." She forced a grin, unnaturally exposing her teeth.

The expression struck Rick as "*I want to eat you*".

"Lab security'll inspect it. Probably contact the FBI."

"The FBI! They—" Rick stopped short of divulging their opposition to his hire.

"They what?"

"They . . . caused this Lab enough trouble and embarrassment. Look at the security debacles. They bungled every one." He sold the lines.

Margie skewed her head and closed the envelope. They signed across the seal and she departed in silence.

Shaken and confused, Rick tried to return to his work. But every cell in his body was jangling, under high alert. What was going on here? The safe had been empty before he deposited his materials in there. Someone else must have the combination. Maybe Ms. Margie was not entirely blameless herself. She had headed to his office first.

Recognizing fruitless frustration, Rick willed himself to his work. He forgot about answering e-mail and went straight to his new model for the grasing cavity. A simple model to accommodate a straight-forward bounding calculation. After nine p.m., Rick was exhausted. He logged out, drove home, and went straight to bed, without dinner. Amid fitful sleep, he dreamed of an old Biblical story, starring himself as Isaac. But the ending was different from the Book's.

CHAPTER 33

Friday morning went much more smoothly. Rick submitted his first bounding run and returned to scale the mountain of e-mail. An hour into the effort, he observed a message on the unclassified partition apparently sent by himself. The message was highlighted IMPORTANT. It was addressed to TEAM GRIT from—WHAT!—Richard Adams' classified e-mail account. Subject: SECURITY QUIZ. Frantic, Rick triple-clicked it.

A cigarette smoking male cartoon-character spy, with attendant dark glasses, attaché, long trench coat, and hat, peered out. Beside the figure was a question:

Q1. John Wayne western from 1969. TRUE _ _ _ _

Rick loved Wayne as Rooster Cogburn. He entered 'grit'. Nothing. Knowing his response was correct, he tried 'GRIT'. The cartoon's cigarette vanished. A second question appeared:

Q2. Rough particles of sand. _ _ _ _

Rick entered 'GRIT'. His mind raced, entering the TOP SECRET project code name on the unclassified computing partition. A major security no-no. This time the cartoon's attaché disappeared before the next question appeared:

Q3. Clench the teeth. _ _ _ _

'GRIT' entered, the hat vanished.

Q4. Pluck. _ _ _ _

Annoyed, Rick entered 'GRIT'. The glasses disappeared.

The cartoon faced him and smirked. Something about its features were familiar. Rick studied it. And then, to his amazement, the cartoon began to leer and open his coat. Wearing only fishnet stockings and high heels, the simpering figure repeatedly flashed him. Rick's jaw dropped, but he didn't feel physically ill. Not until he recognized the character, who now pirouetted while abusing himself, was Gavin Burton in drag.

Rick did a double take . . . a triple take before popping up from his chair. He flew down the hall to Bruno's office, where he stood outside, knocking and shifting from one foot to the other. What was he doing in there, locking his document cache inside his safe? Good luck with that, Rick thought. Bruno was sitting at his desk, morning coffee in hand when Rick burst in. Computer outputs were strewn on tables covered by opaque cloths. His office looked like a morgue for two-dimensional beings.

"Hey, man." Rick asked, "You get a crazy e-mail from me on the unclassified partition?"

"Hold on a—"

"Bruno," Rick interrupted, "is it possible there's a distribution list on the unclassified partition called TEAM GRIT?" He gasped, "Could the damn MRC be on it?"

"There's definitely no distribution on the unclassified partition for the classified group you just mentioned," Bruno said, eyeing his screen. "Remember how security for GRIT works. Even the name is classified. You can't say it or write it, better not to even think it in an uncleared area or on an uncleared network. ZTS!"

"Oh, boy." Rick resumed his dance. "The message apparently originated from my classified account and was sent to God only knows who on the unclassified partition."

"What?"

"The subject is Security Quiz. It's a stupid joke that repeatedly uses code name GRIT as it progressively strips Burton down from a Pink Panther-like spook to a Rocky Horror dancing drag queen."

"Gavin Burton?"

"Uh huh."

"I, uh, would've remembered that," Bruno said. He eyed Rick earnestly, "Tell me he wasn't on distribution."

Rick shrugged.

"Oh, it's from you, all right." Bruno double-clicked. "Let me look into it."

Rick turned to go, but stopped and said, "Thanks for the help. And I forgot to tell you. I got a great idea in San Diego for grasing cavity design."

Bruno stopped up his ears with both hands.

Rick did an about face and trudged away. He closed the door behind him, almost pinching his donkey tail—

CHAPTER 34

THE ADMINISTRATION building's hallowed fourth floor conference room was a place Sam shunned. Bad photography— Bad lighting— Bad decisions— As GRIT's most senior scientist, contributing to the Lab's pre-eminent program *du jour*, as he sometimes thought of it, Sam attended the meeting at the behest of the Laboratory director. But what was he to do among bureaucratic titans? Enjoy the show? He just wanted to hide.

Sam crept through imposing, fourteen-foot-tall wooden double doors fortifying the room. He panned the space. A pair of associate directors were diving for a seat near the conference table's head. The more rotund was beaten out by a ferret of a man entrusted with what Sam considered miscellaneous Laboratory stuff: The AD of Catchall. His darkly circled feral eyes squinted underneath heavy lids and a deeply furrowed brow. Rumor was that one of his divisions was broke and headed for a multicultural staff reduction. The last such RIF had sent the AD for the affected division and the Lab director packing.

Without moving his head, Sam eyed Herr Burton, occupying one of 20 seats at the conference table. Burton doodled thoughtfully on a napkin adjacent to his thick, bound Laboratory-issued notebook. Sam hurried past Burton's cone of peripheral vision to a seat against the back wall. Thrust his face into his notebook and considered notes taken at yesterday's MRC meeting. Compared them with notes he'd taken on GRIT's design from the partial set of drawings acquired by deep cover operatives. Sam had possessed those drawings for a mere four hours, insufficient time to assess their validity and usefulness, but sufficient to develop serious doubts regarding GRIT's performance potential. Of this, he had made no notation; had been reticent.

"John, why can you not trust?" Sam heard director Reynolds say; his voice tinnier than usual. Reynolds dropped his eyeglasses onto the big table at the head and rubbed his baggy eyes before refocusing on O'Donnell. "This intel is gold-plated. He's one of ours."

The rising intonation and emphasis on the final word took Sam aback. Never had anyone openly admitted the Lab's role in administering field operatives. A security *faux pas*. The target of the invective was no surprise. Authority often seeks to pummel into submission strong people who oppose folly and ineptitude. In this case, Sam believed the director was pounding brass balls with a rubber hammer.

O'Donnell said, "Questioning the validity of drawings of the most incredible device ever perfected, or presumably perfected by a bunch of 'stan-atics, does not make me a doubting Thomas or arrogant." He marched toward a seat mid-way down the table, speaking as he walked. "Hell, those drawings fell into our laps. Not an iota of corroborating intelligence chatter. Had to take years to design that gadget."

The director cleared his throat. "For the record: it's only a prototype. But these are not just drawings; they're detailed specifications. Twenty-seven pages of them."

"I'd never stand against investigating a material threat to America's security," O'Donnell said. "I risked my life for this country too many times." He took a slug of water, adding, "Clearly, we're too far into this for a smell test."

Sam glanced quickly to assess the director's reaction, but his eyes were assaulted by brash lighting from so many fat fluorescent bulbs. Although high overhead, the ceiling seemed to press down low, bunkeresque. Sam imagined himself in a Nazi interrogation cell, a pressure cooker for humans. He lowered and steadied his eyes on a nearby photograph: poor color balance, poorer composition. Recreational photography at its worst. He sighed. This was not a place for amateurism. Meetings convened here should be conducted with *gravitas*.

Fully crystallized ideas or carefully dissected problems should be presented succinctly; constructive commentary and vetting should ensue; rigorous conclusions should be developed and efficacious programmatic solutions determined. But after a decade, Sam recognized that whining, grousing, and disparaging were the rule, not the exception.

The director twisted in his chair. Removed and then replaced his eyeglasses. Sam recalled stories of O'Donnell's meritorious military service. Everyone knew them, from this Hill to the one in Washington, DC. Bright, flyboy techie. Sam had mutual friends from O'Donnell's days at Cornell. Scientists and politicos, alike, respected him. That he was the embattled director's heir apparent was a silver lining for the Lab's future.

In a final flourish O'Donnell said, "I've testified before generals, senators, and the Secretary of State, claiming that reliable, written intelligence existed, validating the functionality or expected functionality of the most strategic anti-ballistic missile weapon imaginable." He paused before adding, "I even had to name the damn thing."

"Gamma Ray Intensity Transducer is a fine acronym," Reynolds intoned.

Sam was surprised by O'Donnell's passion in saying, "I told them the scariest truth: A gamma ray laser is the ultimate nuclear defense weapon. It would render America's nuclear arsenal impotent."

Nearly everyone flinched or squirmed, imagining America's steely, powerful rockets as limp duds.

CHAPTER 35

OBSESSED with his endeavor to bound GRIT's performance, Rick struggled for days, nearly living in his office. He was determined to get to the bottom— or rather, the top—of GRIT's performance. He wanted to understand GRIT's maximum destructive potential without months of laborious iterative calculations. Should his calculations confirm that GRIT was capable of marginalizing a nuclear arsenal, like America's, then he could refine them to predict GRIT's threat more precisely. An added bonus of the upper bound that he could generate with modest effort would be to determine whether GRIT should be pursued with torrid intensity and overarching priority.

Rick had arbitrarily increased the probability of grasing for each nucleus, the so-called grasing cross-section, by a factor of 10. He also assumed a massive population inversion of excited atoms. His computer code should have converged on a far overestimated solution for the cavity's maximum power output. An unrealistic upper bound that could be whittled back down in small increments, ensuring convergence all the way down to reality. The result would be information regarding how powerful GRIT could possibly be and how perfectly the cavity must be tuned to maximize the grasing cross-section.

The results could not be believed. If the pitiful power generation he was calculating was anywhere near correct, America could sleep well again. It just wasn't right. Disgusted, Rick refreshed the screen and typed commands to access the numerical solver's statistics, a measure of how certain the code was that it had performed as intended. He must understand why the code refused to work.

The awful scenario prevailed all week. And at the MRC meeting on Thursday, Rick explained that none of his computer simulations had converged. He withheld his new term for the millions of zeros his runs had generated. After his spiel, because no one wanted to hear that the newly hired grasing cavity design genius was a total flop, appropriate steps were taken: Rick's head was severed, smashed, and burned, figuratively speaking. Not by a megalomaniacal evil chieftain, but by his genteel colleagues.

Banging his abused head against a wall early Friday, Rick answered his phone with all of the enthusiasm of an undertaker.

"Welcome back, stranger," Renée said. "How was it?"

"Worth the time, I think." He hesitated, but said, "I, uh, may be on to something."

"That's great. I wasn't even sure you were back yet."

"Came home early. I'm dying for some results."

"Maybe to free up a bit of your time, I'll do your expense report and take it to Jacqueline, your favorite tennis partner— She can get your refund expedited."

"No need. Most of the charges are on my Lab credit card."

"Let me help. You're onto something big. I can tell." She paused before adding, "I have a little selfish motivation, hoping you can come out and play this weekend. Emily's staying with her dad."

"How about dinner on Saturday?"

"Sure. Bring your receipts. I have a blank travel voucher you can sign."

Rick attacked his work with renewed vigor, knowing his weekend was not going to be a workfest. Hours later, and more computer simulations of GRIT's grasing cavity behind him, Rick was convinced that it was incapable of producing an output beam of nuclear warhead kill intensity. A fully participatory grasing volume was not achievable in any variation of grasing cavity design, with any strength of externally applied magnetic field. Even with unrealistically favorable grasing conditions like a super-inflated macroscopic grasing cross-section, only small pockets of grasing nuclei populated the grasing cavity.

Rick reasoned that a cavity in which eighty percent to ninety percent of the nuclei were undergoing stimulated gamma emission would be the baseline for GRIT's operation. But if pockets of grasing nuclei existed here and there, unless those pockets could be expanded and forced to coalesce and form an enormously powerful gamma gas, GRIT was destined to fail, just as all other graser designs had.

GRIT would never qualify as the ultimate nuclear counterweapon. No run-away Rusky Republic, as Bruno called it, was going to launch a nuclear attack and feel immune to the inevitable massive retaliation. It was a fact: GRIT—and by induction, GRIT-like variants—could not develop sufficient energy to blow up speeding warheads, period.

GERRY SAT in his workshop command center, arms crossed, staring at the video monitor. Stained pine in HD. Cursing, he sprang up and paced the floor. Renée's digital video was useless. He glanced back at the image of a wooden divider. Jazz music blared, drowning out background voices, and presumed moans and groans.

The e-mail that Gerry fired off to Burton's classified account indicated that incontrovertible evidence of Rick's intimacy with Renée and continued drug abuse had not yet been obtained. He reiterated his disbelief that the means championed by Burton were sufficient to insure the participation of someone as strong-headed and unpredictable as Rick. Besides, Gerry noted, it was clear that Desiree could not possibly care less about him. And even a love–struck ex could get that. She wanted an MIT professor for a husband. Sooner, rather than later, he claimed that Rick was going to internalize the fact that Barish was her new mark and she would no longer offer leverage of any kind. Even the security breaches being established against Rick might not be effective, Gerry warned. He ended the note saying that he was contemplating implementing more stringent measures.

Burton replied instantly. Gerry liked that, although he didn't agree with his analysis of the situation. He half snickered at Burton's belief that his personal oversight of Rick would solve the control problem. Gerry appreciated that Burton, considering himself a man of the higher mind, did not want the body count to rise. He'd believed that even Fred's demise was unnecessary. Had argued that given Fred's ignorance of the mission's goal, he'd have taken his ignominious participation with the Feynman friends to the grave. Burton demanded that Gerry stand down or else.

CHAPTER 36

SECURITY MEETING was the subject of the classified e-mail routed through a blind server. It was marked URGENT. Not at all what Rick had wanted. He bent and twisted the phone cord until Connie Sanders answered and barked instructions. Sitting in Burton's anteroom, awaiting an audience with the wizard, Rick wanted to tap his shoes together and be back in his office or anywhere else for that matter. Finally, after 35 agonizingly slow minutes passed, Connie ushered him in.

Rick sat relaxed, watching Burton shift in his chair while making small talk.

"Things are difficult. I'm still in shock, regarding Fred's death." Burton sighed. "You two were getting close. How are you getting on?"

"Okay."

"That's good, very good. Even amid tragedy, we must carry on."

A furtive glance from Burton. Rick maintained a neutral expression.

"I wanted to tell you," Burton continued, "that I've come to regard your security efforts within GRIT more highly."

"I haven't seen or heard anything." The Feynman friends' antics burst into his mind. "I mean, I haven't done anything." He took a deep breath and stabilized his eyes.

"Precisely. That's why I believe it best if we meet on a routine basis. We can discuss and implement a strategy."

"That may not be necessary."

"How so?" Burton asked, shifting his weight once more and then tugging at his blazer's fastened middle button.

"I've concluded that GRIT is not a threat to the effectiveness of America's nuclear arsenal. It's not a threat to anything, really."

Burton's mouth gaped. Breaking the silence, he said, "How can . . . I mean, you haven't been working on this for very long." He crossed his legs. Clasped his interlocked fingers around his knee. White knuckles. Bloodless. He asked, "Are you quite certain?"

"Instead of solving the problem of closely approximating GRIT's performance, I decided to bound it. The upper bound suggests unambiguously that GRIT cannot achieve kill energies in or out of the atmosphere. Under all conditions I've studied, and believe me it's been pretty exhaustive, only sparse pockets of grasing nuclei populate the cavity."

"Ah, yes. That's very clever, Rick. I see your tack." Burton's eyes jittered behind his glasses. He pressed his finger pads together under his chin, as if in prayer. "But I'm not convinced of the absolute correctitude of your claim. There is strong evidence that pockets of lasing gammas can produce a powerful, near-instantaneous avalanche through an entire region of gamma gas, creating a grasing cavity nearly full of nuclei demonstrating stimulated emission. Surely, a near complete population inversion would produce terawatts at least. Should the avalanche be prolonged, well, then you're talking an enormous energy delivery capacity."

"Won't happen. Even in an ideal cavity," Rick said, stretching out, glancing down at his scuffed shoes. He needed to get back to work. "You'll see my documentation."

Burton's head beaded with perspiration. "Who else knows of these findings?"

"No one. I'm just starting a draft of my conclusions."

"This could have far reaching ramifications in terms of project morale, even national security. I would like to review these findings before you disseminate them. It would be a shame to see your reputation sullied, in the event there has been an error."

Rick sat up in his chair.

Burton continued, "I do not want to see the momentum of the program blunted. You probably aren't aware that the Lab is securing additional funding for the project. This information could cast a long shadow. I, personally, will verify your findings."

"I'll contact you when the draft is done."

"I'll contact you. Remember, it's essential that these meetings are not publicized. It could, uh, compromise your value as a security asset."

Burton gouged the air with his pen toward a door in the back of the room that Rick hadn't noticed. Without another word, Rick rose and walked toward it. With a buzz, its magnetic latch disengaged.

Rick stepped into a poorly lighted corridor, composed of large, crude reinforced concrete blocks. He felt his way along the claustrophobic maze to a biometrically controlled exit. He stepped out of the building into an unfamiliar parking lot. The sun blazed down, sapping his energy. His bearings were lost. Which way should he go? His hand felt uncomfortable. Looking down, Rick discovered the palm bled from the walls' roughness. Los Alamos National Lab was a grittier place than he'd ever imagined.

CHAPTER 37

SATURDAY morning Rick breakfasted at Becker's Deli. Dining alone in public was one of the things he hated most, almost as much as sleeping solo. But he didn't want to waste time. Polishing off the banana-filled buckwheat hotcakes, he couldn't wait to charge up the Hill and get back at it.

As Rick neared his vehicle, a stick of a man, wearing baggy shorts, bowling shirt, and a cheap straw hat, approached him. The man lifted a half-folded map and said, "Excuse me, sir."

"I've got to warn you. I'm new here."

The man opened the map and thrust it toward Rick's face. Specular darts of harsh sunlight glinted off the surface of a badge.

"Mr. Adams, I'm Agent Jackson of the Federal Bureau of Investigation. Please act natural and accompany me." His head jerked toward the back of the lot.

Rick found himself in the backseat of a black FORD Excursion seated beside Tourista Agent No. 2, a thick, round-faced bundle of tension. "Do I need a lawyer?"

"Do you?" replied a mid-sixties man wearing dark glasses, occupying the passenger's seat. He looked back and squinted, examining Rick. "I'm Director Armstrong, FBI Special Investigations Unit."

Rick blurted, "I can tell you honestly that I know nothing about that missing nuclear data that was in my safe. I got no reasonable explanation. But I'm certain there is one. And I don't want to be the one to say it, but maybe something's up with that."

Jackson, who occupied the driver's seat, scribbled frantically on a little pad. Rick wondered why what he'd said was news. "I'm a little surprised by the way you go about investigating such matters," Rick said. "And if you want to harass me about it, then yes, I do want a lawyer present."

Armstrong spoke slowly, asking, "And when was this incident with the missing nuclear data stuff?"

Who does he think he's kidding? "If you hadn't gotten a call from the Lab, you wouldn't be here, right?" Rick felt confident connecting dots microns apart.

"Okay, Mr. Adams, no questions about the nuclear data today. We would like to know about your relationship with Fred Larson."

"I had no *relationship* with him."

"Excuse me," Armstrong sneered. "I didn't mean to imply . . . . Tell us about your friendship, your working situation with Mr. Larson."

Rick rattled off a laundry list of interactions. Armstrong ogled; Jackson scribbled. The sun beat down through the glass onto Rick's neck. Stifling heat. "So why's this important to the FBI?" Rick asked. "Fred's dead."

"And where were you Friday, June 24th between the hours of 9 p.m. and 11 p.m. MDT?" Tourista Agent No. 2 spewed.

"Boning your sister," Rick replied.

Armstrong cleared his throat loudly. Focused laser eyes on the candy apple red-faced man, who relaxed his posture. Armstrong asked, "Do you think you're a bit confrontational for this high security work, Mr. Adams? That in addition to other, uh, lapses." He held up a voluminous folder, bearing Rick's name on the tab.

Rick's blood pressure spiked. The veins in his neck engorged. A tempest brewed in his head. It was *that* feeling— Rick spoke to the man behind the glasses, behind the goons, behind the refulgent FBI shield. "I know you didn't want the Lab to hire me. But they were dying to get me mixed up in this . . . whatever it is." Rick poked his index finger toward Armstrong's self-righteous glare. Pulse hammering his temples, he said, "So here I am. Whether you like it or not. And I'm staying at the Lab." Rick grasped the door handle. "But, I'm outta here."

Tourista Agent No. 2 seized Rick in a headlock. He writhed for freedom, air. "Sarkowski! Let him go!" Armstrong rasped.

Rick sat up. Rubbed his neck, thinking, this goon has the right moniker.

"Okay, I'll cut to the chase. It's possible that Mr. Larson's death was not accidental. We don't know who was involved. You could help us find out. It would be a great service to your country. Offenses on your record, including ones pending, could be expunged."

"Wait a minute. First, you don't think I'm worthy to have a security clearance. Now you want me to work for you, as a spy?" Burton burst into Rick's mind. This was like déjà vu all over again. Was there a rodent icon tattooed on his forehead?

"The Lab is the target of a foreign entity. We don't know exactly which one or what their designs are. We know they have inroads. Possibly a highly placed operative." Armstrong's glare gave way to the furrowed brow of a man in trouble. "Rick, we've got to understand and foil their plans."

Rick realized this was not about penny ante policy infractions. This was serious business. He forced a breath, asking, "So, why me?"

Armstrong shot a look to Jackson, who ceased scribbling. "We've reason to believe you were going to be included in the plot. Maybe that's still on."

"I'm useless." A Freudian slip? "I mean, I just got here."

"That's more than I'm authorized to share with you. Is there nothing you can tell us?" The gaze was sincere, almost pleading. "You could help save the country, Rick."

The weight of patriotism fell like depleted uranium on Rick's chest. The words resounded in his head, "save the country." When Armstrong removed his sunglasses, his tear ducts brimmed. For an instant, Armstrong's craft had plucked Rick's nationalistic heartstrings. But Rick smelled a smarmy seduction. "Well, you know," he said, "I'd really like to help save the country and all, but I've got a life here. Just want to go on living it. Maybe I've seen too many movies, but bad things happen to spies and secret agents. I'd like to go now."

Jackson scribbled.

Armstrong's weepy eyes turned steely. "I understand that you need to think about it," he said. "Just remember, bad things happen to all kinds of people, not just spies." In an edgy tone, he added, "Very bad things can happen to people who possess inappropriate security information, to people who use illicit drugs and lie about it to the government." He paused, letting the remarks sink in. "And, uh, don't mention this to anyone, Mr. Adams. But do consider it carefully. We'll be in touch."

Rick opened the door, but quickly extended his neck over Jackson's shoulder. In schoolmarmish penmanship, he'd written: "**LANL4 uncooperative.**" Sarkowski shoved Rick's head out of the door. Rick disembarked and Sarkowski followed, smiling full face. He grasped Rick's hand and shook it violently. His eyes darted everywhere. Patted Rick's back like an old pal and waved as Rick moped away.

CHAPTER 38

RICK went home and fell face-first onto the sofa. Was he being played? By whom? Everybody? He was tempted to call Renée and cancel the dinner date. He wasn't even sure it was a good idea. Ah, what the hell, he thought. It was just dinner. And caring company was bound to improve his sagging spirits. After all, she was the one who'd declared that she wanted to be there for him any way she could.

The X5 was flawless when Rick picked up Renée. En route to an out-of-the-way steak house in Tesuque, he asked, "How's your weekend?"

"Quiet. And yours?"

"Interesting. Today, I had a great breakfast at Becker's."

"That's always fascinating."

"Not necessarily, but the really interesting part came afterwards when the FBI, dressed as Miami Vice wannabees, interrogated me in their urban assault vehicle."

She giggled. "Was Bill Murray among them?"

"No, but he could've been." Rick shook his head. "It was so weird."

"You're serious?" Renée shot up straight. "The FBI interrogated you?"

"It was more like importuned me. They wanted to enlist my help, sort of."

"For what?" Her voice cracked. "What did you tell them?"

"Hey, settle down. I haven't done anything, really." Rick's hands left the steering wheel in animation. Renée gasped. "Calm down," he said. "I told them I wasn't interested." Why was she taking this so hard?

"Was that cool with them?" Renée crossed her arms. Her knuckles whitened. "Did they just say, okay, sorry to have importuned you, Mr. Adams?"

"They said sorry to have importuned you, *Dr.* Adams." Rick laughed, trying to diffuse the growing tension.

"This is no laughing matter. What if they follow you or surveil you at work?"

"Shh, there's an urban assault vehicle tailing us. Surveillance has already begun."

"Will you stop kidding around. What's this all about, Rick?"

"Oh, I feel better already. You are so charged up. But seriously, they think Fred's death might not have been an accident. And believe me, I hate to even consider it, but too many strange things are happening around me."

"They think you killed him?"

"Of course not!" This was getting out of hand. "Look, they're on a wild boar chase at the Lab. Like with the Lee guy, I imagine."

"Wen Ho Lee, the so-called spy for China."

"Yeah. They think there're more like him running around the Lab. They want me to help them catch one. I just want to do my work and keep breathing."

"So you told them no, period."

Rick hesitated, but then he said, "I'm just going to keep doing my work." The phrase stuck, "my work." Does GRIT have something to do with all of this?

"What was their final position?"

Rick realized this was more of a grilling than he had had by the FBI. He didn't like it. "They said they would consult their Grand Poobah and get back to me." He looked disgusted, saying, "So, tell me about your day."

"They may try harder to give you grief." She shook an index finger saying, "Remember what happened to Wen Ho."

"Oh, you know all the buttons, don't you."

"What buttons? This is serious."

"I'm not saying another word until we get some food."

Rick hardly touched his surf and turf. He couldn't look at Renée without trying to read her. Where was all that passion when they had sex?

They skipped the bar scene. Instead, they took the long route home. Rick decided to get a read on something else important. A GRIT litmus test.

"Feel better now?" He looked at Renée, whose blonde hair fluttered in the crisp breeze from her open window. "I just thought of something quite stimulating," he said.

"Oh?" She reached over and stroked the length of his thigh.

"My brain's not down there."

She snickered, asking, "When did it move?"

"I think I can prove that GRIT can't possibly work." He cut his gaze to her.

Renée withdrew her hand quick as a cobra strike. Snapped her neck to face him. "Aren't you full of surprises tonight."

"I know it sounds strange. But it just came to me."

"What came to you?"

"How to prove simply that GRIT can't generate enough juice to fry nuclear warheads. So, my dear . . . ." He patted her leg and was surprised when it twitched. "America can sleep safe tonight and for the foreseeable future."

"Who else knows about this terrific discovery?"

"Pretty much only me. I still have to verify it."

"Rick, what if you're wrong? Why hasn't anyone else come up with this in the last six months? You've barely been here a month."

"Some of them don't have the right composite background. Others have their heads too far up their you-know-whats to see a solution of less than Herculean complexity. It's fairly common in the ivory towers of research."

"I'm certainly not smart enough to vet your findings, but if you're wrong, then America's national security and your job are both out the window."

"And if I'm right, the taxpayers' money is right down the drain. A billion bucks by the time this is all over."

"Oh, Rick, don't you realize the taxpayers are screwed either way. The Lab, some other government agency, our *allies* will squander the money."

Rick clenched his teeth. This was an inconvenient truth. But not nearly as inconvenient as what he was finding about Renée.

"Work through the problem conservatively. Take your time."

Once at Renée's place, she disappeared and re-emerged hollow-eyed and sluggish. Her clothing reeked. Soon afterwards she began to sob inconsolably. Rick held her and stroked her hair until she crashed to sleep.

Rick catnapped the entire night. He rose just after five o'clock and slipped out of bed. Drinking juice, he examined a photo affixed to the fridge door. A half-smiling little girl in a tee and jeans stared at him. She held a fluffy kitty to her face. Lucky her, Rick thought, before counting three consecutive weeks that Emily had been away for the weekend. One more curiosity in Renée's unusual existence. He sighed, before draining the juice, scribbling a nice note, and heading off to work.

CHAPTER 39

"AND THEN?" Walter asked Renée. He gazed out the window across from his desk at the tennis club. Dabbed almost daintily at condiments from an overstuffed ham sandwich soiling the sides of his mouth. Renée sat quiet. He turned toward her, brushing crumbs from his lap onto the floor. He watched her play with her salad wrap, before inquiring, "No getting loaded? Playing hide the salami?"

She kicked the toe of her shoe at a leg of the small table in front of the sofa on which she sat. "I just zonked out."

"That's it?"

Her sandwich fell to her lap. "Sex, no. But I had to get high." Waving the wrap, she said, "I think I'm hooked again. I can't live a day without at least one joint."

"That's nothing for you. I know the details of your old habits."

"Not just grass. It has to be *H*-laced. Look at me." She extended her scrawny arm.

Walter eyed her trembling hand. The unsightly blemishes and splotches on her gaunt face were half-masked by heavy makeup. Renée's black-encircled eyes welled with tears that she fought back. He turned. Trained his gaze out the window.

"And what about my case? When will I be able to see Emily?"

"I'm applying significant pressure behind the scenes. I bet you'll be back in court next month. Concentrate on Rick. I'll take care of the rest for you." Walter relaxed his face. Pasted on a thin smile. Even tried to fully open his squinty eyes, turning to face her, administering a warning, "Don't go to pieces or you may only see her on visiting day at the pen. Now you'd better get back to the Lab."

Renée wiped her eyes on her crumpled napkin. She stood and straightened her shirt's sleeves and collar, before setting her uneaten lunch on top of the overly full trash can beside his desk. Walter remained seated until she'd gone. Through the window, he watched her limp past the tennis courts toward the parking lot. Closed the door; locked it. He stuffed the remainder of his meaty sandwich into his mouth, adjusted the window's louvers downward, and made his way behind his desk to a small closed closet. Raked smelly tennis gear from a squatty file cabinet, which he unlocked. He withdrew a large metal document box, containing cash, fake passports, file folders, and a cell phone.

The special cell phone, which he checked frequently yet seldom used, was in play. Sources had told him it was routed through Hamburg. Walter didn't care. All that concerned him was that all the cautious plotting and executing as well as all the ostensible bumbling and buffoonery, his mission persona, was taking a turn toward success. The kettle was coming to a boil.

Walter flipped open the plain black cover of a thin file folder. No name stamped across the top, no number, no photographs, no nonsense. A few details of a Russian operative for rent, name: Alexi Pushkin. Big-time rent, but apparently worth it to the renters. Places and dates ranged from Europe and Asia to the US over three decades. Sketchy biographical history. Classically trained dancer of all things— Walter knew more. A lot more. This was going to be one for the manuals. He annotated the file and closed it, before powering up the special phone.

The call was brief. A few code words. He leaned back and the chair emitted an ominous creak that sounded much like a human neck snapping. He'd heard that before. Renee's face appeared to him. He dispelled the vision, before relocking the cabinet and piling on his yellowed tennis togs, dingy jock strap on top.

GERRY HURRIED to his control console and accessed the conversation recorded in Rick's vehicle a couple of evenings earlier. His ears burned. Burton's ideas were useless. He phoned Walter, using the Helsinki link, and issued concise instructions. Walter promised to set things up for the following weekend. Gerry reminded him that stalkers and rapists were frowned upon in Los Alamos and imprisoned in Argonne, Illinois, where Walter's offenses went unpunished. Gerry released the call, realizing the course of action was heavy handed. But his hand could be so much heavier when he deemed it necessary. That was something that Dr. Adams would soon discover.

Early Friday evening, Gerry stepped inside Angel's back door. A packed house; only standing room. The band was on break. He observed Walter and Renée sitting close at a corner table, sharing a bottle of booze. Two shot glasses: Walter's full, Renée's empty. Gerry wended his way near them. He faced the bar, but used hyper-peripheral vision to spy on them. Renée stared down at the stained table top. Walter nodded discretely to Gerry and his voice rose perceptibly. Gerry's chin dimpled, thinking, he's impressing the boss.

Walter said, "Rick's gone. It's over. How many times do I have to say it." He poured Renée another round.

"I still don' believe it," Renée slurred, picking up the shot. "We have, uh, a thing." She tossed it. Wiped her eyes on her shirt cuff, already blackened with mascara.

"I saw it, myself," Walter claimed. "It's like he's her slave."

"What about the custody hearing? I need to see Emily." Renée bit down on a fingernail. Held the pressure, saying, "You know, supervised is okay." Squeezing her palms together, she said, "I really, really just need to see her."

"It's hit a snag." Walter rapped the table and leaned back. "I've no idea."

"What can you do?"

"It's what can you do, you need to be considering." He refreshed her drink before pulling out his cell and flipping it open. "Gotta go." He stood.

"No, Walter, please." She tugged his arm. Her face contorted. "I'll do anything."

"Then get started." Walter departed, winking at Gerry as he went.

CHAPTER 40

Rick sped from the Lab toward Santa Fe. Careful not to speed through Pojoaque. Equally careful not to drip mustard from his sandwich onto his pants. At nine-thirty he arrived to find Angel's lot overflowing. He parked a block away, behind a shuttered art gallery. From Angel's front door, he forged his way to the bar, three thick. Walter had sounded upset during their telecon. Rick hoped the situation would be quickly resolved at their meeting. Hanging out with him was not Rick's idea of fun.

The band played. Carmen sang. At the song's conclusion, she struck a lascivious pose, extending her hand toward Rick. He kept cool outwardly; melted inwardly. When Carmen blew him a big, wet kiss from the stage, he flushed and looked furtively to see if anyone noticed. He saw Renée standing, her eyes piercing him. She waved wildly.

"Hi, Renée. How's it going?" Rick asked. He stiffened when she melded her blade-thin torso to his, wrapped her arms around his back, and smothered his mouth with hers. Extricating himself, he said, "It's, uh, great to see you, too."

"I thought you'd left town."

"Just really busy." He nodded emphatically.

"Have a sit. Uh, seat. Ah, what the hell."

Renée's behavior and breath coupled with the nearly empty bottle formed a complete picture. Rick said, "Sure, for a few minutes."

"But you jus' got here."

"I can't stay long."

She reached for a lighted cigarette on the ashtray, nearly toppling her glass. "I didn't know you smoked," Rick said.

"Don't lie," she sneered, indenting her bony chest with a shaky thumb. "This is Renée you're talking to."

"Cigarettes," he mouthed, looking into her mascara mussed, sunken raccoon eyes. He thought: Alice Cooper meets Marilyn Manson—

"Yeah Rick, there's lots you don't know. Believe me."

"I'm sure you're right," he said, gazing stageward.

"Looking for somebody?"

"I just wanted to wave to Carmen."

"I suppose anyone who does has a chance."

"What's that supposed to mean?"

"Nothing. Absolutely nothing." From one side of her dry mouth, Renée drew the cigarette nearly down to the filter, flaring her lips in disgust.

"You look tired," he said. "Go home; get some sleep."

"Think I'll stick around. See what the night'll reveal."

"I'm leaving soon. There's a lot riding on my performance these days."

"About five feet, three inches, I'd guess." She inhaled, saying, "No worries." Blew smoke squarely into Rick's face, adding, "Whole town's been there. Why not you?"

"Been where? With who?"

Renée raked the table clean. Bottle, glass, ashtray, purse all crashing to the floor. She screamed, "Don't lie to me. I'm sick of it." She began to sob. In a muffled moan, she said, "The lies . . . deceit. I'm through with it."

Rick stood, noting he garnered all eyes. He tried to put his arm around her. Renée pushed him backward into his chair, which banged on the floor behind him. "I'm taking you home, right now." Rick picked up the purse and lifting Renée from her chair, stuffed the purse under Renée's arm. On their departure, Carmen wailed out familiar lines: "They call it stormy Monday, but Tuesday's just as bad."

Coaxing Renée across the parking lot, Rick asked, "What's wrong with you?" He rifled through her purse, took the car key, unlocked her door. "What is wrong?"

"Everything's wrong."

"No, it's not. You have a home, a good job, a daughter who loves you, friends."

"I've no friends. And neither do you, Rick." She whimpered, "Be careful, please."

"Great. I feel much better now."

"Don't risk your life." She clutched him to her and pleaded, "Get out now. Go back to Boston."

"What're you talking about?"

"I'm so sorry, Rick," she sobbed. "I hate myself. But, I . . . I love you."

A chill raced the length of his spine as Renée collapsed to the ground, disconsolate. Rick picked her up and placed her in the passenger's seat. She fell limp into the floorboard and curled into a ball. He drove to Renee's place in silence, except for her incessant whimpering. A bundle of nerves, once inside the house he quickly undressed her and tucked her under the covers. Renée pawed him. Begged him to stay. Rick looked back from the bedroom door to find her coiled into fetal position, moaning inconsolably.

Fallishly fresh night air slapped Rick's face as he stood on Renée's dimly lit porch. A little pink bicycle with colorful plastic streamers hanging from the handle grips leaned against the same spot as the very first time he was there. Emily was away again this weekend, every weekend. The picture was clearer, although darker.

Leaden heart. Porous thoughts. Rick reassured himself that Renée would be fine tomorrow. Walking toward Angel's, he considered how weird that in her moment of greatest upset, absent of ego filtering and self-consciousness, she would confess her love for him. And to evince a morbid concern for his safety. What could he do? He was a rat in an invisible trap. The Feds, Gerry, Renée, even Sam seemed to know something about it. Everyone, except him. He meant to find out. Just how, was a conundrum he pondered on the way to his vehicle and on the lonely drive home. It continued to dominate his thoughts as he crawled into bed, for a night of fitful slumber.

CHAPTER 41

THE EARLY morning chill invigorated Gerry. He unlatched the cargo door and slithered out of his 4WD Bimmer, which had been pre-prepared: interior lights disabled, a copy of Rick's license plate installed, equipment at the ready. The full-face ski hat was not too warm, although his blood throbbed with excitement, accessing the key that Renée stashed in the left flowerpot near the front door.

Once inside the living room, Gerry heard drunken snores emanating from down the hall. A pale blue diode light, attached to a miner's headband, illuminated his steps. He cleared the way to the garage. Lifted its manual door a few inches, sufficient to get his fingers underneath for quick leverage. Workman-like, he slipped into the bedroom.

Renée lay sprawled across the bed, on her back. Mouth agape. Gerry stared at her naked body. Refocusing, he raised the window, readied a two-foot length of wide cord, covered in blue velvet. Gingerly, he slipped it around Renée's neck. Snapped a shot with a phone camera. A perfect necrophilic pose. More snores. He readied the pre-prepared syringe. Woke her with an injection in the forearm, emptying its entire volume with a forceful depression of the plunger.

"Ouch," Renée cried, springing up.

Gerry silenced her by constricting the velvet covered cord. He said, "Be quiet. Do as I say, and you'll not be harmed. Got that?"

Eyes buldging, darting frantically, she nodded.

"All you have to do is scream, 'Rick'."

Renée resisted, jerking her head side to side; Gerry constricted the cord. Renée coughed; Gerry constricted the cord. Turning pale and feeling dizzy, Renée nodded consent; Gerry loosened the cord. "Scream it, bitch."

With fish-like eyes, bulging from their sockets, Renée looked hysterically from side-to-side; Gerry constricted the cord. She nodded; Gerry loosened the cord.

Renée's desperate shriek could be heard for half a block. "Riiiiiick."

She writhed, trying to wrest free. Gerry lay atop her and covered her mouth with his gloved hand. Waiting silently, he avoided her darting eyes. Soon, Renée was immersed in a psychedelic world. Her struggle ceased. Eyes drooped.

Gerry stretched a reinforced nylon stocking over Renée's head. Gathering her in his arms, he carefully proceeded through the house. Lifted the garage door and his X5's cargo hatch before depositing her on black plastic sheeting, covered by a layer of larva-rich dirt, which he collected by her trashcan. A quick roll and Renée was covered in plastic, which Gerry tied about her securely.

He departed, leaving deep tread marks in her driveway. Scrupulously observing speed limits, nearly half way home, he heard the bundle jerk to life and flail in its bondage. A violent spasm from a horse-killing dose of heroin. Gerry imagined that choking on one's own vomit was an awful way to die. But was there a good one?

He tapped a phone number into his PDA, waited, and then entered a numeric sequence, opening his property's gate. He entered a second sequence, de-energizing the laser-based home security system. He didn't want to waste a second when he arrived with this reeking package. The vehicle's windows remained sealed against leaking the stench of excreta and regurgitation until well inside his gate. Gerry stopped, jumped out, and emptied his stomach in the dirt, leaving no trace of distress in the vehicle. He was a professional, who had perpetrated the perfect indeterminate crime. His exact objective.

CHAPTER 42

THE BEDSIDE telephone rang to life. Rick eyed the clock, thinking even telemarketers don't call at seven twenty-seven on Saturday morning. He managed a groggy, "Hello."

"Rick. It's Gerry, the used car salesman."

"Oh, Gerry. What's up?"

"I don't know if you're busy. But we need to talk about something important."

"I'm heading to work later." Maybe earlier, he thought, waking.

"This is important to both of us."

"Can we talk about it now?"

"I think it's better if we meet. Have a mountain bike?"

"I got an old road bike."

"That's okay. Meet me at the Atalaya trailhead at St. John's. Turn into the College, take an immediate left into the lot. Can't miss it. Say, nine o'clock?" Gerry paused. "And Rick, this is kind of sensitive. Don't mention it to anyone."

Minutes after nine, Rick turned into the parking lot and searched for Gerry's SUV. A full coverage helmet, glasses with iridescent lenses, and half-finger gloves made Gerry barely recognizable when he approached. He directed Rick to park in a remote spot in the lot's unpaved overflow section. To avoid a door ding, he'd said.

Rick, who had stripped to his faded Muddy Charles tee and board shorts, was not enthusiastic. He was bursting to glean the ruination of his day. "So, what's up? This must be pretty important."

"You're a runner, aren't you?"

"Yeah."

"Can you carry your bike to the blacktop on that ridge?" Gerry pointed.

The only ridge Rick saw appeared to be miles away and significantly elevated. He eyed Gerry's bulging muscles. Felt the heft of his own clunky bike. "No problem, but why can't we talk now."

"We can talk up there. It's beautiful. You need to stretch first?"

"I'm pretty stiff," Rick replied.

"I already did. I'm gonna make a pit stop."

Trudging up the poor footpath toward the ridge, Rick enjoyed the fresh currents that excited the prickly foliage of crooked junipers and rustled the lime green leaves of airy aspens, both dotting the landscape. A brilliant sun dominated the sky, more blue than blue. A bird of prey wheeled and eddied on thermals high above as the two men passed a fork in the trail.

"Hey, Rick," Gerry said, extending an ordinary looking cell phone. "I need another pit stop. Answer this if it rings."

Gerry and his bike disappeared around the fork's corner. Minutes passed. Rick jacked a running shoe sole against a wall of stone, cooled by shade. Rested his back, standing straight on one leg, its knee locked. A ground squirrel culled the edible from the inedible atop a sunny crag across the path. Bushy orangish tail, ridiculous white racing stripe. A grave shadow engulfed the feral creature. Rick threw his eyes upward to see the hawk diving, its talons extended like the skinless fingers of a wing-born reaper. And then the squirrel was gone. A single drop of blood bore witness to its existence. Rick winced, thinking how quickly the game can change by a bolt out of the blue.

The phone rang. Rick fumbled it open and said, "Gerry's phone."

"This is your phone now. Take good care of it," Gerry said. "Go back to your vehicle and retrieve the package from under the driver's seat. Then wait for my call."

Rick was dismayed, but not shocked, when the call ended. Hounded by dread, he mounted his bike and began to descend the rain-ravaged, declivitous route. He fell once, scuffing his elbow, twice, lacerating his knee. After the third crash, with both knees bruised and bleeding, he put the bike over his head and ran pell-mell.

Heart pounding and heavy-legged, Rick arrived at his vehicle where he tossed the bike aside, before lashing open the driver's side door. Under the seat, sure enough, there was a plain manila envelope. He prepared to rip off the top. But he felt the weight of the package. A hefty stack of documents, meaning what? Could this be a watershed moment? Voices. Rick crammed the envelope back under the seat. Thrust his muddy shoe on the running board for untying and retying. The duo of hikers passed, chatting animatedly, oblivious to the drama. The envelope retrieved and the top ripped off, a photo floated gently to the ground. It rested face down.

Rick grasped the photo and stared. It seemed to be Renée, but his vision blurred. She was as pale as a cadaver with a velvety cord twisted around her neck. Her eyes ballooned from their blackened sockets. He jerked around, scanning the deserted parking lot for Gerry, onlookers. His pulse quickened, the rhythm resonated throughout his body. Sweat dripped from his face onto the photo. He quickly wiped it away onto his chest, as his mental fog lifted and the situation became clear.

Blood slacked in Rick's veins. He slowly collapsed to the side of his vehicle. His legs shook, knees softly knocking together. A blast of mountain air rustled leaves on the aspen trees. They danced and winked. A massive cloud had blacked out the sun. Rick braced himself against his vehicle. Wiped his face on his soiled tee before pouring himself into the driver's seat. He trembled filing through the packet: a night vision photo of Rick and Renée kissing at the tennis club; another necro photo; a copy of a $10,000 receipt from his Lab-issued credit card from Salsa Sluts of San Diego!

The phone rang. Rick answered, "What's going on?"

"Looks like you like to photograph yourself having wild sex. Maybe a bit too wild, judging by Renée's corpse."

"You know I didn't kill her. If she's dead, you did it!"

"Tell the cops. They'll be by to ask you a few questions any day. You should know that not only did you leave Angel's with her after making a scene but the neighbors heard her screaming your name the night she died. By the way, fresh tire tracks from *your* vehicle were in her driveway."

"That's bullshit. And circumstantial, anyway."

Gerry intoned, "If you beat the murder wrap, there're the drugs, the fraud, the security infractions. Adams, your life is over."

"Wha?"

Rick's head spun. Was he dreaming? He bit his lip hard. Tasted blood, but there was no feeling. In the rearview, he saw a crazed man with a bloodly mouth stare back at him. This was real. This was hell on earth.

"What do you want? Why me?" Rick threw open the door. Exploded out of the suv. Shaking his fist, he screamed, "I'll kill you. Show yourself, you coward."

"Say that louder," Gerry said, perfectly relaxed. "Let people hear you make a death threat."

Rick fell to his knees. His face fell into his trembling hands, the phone smashed against his sagging cheek.

"Do not speak of this to anyone," Gerry continued. "Do as I say, and you'll live just fine. If you cooperate with the cops or assist the FBI in any way, I'll know."

"The FBI. How'd you know?" Rick asked, punch drunk.

"I know everything. But they don't. So if you tell them anything, I may not let them have the pleasure of frying you. I'll smoke you myself."

"Like Fred." His mind a fine mush, Rick demanded, "Just tell me why?"

"GRIT, Adams. Keep GRIT alive or you die."

PART Γ
Squeeze

"You can't squeeze blood from a rock."

—Proverb

CHAPTER 43

RICK'S MIDNIGHT panic attacks ceased after a couple of weeks, but the nightmares persisted. Visits by detective Russell had also stopped. He'd hinted during their last chat that he would be back to arrest Rick once a 'CD' had surfaced. Rick no longer flinched at the thought of Renée's corpse; he simply battled it nightly while sleeping. All in all, detective Russell had provided Rick with plenty of food for thought. Because when Rick considered it, his appetite vanished.

When on the Hill, Rick kept to himself. He pretended to be fixated on his mission to perfect GRIT's grasing cavity design. Answering e-mail early one morning, there it was, sent from an unknown shielded server, Subject "Security Meeting". Rick double-clicked the message and was surprised not to find the grand header used by Connie Sanders. The plain communiqué instructed Rick to come Gavin Burton's office at two-thirty p.m. It was signed 'GB'.

Dread washed over Rick like a tiny tsunami flooding his consciousness. So many what ifs. What if he didn't respond? What if he claimed he didn't produce a report? What if his report persuaded Burton to act against GRIT? What if Gerry found out?

He had saved the document describing GRIT's destructive (in)capacity on removable media and stashed it in the back of a filing cabinet drawer. The safe was as secure as a sieve as far as he was concerned. But he must present something to Burton. While a hardcopy printed, he revisited the most unlikely what if: what if he managed to convince Burton that GRIT and GRIT-like variants were incapable of threatening the pre-eminence of America's nuclear arsenal? Not to worry, his evidence was far from incontrovertible. He possessed only modest computational backing and no experimental data. Yet his case bore the power of simple elegance. As the final pages spooled to the printer, Rick scoured his desk for a rubber stamp. Pressing "DRAFT' across the title page, in big, black type, he was satisfied with having marginalized the report as much as possible.

Rick considered entering the paper's title, Energetic Analysis of the Gamma Ray Intensity Transducer, in the group's log for newly-generated, potentially classified documents. He chose not to. Just in case. Otherwise, he followed security procedures to the letter, double wrapping the hardcopy with a plain outer after marking the inner TOP SECRET. He shoved the half-inch-thick package in his lowest desk drawer and breathed a half-sigh of relief. He held the other half for the meeting's conclusion.

GERRY PERUSED Burton's e-mail accounts from his command center. Things had been awfully quiet at the Lab. Too quiet, given the direct pressure Rick was under and the indirect pressure Burton had to be experiencing. Gerry had decided to let both of them cool down for a bit longer. But when a classified message in the outbox directed to Richard Adams caught his eye, Gerry read the message and immediately fired off an e-mail routed through a university in Romania to Burton. The e-mail header and formatting were identical to those used by Los Alamos's Computing Divison. Sitting in Burton's inbox, it looked like any other message from C Divison; it's Subject: IMPORTANT CALL. It employed code to instruct Burton to call him immediately.

Expecting that his command might be ignored, Gerry activated and self-tested a highly sophisticated audio transmitter he had planted in Burton's office. It was too risky, tapping Burton's phone line. And the Lab's anti-spyware could sniff out a conventional transmitter. So Gerry had installed a microburst transmitter, just to keep in touch. And today could be the most important conversation it had ever transmitted.

The transmitter used extremely brief, low-power microbursts of encrypted information. The info was captured by an intermediate link at the Los Alamos ski hill. The link sent higher energy encrypted bursts to an international satellite, operated by his employer. The info was rained back down to an inconspicuous cell tower disguised as an old windmill on Gerry's property. The trickiest part was to send the microbursts outside the Lab's perimeter without being discovered by innumerable snoop detection electronics. The self-test had worked perfectly. Now, Gerry sat in anticipation of Rick's revelation. Later, in the telecon he had requested of Burton via e-mail, Gerry would compare the actual conversation with Burton's account of it, for diligence's sake.

CHAPTER 44

MORE RELAXED than in previous meetings, Rick sat at the conference table while Burton read the document's Executive Summary. Rick alternated trying to ignore the dimness of the lighting, darkness of the paneling and cabinetry, and fakeness of the soylent green ficus tree. Burton drew Rick's full attention when he leaned forward and peered with steely slate eyes over the upper margin of his faux tortoise shell half-glasses.

"Well?" Rick blurted.

"Based upon this, you would jeopardize America's national security. It's merely a lump parameter description of one of the most complex physical phenomena imaginable. You are a world-class experimental physicist. What is this?"

"You're probably right," Rick said, relieved.

Burton removed his glasses. Held them aloft and eased back into his seat. In a measured, fatherly tone, he said, "Rick, do you recall the acronym for the emergency quenching of a nuclear fission reaction?"

"SCRAM."

"Correct. Do you know whence that originates? What the letters represent?"

"Can't say I do. I'm more of a crane operator than a hermition operator." The physics jibe drifted up toward the ceiling where it died.

"Safety control rod axe man."

Rick nodded.

"That's right, Rick," Burton stressed. "At Chicago nuclear pile number one—the first critical mass of uranium ever assembled—there was a guy with an axe. His only job was to cut a rope used to suspend a control rod, meaty enough to quench the atom-splitting chain reaction immediately, should it have gotten out of control."

"Okay."

"Enrico Fermi, one of the greatest of modern physicists, routed the rope well away from the nuclear pile and stationed the axe man near the exit. Fermi instructed him to cut the rope should people be sickened or keel over. The SCRAM man must cut the rope through, observe the control rod fall into the pile, and then run for help." Burton re-established the half glasses near the ball of his skinny nose. Leaned forward, and gazing over the truncated tops of the frames said, "That's how much faith Fermi had in his and everyone else's bounding calculations, Rick."

Burton's gloomy gaze took hold of Rick, whose eyes sought the floor. His lids felt like those metal shutters on his office window, blocking out everything that was good.

"Get the point?" Burton said. "There are those who question the magnitude of effort dedicated to GRIT, even the program's basic intel. They could undermine the project with one iota of semi-credible scientific backing."

"My aim is not to torpedo GRIT. I'm confident the truth will come out sooner or later." Rick looked up and into Burton's soulful eyes. He appeared to be in pain.

As Burton sipped coffee, the room fell silent, sepulchral. Staring at the cup, Rick recalled the microwave oven and cup of coffee analogy Burton had stressed in a previous meeting, to indicate how easily GRIT might disable an enemy warhead. But even if the pockets of lasing gammas avalanched into a fully participatory grasing cavity, could the output beam penetrate a steel rocket casing and fry rad-hard electronics. Rick thought not. He said, "Mr. Burton, one thing I don't quite get is exactly how GRIT could marginalize a warhead. It's not a ground-borne microwave oven that can destroy a coffee cup warhead in low earth orbit."

Burton donned his half-glasses and his thin lips vanished, saying, "What do you know of inertial confinement fusion technology?"

"Uses laser beams, not magnets, to compress fuel and force its atoms to fuse. When they fuse, the reaction liberates energy. The opposite of nuclear fission that blows atoms apart."

"What's the most effective way for the laser beams to compress the fuel?"

"Um, focus the beams very precisely and symmetrically on the . . . the fuel."

Burton shook his head slowly, steadily eyeing Rick. Time moved at a glacial pace. "That's completely naive. The fuel is contained inside a *hohlraum*."

"Cavity?" Rick's German was pretty rusty.

"In the ICF business, it's euphemistically called the "empty can." But, yes, Rick. The fuel is not sitting on the head of a pin, like so many angels, awaiting compression."

"So, how's the *hohlraum* designed?"

"You've neither the background nor the clearance," Burton snapped. Off came the glasses. "But, do get this: we don't know the details of the design of the other sides' warheads. And hopefully they don't know ours." Burton paused. "That is to say, we don't know where the detonation electronics package is fitted onto the warhead."

Rick couldn't sit still. He said, "But the beam has to penetrate at least some marginal thickness of metal radiation shielding for low earth orbit. And then the electronics are bound to be rad-hard. GRIT just can't do it."

Burton's eyes grayed. "You've completely lost faith in technology, haven't you?"

Rick's head hung. He couldn't bear to admit that what little faith he'd ever had in anything good was all but gone.

"I'm telling you that GRIT need only illuminate the exterior of the warhead and deliver, say, a megawatt of photonic energy over its outer casing for an instant. The casing will absorb the exterior light energy and re-radiate it as powerful X-rays on the interior. The shielding of the detonation electronics package inside is designed to ward off cosmic rays and such, not a direct blast of hard X-rays coming from inside the casing."

Rick's head snapped up. "Indirect drive!"

"Exactly. Just like an ICF shot. X-rays couple the laser beam energy into the fuel more effectively than a direct blast from the beam itself."

Rick's hands involuntarily shot into the air. "And the warhead casing becomes a *hohlraum*, enabling a smaller amount of externally applied energy to destroy the detonation electronics inside."

Burton's fingers interlaced as though in prayer. "Rick, GRIT was never intended to kill a warhead. Even destroying the detonation electronics is not strictly correct. It need only disable or confuse them to effectively neutralize the threat."

Rick sighed, awestruck. "It's . . . beautiful science."

"Every day we are provided with opportunities for failure." Burton swept his arm in a generous arc, saying, "But Rick, golden opportunities to achieve excellence are few." He looked as though he inspected a gnat held between his thumb and forefinger pronouncing, "GRIT is a rare occasion for multiple forms of excellence: research, national security, aggrandizement of this Lab— This opportunity must be seized."

Rick nodded.

"You're a very talented, multidisciplinary contributor, Rick. The program needs you to help design and build the most powerful GRIT possible. Only then will you have given this Laboratory and the country your best."

Hair raised on the back of Rick's neck. His fingers tingled. He had to play this stupid game or have Gerry ruin his life, if not end it. Why not play to win? He said, "Maybe these calculations can help define a more efficient grasing cavity. Anyway, I know my job." He reached out to retrieve the document.

"I'll retain this," Burton said. "Please destroy the files used to create it and delete any written references to it. The last thing we need is another security slipup."

CHAPTER 45

GERRY listened hungrily as the final burst of audio came through. He appreciated that Burton was continuing to try to handle the matter psychologically. Gerry believed that Burton eschewed the wet work that sometimes had to be done.

He stood and stretched. Felt the constraint of his shirt as packs of shoulder muscle shifted. Adams was securely in the fold. And the FBI might have bluffed and been called again. It took them years to move on Wen Ho. And then they blew it. Gerry prepared to silence the reception of the communications from Burton's office when he overheard Connie Sanders on the speakerphone.

"Dr. Burton, may I interrupt you?"

"Yes, Connie."

"A Mr. Armstrong, Director of the FBI's Special Investigations Unit is here."

"Does he have an appointment? I don't recall—"

"Says it's urgent, sir."

"Well, uh, give me just a minute."

The tension in Burton's voice was perceptible, Gerry thought, ceasing to admire his bulging muscles in the mirrored wall. Awaiting the conversation, Gerry grit his teeth and filthily cursed Armstrong's mother.

CHAPTER 46

THE TA-3 cafeteria was on Rick's way to his vehicle. He decided to get a bite of lunch and mull how best to proceed. Nearing the cash register, he turned to find Sam holding a cup of coffee. He said, "Hello, Sam. How are you?"

"Very well. And you?"

"Ahhhh. Let me buy you that coffee and if you have time, I'll give you a core dump." Rick tacked, "Or, even better, I'll spot you a coffee for a little insight."

"How about if I join you for your lunch and you come back to my office for a little chat? If *you* have the time." Sam's thick eyebrows arched in expectation.

Soon, Rick found himself in Sam's claustrophobic office in the CMR building, barely 50 meters from a guard tower. Rick didn't object to the metal blinds, he knew they obscured the view of what looked like a prison yard. It was complete with armed guards and a 20-foot fence, topped with razor wire—outlawed by the Geneva Convention for use with prisoners of war.

Sam served up the first meaty observation. "Rick, this non-convergence situation has persisted for a while."

"Uh huh."

"Even after your parametric studies and sensitivity analyses, you don't seem to be able to come up with an acceptable solution for a successful design. Certainly not an enormously powerful configuration that achieves a substantial population inversion, in the macro-sense. Is this a correct assessment?"

"Yeah. But I'm able to model pockets of lasing gammas that might be capable of avalanching into a fully participatory grasing cavity."

"Only pockets so far, though."

"Yes. But that's better than what I had before."

"Have you thought about bounding the performance of a device that does not achieve macropopulation inversion? Just to understand its upper limit of intensity. Then maybe you could progressively solve for the grasing cross-section and nuclei inversion fraction necessary to sustain grasing, of sufficient duration to be useful."

Rick was quiet, unsure what he could, should reply. "I, uh, have done some computing along those lines."

"And?"

"Let's say it was inconclusive."

Sam drew a finer bead on Rick's face.

"Well," Rick chuckled, "I'm hardly sure of anything these days. I could've made mistakes. America's security could depend upon our rigor." Rick sold the line . . . even to himself. He fidgeted, asking, "Have you put pencil to paper on this, Sam?"

"Oh, no. Solely *gedanken*."

Rick understood Einstein's term for intellectual musing, but wasn't certain Sam was being truthful.

"As a Senior Laboratory Fellow, my security compartment could easily be enlarged to include your work. I'd be happy to review your bounding calculations, if you'd like. Just between you and me. No need to report the findings to the Review Committee. Not until we're certain."

Rick believed that of all the new people he had met at the Lab, Sam was the most sincere and the least politically motivated. He was at the top of the scientific ranks with no apparent managerial ambition. Lowering his voice, Rick said, "I've been asked not to share those results. May not be healthy for GRIT, the program."

"I see. You've shared your findings with Arthur."

"No."

"Of course not." Sam tapped his finger tips together. "He is a bit of a glass blower; not much of a computational man."

"That's not it at all," Rick said. "Arthur has a great nose; experimentalists always do." Rick paused. "Mr. Burton asked me to keep the results private."

"Burton, he's a sharp one." Sam crossed his legs; clasped his hands around his knees, asking, "How, uh, did you manage to get his ear? Such a busy man, wouldn't sully his hands with technical work, I would think."

"This is strictly between us." Rick's eyes searched the room involuntarily. Even Sam's thin smile looked suspicious at the moment. "Burton asked me to act as a security asset within GRIT. I report directly to him on certain security matters. Kinda like a derivative classifier."

"Good heavens, I . . . ." Sam glanced at his watch and popped up. "Rick, I'm going to be late." Picking up his letter carrier cum briefcase, he fumbled it to the floor.

Rick picked it up and handed it to him. "Be careful. This experiment needs you."

Flustered and inching toward the door, Sam said, "I was just going to say the same to you."

CHAPTER 47

THE GESTAPO from Washington having just left his office, Burton sat stone-faced. His heart thumped in his chest, neck, head, all the way down to his toes. Armstrong had been unrelenting, and his questions tough: Had Adams pilfered classified nuclear data? Was he on drugs? Had he solved the big problem? And the why of all whys: why had the Lab hired him against the FBI's recommendation in the first place? Burton had allayed most concerns, but one request could not be circumvented. It was compulsory to provide Armstrong with detailed information on all of Rick's Lab activity.

Burton unmeshed his tightly interlaced fingers. His blanched, blood-starved knuckles cracked. He had a question: Why had Rick divulged the trumped-up security infraction to Armstrong? Of course, Rick was caught off guard, but he could've dummied up. Now, Armstrong's plan to extract every shred of information on Richard Adams collected by the Lab since his hire provoked Burton to wish he had not generated the report on the missing disk drives, subsequently found in Rick's safe. The Renée Roxbury questions were not that easy to dodge. A horny, bean-counting contractor who had just disappeared. What could he say? And Rick's falsified travel records would be another prickly issue. Burton knew that he could stonewall Armstrong for a long time. But everything would have to be handled indirectly. He must not attract suspicion to himself.

He was calming down at last. Thank God Armstrong hadn't detected his panic. The front had been good. Especially the story of personally keeping his eye on Rick by periodically calling him into his office for observation. Good cover for himself, too.

LATER, BURTON perused his classified e-mail inbox and double-clicked a message ostensibly from C Division. As he read, he pursed his lips, set his chin. He didn't like dead drops in Santa Fe and certainly didn't want any more telephonic or electronic communication with Gerry than were absolutely necessary. He gloated that the convoluted routings and mega-bit encryption the Lab applied to all of his communications were sufficiently arcane that he could e-mail and instant message Bin Laden in Tora Bora all day, every day, and never be caught.

But the point was that there was nothing significant that he needed to relate to his counterpart. Gerry was not his handler, Burton told himself. Everything was under control, including Rick's brainy discovery. Burton mused that if need be he could quash any story and squash any staff member, including Richard Adams, without ever firing a shot. A man of the higher mind, like himself, could surreptitiously achieve all his ambitions. Always had.

CHAPTER 48

A DREARY Dulce night. Rainy outside. Cold inside the little cabin. Sunflower was worlds away, communing with the ancestors. Her ritual was interrupted by a muffled thud at the door. She opened it to find Big John, lying prostrate at the threshold. Now she understood the severity of Their warning. That Big John was hurt, she knew. What she hadn't known was that he was nearly dead.

She stoked the fire and nestled Big John beside it. Sunflower believed he'd been in the Jemez Mountains, 100 miles away. So strong, yet so weak. But he was only a man. A man shivering, fevered, and curled up like a stillborn baby. A putrid scab harbored proud flesh on his thigh. She sterilized a skinning knife and went to work, cutting and scraping. Afterward, she used her saliva to mix a soggy paste from the dried medicine brew she had concocted weeks earlier. She filled the cactus pockets and bound them to Big John's leg with root stock. His forehead burned and his skin was colorless. Sunflower reckoned that Big John's chances of surviving the night were slim. And his chances of surviving the coming days were slimmer.

Later, lost in the firelight, it came to her. She must hold a medicine feast. A woman had not held one on the reservation for over a hundred years. Sunflower owed Big John every possible chance for redemption. For his and T'Bird's sakes, the sins of the father inevitably being visited on the son. Her path was spiritual warriorhood. She continually gave thanks for the Ga'an sparing her family from their most rigorous wrath. But her husband's redemption and the reinstatement of her son's birthright, endowed by the mystical Thunderbird, were still in the balance. Sunflower recognized that she was going to need help. Not just from the ancestors, but from other humans, too.

CHAPTER 49

ARMEN sat at Angel's bar, listening to the lonely sound of raindrops on the roof while staring soulfully at her lipstick-smudged tumbler. Jeans and an oversize sweatshirt replaced her provocative stage getup. Hair and makeup, perfect; mood, miserable.

"So what's your big plan?" Diego asked, checking the tally, his eyes popping.

"This is it for me, Cuz." She stole a glance at T'Bird, still in his beaded buckskin stage garb, chatting with a massage therapist from a local high-dollar Japanese bathhouse.

"Want something to eat?" Diego asked. "There's more piñon meatloaf."

"Don't think so," she said, tilting the scratch-laden tumbler from side to side. "Besides, I've a bone to pick with you." She cast a glare his way. "About Chico . . . ."

Diego disappeared into the kitchen.

Carmen saw a young couple necking at a distant table. Drained her drink. Looked over at T'Bird, who stood, whispering through wavy red tresses into the woman's ear. Her fine features animated with anticipation as he strode toward his leather motorcycle jacket. He looked at Carmen, his eyes atwinkle. She stared back, dead eyed. He flipped open a tiny cell phone and a moment later his expression grew grim. Carmen's brow wrinkled instinctively. An instant later, he slapped the phone shut and gave the woman a consolation pat on the shoulder. He approached Carmen and said, "Have a good night, Baby. I'm headed to Dulce."

"What's the matter?"

"It's Dad."

Carmen was puzzled. She understood that tensions hampered T'Bird's relationship with his father. Had for a long time. Since before she knew him. The solemnity of his face, the fixity of his gaze both suggested that whatever had gone before, now, he was committed to aiding his father.

Thunder rumbled. Heavy raindrops pelted Angel's flimsy roof as if a hoard of monkeys had begun hammering it. "I'll drive you," Carmen said, hopping off the stool.

"No thanks. But you're the best."

"You can't ride up there in the middle of the night in this weather."

"May be too late, already," he said, making for the front doors.

"May be too late for you, if you don't listen to me." She watched, paralyzed. He burst through the doors into the downpour. She screamed, "T'Bird!"

The rickety entrance answered with a rude slap against itself. And then another.

"He'll be okay," said a tall, slightly graying gentleman sitting a few bar stools down. "Besides, what's he got that I ain't got?" He smiled pleasantly.

Carmen recognized the voice although she stood with her head and eyes lowered, thinking, MEN— She'd already exchanged greetings with the man, who wore his uniform: chinos, a white, button-down collar oxford cloth shirt, smooth black calf laceups and coordinated leather belt. He'd worn it to work at the Santa Fe Regional Bank, where he was President. He'd ditched his perfectly knotted Newt Gingrich stripe tie at five o'clock, she was sure.

"Oh, Scott, what's a girl to do?" Carmen said, turning to face him.

"You're too young and pretty to even consider such thoughts." He added quickly, "And intelligent, of course. Don't forget, I'm a big-brain defense attorney, masquerading as a dumb banker."

"Ah, yes, Mr. Scott McLaughlin, Esquire," Carmen replied. "Everyone remembers how well you defended Diego in the food poisoning drama of the century."

"Cases like that are one of the reasons I bought the bank," he chuckled. "But seriously, if you ever need me, just call . . . night or day. Still have my home number?"

Carmen patted her purse. "Right here."

He sipped his pinot grigio. "Good. Now come down here and tell me all about what's troubling you."

"You're a sweetie, but I'm calling it a night." Carmen managed a smile, thinking T'Bird was probably the one who should be drinking with Scott. She feared a lawyer was in T'Bird's future, once he broke Chico's neck. She grabbed her purse and headed for the back door. Launching into the torrent, she wondered, "What, indeed, is a girl to do?"

The Cherokee's starter ground futilely. Carmen backed off the throttle. Squeezed her nose against the stench of gas fumes. She sat soaked, rain pelting her face, streaking her makeup through the open driver's window. She searched the floorboard in vain for the crank. Time dragged before she turned the key and the engine burst to life. Splashing out of Angel's lot onto the paved surface, she noted the low, wide-set, yellowish headlights of a car turning in behind her.

Wind rushed into the cabin, flaring and tossing her hair into a tangle. Her running makeup resembled war paint. When Carmen approached the El Matador Apartments, her mind and the night sky were equally cloudy. The lot was full, again, so she parked parallel to the street. Flung open the Jeep's door, blunting its recoil with her hip.

A rusty '64 Chevy lowrider raced up and skid to a stop, splashing and nearly sideswiping her. Pinned between the vehicles, Carmen could see Chico's snaggletooth smirk when he said, "*Hola, Chiquita.* Wanna fuck?"

The trio, shoulder-to-shoulder on the El Camino's bench seat, burst into hysterics. Through his open window, a passenger reached for Carmen's breasts. She slapped away his hands. Menacing, he drew back his fist. She covered her face with her purse. Waited what seemed an eternity for the blow. She could see nothing. Only the lope of a big engine motorcycle registered in her consciousness. And then a loud thud. The dull sound of wood or rubber striking hollow metal. Over the throaty engine's persistent cough, came a battle cry, "Come and get me, Chico. Pencil prick!"

Carmen recognized the voice. She yanked down her purse and saw T'Bird's Harley fishtailing, his leg still extended from having kicked in Chico's door on the fly. T'Bird gunned his bike. Its powerful engine growled speeding away.

Chico hit the gas. His bolt bucket backfired and then lurched forward, barely spinning a rear tire on the sandy roadside. Although his taillights faded quickly, Carmen didn't bother to watch them disappear. T'Bird was long gone. She just prayed that he wouldn't overdrive his bike on the treacherous ride to Dulce.

CHAPTER 50

S AFELY inside her apartment, Carmen ignored the bills and catalogues on the kitchen counter. Only National Geographic made it to the bedroom nightstand. Water poured into the tub as phone messages spilled from her machine: a telemarketer, a stalker weirdo wanting her to model for his tattoo shop, three hang-ups from Vlad—would he ever stop calling her?—and her mom checking in.

Could her parents really have been married for almost 30 years? Right out of high school for him, not even for her. Whenever relationships had gotten too close for Carmen's comfort, she'd backed off. Said she wasn't ready to begin perfecting her biscochitos, the delicious lard-based cookies her mother made to perfection for her father.

Carmen disrobed en route to the bathtub. The heels hit the living room floor. She extended her smashed toes. Once in the bedroom, the tight jeans were off. Why look? She knew the welt circumscribing her waistline was deeper than last time she'd worn them. Next fell the sweatshirt and then the bustier. Its wire understructure was stiff enough to qualify it as nuclear reactor containment rebar, Vlad had joked, adding that its shape was identical. She rubbed the barbarous bearing points on her torso, before dislodging the frilly wedgy, another Vladism.

Once between her multicolor 'happy' sheets, Carmen listened to the rhythm of raindrops striking her balcony; it lifted her spirits. Vlad had told her that rain generates white noise whereas water fountains generate pink noise. Rain is completely random whereas every fountain has a characteristic spectral signature. Seemingly, Vlad knew everything about the physical world. Stark relief to how little he knew of love. Maybe if he'd been able to say the word? But he'd been gone for months, hadn't he? Nine weeks, one day, and—glancing at the bedside clock—nearly five hours.

For a change of perspective, Carmen rolled to her side. The night stand's familiar array: Chinese lacquered box bearing pens and pencils; paper pad; super-size plastic cola container half-filled with water and Dan; self-help book mostly obscured by the new National Geographic. She grabbed the mag and opened it mid-way. Black-skinned women with tiny nose bones and pendulous bare breasts, boasting prominent nipple piercings, stared blankly. They probably didn't give a hoot about whether their husbands were capable of telling them they loved them. But Carmen would bet that there were other things, perhaps things no western woman could fathom, that were absolute requirements for these women to commit to a man. She sighed. This was not the change of thoughts she'd sought.

T'Bird's face intruded. Racing northward on tortuous mountain roads in the middle of the night in the rain. She should've insisted on driving him. What the hell . . . she did insist. He'd ignored her. "Men," she huffed aloud, throwing off her colorful covers. She sprang up and headed for the kitchen, returning with a mug of steaming white tea. She selected track 11 using the stereo's remote and lowered the volume to force herself to concentrate on the music. It was her favorite song on this classic Selena CD.

Carmen knew that she could write this music. Could sing it, too. She could never perform just like Selena did. After all, since her death no one else had taken the mantle of *Tejano* and done it justice. Now under the music's spell, Carmen closed her eyes. She sat up and reached the pen and pad. Aching and longing flowed from her heart onto the page. Predictably, tears flowed from her eyes onto her cheeks.

RAIN POUNDED the serpentine pavement of West Highway 64, leading to Dulce, New Mexico. T'Bird wore sunglasses against the assault on his eyes. A black night. The mountain's jagged contours were hidden from view, excepting when spider webs of lightning illuminated the sky in violent bursts.

Were those oncoming lights he saw? A sharp left curve ahead, a declivitous drop-off to his right, T'Bird inched closer to the centerline. Dingy lights glowed ahead. T'Bird moved toward the outer margin of the narrow road. An abyss below. He slowed. Rounding the curve, the truck's front end drifted toward the roadway's center. T'Bird saw the grill pass the solid white centerline. He hugged the shoulder; his bike unsteady from rocks and debris. The abyss loomed. The truck faced him, head on. T'Bird yanked the wheel left, cutting across the truck's path, toward the mountain. The bike fishtailed and went down in a spectacular scintillation. The driver slammed on the old truck's brakes. But it was too late.

CHAPTER 51

Sᴀᴍ ᴅʀᴜᴍᴍᴇᴅ his fingers quietly on the arm of his chair, his back against the wall. Another momentous *fourth floor* meeting. He glanced at his wristwatch, noting that less than half an hour had elapsed. Typically, ADs made overtures to the director, hoping to inflate their budgets. They took turns in the limelight or on the hot seat. A continual spotlight did not bode well. And, yet again, director Reynold's gaze had seldom wavered from John O'Donnell.

Reynolds erupted, "John, you've championed GRIT well. We all appreciate your contributions." He panned from side to side, eliciting a hear-hear or two from green-eyed *schmeggeges*, the most vocal of which was the AD of Catchall.

"And your earlier statements regarding the intel upon which the program is based were absolutely correct."

Reynolds's paused to survey his audience. At the heat of his gaze, Sam dropped his head and kept his eyes down. Scratched his forehead, as if amid deep concentration.

The director said, "Gavin, weren't those statements absolutely correct."

Burton hardly looked up from his scribbles. "I'm convinced that they were," he said, in a sort of yawn.

"You, personally, can verify the nature of the sources," the director continued.

"While I believe the statements to be correct, it is strict Laboratory policy to comment neither on the identity nor the nature of intelligence sources."

Sam was stunned. Not by Burton's circumspection, which was, as always, in keeping with stringent Laboratory standards, but by his supercilious tone. And although O'Donnell's statements were factual, Sam had to admit that the picture painted by the intel remained suspect. In his capacity as a roving problem solver, having access to many different scientists in differing security compartments, Sam had learned that the drawings had been provided by a double-agent. Bottom feeding, in the hierarchy of intelligence credibility. This was known to a precious few, excluding O'Donnell. Sam was convinced that had O'Donnell been aware, he would not have been willing to jeopardize his reputation in DC for overselling GRIT's viability. But, of course, Sam could not have warned O'Donnell. Such was against Laboratory policy.

"There, John," the director said. "Gavin, uh, agrees. All you need do is stand by those statements of fact." His voice thinned and his otherwise saggy, gray cheeks had become taut and pink.

"I'm not reneging on my statements," O'Donnell replied. "I'm just not inclined to go back begging before we've delivered anything, even paper. I'm not budging until we at least have a feasible grasing cavity design."

Sam swallowed hard. Rick's visibility was on the rise.

"I'd go myself," the director said, "but with the National Nuclear Security Administration still breathing down my neck about the recent security violations," focusing on O'Donnell, he added, "I just don't have time to go beat the big drum."

"You mean pass the big hat," O'Donnell replied.

Reynolds's pink cheeks reddened. "This is our chance to put the nation back on equal footing. To achieve military parity. That's the biggest deterrent to nuclear attack."

"If they have a functional nuke killer, then the balance has been disturbed," O'Donnell said. "Let's determine that first. Even the idiots at NNSA can get that."

"NNSA's done nothing right from the get-go!" stormed the AD of catchall. "They had no clue that we had no clue how to protect top secret nuclear weapons data."

Sam could almost smell searing flesh when O'Donnell's eyes flashed toward the man. Burton continued his doodling, undisturbed by the pathetic outburst.

Reynolds said, "We require a contingency fund, to ensure a success oriented program. Fifty million max. A veritable drop in the bailout bucket."

Sam recognized that the director's 50 percent tax on incoming funds would give him an extra $25 million to shore up Catchall's shortfall. Although the DOE had abolished slush funds, this was the way the Lab operated: a socialist demagoguery.

O'Donnell said, "GRIT is under my purview. I'm confident my cowboys and buttheads can vet the design using computational analysis, rapid prototyping, and experimentation, all within our present funding."

"But what about mine?" Erupted the AD of catchall.

Reynolds visually stabbed the AD. And then the unthinkable happened.

Without looking directly at him, Reynolds said, "Sam, you're awfully quiet back there. What do you think about GRIT's funding level? No one has a better feel for the scientific complexity of this project than you."

Sam's tongue and stomach knotted. Silence. He stole a glimpse of Burton, who abruptly ceased his scribble.

"Sam, did you hear me? GRIT's an incredibly tough technical challenge, yes."

"Well, there is, uh, scientific uncertainty," Sam's heart throbbed. From the corner of his spasming eyes, he saw Burton smirking. Sam muttered, "*Schmuck.*"

David Goldstein, a directorial aide, who sat beside Sam, choked sipping water.

Sam panicked. He'd never broken this cardinal rule of public comportment espoused by Uncle George: Dress British; think—but never speak—Yiddish. Sam cleared his throat loudly, tugging the bottom of his waistcoat. "As I was saying, smugness is inadvisable. We can, uh . . . we can always use more money."

Quelling his self-revulsion, Sam glared at Burton, who seized the spotlight, saying, "Should we have at-risk staff because of a budget shortfall, this may be a perfect opportunity to use the additional monies that John could obtain from Washington. At-risk staff could be transferred to GRIT, thereby avoiding an administrative logjam. They can bill to GRIT full-time even though they, of course, will have to work almost exclusively at completing their previous assignments."

It sounded to Sam more like a rehearsed speech than an extemporaneous expression of an idea that had popped into Burton's head.

"If it turns out GRIT does not require the additional staffing," Burton continued, "ultimately they can be returned to their former charge codes. They will never have to move an inch or alter their duties. And no workforce reduction."

Reynolds lightly clasped his hands and rested them on the table. "John, you're going to have to carry the ball." He added, "Know this will not be forgotten."

Sam believed truer words had never been spoken. He fingered his collar, as though he could feel the edge of a razor make its first pass across the width of his neck. But it was not his neck on the block. Should GRIT fail, a political guillotine would decapitate O'Donnell. Or more likely, a swinging pendulum blade, in innumerable passes, each infinitesimally deeper than the preceding. Purely Poesque. Enacted at successively higher level meetings, the decapitation would culminate in a closed door testimony before a congressional committee. O'Donnell would explain GRIT's failure, why he'd oversold the program, and where the squandered money went. Sam shuddered at the thought of his friend having his livelihood destroyed and his political throat cut. But what could he do?

CHAPTER 52

T'BIRD and Sunflower worked quickly to prepare a medicine lodge for the healing ritual. T'Bird's head still throbbed from the mild concussion sustained in the crash. As he placed a match to the neat pile of brush and cedar arranged at the center of the lodge, the sun fire, he eyed Big John. His father lay on a cot near the wall of the squat adobe hut. He drifted in and out of consciousness, eyes fluttering open, groaning in a way that gave T'Bird chills. His mother's sacred ritual seemed his father's only hope.

Together they moved Big John closer to the sun fire. When Sunflower began to chant, T'Bird exited the lodge. He returned later to watch his mother carefully singe a small bowl of chili-laced blue corn meal, using a glowing ember. She blessed it and inhaled its sharp scent. She trembled as Spirits entered her body. She placed the bowl under Big John's nostrils. After inhaling, he writhed and convulsed, before retching uncontrollably. Spirits had entered his body and begun their cleansing. When Big John lay still, Sunflower covered him with a worn bear hide. He slept immediately. She thanked her ancestors and the Spirits that her medicine was still strong.

T'Bird took up the bowl, inhaled. It was nothing like the banal drug-induced altered state of consciousness he often sought. No need to hide or to run away. His headache eased and he lay down to blissful sleep.

At daybreak, T'Bird woke and went into the cabin where he found his mother sitting cross-legged, rocking in front of the fire. He said, "Good morning."

"Feel better?" She asked.

"Hungry."

"Come outside. I got something to show you. Then I'll fix breakfast." She rose and strode toward the front door.

T'Bird followed. He stopped on the porch and gawked. "Where'd you get that?"

"Oh, T. C. brought it over this morning," Sunflower said, standing underneath a 200-year-old pinion.

"That's not what I meant." He gave her the eye. "A mid-fifties convertible. My bike in the trunk . . . half-way." He stared down the little woman. "What's the story?"

"So many questions. It's nice, no?"

"No. Yes! It's beautiful!" He approached the car. Dared to run his hand over the smoothness of the finely polished fender. "Whose is it anyway?"

"Yours."

"Oh, yeah. Then why haven't I ever seen it?"

"Told you. T.C. had it. Brought it over this—"

"Got that. He had it for 50 years?"

"More like 25. Your father and I bought it used when you were a baby. It's a Thunderbird; just like you."

He could hear no longer. Glistening red and white paint. Supple red leather interior with white piping. Flawless. He opened the door, jumped in, and eyeballing the analog speedo, said, "Less than 20,000 miles. It's like new."

"Guess T.C. don't drive much. A while back I asked him to get some new tires and clean it up a little. It's a '57. Open the hood; take a look-see." Studying the old tree, Sunflower added, "Be a nice college car, I think."

T'Bird ignored the hint. "Fifty-seven, huh," he said, launching from the driver's seat. He unlatched the hood and carefully eased it up. A chromed engine, blinding in sunlight. He squinted against its radiance. "It's supercharged. A supercharged Thunderbird." He refocused on her. "Why didn't you tell me?"

"Wasn't time."

"And now?"

"Now it's time for you to eat some breakfast and head back to Santa Fe. You have commitments there. And don't race all the way. But it probably wouldn't hurt to blow the cobwebs out of the engine, when it's safe."

He dashed over and lifted his mother two feet off the ground. Squeezed her frail frame to his chest. "I'm gonna miss you."

"Enjoy yourself. Do what you do," she said, flapping her pinned arms. "And put me down." She smoothed her shirt, adding, "Change is on the wind. It's gonna sweep you up and take you someplace you didn't figure on."

"You know it makes me feel weird when you talk like that."

"Trust the Mountain Spirits. They'll guide you. "

Soon, he was crawling the Thunderbird over the rutted road leading from the cabin to the highway. He lingered for a moment when he reached the pavement. No people, no cars. T'Bird glanced up into the cloudless sky and saw a large bird circling. An eagle? No, bigger. It rode a high thermal, nearly stratospheric and then vanished.

T'Bird's head was clear and his heart beat strong. Accelerating slowly, he headed south. His heart leapt with another strong emotion when he flexed the throttle and the little convertible rocketed forward. T'Bird slowed and counted his blessings until he hit the Santa Fe county line, where he yelled joyously and again punched the accelerator.

CHAPTER 53

Rick shuffled onto Water Street from an exceptional trout hash brunch at Pascual's, near the Santa Fe plaza. He hadn't gone near Becker's since that fateful Saturday— His hunger well sated, memories of both the distant and recent past tormented him. Thoughts of Desiree and Renée, their merits and demerits, occupied the little free time he'd had. To think that he'd purchased illicit drugs for one and sat by while both of them used harmful substances was depressing. What enormous holes in their lives were they trying to fill with drugs, he wondered? What could he have done to help either one? Enough! He was going to the animal shelter this afternoon. Certain to find an abused, incomplete animal there, who desperately needed him. Maybe a fish? No chance of abandonment there.

Turning a corner, just up the street from Angel's, Rick observed a faded sign:

¡Fantastic Sunday Afternoon Jam!

Could this be the ticket to dispel his gloom? Rick entered Angel's and found it packed. He maneuvered himself against the wall, near the PA cabinets. The Taos T'Birds wailed out a blues jam. Rick marked time with his toes, seduced by the music. But was yanked back to rude reality by the noisy entrance of a group of middle-aged men. The ringleader was a portly, fifty-something hipster, wearing holey jeans and a tie-dyed tee. He sported a gray goatee and a balding blondish pate. A frayed, stubby ponytail appeared to poke out the back of his neck. Two bone-skinny posse members seemed to have benefited from a Tommy Bahamas clearance sale. The crew included roadies, who carried guitar cases and electronics boxes, and a duo of business-types in chalk stripe suits, no less. The group crushed the squatty stage, blocking Rick's view.

At the song's conclusion, they applauded boisterously and the ringleader called out, "My man, Diego. Hello, T'Bird, Doc." He ignored Wilmer.

"Hey dude, good to see you," Diego said, nearly tripping over his crash cymbal stand getting around to greet him. "Been too long, man."

"Jamming today?"

"Just being cool, man," Diego studied the fractured drumstick he'd been using.

"Flew in for the Opera and checked on my house. I'm leaving tonight."

"Too bad, man. You see, T'Bird here crashed his bike."

"I was run off the road in the middle of the night," T'Bird said.

"Bummer, 'Bird," the leader said. "Didn't dull your touch. But if you need a rest, I, uh, brought my axe. Or you could stay and play backup."

T'Bird eyed Diego, who said, "I don't know, man. Check out all these people. They may not dig that Hendrix stuff."

"Put their drinks on my tab while I play." He winked.

Rick noted Diego was trying hard to disguise his delight. Bona fide bid-nessman. T'Bird's curly red jackcord hit the floor before he gingerly stepped offstage. Wilmer followed, tail firmly between his legs. Doc rose, but was busted.

"Doc, stick around," the leader said.

A burly biker in dusty black leather barked, "Who's the fuckin' fruitcakes. Get T'Bird back onstage."

"Drink on the house, Bro," Diego yelled from the bar. "Free drinks for everbody!"

"They that bad?"

Rick turned in time to dodge the swinging neck of the leader's squealing guitar. Relaxing the pose and noise, the leader called out, "Diego, need you on the skins."

"Can't do it, Bro. Gotta get these drinks out."

Rick turned to see Diego popping tops off beer bottles like Gatling gunfire.

The leader shouted, "Anybody here know the *real* king of rock and roll?"

Rick called out, "Are you experienced!"

"A fan." The leader asked, peering down skeptically, "You a drummer?"

Rick nodded.

"Wanna play?"

Catcalls and whistles greeted Rick as he mounted the stage. He believed that his jeans and button down collar shirt were hardly less congruous than Bermuda shorts and silk beach shirts. From the drummer's stool, Rick looked out over the crowd to the rear of the room. He saw Diego, T'Bird, and Carmen, whose mouth was agape.

CARMEN LEANED against the bar, supporting her bosom on folded arms. She slumped onto one leg, in disbelief that the guest drummer was Dr. Dick.

"Let's see what this *huevo* can do," Diego said, slapping open bottles onto the bar. "And hey, how about a little help here."

Carmen grabbed a longneck and gulped.

"Servin', not drinkin', dammit."

She said, "Silicon Valley has descended on us yet again."

"And I'm gonna milk him for all he's worth," Diego replied.

"Twenty billion buys a lotta beer," Carmen said, her eyes flashing as Rick clicked off the tempo using his drum sticks.

"Two, three, four." Bam! Bam! Ba da dada . . . .

"Holy shit," Diego cried. "He's gonna trash my set."

"Your set's already trash," Carmen said, taking another swig. "It's just being played for a change."

CHAPTER 54

A BURGEONING load of mail collected from his neglected box on Monday morning, Rick made his way up the Hill. Once in his office, he commenced establishing a flight of parameter sensitivity runs that he'd envisioned a month ago, before abandoning an optimal grasing cavity for GRIT in favor of simply bounding its performance. He initiated execution and extracted the mail bundle. Bills, a come-on, discount coupons, more bills . . . . A hand-scrawled envelope in Frankensteinish penmanship caught his eye. Obviously it was from a physician or someone famous.

The brief note, scribbled on the letterhead of Chief R. B. Martinez, informed Rick that he was expected at the Chavez Auditorium at the Tesuque Community Center at 7:00 p.m. on Thursday. He would address an audience of fellow traffic offenders on the engineering of hotrod engines. What a waste of time, Rick thought. Then he recalled the magnitude of the fine and that he'd actually asked for an opportunity to mitigate it when he entered his plea. That the wacky judge had asked him to speak about hotrod engine design was a hoot. Oh, well, an hour of his time had never been worth several hundred dollars to any employer.

The spate of computer runs that Rick executed over the following days proved fallow. No convergence. No insight. No story for the MRC, who hammered him mercilessly on Thursday afternoon. His spirits were more resilient than before, recognizing that none of them could do any better and that he was accomplishing one very important mission: staying alive.

THE TESUQUE Community Center was a grouping of squat buildings, surrounding a taller, gymnasium-looking structure, all encompassed by a graceful adobe-look wall. A new parking lot with smooth pavement and stark white markings stretched from the compound out into rugged desert landscape. As he hustled toward the building cluster, Rick could almost hear the shouts and groans from the nearby casino.

He brought a few transparencies and a stack of stapled papers. The foils would be useful in the unlikely event this place had an overhead projector. The hardcopy he would present to the Judge, Chief Raging Bear Martinez, for him to round file.

Rick stopped inside the Chavez Auditorium's door to admire its orderly interior, clean, spacious, and well lighted. Several older people were already ensconced near the front in colorful molded plastic chairs with shiny steel frames, same speed as the ones in the Building Two conference room. He proceeded toward the generous stage, bearing a trendy Plexiglass lectern.

Gonzales's sing-song voice resounded from a public address system. "Richard Adams, please approach the podium."

Rick ascended the stage and placed his materials on the lectern.

"Test the mic, please."

"Testing . . . testing."

"That as loud as you're going to talk?" the familiar, unamplified voice of Chief Martinez asked from the rear of the room.

Rick said, "I can speak louder."

"More volume," the Chief roared to Gonzales, who sat at a professional mixing board.

"*Muy waino,* R. B.," Gonzales's amplified voice replied.

"Does your notebook computer have IR that can link to our high intensity projector?" The Chief asked Rick.

"Well, no, R. B."

"That's Judge Martinez."

"Sorry. Actually, I brought these." Rick held up the foils.

"And what kinda Los Alamos scientist are you anyway? Transparencies." The Chief shook his head, saying, "We're going to need an overhead."

"*Muy waino,* R. B."

Panning the sparsely-filled space and eyeing his watch, the Chief grabbed a cattle prod and marched out the front doors. A moment later, a swarm of dilatory youths and ne'er-do-well young adults, whom Rick had passed while they smoked out doors, filled the auditorium to capacity, excepting the Chief's two large, padded front-row chairs.

Rick introduced himself to the audience. At his side, he held the first foil, bearing his presentation's title, taken from a famous, non-threatening lecture series called PHYSICS FOR POETS. Rick had added a special twist for this assemblage, which he expected to resemble Angel's crowd. The room quieted, but before Rick could project the first foil, a kerfuffle erupted when Carmen entered. She wore candy-apple-red leather Capri pants and matching four-inch-high heeled boots, which sparked the floor as she strutted forward, scanning for an empty seat.

CHAPTER 55

" . . . AND DR. BURTON, we're honored to have you present this evening," a genial man said from the small podium in a meeting room at Santa Fe's elegant Hotel Eldorado. "Thank you for everything you've done in support of the Santa Fe Technology Alliance." The local businessmen, all crowded together in folding metal chairs, some of whom craned their necks gawking and waving at the Lab's computing and security Czar, applauded vigorously.

Burton nodded acceptance of the credit conferred by the comment, although he had neither assisted the organization at large nor any of the companies who schmoozed here. He assumed the organization's president had spoken in the hopeful tense. Burton seldom attended these monthly get-togethers, although he possessed a standing invitation. He was, after all, a by-the-book guy. Further, he had nothing to gain from helping them. But tonight, he thought a little adulation from local techies might raise his sagging spirits.

Five minutes into the featured speaker's broad-brush bloviation on how nanotechnology would rejuvenate America's ailing economy, Burton eased out the back doors. He proceeded around the hotel to his car, which he'd parked on a side street. To enhance his driving pleasure, instead of his clunky SUV, he'd driven his wife's new Lexus. He flicked the throttle, revving the engine, and accelerated onto San Francisco Street. Felt the security of performance tires gripping the pavement. Indulged himself in the luxury and smell of new, oversized leather upholstered seats, firmly caressing his puny lats and lumbar.

Soon he missed the familiar smell of his vehicle. To be precise, Kelly's scent, which permeated the passenger's seat. She loved to ride with her muzzle poked out of the half-open window. He could feel her unconditional love. His caring for her was the closest thing to real love he'd ever experienced. Approaching the cemetery on Paseo de Peralta, he accelerated rapidly and a wide grin spread across his face. Kelly would love this, he thought.

"What's the rush?" A voice asked from behind.

Burton crushed the brakes. "Who are you? What do you want? Do you know who I am?" He snapped to the rearview mirror, which had been tilted roofward.

"I want to have a little chat. And, yes, I know you much better than you think."

Burton recognized the Eastern European elocution. "So you're not Gerry the German tonight. What the hell are you trying to do, expose us both. What if I'd crashed?"

"Then I'd have saved your ass, again. Just like all those years ago. Or maybe this time, I'd just torch this piece of shit with you inside."

Burton reached to adjust the rearview mirror.

"No need. I've got your back . . . covered."

"I suppose another corpse would be no problem for you. You're never around during the investigations. I'm the one who goes about his routine like nothing happened. Cambridge, Los Alamos, Santa Fe. Why should you care about the body count?"

"Nice attitude. Let's head up Hyde Park Road and visit the ski lifts. Be careful. When you have a bad attitude, like Fred's, the slope gets a bit too slippery sometimes."

"You can't do this," Burton said bravely, while suppressing a shudder. "Your contract is to protect me, aid me. The North would hunt you down and—"

"Shut up! You know nothing of my contract. If I wanted to take you out, you'd already be a grease spot on some back road. Maybe a stuffed doll in a basement."

Gerry emitted a high pitched giggle that unnerved Burton. Was he high? Burton felt perspiration beading on his forehead, thinking that Gerry was too dangerous to be out of control. "How, uh, can I help?" Burton asked.

"I'm just touching base with you, as they say here in America. I recall asking you to contact me. You did not." Gerry's accent thickened, asking, "Has your encrypted e-mail malfunctioned? Are there other malfunctions I should know about?"

"I'm in complete control." As he lied, Burton's fleshy little hands perspired onto the leather wrapped steering wheel. He gripped tighter.

"That's good news. Has anybody figured out that GRIT is a bogus sack of shit or is that still our little secret?"

Silence.

Gerry scoffed, "Since Fred's death was ruled an accident by the LAPD, I suppose that's behind us, too."

"Needless. Messy. Of course, it raised eyebrows." Burton used the best defense.

"Whose eyebrows? Armstrong's and his morons'. And now they're going to cull through every shred of paper related to Adams, because they're onto him." Gerry screamed, "You lying fuck-up!"

Burton's mind overloaded. He felt as though he was blacking out. The car swerved into oncoming traffic. He yanked the wheel. Tried to shake clarity into his head. "How do you know?" Seconds later, he said, "You son-of-a-bitch. You bugged my office. How incredibly stupid."

Gerry rammed a cold pistol muzzle into Burton's right ear.

Burton shuddered. "The admin building is the most closely monitored place on the entire site. If that bug is detected, there'll be a national inquiry. I'll be blown."

"Stop the car."

"Why?"

"You heard me."

Burton accelerated, but when he heard the pistol's hammer cock, he hit the brakes and steered to the roadway's shoulder. The muzzle was still jammed into his ear when Gerry monotoned, "Kill the engine, lights." Burton bit his lip. His hands dripped.

"This mission is already just about blown," Gerry said. "If I eliminate you, to keep you from squealing, I'll be paid double."

"What can I do?"

"I want a drop of everything the Feds are going to get on Adams from the Lab."

"That'll take at least—"

"Twenty-four hours. Man up! It's the only way you're going to survive your bumpy ride to the top."

The barrel penetrated further into the ear canal. Burton's head and neck ached when Gerry whispered, "Right now, I have no different feelings about sending you up as putting you down."

His senses numbed. Burton didn't even feel Gerry withdraw the muzzle. Didn't feel the blood trickle down his neck. He only heard the rear door slam, before his stomach began boiling, churning. Burton yanked his door handle and tried to kick it open quickly with his foot. Salmon mousse, fumé blanc, and chunks of brie hit the window and slowly drizzled down past the armrest into the map pocket. An awful stench permeated the vehicle on his drive up the Hill. It reminded him of the stink of death.

CHAPTER 56

R.B. STOOD, quelling the din that Carmen's entry had excited. When he waved her up front, she beamed at him. Rick was amazed that for the first time he'd witnessed, the Bull blushed like a lamb. Rick threw up his initial projection, *Physics for Bankers, Bikers, and Lowriders:*

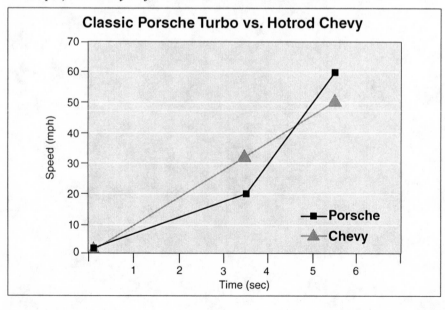

Rick focused on Carmen while R. B. helped her remove her black leather jacket, revealing a skintight, nude, cut lace top. Stammering into his presentation, he said, "There are, uh, many important engine performance questions that can be answered by a plot of time versus speed. I'll answer six and then each of you will be required to answer one question—the most important one—before leaving." Rick eyed the front row.

R. B. said to Carmen, "I didn't know there's a quiz."

"How exciting," she replied, batting her eyelashes.

Rick spoke simply, yet eloquently. The area encompassed by a triangle miraculously revealed by how far the Chevy led the Porsche after three seconds of racing. And the slope of a line indicated the muscle car's quickness off the line. Rick described it as, "neck-snapping acceleration."

"That's what I'm talking about!" R. B. had exulted.

Rick watched as Carmen appeared to struggle with terms like "normal aspiration," which led to the straight-line plot of the Chevy's speed, and turbo-lag, which gave the Porsche a hockey stick speed profile. But he sensed her understanding as he correlated the graphic with a straight-forward explanation of the physical effects.

When Rick confirmed the Chevy's early domination of the hypothetical race, he heard R. B. boast to Carmen, "I could kick some turbo butt in my Chevelle."

But R. B's. smile ran away when Rick indicated that after three seconds the Porsche's turbo would operate at peak efficiency and leave the muscle car in a dust cloud.

"Hey Bro, how that turbo work?" a young man asked from the back row.

The Chief beamed at hearing a question. It was a first at one of these sessions.

Rick provided plain-English responses to several inquiries before saying, "If there are no more questions from you, it's time for one from me."

Carmen stood to her feet. "Professor Dick," she said. "Can you elucidate how the fundamental theorem of calculus can be applied to this plot?" Shrugging girlishly, she looked down at the Chief's popping eyes.

"I'm so glad that you asked," Rick replied. "Let me begin by recalling that the essence of that theorem whereof you speak is that the integral can sometimes be expressed as the anti-derivative." Two minutes later, a few in the room believed they had a modest grasp of how the speed of the Chevy at any particular time was the derivative of its position evaluated at that time whereas the speed could also be expressed as the integral of the vehicle's acceleration, all owing to the fundamental theorem of calculus.

Rick asked, "How do you take attendance, Judge?"

"Everybody initials beside their names when they leave."

"Please answer the following important question by placing a 'C' or 'P' by your name on the roster." A hushed room. "Which car would you rather own?" Rick tapped the graph twice with his marker and thanked the audience for its attention.

"That was great," R. B. boomed. "What would you know about planes? Can you draw the graphs for a GS V and maybe a Lear 60? I know I'll win that one."

"Sorry, Judge Martinez."

"Hell, call me R. B. But consider it. Meantime, I'll have officer Gonzales keep an eye out for you."

R. B. winked. Rick winced.

CHAPTER 57

"WELL DONE," Carmen said to Rick, as they strolled side-by-side, in matching strides. "You might have a future in this lecturing business."

"I might get into trouble with the attendees."

"That might be fun," she said, coquettishly whirling her jacket over her shoulders.

Arriving at Carmen's dusty Cherokee, Rick reached for her key in anticipation of unlocking her door. Windowless. They exchanged a glance before he opened the door and helped her up into the cabin. He drank in her perfume.

"Want to come see the show? Maybe work out on the drums?"

"I'm headed back to my office."

She eyed him dead on. "Sure you can't come out and play?"

"Quite."

Rick watched Carmen turn her head. She closed the door with a bang, which he interpreted as a face slap. He turned to walk away without looking back. The starter ground fruitlessly. Drawing a deep breath, he turned to see her determined expression as she drained the battery.

Rick approached the vehicle and asked, "May I be of assistance?"

"Thought you had a hot date with a fast computer."

"Shouldn't take but a minute to be your knight in shining armor." He ground the starter without avail.

"Did we find a chink already?"

"I've a backup plan." Rick eyed his watch. "I'll remove the air filter and we'll have a cup of coffee while this thing dries out. How's that?"

"Been there. Done that. I'll call T'Bird."

"That's ridiculous. I'll take you to the gig. He can bring you back out here later."

"Off to Los Alamos with you," she said, flipping open her cell phone.

"Okay." Rick turned to see yellowish headlights rounding the building. They stopped well short of Carmen and him. The engine loped and smoked. Rick thought it the funniest lowrider he'd ever seen. A suspensionless El Camino with a cabin chock full of . . . of how many, he couldn't tell at that range. Rick was confident that either a 911 Turbo or Hot Rod Chevy would be just fine with them.

He glanced back at Carmen, who stared at the jalopy, a fingernail jammed awkwardly into the corner of her mouth.

"Well, on second thought," she said, "I'd love a ride."

Rick smiled. "Collect your things. I'll bring my vehicle over."

He wheeled the gleaming X5 next to her dirty Jeep's rear bumper. Assisted Carmen into its luxurious cabin before securing the door. When she ran a delicate hand over the smooth kid leather of her seat, Rick swelled with pride. He rounded the X5's rear, thinking nothing of the lowriders inching toward them. He started to back up, but their exit was blocked. Rick sounded his horn and the El Camino's dim lights went off. Rick glanced to Carmen, saying, "I wonder what this is all about." He opened his door.

"Rick, wait. Don't go out there."

"We can't sit here all night."

Rick turned to face the trio, crammed onto the cabin's bench seat. He forced a smile, saying, "Excuse me, but can we get out?"

The passengers snickered.

The runt said, "Don' know, Bro. Can you?"

The remark fired up Rick's spine like an electrical shock. And to think he'd felt sorry for the guy. "You know Goddamn well, we can't. And we don't want any trouble. So, why don't you move."

Three sullen faces stared at him as Rick approached the vehicle. The moonlight cast a sliver of illumination on a scuffed, yet shimmering hunting knife blade. Rick stepped back from the swinging arc of the caved-in door panel. He stood motionless, his eyes locked on the crazy chocolate-color eyes of the runt.

When the El Camino's doors swung wide, Rick searched the ground stealthily for a weapon. The blinding lights of a police cruiser lit up the scene. Officer Gonzales drove by slowly and waved.

Rick returned the gesture and turned to retake his seat in the Bimmer. He backed up just enough to clear Carmen's vehicle's bumper when he drove forward. In the rearview, Rick could feel the heat of the runt's glare. "That guy's crazy."

"Yeah, don't mess with him."

"You know this person?" Rick's face snapped to hers.

"Unfortunately. Chico comes to the bar now and then."

"Well, one of us has apparently pissed him off."

Silence.

Rick proceeded north on highway 285 to avoid crossing heavy traffic on the Pojoaque speedway, as that stretch of road was known. They'd driven a mile or so, waiting for an opportunity to turn back toward Santa Fe, when Rick noted yellowish headlights riding the BMW's tail. He juiced the engine, but hit the brakes almost immediately, encountering a slow poke in the passing lane. Rick watched helplessly as the El Camino gained on them. The yellow lights disappeared from the rearview just before their bumpers collided. "Damn him!"

"Be careful," Carmen said, restoring her fingernail to her now-pouty lips.

"I'd like to kick his ass," Rick said, flooring the accelerator. He maneuvered around the idler into the outside lane. No room to break free. Just then, the slowpoke speeded by, Chico glued to his tail. Rick looked over to see the grinning faces of the passengers. Chico swerved into Rick's lane, forcing him to the shoulder. Dirt boiled behind them as Rick crushed the brakes.

"Whoah!" Carmen said, bracing herself for impact with the dashboard. Her eyes bulged when the restraint system caught her.

The El Camino roared past. Rick noted a break in following traffic and swerved across both lanes into the median. The Bimmer bounced and thudded across the rough divider. White knuckles on the steering wheel and red nails in Rick's arm. They made the southbound lane and Rick coolly steered into the flow of traffic. Once at speed, Carmen brushed lustrous hair back from her face with a shaky hand. Rick took it and caressed it firmly. Suddenly, Chico and the unfortunate encounter seemed ancient history. After all, it was a romantic moonlit night.

CHAPTER 58

Rick stopped outside Angel's front entrance. The bimmer's engine hummed. "That wasn't so bad, was it?" he asked. "We'll have to do it again sometime."

"Not the first part," Carmen said, shaking her head firmly. "Coming in?"

"Got to go."

"To Los Alamos? I thought you wanted a coffee. Did you have dinner? The enchiladas were yummy today. It'll be my treat, in honor of your gallantry."

He eyed his watch, before stealing a glimpse at her slender legs, tiny waist. Rick patted his stomach, saying, "I don't think missing a meal will hurt me."

"I like some meat on my men's bones."

It was only a dinner invitation. And after all, he'd driven her all the way up from the valley . . . of death. Besides, he was starving. Had he heard correctly? Carmen liked men with some meat on them. Rick said, "Sounds like a plan."

Carmen delivered piping hot enchiladas and cold beer. She sat across the table from Rick, who devoured the food with his mouth and her with his eyes. Soon the clank of saggy saloon doors, clunk of cowboy boots, clink of spurs, dissonance of guitar tuning, buzz of conversation, and howl of organ riffs announced the show was soon to begin.

Carmen sang every note for him, Rick believed. During the first break, the two sat alone at a tiny table, chatting. During the second break, talk was scarce. They held hands and gazed into each other's eyes. Rick stole glimpses of T'Bird and Diego, who shook their heads and exchanged bewildered glances. Before the third set, Carmen announced to the crowd that her car was stranded in Pojoaque and that she was off to retrieve it.

The drive to Carmen's apartment was subdued. Rick mentioned her vehicle, but she insisted that situation would take care of itself. They were more like two teenagers, who were not well experienced with the scenario. The anticipation. The apprehension. Once inside the apartment that changed. There was neither a nightcap nor mood music. Carmen didn't excuse herself to freshen up or slip into something more comfortable. Rick didn't channel surf or tell funny stories. He was up for her immediately.

They fell onto the sofa and ripped into each other. Carmen's mouth smothered Rick's, their tongues lashing and probing. He caressed her breasts, supported their weight in steady hands. Titillated her nipples, with his fingers before gorging his mouth with their fullness. Carmen ravished him, massaging and teasing his prick. Rick recognized it was more than sexual chemistry. They were starving souls preparing to feast.

Forefeast was brief. Carmen pulled Rick into her. He locked eyes with her while gently inching his way inside. An eternity of pleasure. Pearls of perspiration beaded on Carmen's. Rick licked them with relish. He tenderly kissed her voluptuous lips. Carmen disengaged their bodies, and stood. Smiling, she led him by his monumental erection into her bedroom. They tumbled together on the bed and re-engaged, squirming, straining, struggling. Carmen wrestled herself atop him and writhed rhythmically. She exploded in a deafening shriek of ecstasy.

Rick froze.

"Don't stop. Ricky, don't stop." Carmen huffed, heaving herself into him.

In a single muscular coordination, Rick whisked Carmen underneath him. And in a bone-crushing frenzy, he succumbed.

Rick rolled to his back, emitting a low groan. Carmen stretched across him to turn on the nightstand lamp. Rick spied the super size cola cup and made for it.

Carmen yanked Dan out, with a splash. Flung him—it—under the bed.

"What's that?" Rick asked, foggy with ecstasy.

"Oh, nothing."

He grasped the cup and gulped.

"Don't!"

"This well water or something?" He pruned his face, smacking his lips.

"Let me get you some fresh water, Ricky. That's been there a while."

"Don't be long. I want you again," he said, puzzled by her naughty snicker.

CHAPTER 59

SAM CONCLUDED himself a simple man caught in a complex struggle. He must settle down. Put it all in perspective. No yearning for books; no desire for tea. Even the photographs adorning his study's walls and those of Wallenberg in the open book on his desk held no interest for him. He thought only of the Lab, justice, and Rick.

The Lab had been guilty of programmatic blundering and poor planning for decades. Harbored patently incorrect scientific and political beliefs. Even acted on them. Yet it had endured. And the science was still world-class. But to an individual, truly bad things could happen. He removed his eyeglasses. Massaged his temple, contemplating those bad things, recalling ones he'd seen. Roving scientific genius, ha! Sam was no genius and knew it. But neither was he blind nor stupid. And certainly he was not the guardian angel of Los Alamos National Laboratory. He believed that would be a daunting task for Michael, who had his wings full with the Jews.

A bitter thought intruded. Sam chewed it; tried to spit it out. Couldn't. Was he Rick Adams's savior? Was it too late to try? Maybe. Gavin Burton's personally appointed derivative classifier. Phhh. A ring of co-conspirators? Possibly. And if Sam were to speak out against what he was confident was bogus intelligence related to GRIT, his head would be served up on a platter to Burton. Having avoided that all these years, he was not about to bungle there now. And if Rick were the one to sever it? Well, stranger things had happened.

And if the Lab crumbled completely? Society wouldn't understand the magnitude of loss. Never. Mostly because the Lab's greatest successes could not be touted. Only its failures were visible. Political fodder. Cable TV news hysteria. Sam believed the director soon would be swinging by a golden parachute. No great loss. But Sam's friend, John O'Donnell, an upstanding man and fine colleague, would also be out, swinging by a millstone sufficiently massive to sink his professional future. John's kids were in college, all four of them. Dismal prospects. But, neither was Sam the savior of John O'Donnell. Reba and he were from families who were apparently not intended to save the world. Half of them couldn't even save themselves—

Reba's soft mezzo-soprano colored the background. Sam closed his eyes in deep concentration. She sang along with a recording that she had considered introducing to her high school chorus class. Her voice, clarion clear, effortless. Sam ambled down the hallway, awaited the piece's conclusion, and then poked his head inside Reba's matchbox-size music room. "You know how much I love beautiful music, especially when sung by a lovely lady."

"You like this one especially or just coming up for air from your cogitations?"

"A bit of both," he hedged, moving toward her. She sat on the edge of a well-worn wing chair. Supple burgundy leather. Padded and deep. In slacks and blouse, she looked to Sam every bit as beautiful as the day they were married. He drew up beside her. Rested his hands on her delicate shoulders. Haltingly, he asked, "Reba, are you happy?"

"What on earth do you mean?"

"You could be rehearsing for a somewhat more magnitudinous venue than the high school music room or the Fuller Lodge in beautiful downtown Los Alamos."

"Oh, yes, having spent my life under a media microscope. Rushing to concerts, recording sessions, traveling constantly, pulling my hair over critical reviews. No thanks. It's clearer now than ever, this is a meaningful existence."

Sam observed Reba observing him. Read her thoughts. Awaited the inevitable.

"Are you unhappy?" She asked with almost practiced nonchalance.

"Not at all," he replied. "Why, I have you and the twins. Books, photography, work. My word, that's a lot. I'm blessed. Haven't missed out on anything other than a lot of vapid cocktail party *kibitzing.*" Sam studied his slippers.

"Is something brewing at the Lab?" she asked.

His nod was barely perceptible.

Reba kissed his hand and then held it to her warm cheek. "Keep a low profile. In time, all will be revealed." Sincere eyes. Her head bobbed knowingly, saying, "How many times have you seen it before?"

Sam nodded agreement.

Reba released his hand and looked back to her lyrics sheet.

Sam rubbed her back and let his hand drip from her shoulders. Wistfully, he padded down the hall, thinking it had been her choice to seek a quiet life. He'd not cajoled her, rather she'd cajoled him. Willing for her to spread her wings, to embrace heights of success, he was her staunchest supporter. She had demurred.

And the lovely melody that she sang aloud to herself would never escape the room's faded walls. As on so many occasions, Reba would ultimately opine that although talent exists in the young, maturity and experience are generally absent. Sam concluded that it was not so different from his visions of bravery, which were confined to his study.

Seated at his desk, Sam glanced sideward at the open book. Eyes, accusing eyes stared out from the page at him. His stomach began to churn. A familiar sensation. It would pass. But the eyes, they seemed to narrow, to grow more accusatory. Sam blinked when he perceived Wallenberg's lips turning down in disgust. A tidal wave of grief, frustration, self-loathing crashed over him. And then, his chest heaved with pain.

Hunched from the weight of the ache, Sam groaned. His breath shallowed. Fire seemed to course through the veins of his left arm. He felt worthless, grotesque. Sam fell backward, crashing into his chair and onto the floor. Clutching, he wiped the book from his desk. It slapped the floor flat, pages unturned. There on the floor, face-to-face with Wallenberg. In the pool of dingy lamp light those eyes continued to bore into Sam's rawness. Gasping for air, he heard Reba's faint mezzo-soprano. Nothing but a dirge. Was this his fate? To be enshrouded by mediocrity. Emasculated. The fire pulsed throughout his chest. And as the room swirled to black, Sam thought that if his time was up, so be it. He could tolerate this life no longer.

CHAPTER 60

THE WORKSHOP command center, Gerry's private retreat. He reviewed the lovebirds' meaningless chatter in Rick's vehicle the previous night, thinking, "lying American hedonists." Rick's ex was completely worthless to the mission now. And if Renée's murder didn't keep Rick reeled in, Carmen might have to be next. It would be her fault for being a slut.

Later that evening at El Meson, waiting to access the dead drop, which already lay outside in the usual place, Gerry missed the dancers. A guitarist played sleepy Latin American ballads. Nursing quality vodka, Gerry watched the window outside. Nothing for half an hour. After nine, he strolled out of the rear door and headed behind the building. He neared the unused newsstand, but heard quiet voices. A cough.

Gerry hugged the wall and ran a hand inside his jacket's inner pocket. More whispers. He gripped the small firearm, no bigger than a peashooter, lightly and slid it from his jacket. If they were Armstrong's goons, he could taste the pleasure of offing them in a murder/suicide contrivance. He could engineer the crime scene, secure the drop, and disappear, all in 90 seconds. Maybe he'd set a personal best?

Peeking around the industrial trash bin, Gerry saw two dots glowing red, about five feet from the ground. Then the overstuffed faces of pre-teens, who choked quietly as they inhaled, came into focus. He slipped the weapon into his pocket, stood tall, and stretched a menacing scowl across his face. He stormed toward the youths. They threw down their smokes and raced down the alley. Gerry extinguished the cigarettes and from the paper dispenser he withdrew the drop, which he stashed inside his jacket.

CHAPTER 61

SUMMER had segued into fall, which in Northern New Mexico brought golden aspen leaves that shown like billions of doubloons against the cloudless sky. The air was brisk for Halloween and a paper-thin, erminesque layer of moisture blanketed the plaza. It was the first carefree evening Rick had spent with Carmen since they had become intimate. She'd accused him of being distant, of playing mind games. He couldn't tell her the truth for fear of endangering her life. There'd been neither accusations nor questions regarding his sudden transition from lancer to cuddler.

Rick's mood had been hampered by the reappearance of Detective Russell. He seemed to be everywhere, watching, asking questions, looking sullen. His opening gambit was usually a question about whether Rick had forgotten to relate anything to him about Renée's disappearance . . . in the previous dozen interviews and telecons. Rick took comfort in that there was absolutely no evidence of a crime. Neither in Renée's house nor vehicle. Neither in Rick's house nor vehicle, all of which had been examined thoroughly. There was no body, no CD. Yet Detective Russell's affect and innuendo was that when a CD was discovered, he would gladly punch Rick's ticket to the slammer.

Rick strolled into Building Two at 9:30, prepared to fake a little more prog-ress on GRIT. None of his legitimate efforts had borne fruit. And he had taken to falsifying results, mostly to keep the MRC off his back. Door unlocked, briefcase still in hand, Rick heard Bruno shouting him out, "So glad you could make it."

"The weather . . . snow," Rick replied.

Bruno glanced down at Rick's barely damp shoes and said, "All ten flurries. My Subaru ate up the road, man. Your fancy Bimmer have trouble? Like all last week? Did it overheat then?"

"What idiot recommended me for this job, anyway? He should be ashamed."

"I resemble that comment. And grapevine has it that the cavity design is coming along. That's why I'm inviting you to lunch. Got to keep your strength up. You're losing weight, Buddy." Bruno patted his blossoming paunch. "Apparently there's a conservation principle in play: the more you lose, the more I gain."

Rick didn't need to glance at his trimmed waist to know it was true. It was miraculous he could digest food at all. "I'd like to help you out, but too much to do. Maybe next week."

Bruno stood, palms up, shoulders scrunched. Rick understood his friend was just trying to be supportive. Rick also knew that Detective Russell had grilled Bruno a couple of times, asking details of Rick's professional and romantic interactions in Boston. It was embarrassing. Rick knew he'd not harmed Renée. But others, they just read the papers and listened to gossip. Ouch—

Fact was, the FBI had also questioned Bruno, Sam, and Arthur, regarding Rick's potential security infractions. What could he do? The short-term goal was to keep GRIT, thus himself, alive, by falsifying research results. This supported his longer-term goal, which was to live long enough to devise a real plan.

Rick watched Bruno walk away. I used to be able to tell him anything. But now, what could I say to him or to anyone that wouldn't put their lives in jeopardy? What if during lunch with Bruno or more likely Sam a bomb was dropped? Sam had asked him for coffee, but had Rick declined, citing too much work. Sam's silence and the weight of his scrutiny during MRC meetings, while Rick spun his web of lies, always left Rick queasy. For some reason, it was as though Sam had it all figured out. Just like the bounding calculation they had discussed a while ago. Sam knew, but was unwilling to open his mouth, to blow the whistle on the bogus claims. Why? Whose side was he really on? Just one more piece of Rick's sordid life puzzle.

Of all his accusers, the most passionate was inanimate. The GRIT experimental device, the vacuous mastodon skeleton as Rick thought of it, stood in constant complaint, languishing without a grasing cavity. The volume enclosed by the beast's tall, slender, inwardly curved superconducting magnet *ribs*, remained vacuous, empty.

CHAPTER 62

THE PLASMA monitors glowed. Their power supplies hummed in seeming anticipation of a ground-braking calculation. Rick doodled, surfed the WEB, and listened to music for a couple of hours. He headed to the locker room about 11:45 and was on the trail before noon. Showered and ready for lunch shortly after one, he cruised into town.

An hour earlier, Tony's Pizza, a joint with splintery, high-back wooden chairs and plastic white and red checked table cloths, would've been filled. Its garlic- and basil-laced atmosphere would have enveloped scientists scribbling on napkins and arguing fine points of theory, technicians laughing and making fun of their managers, and crafts people glad to be out of the elements. Because Rick had been avoiding his colleagues—everyone at the Lab, really—the 1:30 desolation was comforting. His order placed at the counter, a meatball sub with chips and iced tea, Rick surveyed the small red and white sea. Sam perused a journal at a corner table. Damn.

Rick sipped tea, approaching the table. Sam's face appeared drawn. His full lips seemed to pull downward at the corners, unlike what Rick had seen before. "Late lunch."

"Join me?"

"Oh, I just ordered. Don't want to hold you up."

Sam's burgeoning plate of spaghetti steamed. "As you like."

The words were nice, but the tone gruff. Rick said quickly, "Why not." Neither man was a master of small talk, but Rick gave it a shot, asking, "Late meeting?"

"Doctor's appointment."

"Everything tip top?"

"I expect to be around a while longer. At least until Thanksgiving. My grandchildren were supposed to come up this year." He looked down; poked the pasta. "They cancelled last night. Maybe I'll make it until New Year's, the rescheduled date."

Rick chuckled nervously. "Where do they live?"

"The West Coast."

"Not so far."

"Too far. But my son and his wife have excellent jobs, many friends. The twin boys are thriving. Last time they were here, we taught them some traditional songs. They harmonize beautifully. But, it's probably better for them out there."

"Uh huh."

"Heading back East for the holidays? Or is your sweetheart coming here?"

"I'm staying put. My reasons to return to the East have e to the minus t'ed for a couple of months." Rick quoted the expression, before jabbing his tea with a straw. The terse terminology of mathematics transformed the truth of love on the rocks into a tractable academic matter rather than a personal failure. Exponential decline was about the fastest route for something to go downhill that mathematics could express. The smaller the time constant, the quicker the decay. In a matter of months, Rick had gone from desperately needing Desiree, radically altering his life for a chance to be with her, to accepting their ill fate.

"Ah, yes. But there's a broad range of time constants," Sam said, "that dictate exponential decline. Some so large the effects won't vanish in just one lifetime."

Sam's tremulous voice and his contorted facial expression suggested to Rick they'd struck a deep chord. Rick absorbed the moment, until, as if on cue, Sam changed the subject.

"Are you enjoying your work environment?" Sam asked.

"I suppose."

"The Lab has its warts, but it's hard to find a better place to pursue scientific excellence."

"I . . . couldn't agree more."

"However." Sam dragged out the word slightly.

Rick tensed.

"No matter where you are or what magnitude of resources are available," Sam said, "the insoluble remains insoluble, doesn't it."

The rhetorical question demanded not an answer, but amplification that Rick was unwilling to provide. He gulped tea.

"If a solution does not exist then you just can't make one up."

Rick choked. His face reddened. He covered his mouth and stood. Sam moved to strike his back, but Rick turned and raced toward the men's room.

CHAPTER 63

CARMEN cradled Rick's head in her lap and stroked his curly hair. She was quite pleased with the little designs she made on his forehead. But he kept sweeping them away with his hand. He lay relaxed with his bare feet extending beyond the sofa's end as Carmen sat, considering the upcoming Thanksgiving holiday. She was no chef and knew it, but was determined to prepare a fitting meal.

T'Bird had announced that he was heading north to Dulce. That had surprised her. But then, he'd been full of surprises lately. He'd said that he would be back for the weekend bike race and was determined to win. Carmen said to Rick, "I've never seen T'Bird so bent on winning a bike race."

"Thanksgiving weekend?"

"It'd be good for him. You know, self esteem."

"I never noticed a problem with him in that department."

"I think I know him a bit better than you," she said, teasing up an unruly lock, à la Nero. "Something's up. He's even going to Dulce."

"Have you been there?"

"Several times. His mom's so cool. She's a healer. A shaman . . . shawoman."

"What's the story on that?"

"Sunflower is Jicarilla Apache. Her kinsmen were powerful medicine men."

"Uh huh."

"She told me that when she was a girl, she saw her father, Stillwater, sink to the bottom of a mountain lake to interact with sacred mountain Spirits."

"The Gunn."

"That's Ga'an. Rhymes with kahn.

"Sunflower, when she was a teenager, had an amazing encounter with the most powerful of mountain Spirits, a Gray Ga'an. Most women were relegated to child-bearing, -rearing and basketwork, as the name Jicarilla implies."

Rick dusted his forehead with the back of his hand.

"Anyway, Stillwater was visited by Sotli, a powerful Apache medicine woman already in the spirit world, who instructed him that her blessings and powers would be bestowed on Sunflower if he instructed her in ancient medicine."

Rick said, "Well, I guess T'Bird's dad was pretty happy about not having a bunch of doctor bills. Or maybe he was like my old man. Just wore through everything. Besides, when I was a kid, medicine usually made me feel sicker than I was already. Crazy dreams. And I'd feel more like jumping off a bridge than anything. "

"*Pobrecito* Ricky," she said. "Turns out, neither the Jicarilla warriors nor the other women appreciated Sunflower's calling. And only after T'Bird's birth was she confident enough to stand up to Big John and the tribal leaders."

"How so?"

"She warned that the Ga'an would exact revenge should they desecrate sacred tribal lands of Southern Colorado and Northern New Mexico."

"How were they going to do that?"

"The elders and braves had a scheme to sell development rights to build a lodge and casino and to lead hunting parties close to sacred burial sites. Sunflower's ancestors had sold crude oil leases, but they were well away from sacred sites. Finally, even Big John went along with the elders."

"What was he going to do? Piss off his cronies?" Rick sat up. His hands spread wide apart. "Big John lived in the real world with the other men, not the lady in the lake."

"Very funny. But that was exactly it. Apache society is matriarchal. Big John was a Chiricahua and had moved from Southern New Mexico just a few years earlier to join his bride's family in the northern mountains. He had to earn acceptance."

Rick drew his face toward hers. They kissed. She felt the warmth of his hand caress her breast. He massaged it circularly. She thought, oh God, sex would be so good. But my story. This is the really good part! She ended the smooch with a loud smack and said, "Now, let me finish."

Rick slid down to her lap. "So, Big John and the Big Shots ticked off the Ga'an by selling hunting licenses in the Happy Hunting Grounds."

"Pretty much. That was before Sunflower inherited her parents' oil wealth. The expensive game licenses and big casino enriched all the tribesmen."

"So T'Bird's mom is a millionaire."

"Oh, yeah."

"BJ sounds pretty level-headed to me."

"That's really setting the bar high," she snickered.

"I don't mind a high bar. So long as I can reach the bottles and glasses."

"Will you stop it." Carmen mussed her latest hair sculpture. "See, Sunflower said that she'd assured Big John that T'Bird was destined for greatness. It was more important for Big John to be a steady moral compass for him."

"Whatever."

"At a tribal gathering and feast the night before signing the contract, Stillwater roused from his wickiup to warn the tribal leaders of disastrous consequences for those who signed. He was ignored."

"All that money on one side of the equation; hocus pocus on the other."

"Well, Stillwater imposed a curse on all those leaders and tribesmen in the names of his dominant ancestors." Carmen sighed. "And Big John signed the accord to make the sacred land of Sunflower's ancestors a hunters', golfers', and gamblers' Disneyland."

"Looks like it all turned out okay to me. T'Bird's okay. And BJ?"

Carmen frowned. T'Bird was all right, but all was not right—

"Is BJ alive?"

"Yes. But the other tribal leaders and warriors were razed."

"By a razor-toting, big-game hunter?"

"Rare illnesses; freak accidents; the inexplicable. Sunflower herself told me. T'Bird won't talk about it."

"Incredible."

"Ricky, these are the same Spirits who're angry with the Lab for desecration of Northern New Mexican land. Sunflower believes the Lab will be destroyed."

Rick blurted out, "I'm more worried about my survival than the Lab's."

Carmen sat up. She looked him in the eyes. "What does that mean?"

"Just a bad joke. Now, what happened?"

Carmen relaxed her gaze, but her mind was making connections. Rick's hellish nightmares of the Lab. Did he fear for his safety? What was the root of it all? She suppressed her negative thoughts. Rick needed to hear this. "Sunflower prevailed on her Jicarilla ancestors to appease the angry Ga'an, to spare Big John and T'Bird. Her supplications were granted for a price."

"Big time wampum?"

"Big time misery! Big John was cursed to suffer shame and disorientation, as though his giant head had been severed from his body like his ancestor's. They're both big, strapping men. T'Bird lost his special birthright."

Rick stared blankly. He asked, "Giant head? Just how strapping is BJ?"

"I've never seen him. No photo, *nada*." Carmen could almost see the gears in Rick's mind wheeling. "He's bigger than T'Bird, Sunflower says."

"Interesting. And the headless ancestors? Was it congenital?"

"There was only one, smartass. Big John is descended directly from one of the most feared Mimbreño Chiricahua Apache Chiefs, Mangas Coloradas. The name Apache was derived from the Yuma word for fighting men."

"Were they just bloodthirsty or relocation holdouts?"

"They killed mostly for necessity; sometimes revenge. The sight of Mangas's red shirt sleeves leading a charge was said to send the enemy running."

"What happened to him?"

"Mangas was deceitfully captured and decapitated by General West and his men. His head was boiled and his skull was sent to the Smithsonian Institution. It's one of the largest skulls ever examined. His brain was larger than Daniel Webster's!"

"Wow! I guess that would disturb the lineage."

"The mutilation of Mangas's body meant that he would forever roam the *Happy Place* headless. And his progeny were doomed to bear his burden of unrest."

Rick raised his face into the softness of her bosom. She could feel her nipples responding. She closed her eyes. Ran her fingers through his thick, mussed hair. She gripped it firmly and pulled his face into her. Relating the cautionary tale had been enjoyable. And now, for the first time in too long, she was about to enjoy some belly-smacking sex.

CHAPTER 64

IN THE WEE morning hours, cozy in bed, Carmen felt safe in Rick's embrace. Her mind drifted in the silence. She was surprised when abruptly Rick asked, "Would you mind if we changed our Thanksgiving dinner plans?"

She couldn't help her rigid posture, asking, "Something come up?"

"My friend Sam Smith, I told you about him, is being stiffed by his kids. They were supposed to bring the grandchildren to Los Alamos. Sam was really down about it when I spoke to him. You can say no. But can we invite them to dinner here? You can still cook, if you want, or we can buy food out. Good food."

Carmen bolted up. "Maybe I will cook." She immediately settled back in. "But, they probably have lots of friends in Los Alamos."

"But their plan is busted. And I don't know how healthy Sam is these days. Hey, they might enjoy some different company. I'm sure we're younger than their friends. His wife teaches voice at Los Alamos High."

"What's her name?"

"Reba."

"Reba and Sam Smith." An image of Reba McEntire's orange hair and her twangy voice entered Carmen's mind. And then the Grand Ol' Opry dominated her mental landscape. "Should I make barbeque? I'll definitely read up on panhandle real estate prices. Oil futures, too."

"I don't think so. Like many Labites, they moved here from the East Coast. And Sam is a dead ringer for my freshman physics professor Howard Goldstein."

"I get the picture," she said, relieved.

Long after Rick had gone to sleep, Carmen continued to devise her plan for the perfect holiday feast. It would require a visit to her friend, Mel the butcher. Rick thrashed and mumbled. Another nightmare. Carmen listened as he battled the usual cast of characters: Burton, Graser, Ger. She sat absorbing the gibberish, before reaching to stroke his head, wondering what he was hiding in there that was so unsettling.

THE FOLLOWING afternoon, Carmen and Rick sat on his veranda, wearing polar fleece jackets, zipped to the throat against the fall chill. The sun floated like a brilliant golden beach ball above a cleft formed by two western peaks. Warmed by the glow, Carmen said, "Let's talk about Thanksgiving. I'm getting excited."

"It's a non-starter. I called him today. Said they've decided on a quiet holiday."

"Oh, no. I ordered the most beautiful lamb chops. My friend Mel cut them especially for us. He even started marinating them right away, so they'll be extra delicious grilled or baked."

Carmen thought of her deceased grandparents and despaired that Sam and Reba would have a miserable holiday dinner, alone. In a moment of inspiration or sheer pluck, she raced inside and returned with a cordless phone. After a quick call to directory assistance, she dialed. Rick put a finger to his nose and appeared to be holding his breath.

"May I speak with Reba Smith, please?" Carmen used a tone of voice evocative of East Coast breeding.

"Speaking."

"Hello, Ms. Smith. I'm Carmen Cdebaca, a friend of Rick Adams. He's a colleague of your husband's at the Lab."

"Yes, Sam has spoken of Rick. What is this regarding?"

"It's just that Rick has spoken so highly of Sam. He's actually a role model for him at the Lab. You know, Rick works hard and has made few friends."

Rick grimaced. He made a funny gesture with his hands, like indicating a 'tee' intersection or something." Carmen smiled at him and continued. "I'm so sorry that we may not be able to have Thanksgiving dinner together. Today I ordered some wonderful lamb chops from my friend, a former surgeon turned kosher butcher."

"Who is he?"

"Dr. Melvin Richwein, a retired neurosurgeon from back East. He jokes that a surgical residency should be required for all kosher butchers."

Rick waved violently at Carmen. She smiled again. "He's a delightful man."

"I don't know him," Reba replied. "Where's his shop. Now, what's it called?"

"It's just off Cerrillos Road. Called Dr. Mel's—" she hedged.

"And how do you know him?"

"He presented a series of extracurricular lectures at St. John's on the stomach configurations and digestive processes of humans and various quadrupeds. He's a world expert. But you may've seen him at the Opera, quite handsome with an arresting . . . smile." Leer, nearly slipped. "He usually wears a hand-beaded kippah and coordinating beaded moccasins. Very chic." Carmen refrained from mentioning Mel's visible tattoos and body piercings, especially the diamond tipped tongue stud, responsible for his lisp.

Reba asked, "Do you attend such lectures often?"

"As a student, I did all the time. I'm too busy now." Carmen thought she might have Reba cracked. This broad was a tough nut.

"Well, it was thoughtful of you to go to all the trouble," Reba said. "But I think we're just going to relax. Sam and I have been a bit too busy lately, ourselves."

"I understand. I've been working two jobs and studying voice."

"Really?"

Carmen tacked, "You know, I've already purchased the chops. Would you be kind enough to take half of them? It'd be a shame to freeze freshly butchered meat. It's more like culinary art."

"Ahhh, no thank you. Even though that's awfully generous." Reba sighed. "Why don't you and Rick come to our place? Bring your chops and I'll prepare them."

"Wonderful. What time?"

"Four p.m., sharp."

CHAPTER 65

THREE fifty-nine, Thanksgiving day: Rick rang the Smith's doorbell. After brief, somewhat stiff introductions, he watched Carmen present the chops to Reba. Carmen had wisely substituted a plain outer brown paper bag for Mel's advertisement bag. Thus avoiding Mel's off-beat slogan as an initial topic of conversation. Although Rick had been amused, reading how the good doctor touted his "unbeatable meat," he was pretty sure Reba wouldn't appreciate it.

Dinner was sedate. Sam held forth on the Lab, and Rick on his doleful adolescence. Carmen was subdued while Reba sat quiet, looking embarrassed most of the time. Her contributions to the conversation were generally to inject skepticism. Rick found Sam's body language and commentary more sympathetic than before. Had he endured an abusive childhood, too?

After-dinner talk was small, considering the big brains present. Rick would've been delighted to see Carmen open up with some metaphysical or even real physical questions for Sam. She was enthralled by modern physics paradoxes like why electrons, with their negative electrical charge, don't get sucked up by an atom's positively charged nucleus? And she and Vlad, her ex, had apparently argued for hours over how atoms can be 99.9999% void, yet compose very dense materials. Although real answers to these questions were given in incomprehensible terms, she loved hearing educated perspectives on them. But she didn't inquire.

The atmosphere of the nice, clean, orderly home was oppressive. It discouraged inquiry, even curiosity. Rick found himself examining the living room for clues defining who these people were, really. There were none. Neither Reba nor Sam had commented on their backgrounds or personal lives at all. When Carmen asked to see photos of the twins, they were retrieved from out of sight. And when Carmen, apparently trying to liven up the party, withdrew a CD from her purse, Rick froze. She extended it toward Reba, saying, "This may interest you."

Rick watched while Reba eyed the jacket. Her expression disfigured as she mouthed the title: "Meshugga Beach Party: Sixteen Songs of the Chosen Surfers."

She thrust the disk toward Sam.

"How, uh, interesting, Reba. Some of your favorites are here."

Carmen said, "Rick told me that you teach voice in Los Alamos. And that you'd taught your grandchildren traditional Jewish songs."

Reba glared at Sam, who shrugged.

"I worked on a couple of these pieces with a choral group in Santa Fe," Carmen said. "It's a radically different interpretation, of course. I thought you might like to hear some. Just for fun."

Reba declined. Rick drew an easy breath.

"I'd like to hear some," Sam said. "It's very thoughtful of you to bring this."

Rick nearly held his breath as the beat thumped and garage-inspired surf music wailed from the powerful little speakers of a bookshelf stereo. Savage guitar. Reba must've thought the musical mayhem a satanic perversion of the world's most sacred music, because she covered her ears.

Sam mashed stop.

"Isn't that crazy," Carmen enthused. "The Big Kahuna guitarist is Waldorf from LA. He's performed surf music for Nickelodeon and a Disney film."

Rick shot her a look. His eyes pleaded for her not to mention Randy California or his cohort Clit McTorius.

"Try track seven, Sam," Carmen said. "*Kol Nidre*."

After a moment of a percussion-dominated, martial rhythm, Sam said, "I recognize the music, but not the beat."

Rick asked, "Is this always sung as a bolero?"

"It's never sung to bolero," Reba burst.

Sam mashed stop.

"It's actually a very solemn chant, sung on Yom Kippur," Carmen said to Rick. "I'm sure Meshugga didn't mean any disrespect by their rendition. Waldorf says he's trying to reach a larger, more youthful audience, who may overlook this important music unless it's modernized."

Silence.

Rick said, "Well, it's been a wonderful dinner."

Carmen said, "Do you want to hear the vocals?" She cleared her throat and moved to the edge of her seat. Straightened her back and rolled her shoulders downward, elongating her neck. "It goes like this," she said, beginning the chant.

Rick winced, seeing Reba cross her arms, her eyes drilling Carmen. Amazingly, she ignored the imperious glare and enriched the tone. Rick was impressed by the way Carmen handled the pressure. He looked on in amazement as Sam's head bowed in reverence. It was as though Carmen were one of the heavenly host. Her vocal timbre was completely different from the rock and roll rants of Angel's. Maybe it was good, he thought, that there was more of Carmen to know. When Rick stole another peek at Reba and found her eyes closed, he shut his eyes, too. And thanked his lucky stars.

CHAPTER 66

GERRY had been under the weather all week. Thanksgiving night was falling and his day had been a waste. He shuffled from the computer console of his command center around the corner to a desiccator, located underneath a gleaming fume hood. The spot-free floors, smudge-free steel cabinets, and streak-free mirrors of his surroundings helped his feelings, but his immune system required a serious boost. He was precipitating a potent salt of tauro-ursodeoxycholic acid, which he would ingest over the coming days. Gerry hoped to perk himself up in preparation for the bike race Saturday by supplementing his less strenuous preparation regimen. He considered TUDCA to be Echinacea raised to the tenth power.

That morning, as ordinary folks trussed turkeys and would-be chefs marinated exclusive cuts of meat, Gerry had begun to prepare a rare meal. He'd removed a veiny tissue sack from the freezer, placed it in a thermostatically controlled infra-red oven, and slowly, precisely elevated its temperature from -18 °C up to +40 °C. The oven heated the soggy mass evenly, raising its temperature at the steady climb of 10 °C per hour. From the warm pouch, he had extracted almost a hundred milliliters of tauro-ursodeoxycholic acid. He centrifuged it and allowed it to rest before being placed in a desiccator, where it lay until completely evacuated of moisture, producing a super salt.

Gerry engaged with the lilting melody of waltz that filled the air as he accessed the bladder from his laboratory refrigerator. No one—other than Maestro Tchaikovsky—wrote waltzes like Glazunov, he mused. And *Raymonda*, only Nureyev understood its power. Gerry became animated and nearly floated to a nearby cabinet, his small, thickly calloused feet lightly stroking the tiled flooring as he went. He withdrew a sterile plate upon which he carefully placed the purplish pouch before introducing it under a short wavelength heating lamp. In minutes it was sizzling, oozing, and emanating an obnoxious odor, captured by the closed-loop fume hood. Venting the putrid vapors outside might spark concerns of his cooking crack. Or worse, his neighbor might suspect him of cooking and eating menudo. This dish was infinitely more expensive than cocaine or heroin, and according to traditional Chinese medicine, bolstered one's health instead of destroying it.

Standing well away, Gerry used forceps to rotate the oozing bladder, which resembled a rotten eggplant. He considered that people in his employer's country were generally undernourished and many starved to death every day. But he was supplied this fountain of youth, as he liked to think of it, whose black-market value exceeded $25,000, via contract. Just as his plastic surgeries had been a matter of contract. It was to his and his employers' advantage that he appear youthful and optimally vigorous. Better to deter challenge, than to offer a crushing retort.

Unlike China, there were no indigenous black bears in Gerry's current employer's country. For super potency, his medicinal gallbladders were extracted solely from wild Asiatic black bears, vigorously protected by international animal rights groups. What's more, Federal Express had delivered it via Singapore right to his gate.

After removing the bubbly blackened pouch from underneath the lamp, Gerry ceremoniously raised a vodka shot to the Motherland and drained it before devouring his healthful feast, using forceps and a scalpel and pinching his nose tightly.

CHAPTER 67

Rick sprang up. Carmen was watching him, sitting up, beside him in his bed. He tried to shake off the eerie veil of fitful sleep. At last he asked, "Wha', wha'?"

"What were you dreaming about?"

"I dunno . . . the Lab, stress." Rain gently patted the roof. He noted the time, only 7:40. "Why are you sitting up? *Vamos* to sleep." His head hit his pillow.

"I can't sleep any longer. I'll make coffee."

The stout French roast perked Rick up within sips. Carmen was unusually quiet. Her countenance contemplative. He asked, "What's going on in that big brain of yours?"

"Just thinking. Do you have to go to work today?"

"It's a holiday, remember."

"You used to work every day and most nights," Carmen said, turning to face him. "Are you going to work some here?"

"Nope," he said, eyeing her carefully.

"Don't forget, tomorrow's the bike race."

"Yeah. We can treat T'Bird to a whopping lunch at Annapurna Café, in honor of his transcendental victory."

"Hopefully." She took a tiny taste of coffee. Arched an eyebrow, asking, "Why don't you bring your big laser book home any longer?"

"Ah, yes, venerable Siegman. I've mastered that one."

"Really?"

"Truthfully, there are plenty of so-called laser physicists out there who have not mastered that one completely. You connect the dots."

"So, lasers aren't important to you any more?"

"Go easy. It's only my first cup." Rick cut his gaze to the steamy brew. "Sure they're important. And gas lasers have some very critical gas dynamics considerations, as I'm certain you're aware from your intense modern physics at St. John's."

"It was called a modern physics intensive." She hooked a strand of hair behind her ear, saying, "Tell me more about lasers."

"Caaarmen, we've talked about this before."

She scrooched beside him and whispered, "Remember how hot I told you I got during your hotrod lecture."

Rick's mind leapt back to their first night together. If he could only recapture the magic. Now it was as though his life was a ticking bomb. Rather than be a dud, he said, "Why don't you recap our previous chats on the subject."

Carmen elevated an index finger. "Laser is an acronym for light amplification by stimulated emission radiation." The thumb popped outward when she added, "Laser light is *muy especial* in that it's monochromatic, well-collimated, and coherent. That makes it much groovier than, say, a light bulb." She beamed.

"*¡Muy bien!*" Rick's eyes sparkled. "*Más.*"

"Gas lasers use a gas for the lasing medium." Carmen crinkled her brow, saying, "But, you know, my mom's ophthalmologist used a helium-neon laser to—"

"Let's crawl before we fly, shall we. But, you're right. Multiple gases can be more effective for creating a . . . a . . . ."

The crinkle transformed to a crease.

"Remember that stimulated emission is the Nobel Prize-wining discovery describing a photon, whose energy is identical to the differential energy of the excited and ground states, smacking into an excited atom and inducing it to de-excite by emitting two identical photons with the exact same energy as the incident photon."

"Right."

"So, you need a big supply of atoms in the ideal excited state, otherwise called the lasing state. And the use of multiple gases can promote a larger reservoir of atoms in that state. This is key." Now, Rick's fingers were popping up in emphasis. "To sustain the lasing reaction, there must be more atoms in the excited lasing state than not. It's called a population inversion and enables the amplification of the stimulated emission radiations." "Sick of this yet? Want breakfast?"

"Wait, no. I just forgot that one thing." Carmen's brow relaxed. "How about you pontificate while I make breakfast?"

"Deal."

Rick watched Carmen stepping lively, crossing the room, bouncing all the way. In what seemed an instant, she called him to set the table. She had seen to it that Rick's refrigerator and pantry were stocked with bare necessities and a luxury or two. Aged balsamic vinegar from Italy, and from Spain, Manchego cheese. They were both firsts for him. And they were in play in the omelet, along with some wilted spinach.

More coffee brewed, Rick sat at the breakfast nook table, thankful the drizzle was nourishing his neglected outdoor plants.

Carmen had barely taken a seat when she asked, "Now where were we?"

Rick waved her off with his fork, savoring a bite. Food hadn't tasted this good for a while. "Regarding helium-neon lasers," he said at last, "the electrons jump up to a certain energy level in the helium and then quickly decay to an ideal energy level, lasing state, in the neon that produces a 0.6 micron lasing line. It's an optimal wavelength for reattaching retinas." Rick made a mock smacking sound, reached over to give Carmen a smooch, and then fell silent. "One step back. What's special about laser emissions?"

"They're monochromatic."

"Meaning they're all the exact same—

"Color."

"Same color *ergo* same wavelength and energy, which are probably more important considerations for your mom's ophthalmologist, unless she's having her eye color changed." Rick grinned.

"That's hysterical," Carmen yawned. "And they're highly collimated: lined up real tidy."

"So tidy you can propagate a laser beam from earth to the moon and the beam only spreads out one mile. That's one part in about 250,000. Without that, you just have an expensive flashlight."

"Tell me again how the light, the *emissions* escape to reattach my mom's retina or blow up enemy missiles in outer space in President Reagan's Star Wars pipe dream?"

"Recall there are mirrors at either end of the lasing cavity. In a typical laser, they reflect the stimulated emission beam back and forth about a million times a second. One mirror reflects almost 100% of the photons and the other reflects about 99% and transmits 1% of the beam for use."

"Is the laser beam like an x-ray beam?"

Rick stared at Carmen for an instant before answering. "They're both generated by electrons de-exciting. So technically, they're both chemical phenomena. But, unless the x-rays are produced by an x-ray laser, the beam is not highly coherent."

Carmen raised her coffee cup to her lips. Rick caught her peeking over the rim at him. The glance seemed furtive. He didn't like it.

She asked casually, "So how does a laser differ from a graser?"

Rick snapped his head up and glared. "Well, well," he said. "That was a hell of an intensive course you took at St. John's. Or did you learn about grasers elsewhere?"

Carmen blushed. "I, uh . . . Vlad may have mentioned them."

The insincerity floored Rick. "Vlad is a theory guru, I was told by you. Why would he care about some applied physics that might actually be of use to somebody?"

"So, you don't know the difference, I take it." She set her jaw.

Rick reckoned that her best defense was in force. "That is absolutely incorrect. The fundamental difference in the two is that while a laser uses stimulated electronic transitions to produce low energy photons or x-rays, a graser uses stimulated nuclear transitions to produce high energy gamma rays. Hence the acronym: gamma ray amplification by stimulated emission radiation." He continued in a robotic monotone, "Further, although lasers and grasers generate electromagnetic radiations, the nuclear transitions produce wavelengths 1000 times more penetrating than any lasing line achievable by electrons." Rick stared at the wall. His mind raced so fast it ached.

"Is there a special kind called a burton-graser?"

"What are you asking?" Rick sprang up. He banged the table with his fist. Staggering backward, he toppled his chair to the floor. "Who do you work for? Tell me what the hell is going on!"

"Nobody. Just forget it."

"Forget it? Did Ger—" Rick checked himself, fearing the worst. It was not bad enough that his sleep was tormented by Gerry, Burton, and grasers; once again they had pervaded every aspect of his life. "I'm showering, then heading up the Hill," he said, storming out of the room. He considered that if he were alone, at least he'd know who in present company he could trust.

CHAPTER 68

SATURDAY night at Angel's was flat. Rick and Carmen were not the love birds they had been before the blowout. He wasn't completely certain of anything anymore. And he wasn't in the mood for playing pretend. His life was on the line.

Carmen seemingly sleep-walked the last few numbers of the set. The band's energy was low; the few patrons' lower. T'Bird was physically, but not mentally, present. In the afternoon, he'd claimed to Carmen that Gerry won the Thanksgiving bike race only by deliberately causing him to wipe out. T'Bird had reinjured his leg, which was not fully recovered from his motorcycle crash. When Carmen told Rick the story, he assumed it was true. T'Bird wasn't a liar. And what he didn't know was that he might be lucky still to be alive.

During the final set, the handsome young man that Rick had seen at the bar and more recently lunching at the Lab with the theory division genii arrived on the scene. To Rick's dismay, the man whooped and loudly applauded Carmen. After the set, T'Bird, Carmen, and Rick sat quietly together when the young man staggered over to their table.

"*Bon soir, ma Chérie,*" he said, taking and kissing the palm of Carmen's hand.

The words were correct, but, in Rick's mind, the accent was all wrong.

"Vlad, this is my friend Rick Adams," Carmen said, blushing.

T'Bird studied his tumbler of grapefruit juice.

Rick offered his hand and said, "Pleased to meet you." The man appeared to be about half-a-dozen years Rick's junior and he was profoundly schnockered.

"*Enchanter, Monsieur*," Vlad said to Rick, before chuckling to Carmen, "So this is your new love?"

"I said Rick is my friend."

"For you, this is a meaningless term, suggesting someone that you've known for five minutes or someone you've screwed fifty times. I'm confident you would refer to me as your *friend*."

T'Bird twitched, shooting a look at Carmen.

"Thanks for stopping by, Vlad," she said.

"*Mi amor*, I'm not just stopping by."

Rick caught a whiff of Vlad's breath. Nothing. He'd been drinking Vodka.

"No, I wanna talk," he said. "About sex or maybe physics, like we used to after sex." He reached for the free chair.

T'Bird's boot crashed into its seat.

"I see he's still your knight in buckskin armor. All that pent up lust for his *sister*. I don't know why you would bang me and Rick here, even Doc, but not T'Bird." Vlad shook his head and grinned.

In a flash, T'Bird had Vlad by the throat with both hands. He lifted him inches off the ground, fixing menacingly on his reddening face. Through gritted teeth, T'Bird said, "Apologize to her, you little shit, or that'll be your last insult."

"T'Bird, stop." Carmen yelled, scrambling around the table.

Vlad's eyes bulged. T'Bird squeezed the boy's flimsy neck tighter.

"Please, T'Bird, stop."

Vlad's face continue to redden and then it began to blue.

Carmen screeched, "You're killing him!"

Rick took a deep breath, preparing to enter the fray, but Vlad croaked a phrase to someone behind Rick. Vlad's eyes pleaded. Rick thought the phrase Baltic. Czech?

Gerry approached the table and asked, "Is my friend troubling you?"

T'Bird released the death grip. Vlad crumpled to the floor, like a marionette whose animator had lost interest. Carmen knelt beside him. Rick watched as she stroked his face and smoothed his mussed hair. And when she whispered,

Rick felt a pang of jealously as potent as lightning crackling up his spine. His relationship with Carmen was more complicated than he'd realized. And was Vlad so drunk that he didn't know what he was saying or had he spoken the truth? *In vino veritas.*

"Vlad, get up," Gerry said. "Time for you to go."

"He's not the only one who causes trouble and should apologize," T'Bird retorted.

"Is that so," Gerry replied.

"Yeah. Is there anything you want to say?" T'Bird bowed his chest. "Or should I be more specific?"

"Not every neck in this place is as thin as his," Gerry said. "The next one you grab could be your last."

"Maybe it's time to find out," T'Bird said, starting toward Gerry.

Rick's heart beat double-time, watching Gerry assume a martial arts pose, weight on his back leg, front leg free. He wasn't playing around. Rick didn't want to get involved. T'Bird was a strong man. And an heir of Mangas Coloradas, according to Carmen. He could take care of himself under typical circumstances. But Gerry was anything but typical. Lethal. Maybe bloodthirsty. Rick sucked air between his teeth. T'Bird crouched, preparing to spring toward Gerry. When T'Bird's eyes widened, Rick shot up from his chair and interposed himself between the two men. He faced T'Bird.

"Wait a second," Rick said. "Take a deep breath."

"Get outta my way." T'Bird used his beefy forearm to brush Rick aside.

Rick hurled himself again into the breach, chest-to-chest with T'Bird, whose neck veins pulsed visibly. Warm air expelled from his flaring nostils bathed Rick's face. "You're going to have to fight me first."

"I ain't scared a him," T'Bird said.

"For Carmen's sake, leave it alone."

"Come on Big Man," Carmen said. "We got to play."

T'Bird turned, rudely brushing Rick backward. Gerry relaxed his battle stance; remained silent. He stared down Rick with icy cold eyes. But instead of wilting, Rick returned the glare.

CHAPTER 69

THE RIDE to Rick's place was quiet as were preparations for bed. Unable to sleep, fighting the covers and his mind, Rick obsessed over his torturous conundra. Was Carmen involved with the conspiracy as a backup for Renée? What was Gerry's relationship with Vlad? Was anyone at the Lab not a spy? Surely neither Arthur nor Sam, but Sam was definitely hiding something. What? And the most maddening question of all: Had Carmen actually slept with Doc?

During morning coffee in bed, Rick repelled Carmen's attempt at feminine magic. Although his head was thick, negative thoughts raced rampant within it. He pretended to be absorbed by the sports page of the New Mexican. During his second cup of coffee, he'd stewed so thoroughly in his own fat that he was just about confited.

Carmen asked, "Does Heisenberg's uncertainty principle preclude a particle from being in two separate quantum states simultaneously?"

"Didn't we discuss that already?"

"Well, you said that quantum mechanics only suggested probable outcomes. How definite is that?"

"Maybe you should ask Vlad?"

"Oh, is my Ricky jealous?"

"Confused."

"And here I thought you knew all about QED and QCD."

"You know what I mean. You, the Lab, this town . . . ."

"I hate to be the one to tell you, but plenty of people are mystified by the Lab. What it does; what it doesn't do. And you haven't been in this town nearly long enough to understand it. So, that leaves me."

Rick flapped down his papers. "Is Vlad crazy? What's his deal?"

"I've told you. His father's a high-level Russian politico."

Rick stirred the world's weakest tornado using his index finger.

"And he's really sorry for the way he treated me," Carmen said. "That's about it."

"Is that it, really? Is that why he verbally abuses you publicly? Why do you take it?" Rick stared her down. "Are there other interests you two have in common?"

"Like what?"

"Does he still call you?"

She averted the intensity of his stare. "Well, he's my friend."

"And what *exactly* does that mean?"

Carmen glared. "Bastard. You want to abuse me, too?"

"I just want to know you, first." Rick's eyes narrowed to razor slits.

"What are we doing here, together?" Carmen kicked the covers to the floor.

"I'm not entirely sure. Maybe the same thing I was doing with Renée." Rick watched for a revealing twitch, a hesitation.

"Screwing?"

"Like you and Doc?"

"That's none of your goddamn business."

"You're not denying it."

"Doc's very intelligent. He knows more about music, real music, symphonic, baroque, jazz, than anyone in town. He knows everything about music theory."

"Doc, the brilliant, minstrel, druggie douche bag."

"Your *friend* Renée didn't seem to mind. She was his biggest 'H' customer. I'm sure when she didn't work for the Lab she paid other ways. But I suppose a junkie slut, who works at that Lab, is better then a druggie musician."

"That's a lie," Rick shouted. The mere mention of Renée stressed him into orbit. "She'd no needle marks on her."

"She smoked it. And you probably did, too. So don't be so self-righteous."

"What I did with Renée is my business."

"Your fucking business."

"We can't all be perfect, now, can we?" Rick leapt out of bed. He stormed out of the room, smashing his coffee cup into the kiva fireplace as he went.

CHAPTER 70

DECEMBER dawned with a blanket of new snow. The spirits of Angel's patrons were warm and high, but Carmen's lulled. It was early afternoon and the bar was dead so she sat scribbling *Tejano* lyrics on a cocktail napkin. And this was a real tearjerker. She hadn't seen Rick since that Sunday morning more than a week ago. She kept reliving his violent aggression. The accusations; the acrimony. She'd never for an instant suspected Rick in Renée's disappearance. But sitting in bed quaking, after his eruption, had been tough.

One picture was indelible in her mind. A jagged splinter of ceramic from the shattered cup lay on the bed, bleeding coffee near her foot. Ceramic is so brittle. Just like our relationship, she'd concluded. The splinter's crenulated edge had glistened in the sunlight. A dirty, dangerous shard. Carmen believed that Renée had probably been stoned out of her mind and fallen in the acequia near her home. She'd drowned and had been covered by falling leaves. While dredging next spring: *voila*. But now, regarding Rick's innocence, Carmen had to admit to herself that now she wasn't certain.

In Carmen's last phone conversation with Rick, he'd said that he was terribly busy, preparing to go to Cambridge for some guy's dissertation defense. Said he'd stay through the holidays because the Lab was closing the last week of December because of the budget crunch. Carmen had never heard of Rashid. She assumed Rick just wanted some time to think things over. She hoped he hadn't made up the story about Rashid's blinding himself in one eye in Rick's lab. She also hoped that Rick wasn't just plotting to see his ex.

Diego mopped happily up to the legs of the stool on which Carmen sat. She glanced down; couldn't tell which was dirtier, the floor or the mop. When he bumped her stool for the third time, she said, "Excuse me."

"You gonna sit there all afternoon? I ain't paying you no extra time," he quacked, leaning against the mop. "A little sunshine do you some good. Maybe get your bottom lip off the floor."

Carmen cringed. She scourged herself from the stool and crumpled the napkin before throwing it into the trashcan behind the bar. Grabbing her purse and glancing toward Diego, she said, "*Besos.*" The saloon doors banged together. José Maria entered, carrying his guitar case and smiling.

Carmen said, "*¿Que* pasta?"

"*Hola* Carmen, Diego." He approached his folding chair and carefully removed his guitar from its case.

"Something to drink, José Maria?" Carmen asked.

"*Agua sólo, por favor.*"

Carmen headed toward the cooler.

"He didn't say bottled water," Diego snapped.

Carmen brought over a bottle. She turned her head away to hide her swollen eyes. She felt José Maria's observant gaze appraising her.

"*Gracias,*" he said.

Carmen nodded and turned to go.

"*Momento, por favor,*" he said, cording the strings, strumming a rhythm and melody different from his beloved flamenco.

Carmen liked the feel. Latin, like Tejano. "Do I know this one?"

"*Sí y no.*"

Carmen was baffled until José Maria sang the lyrics from one of her ballads. And his music was so beautiful, a perfect compliment. Although the song was a crusher, in classic Selena style, Carmen's eyes filled with tears of joy. On the second verse, she rested on her knees beside him and assumed the vocal.

Carmen was nearly in shock. "I have more songs. Lots more!"

"¡*Yo, también!*"

José Maria began an upbeat ranchero-style tune. Carmen waited anxiously for a clue. Again, he sang a line of her lyrics.

She grabbed the guitar's neck, muffling the strings. "How'd you get these?"

"*Tengo un método*," he said, removing her hand and launching into a third moving melody.

Moments later, still stunned, Carmen made her way outside. It felt wonderful to be alive and to breathe brisk mountain air. She reeled at the possibilities for her life. Just couldn't wait to tell the good news to Ri . . . her mother—

CHAPTER 71

Rick struggled to free himself from bondage. He was constrained from torso to toe. He lay on a table, flailing his head. His forehead steaming hot. The lacerations on his face burned from salty sweat that streamed down his face. His jaw ached. It was clamped shut inside an iron facemask. His eye, swollen shut from a massive blow, throbbed. Renée and Gerry stood watching. Her head sagged at the same unnatural angle it had assumed in the necrophotos. She moved closer, a bony finger extended toward an eyehole in the mask, toward Rick's injured eye. She guided her finger through the hole. Pressed hard. Put her weight on it. Rick flailed, trying to break free. Had to break—

"Hey, buddy, do you mind," the man said.

Rick woke and froze. "I'm, uh, sorry," he said for the third time during the red-eye flight from Boston's Logan Airport to Albuquerque. He was stuck in a middle seat with a thin, too short blanket twisted tightly about him. His head pounded. His eye oozed, the midnight blue and ebony corona encircling it damp with discharge. Had he really called Barish a douche bag right to his face?

Rick hacked. Covering his mouth, he touched his sore cheek. He recalled the oral defense nightmare. Rashid had been brilliant. But Rick had bitten his tongue bloody, not lashing out at the tenured peanut gallery, who showed up, apparently eager to make known their ignorance of quantum superfluids. At least Rashid got through, and had fared better than himself.

Rick wondered why he had to rush over to Desiree's apartment. It was stupid. But who would know that Barish would be there? And when Barish tried to pull Desiree away from the final face-to-face, his pock-marked, cucumber-size nose was just too juicy a target. He must have felt the same about my bristling face, Rick thought, recalling the blow. Truth be told, Rick had taken the harder lick.

But then, the looks on the faces of Rashid's other doctoral committee members when Rick entered the conference room the following day, they were priceless. There was some poetic justice in Rick's eye looking much worse than Rashid's. Although Rick's would be fine. But in the meantime, Rashid had a healthy settlement from the Instutute, a shiny new Ph. D., and a job offer with a hot California tech outfit.

The rest was kind of a blur. The Kendall Square Marriott's sterility, the tastelessness of Legal Seafood's best, and the weirdness of paying off Desiree's coke debt with Joel. Rick had thought buying her drugs was over. But there Joel was at the Muddy Charles, as if on cue. His pitch was, "She don't pay, I'm gonna screw it up for her wid' the new chump." Rick couldn't take pleasure in Desiree's downfall. And it was just a couple of hundred bucks. She was obviously cutting back.

Joel had followed him to a cash machine where Rick withdrew the money and handed it over. The strangest part was the hand scrawled note that Joel handed him in return. "Pleasure doing business with you." It was written on a lined, 4" by 6" piece of notepad that had been rolled, and judging by its powdery feel, used for snorting. Joel had walked away without another word. Rick had immediately tossed the note in the trash. It was all too weird, Rick thought, as his head fell to the side, and he descended into hell.

AFTER HIS ARRIVAL to Albuquerque, Rick drove straight to the Lab and trudged toward his office. And who, but Bruno, stood smirking. Rick thought about clicking his heels together, but remembered this was home.

"Long broom-ride back?" Bruno asked.

Rick managed a Cycloptic glare.

"Lemme see, it's Monday morning. Am I wrong or are you back early?"

Rick could tell Bruno was enjoying the encounter.

"Let me guess." Bruno croaked bluesily, "Couldn't stand the weather . . . ."

"Taking that on the road? Why not leave now?"

"I know it's none of my business, but are you okay, really?"

"I'm here, ready to sweat." Rick tried to suppress a cough with a shaky hand.

"How about the other guy?"

"Wasn't worth the trouble," Rick hacked. "Neither of them."

"Would 'I told ya so' be in order?"

"I got plenty of work to do. I can feel the love of the MRC already."

"You should go home and get some sleep."

"I'm fine, really," Rick said, nearly choking on phlegm.

"You can bullshit some of the people all of the time. Don't matter. But I'm going to call you on it when you bullshit me. Besides, Carmen called Mary every day you were away. So I'm here to offer my services in an unofficial mediation capacity. Bruno's head cocked and his hands rose to his chin, saying, "Think of me as an exchange particle. Sorta like in the Feynman model of atomic interactions. I can be swapped back and forth carrying vital information, mediating the transmutation of romantic strife to romantic bliss."

"You can't imagine what a horrible analogy that is." Rick grimaced. Fred's and the other Feynman fanatics' faces flashed before him. Fresh out of good humor, Rick said, "Besides, that's none of your business."

"Great. Now you got a persecution complex. Look, I said nothing about all the bad security rap that's been dumped on you. I know you man. You probably deserved most of it."

"Got that ri ... ahr . . . right."

"But I ain't watching you go under and not try to grab you for a breath o' air."

"Is this where we embrace and declare, 'I love you, man'?" Rick turned to his door. Tried in vain, with his shaky hand, to fit his key into the lock.

"Hey, asshole, I'm trying to help here."

"I'm not worth the trouble, either." Rick finally unlocked the door and swung it open. He stepped inside. Bruno was close behind. Not bothering to hit the lights, Rick dropped his case on the floor, clunked into his chair, and related a thumbnail sketch of the Boston debacle.

"No sweat, man," Bruno said. "I knew that chick was bad news. Everybody did; even you." Before exiting, he added, "I don't know much about your beef with Carmen. I do know she ain't a saint, but she ain't a liar. Give her a call. And if you need me, I'm here."

CHAPTER 72

DIRECTOR ARMSTRONG sifted through the photos, the products of a predictable sting. Inevitable, perhaps. Frustrations with the Lab, a missing druggie lover, a pressure-packed trip to Boston. The fist fight with Barish was icing on the cake. Faced with an opportunity to be a woman's saviour, what was he going to do? It was obvious. Now, Joel was headed for a suspended sentence for his latest drug trafficking conviction and Armstrong had decided that Mr. Adams was headed for a head banging. A squeezing, like an overripe pimple.

Bad boys crumbling were nothing new for Armstrong. The high probability of a lost paycheck or a lengthy incarceration was more than enough. In Adam's case, there was espionage, good for some unnerving treason talk, and the missing girl, adding murder to the mix. Breaking him would be like breaking matchsticks with bowling balls. Maybe like turning brass balls into glass balls.

WHEN RICK PULLED into the Administration Building's parking lot at about 11:30 a.m., seeking soup at the cafeteria to quell his burning throat, a white, windowless van pulled directly behind him. When its side cargo door slid open, Agent Sarkowski emerged, badge blazing. He commanded Rick into the vehicle and slammed the door shut. After nearly an hour of driving, they disembarked at a deserted industrial park. Once inside the prefabricated metal building's interrogation cell, Rick insisted, "I want a lawyer, now!"

"Your lawyer is present, Mr. Adams," said an attractive woman in her thirties, dressed in a dark business suit. There was a hefty accordion-type folder under her left arm. She extended her right hand, saying, "I'm Vera Johnson, special prosecutor for the State of New Mexico."

Rick nodded.

"I know this is tough for you. We can get through it more easily with your cooperation." She paused to remove her eyeglasses. "Frankly, you're in serious trouble. I'm not saying that I can cut a deal to get you off scot-free."

Mucous rattled in Rick's throat. He hacked loudly, his head resounding. Still, his wits were sharp enough to be certain that his legal rights were being violated. Maybe he could force an incident that would provide ammunition against these goons. Sooner or later, he was sure to see them in court. He said, "Thanks for the reassurance."

"Rick, I really want to help you. I believe that you have no idea how many charges the State could file against you. If even one sticks, it'll ruin your life."

"My wonderful life?" Rick wandered around the little room. He glimpsed Ms. Johnson using his peripheral vision, wondering what was her real name.

She pointed to a table, secured to the floor using bolts. She sat on a bench similarly secured and invited him to sit across from her.

Rick stood.

"You must put your upset aside for me to help you," she said, examining a legal pad of notes. "We have reason to believe that you have committed an array of offenses against the United States Government, including—"

"Charge me or let me go!"

Ms. Johnson's jaw slacked, her gaze reminiscent of a deer facing high beams.

An instant later, Director Armstrong burst through the door. "Thank you, Vera. Mr. Adams apparently has no appreciation for your efforts to assist him." Silently, she gathered her things and departed.

One down. "I want my own lawyer," Rick said to Armstrong.

"Mr. Adams, you are not entitled to a lawyer. We're having an off the record chat." Armstrong dabbed at his right eye and grinned. "If I decide to come down on you, it will be like a megaton of bricks and all the lawyers in Santa Fe and Boston together will not be able to save your ass."

"Like you came down on Wen Ho? That was a grand success."

"That wasn't me. Let's get to the point. The Bureau has reason to believe that you are working in league with an international espionage contingent that has infiltrated Los Alamos National Laboratory. Among other things, you intend to access national security information with intent to sell it to foreign powers and ultimately foment the Laboratory's and the United States' ruination." He rolled his hand and pursed his lips. "Help me out with the details."

"I've no idea what you're talking about."

"We have reason to believe that Renée Roxbury was your espionage contact within the Laboratory and that she was also your local drug supplier. She was killed by you and her body hidden by you . . . for what reason?"

"I bet Renée's in the Caribbean drinking piña coladas right now." Rick tried, but just couldn't sell the line. He hoped that Armstrong didn't smell blood.

Armstrong stopped dead. Locked eyes, saying, "We found her body."

Rick nearly gagged. His knees weakened.

"That's why you're here, Rick. We have her and can hush it up or let it out. The decision is yours. They'll be able to shoot for murder one. The circumstantial evidence against you is overwhelming: public outburst, tire tracks, tormented screams of your name. And the co-conspiracy goes to motive."

"You're lying."

"And you're pissing your pants," Armstrong replied. "She was out of control and you silenced her to save your ass and your espionage mission. You knew she was dead and went to Boston to buy your own drugs." He tapped the slim folder he held. "Look, Rick, we got the photos."

Ice water seemed to shoot up Rick's arms. He somehow managed to suppress a shiver. How could Armstrong have gotten the necrophotos from Gerry? Did he really have Renée's corpse, too? Oh, God, Rick began to panic. When I was away, they broke into my house and found them. Sweat developed on every pore of his body. Rick tried to turn and walk away, to clear his mind. But it was as though his feet were cast in lead. He couldn't move. Should he just spill his guts? Armstrong didn't really want him. He wanted Gerry. Seconds dripped by.

Armstrong's gaze pierced him. Rick took a deep breath, determined not to say something stupid, again. He asked, "What photos?"

Armstrong opened his thin folder and filed through its contents. Rick's eyes were wide. If he saw Renée's photo with that cord strangling her broken neck, he was going to faint or puke or both. Armstrong pulled out a typewritten sheet of paper. It was an affidavit bearing Joel's name, accusing Rick of purchasing cocaine with intent to distribute. Next came the photos . . . of Rick handing money to Joel in Cambridge, a few days ago.

Rick beamed. "What's so damning about loaning an old buddy a few shekels?"

"We have the coke laced note, bearing Joel's and your fingerprints."

Rick stared down Armstrong. "If you were tailing me and watched the transaction, then you know that I didn't do coke with Joel. It was entrapment."

Armstrong looked at the papers. "I could detain you right now on the strength of this affidavit. You see, you lied to the Federal Government on your security clearance affidavit. We could hold you until we prove our real case." He didn't sell the line.

"You're sick."

In a low voice, Armstrong growled, "Forget Lee, Rick, you're looking at Rosenberg-like treatment. We got espionage and murder one to play with. That's even nastier than the Rosenbergs."

"The Rosenbergs were also framed."

When Armstrong grinned, Rick shuddered.

"You know, Rick, those who were close to the Rosenbergs understood that their deaths were merciful after all the torture they endured. They kept them on suicide watch every minute of every day so they didn't get out of this world too quickly or easily."

"I'm not a spy. And you know I didn't kill anyone." He lowered his head and bit his lip. "I'll take a polygraph. That'll clear me."

"It's not even admissible in court. There's only one way to save your ass. Tell me everything you know, starting with who the deep cover mole is at the Lab."

"How would I know? You're the fuckin' FBI."

"Okay, let's hear what you do know. Who killed Renée Roxbury? Who's running the operation outside the Laboratory? How were you recruited? How do you get paid? What's the objective of your mission?"

Rick's head spun; his vision blurred. He managed to turn and take a step or two, trying to distance himself from Armstrong's psychological assault. He turned to see Armstrong looking down his nose at him. Smug. Self-satisfied. A bolt of rebellion shot into his brain. Rick wheeled around and glared at Armstrong.

Armstrong's smirk disappeared. His tone grew fatherly. "Come on board and help us root out these evildoers," he said. "I promise you, I'll personally take the stand on your behalf if you go to trial. I'll make you look like a goddamn national hero. For Chrissakes, man, it's the only way for you to survive."

Rick's guts swirled. Disgorgement seemed unavoidable—verbal, organic, both—until a thought of Gerry pierced his consciousness. Armstrong was a brutalizer, but Gerry was a killer. And how had they found Renée, unless Gerry wanted them to? Armstrong liked photos so much, why hadn't he shown photos of her decomposing body? Rick reasoned that if he ratted out Gerry today, it was a death sentence tomorrow. In time and with enough preparation, Rick might be able to deal with Armstrong and even the wacked-out American criminal justice system. No amount of cogitation or preparation could keep him safe from Gerry. Rick said, "I, uh, need to consider this."

"We need your answer now. The clock is ticking. National security is at risk every moment we delay."

Rick crossed his arms. "I need a week."

"You got days."

CHAPTER 73

RUDELY DUMPED at his vehicle, Rick drove to a local drug store and purchased a little bottle of purplish cough syrup. He slugged it on the way home and before crawling into bed for fitful sleep. The remainder of the work week, his routine consisted of getting up and going to play at working, drinking cough potion, and going home to crash.

Friday morning the drive up the Hill seemed to take forever. At the turnoff for TA-38, Rick sat zoned out at a traffic signal. Suddenly, his passenger's side door jarred. Sarkowsky worked a slim-Jim between the outer glass and door panel. An instant later, he sat in the passenger's seat. In the rearview, Rick saw Agent Jackson wave from behind the wheel of a giant black Excursion SUV. Rick thought, Mutt and Jeff.

"Go straight, Adams."

"I, uh, contacted my lawyer and he says—"

"Can it, Adams. Director Armstrong wants your answer. Yes or no?"

"I'm trying to explain my position on the matter."

"If yes, continue straight to White Rock. No, pull over at TA-18, at the bottom of the Hill."

Rick tried to laugh it off, but coughed up green slime and nearly had a choking fit. He mashed the gas before unscrewing the white cap on a big bottle of burgundyish brew. Took a long gulp, slowing near TA-18. "You just don't get it, do ya?"

"Turn and you're the one who's going to get it."

"I have rights, Sarkowski."

Rick turned onto an apron and stopped. He faced the agent, who withdrew an official looking envelope from inside his coat, and shoved it toward Rick. The agent produced a mini digital video camera and began reciting, "You are hereby served—"

"Forget it," Rick said, slapping the camera away.

Sarkowski dropped the summons in Rick's lap, opened his door, and hopped out. "Welcome to hell, Adams." He turned and walked toward the waiting Excursion, leaving Rick's passenger door open wide.

Rick seized the letter and threw it out, before fishtailing onto the roadway, closing the door with a loud bang. He headed home.

So many attorneys advertised pro bono services on the WEB. Rick was screened out by the personal assistants of the first five he phoned. When they asked similar questions regarding the heinousness of his potential crime and his fame factor, it became clear Rick was going to have to pay an expensive attorney to represent him. That meant finding a realtor who might be able to sell his house fast. No bank was going to loan him money. The house, the car, the furnishings . . . he was up to his ears in debt. It was eye-opening to find that for a ten percent commission and at a sub-appraisal selling price, his house could be unloaded in a week. He learned that furnishings, if they were tasteful and immaculately maintained, could bring as much as 50 percent of their new retail value.

Next online stop, a cash for auto title company. Rick was told that for a five percent fee, same day cash equaling the NADA Book wholesale value was available if the vehicle was cherry. It would be a couple of thousand in a pinch.

After coughing up a wad of gunk, a generous gulp of medicine left Rick feeling drowsy. He curled up on the living room sofa only to experience the most horrific nightmare of his life. A Dawn of the Dead-like chase, where Renée, Gerry, Sarkowski and other undead clawed and gnawed at him while he tried to escape quicksand on rubbery legs. He woke wondering how such nonsense could seem so real.

Rick lay with his feet extending over the sofa's edge, the way he had when Carmen had held his head in her lap. He imagined her caress. Thoughts of her were his only solace. He considered that groveling and begging for forgiveness was not in the cards. But, if he were to catch a set of The Thunderbirds at Angel's and if the opportunity to speak with Carmen presented itself, he would be game to admit that he had acted selfishly and insensitively and promise never to do that again.

Later that evening at Angel's, when Rick saw Carmen, he suppressed the urge to grab her to him with urgent passion, an embrace of self-preservation. He nursed a single beer as she let her love flow to him from the stage. Why had he not sensed her saving grace before? Perhaps he hadn't needed it so desperately until now. He could tell that she still cared.

Engrossed in Carmen and the music, Rick didn't notice Gerry slink into an adjacent seat, until he said, "She's really pouring it on tonight."

Rick refused to speak. Refused to alter his gaze from the stage.

"If something unfortunate happened to you, I might take care of that myself."

"Don't bet on it," Rick retorted.

"That's up to you. Does she know you're looking for a realtor? A used car dealer? I have some expertise in the latter, you may recall."

Rick flushed. But kept his gaze fixed on the stage.

"I asked you a question."

"No."

"Good. Then she also doesn't know about your new pals from Washington?"

"Don't have any." Rick shifted in his seat. He tried hard to focus on Carmen, but the knot in his stomach grew by the second.

"It's useless to try and deceive me. I thought you knew that." Gerry inched closer. Rick could smell his breath. Feel its warmth when he whispered, "Armstrong can harass you, but he won't kill you. Don't spill your guts to him or any lawyer. Got that?"

Rick expected that Gerry was not in Los Alamos that morning. He must have somehow known about Rick's joy ride in their van earlier in the week. He tried to mollify Gerry, saying, "I told them to go to hell. They haven't bothered me since."

"And the summons?"

Rick froze. He was a rat whose neck was firmly lodged in a trap. He wanted to pinch himself, make certain he wasn't having another nightmare. By rights, this was a nightmare, he just wasn't asleep.

Gerry murmured, "A mistake will cost you your life." Pointing toward the stage, he added, "Could cause her more than a little pain, too. So, go to work tomorrow, keep your mouth shut, and keep GRIT on track."

Rick nodded, still looking straight ahead. He swallowed hard and choked violently. Gerry stood and patted Rick on the shoulder. Rick looked up to see his lumber-size teeth glistening and his chin cavernous with satisfaction. As Gerry went, Rick spotted Walter, sitting alone, watching, his face pushed into his beer.

CHAPTER 74

THE MRC meeting was a joke, starring Rick as principal jester. He spun a tissue of lies that were gobbled up heartily and then tried to escape quickly. Nearly giddy, the attendees shuffled slowly toward the massive exit doors, abuzz with the wonderful news that a fresh tranche of money from DC authorized for GRIT had arrived. Associate Director O'Donnell, the hero, had garnered another 50 megabucks for the Lab to burn.

Rick overheard one of O'Donnell's minions giving a blow by blow of the impassioned plea to save America's nuclear arsenal that his boss had delivered in front of a heavy-weight DC audience. The military and the politicos were impressed sufficiently to lend their full support to GRIT. The underling said now GRIT was the Pentagon's highest priority. Rick's stomach began to ache as though he had a bleeding ulcer. GRIT was going to give a lot of people heartburn. And O'Donnell was at the top of the list.

There were other more quiet discussions, regarding the Lab director's imminent ouster over the most recent security debacle. Operations Security had promulgated few details, but the scuttlebutt was that recently-derived nuclear weapons design parameters, mostly chemical processing specifications, for small, tactical devices—the kind most useful to terrorists endeavoring to sneak a weapon into the country—had been mishandled at the Lab and possibly copied for distribution. Rick heard a whisper that the director might be stepping down voluntarily before the perpetrator was charged. It was speculated that O'Donnell could be bound for the director's office at the beginning of the year. All concurred that he would be a strong, disciplined leader. That was crucial. Especially now, with the Lab back in DC's focus, where it belonged.

CHAPTER 75

THREE A.M. on their first night back together at Rick's place, Carmen pleaded with him to see a doctor. He knew her heart was in the right place, yet he refused, citing how well he'd lived during the many years in which he'd avoided them. Rick finally gave in when Carmen suggested that she had a female doctor friend who would see him first thing in the morning. He took a grand gulp from a big bottle of cough medicine and fell into a horrific stupor until his next coughing onslaught.

The following morning, Carmen drove them northward. Rick jostled around in the Bimmer, feeling nauseous. His stomach was so full of chemicals and alcohol from the cough preparations that he could barely keep down his breakfast. Snow was threatening for the third consecutive day and the air near the Colorado border seemed much colder than that of Santa Fe. More than once Rick asked Carmen where they were headed. Each time she simply reminded him of their agreement. When she pulled up to a dilapidated little cabin and shut off the engine, Rick sighed. When Carmen told him it was Sunflower's place, he nearly reneged.

The cabin was comfortable inside. Rick stood by the fire, trying to quell a chill. The introduction to Sunflower had been relatively painless. She hadn't stared at his swollen eye. Hadn't asked any questions . . . yet. But she and Carmen had crept out of sight after greeting. The pair reappeared and Sunflower offered Rick a steaming drink. He held the warm cup in his hands and drew it toward his nose. It was a dark potion, pungent, smelling of berries.

"Carmen says you have a cough and a fever," Sunflower said. "This'll help quiet the cough."

"What is it?"

"A concoction of juniper berry juice, honey, and wild herbs."

"Just a bad cold," Rick replied, tasting. He took a bigger sip. "Soothing."

"She says you're a doctor who doesn't like doctors."

Rick blushed. "Maybe it's because when I was a kid and went to the doctor, the medicine sometimes made me sicker than the sickness."

"Sit." Sunflower pointed to her easy chair, near the fire. "You look a bit tired." She moved toward Rick; he started. "Heavens, I'm not going to hurt you."

"I just . . . uh . . . ."

Sunflower felt his febrile forehead. Looked closely at his eye. "Did you fall?"

"No."

She stepped back and looked Rick over. "The mind is capable of helping heal the body. If the mind is not ready or willing, I don't think I can help."

"I just don't know if I can believe in this."

"Rick, you've no idea how powerful Sunflower is," Carmen said. "She healed me when I thought I was going to die of pneumonia. And she knows everything."

"Hush, child. It's Rick's decision. He must believe or he can just keep taking that cough syrup crap and spiral down, probably end up in the hospital or worse."

Rick sheepishly asked, "Carmen, did you tell her I take that stuff?"

"No, I didn't. She knows everything. Just try her."

"How did you know?" Rick asked.

"I smell it on your breath."

Rick felt ridiculous. And what was the point in trying this old woman living in a mountain shack, he wondered to himself.

"It's okay," Sunflower continued. "A certain amount of skepticism is healthy."

Seeing no way out of this, Rick tossed a softball. "Where did I pick up the germs that gave me this cold?"

"It's not a cold, Rick. It's infection. Your body is exposed to germs everywhere. Normally, you're strong enough to ward off sickness. But your system has been overwhelmed. It's always on high alert, like battle fatigue. You're worn down. You need to rest your body and more importantly, your mind."

"Rick's work is pressing. But he's got a lot on his mind," Carmen said.

"Death," Sunflower said. "Rick sees death everywhere. It's all around him."

Carmen caught her breath.

Rick choked and coughed up a mouthful of phlegm. He sprang up and headed toward the bathroom.

After flushing the antiquated toilet, Rick splashed his face with water and quietly reprimanded himself, "Get a grip. You're an MIT graduate. Do not be rattled by this Indian hocus-pocus." Cold fusion darted into his mind. Especially the way MIT had given it thumbs down after a nanosecond of consideration. He was ready to get away from this circus. And believed he knew a means to do so.

When Rick returned, Carmen paced anxiously while Sunflower sat composed in her rocking chair. He said, "Since we're here, there is something I've wondered about for a long time."

"Well then," Sunflower replied, "Let's go to my medicine lodge and try to sort it out." Silently, she rose and walked toward the back of the cabin to its rear door.

CHAPTER 76

T HE MEDICINE lodge was little more than a dirt floor hut. Yet, Rick didn't find it dusty. It was more like cozy. Similar to the cabin, only more so. A small fire blazed in the center, apparently prepared by Sunflower some time ago, because the space was warm and surprisingly not the least bit smoky. The trio sat on the ground, facing the fire.

Sunflower said, "Ask me."

Rick rolled his hand in front of his chest. "How does the world work, really? More carefully stated, how does matter interact? There's a theory called the standard model of particle physics."

"Okay," Sunflower replied, wide-eyed.

"It turns out that electrons, protons, and neutrons are composed of constituent quarks and leptons whose flavors are up, down, strange, charm, bottom, and top, in order of ascending mass."

"Whimsical names," Sunflower said, smiling to Carmen, who frowned.

"Quarks have unusual electric charge characteristics, 1/3 and 2/3 of a proton's unit charge, and can compose hadrons depending upon whether the strong or weak force prevails. Now, QCD, quantum chromodynamics, as the name suggests, defines the color forces acting upon the quarks."

Sunflower sat quiet. She appeared amused. Rick could see that Carmen was not. Finally, Carmen said, "Riiick."

He finished his condensed, 20 minute exposition on the 'sm,' as he had begun to call the convoluted standard model. Rick ended his dissertation with a brief discussion of quantum field theory and the impact of gluons on quark and anti-quark color: red, blue and green. At last, he posed a question: "Can this possibly be correct?"

Sunflower smiled warmly. "I don't know anything about all of these fanciful terms you've used. I suppose some really smart and highly educated people spent a lot of time dreaming all of this up."

"I bet you're right about that," he agreed, sitting composed, resting his back and his case. "It was a long shot."

Carmen exhaled in disgust.

"For those fellows who waste time on this theory," Sunflower said, "I might recommend whistling and gardening."

Rick tensed at the denigration. He knew personally some of the brilliant researchers who devised the sm. "I don't believe this theory is a waste at all."

"If what you meant to say is that the pursuit of truth is no waste, I agree. It's just that all of this stuff they've come up with is wrong. I had more faith in the God Particle, they call it, years ago, when I first read about it in the papers. Now, it's in all the books and movies. It's kinda like that nanotechnology. Was supposed to change the world. What's it done for anybody? It's just hype."

Rick had to admit that the overblown claims of nano-everything had been another jab at scientific credibility. But that wasn't at issue here. "On what do you base your assertion that the sm is all wrong?"

"Their theory is just too jumbled up to be right. If they build a bigger machine to test it, like you talked about doing, they'll undoubtedly reveal another layer of more complicated particles and color and ahhh bull. Then they'll look for another bosonhiggsathon thing to explain it all." Sunflower laughed heartily. "The ancients only needed four fundamental quantities to describe the world, and that was too many. The masters need only one."

"And what's that?"

"Breath. Tell your friends if they want to squash down their over-complicated theory, they should study their breath while whistling. Tell them to feel the vibrations. That's all they need."

Carmen sat up to her knees, her head down. She seemed embarrassed for Sunflower. "Okay, Rick. If you're happy, we can leave now." She turned to Sunflower and said, "Sorry to bother you. It's just this Los Alamos kind of mind." She screwed her temple with an index finger.

Rick watched the exchange, but then closed his eyes in contemplation, uncertain whether he'd been had or whether greatness had been uttered. "No, Carmen. What she said is at least partially correct. Remember Ockham's razor?"

"William of Ockham? The English Franciscan friar?"

"Showoff. Tell Sunflower what he said."

"Given two competing theories that produce the same results, the simpler of the two is better."

"Exactly," Rick said. "Rival researchers of the SM have proposed vibrational models to successfully describe matter's interactions. They call it superstring theory."

Sunflower guffawed. "They have imagination all right."

"Both theories agree, except the SM can't handle gravity." Rick went on excitedly, "But if Sunflower is correct, and only one quantity, vibration, is required to simultaneously satisfy the equations of all four forces, then not only is it far simpler but it is the basis for a GUT, far exceeding the SM."

"Wow!" Carmen said.

Sunflower asked, "What is agut, please?"

"The grand unification theory sought by Einstein." Carmen answered.

Sunflower waved off the idea. Rick had to access the very marrow of her sage remarks. "Gardening? You talked about gardening. I don't get the connection. Do you believe that gravitons can be observed terrestrially?"

"I just thought those researchers might try to relax. They must be really stressed, trying to be so creative and continually demonstrating their brilliance. They need some rest, too."

Rick laughed, but was overcome by a terrible choking spell. His face reddened as his chest rumbled and he fought for air in the claustrophobic lodge.

Sunflower produced a leather pouch filled with what looked to Rick like blue cornmeal. She singed it, little by little over the open fire, chanting all the while. The unmistakable scent of jalapeños filled the space. She poured the smoking meal into a small bowl and placed it up to Rick's nostrils. He inhaled. His cough subsided.

Sunflower said, "Breathe deeper. Take this into your spirit." She added, "You should stay away from those goopy syrups and pills, too. They won't do you any good. May do you some harm."

Rick nodded, continuing to ingest the healing smolder.

Sunflower eyed him sympathetically as she filled his coat pockets with sanctified cornmeal. Rick looked puzzled.

She said, "This is for healing and protection from evil."

Rick nodded acquiescence. He understood that he was a sick man. And death was all around him. But he was far from certain that anything—much less cornmeal—could protect him from Gerry.

CHAPTER 77

GERRY tugged a massive 50 pound dumbbell, gleaning bursts of a conversation delivered to his command center via satellite-linked snooper. He scowled into the full length mirror in front of him. His skin appeared to be an expandable sheath, constraining bone and bulging muscle, desperately wanting to break free.

Although Gerry knew none of the details of Rick's detention by the FBI, he was certain that Burton, in his capacity as Lab security Czar, would be contacted by the Bureau, seeking his help in their investigation. His continual monitoring of Burton's office finally was paying off. He began another set of 20 reps and listened intently.

Armstrong said, "I've had a little chat with your Dr. Adams."

"What did he say?"

"Sorry, Gavin, I cannot release that information. Besides, the operative element of this, from your perspective, is that Adams, who never should've been allowed to work here in the first place, is going to sweat a little."

"The security of the Laboratory is within my purview. I have a right and a need to know about covert operations executed inside my Laboratory." Burton paused. "Every day that passes, the Lab's security, for which I am ultimately responsible, is jeopardized."

Gerry recognized that Burton's consternation was real; only the reason had been perverted.

"Don't you worry about that," Armstrong replied. "I expect this to bear fruit quickly. He's going to lead us just where we want to go very soon. And if not, he's going to be jammed down the deepest, darkest rat hole—one that would make Saddam's spider crack look like a luxury suite—until he tells me what I want to know."

"But, uh, I have a great deal of experience with all kinds of operations," Burton said. "If I understood your objective and how much info you have to work with, I assure you we would be a powerful team."

Gerry was impressed by Burton's sincere delivery.

"I appreciate your attitude. These government labs need more security-wise hounds like you, Gavin."

"So what's the plan?"

"Uh-uh. This is strictly Bureau. Keep your hands off or you'll find yourself on the outside looking in. Clear?"

"Crystal."

"Got to go, Gavin. We'll be in touch."

Gerry's 50 pound dumb-bell hit the padded floor with a clunk. He scoffed into the mirror, "Clear? Crystal." He considered the American intelligence community a bunch of oxymorons, Armstrong and Burton included.

Burton had done the right thing, Gerry admitted to himself. Very soon, once it all came tumbling down, Burton would be subjected to scrutiny before ascending the Lab's directorship. No need to instigate a dustup with the Feds. Besides, all they could do was make Adams's life miserable, not such a grim prospect. And by the time he was ready to crack, Gerry would have taken care of him quietly.

Besides, Gerry understood that Rick hardly knew anything worth telling about anyone else anyway. Maybe the pervert Walter, but who cared. Rick just needed to keep it together a while longer. All was well: the director was already sunk and O'Donnell had a $150 million anchor wrapped around his neck. Gerry resolved to relieve some pressure from Rick, without letting him off the hook entirely. It would be like telling someone he'd won the lottery, just before pushing him in front of a bus.

CHAPTER 78

RICK sat at the little conference table in Arthur's office. It was the same table where Fred, Bruno, Arthur, and he had sat fewer than six months earlier, at Rick's interview. The slight nervousness he felt then was nothing in comparison to the heart pounding distress he felt now.

"Richard, I've some bad news for you," Arthur said. "Your clearance has been revoked, pending an investigation into your alleged security infractions."

"But I thought that was being handled," Rick replied. "It was all a mistake."

"Apparently this is coming from DC. I'm confident it all will work out in your favor." Making eye contact with Rick for the first time, he said, "Believe me when I say, I'm behind you a 110 percent."

Rick was dazed. "What does this mean?"

Arthur exhaled forcefully and returned his gaze to the dull, scuffed table top. "You're off GRIT, Rick. One of the new staff that we're adding to the project, thanks to the recent budget increase, will assume your responsibility. I don't believe you'll be allowed to brief her on your progress."

Rick's head drooped. "Is there no other way? Can't you do something?"

"I don't like it either. But I have no alternative," Arthur said, eyeing the ceiling. "I love this Lab, but have never particularly cared for the way it conducts business."

"So, that's it?"

"Unfortunately, no." Arthur's eyes hit the table.

Rick felt woozy from the rush of dread.

"They're garnishing your wages, pending an investigation of your travel disbursements."

"I've only been on one friggin' trip."

"I'm sorry. It's straight from the top. The review probably won't take very long. They'll see everything is copasetic, I'm sure."

"Not if Armstrong has his way," Rick mumbled to himself.

"Pardon?"

"Nothing. What do I do?"

"Margie'll collect your badge by the end of the day. Your classified partition computer access has already been denied. For the time being, you can sit in Building 87, just outside the fence."

Arthur fell silent, as though in a trance. Rick assumed the meeting was over. He dashed from the office down the hall, his brain afire. "Outside the fence," burned in his ears. He was a pariah. Rick picked up his case, not bothering to log out of his computer, and flew from the building.

In his hierarchy of needs, cash was king. Cash for a lawyer, a plane ticket, maybe a hit man. Soon Rick stood in front of a bank teller, requesting a tally of his available cash. He knew the news was bad when a well-dressed woman approached the window and asked that he follow her to her office. Rather than create a scene about his frozen assets, which he knew would avail nothing other than getting him into jail sooner, Rick headed down the Hill. After a brief stop at home, where he tore through a yet-unpacked box marked, 'IMPORTANT' and his home safe, he was at a Cerrillos Road pawnshop with a small treasure stash. A couple of class rings, an old wrist watch in need of repair, and his portable music player. He netted ten percent of their value.

The small wad of cash still in hand, Rick spied a nearby gun case. The cheapest was a scratched 9 mm with a nasty gash across the barrel. Looking at the cracked handle, he assumed it'd probably been used to open up someone's head. Rick recognized that he had dangerous enemies from whom protection was paramount. And if the enemy got the worst end of the deal that might not be so bad. But, he'd always been a lover not a fighter, and certainly not a killer.

There had to be a better way than violence, he thought, gingerly pressing his still-swollen eye socket. He cast a lingering glance at the firearm and exited the shop.

A dark, dismal day. Frigid north wind howled outside the dilapidated shop. Rick buttoned his coat before mounting the Bimmer. Distracted, he withdrew his key. And then, from out of nowhere, a gunshot resounded. He hit the floorboard, his heart hammering. He waited. Nothing. Rick raised his head slowly and saw a duo of teenagers bent over a vintage Pontiac lowrider. The vehicle backfired again. Rick paused for an instant, thinking, what if? He re-entered the shop and traded his cash for the pistol and 100 rounds of ammo. Returning to his vehicle, he considered what good the cash would do him dead.

CHAPTER 79

EXHAUSTED, lying on the sofa in his lonely living room, Rick stared intently at the roaring fire in the fireplace. He quaked and pulled the colorful Chief Joseph blanket up to his chin. Although his body was lethargic, his mind was hyperactive. No more obsessing about selling the house and furnishings, the suv. He could stay in a motel or with Carmen until this mess blew over. And the Toyota was drivable. Thank heaven he hadn't sold it. Everything else about his situation seemed insoluble. Like how to save himself once Gerry found out about his dismissal from GRIT. How did Gerry know everything that happened? How Sunflower knew the stuff she did wasn't far behind, but at least that wasn't life threatening.

Chewing the fact that no one was present when Sarkowski and he went at it over the summons in the Bimmer, Rick smacked his head. What an idiot, he fumed all the way to be bedroom, where a pile of potential pawn junk that didn't make the cut confronted him. He found the AllTrac's keys in the back of his underwear drawer. Its plain key-head possessed no plastic cover, no fancy logo, and no electronic functionality, like a microphone, hidden camera, or both. Rick attached it to his fancy Bimmer key fob. He felt bad for having dismissed the reliable, if not rust eaten, vehicle. There was yet another lesson for him. He resolved to be smarter, should he live much longer.

Piling his things back into a box, a rattle piqued Rick's curiosity. He delved deep into the rat's nest of CDs, wires, folders, tee shirts and withdrew a vial of pills. Antidepressants he'd confiscated from Desiree a year earlier, after her talk of suicide. He recognized that he was already in enough trouble, partially because of substance abuse. He didn't want to give up any more intellectual or psychological ground to drugs. But maybe one of these would give him some badly needed running room. Maybe a decent nap. He popped the cap and then a pill.

Back on the sofa, covered toe to throat, sleep came easily. But with a price. Rick was back in his childhood neighborhood, running, running, running. It's so far. I've got to . . . got to get it. His lungs were ablaze and his legs cramped. The scene at the baseball diamond, when he was only eleven years old, inflamed his brain.

In the dream he was always completely out of breath from an asthma attack, but would run with all of his strength to catch a fly ball. It always hit the ground just as he fell, face first. He could hear screaming from the sidelines, "Get up! Get the ball! Rick, get up!" He couldn't move. Lay prone, tasting blood from his smashed nose that dripped onto his lips as he gasped for air. The cries faded into the background as Rick spiraled downward into a pit of darkness.

"Get up! Get up!" they yelled when, coughing and groggy, Rick woke, his shirt drenched with perspiration. He tried to relax, to calm his nerves and clenched bronchia. No use. The fire in the fireplace had smoldered and the atmosphere was thick with black smoke. Rick couldn't coax a breath of life-saving air into his lungs. He rolled from the sofa, hitting the floor hard. He wondered where was Carmen, Desiree, his mother . . . anyone. He was dying alone. No one was there to care for or about him. Rick considered that he'd borne disgraces and affronts that would turn a typical man to seclusion, just to ennsure companionship. Despite that, here he was, dying unloved, unwanted, and completely unworthy.

Rick summoned his strength and crawled to the lower window. He struggled with the latch. Finally, he managed to crack it open. The frigid air slapped his face, shocking his constricted bronchia. He angled his lips to the crack; gasped for air. After a few breaths, he collapsed to the floor. Lay still, feeling his pulse returning to normal.

THE FOLLOWING morning, a half-pot of coffee downed and another pill popped, Rick determined to be dumb like a fox and proceed to work as though all were well. He and Carmen would perform a little skit to keep Gerry off his back for a few days. Small, yet important, steps for staying alive.

Searching his coat for the throat lozenges he'd purchased, he found only a gun, ammo, and singed jalapeño cornmeal. Deciding to test fire the pistol, he loaded a single round into the chamber and stepped out onto the back balcony. He raised his arm skyward, in the general direction of a pinion wood. His neighbor's handyman, carrying a bundle of trash, tromped by. The man looked up and Rick, feigning a yawn, hid the weapon behind his head with one hand and waved with the other. Rick stuffed the gun in his pocket, planning to test it later. Back in his bedroom, he stashed the pistol and ammo in the lower drawer of his bedside table, good company for his special cell phone. And handy, just in case.

CHAPTER 80

EMBRACING CARMEN in Angel's parking lot was Rick's first restful moment of the day. He kissed her passionately before leveling his eyes on her. He explained the little skit he wanted to enact in his vehicle. Her eyes told him she thought it was mindless. And she was worried. His told her it was essential.

"How was work today?" Carmen asked, her voice wooden.

"Just great."

"Did you solve any differential equations?"

"Nope, but I made good progress on a challenging problem. That's when I'm happiest, I find."

Carmen shook her head, not wanting to continue.

Rick waved her off and looked dubious, pointing surreptitiously to the car key, using his right pinky. He wasn't sure, but hoped the smart key couldn't feed video from the tiny LED that acted as a flashlight. He was convinced the key was a sensitive audio transmitter, maybe more.

"I suppose this is a long term project, huh?" Carmen said.

"I'm gonna keep it going as long as I can. It's interesting."

"That's great."

Rick noticed her expression of relief as they entered the El Matador Apartments.

"Well, here we are," she said, unlocking her door as they rolled to a stop. "See you later."

"Yeah. I'll try to make it for the second set."

Once out of the vehicle, Carmen made a monster face at him.

When Gerry reviewed the conversation, he had to laugh. Why was Adams putting it on so thick for Carmen, he wondered? Gerry chose the Amsterdam connection to call Rick's special cell phone; just to reassure him a little. The phone rang and rang. He didn't want to waste more time in Angel's, stinking barroom that it was, but it was important to interact with Rick. Gerry believed that he needed to gauge his mindset and ensure that Rick was not too close to the edge.

Later that evening, Angel's crowd was sparse. Gerry waited in the back of the lot for Rick to arrive and settle in before entering and taking a seat next to him. Expressionless, Gerry observed Rick, who ignored his presence. Between songs, Gerry asked, "Still under the weather?"

Silence.

Gerry tried again. "Everything okay?"

"Ducky."

"You must have a really bad cold."

"I'm fine."

Carmen looked over. Gerry acknowledged her stare with a small wave. In an elevated voice, he said to Rick, "I have some cold remedy in my vehicle. Come on. I'll give you some."

"No thanks."

"It's good stuff, Rick. Come try it . . . now," Gerry said, standing.

He moved aside, allowing Rick to take the lead toward the back door. Rick shuffled along, dragging himself out of the building and into the parking lot.

"What more do you want?" Rick protested. "I'm keeping GRIT alive."

"Shut up," Gerry whispered. Once at his SUV, he growled, "Get in."

Gerry watched Rick slowly round the back bumper. He hacked, reaching for the door handle, and paused to spit out a wad of gunk. Out of nowhere a dusty old Suburban pulled up beside him.

Lowering his window, Walter said, "Rick, glad I caught you."

Gerry was startled. He said, "We're busy."

"Hello, Gerry. Sorry to interrupt, but I have a question for Rick."

Gerry's expression turned stony.

Walter said, "Gerry, this is important Lab business." He winked. "Rick, get in."

"Okay," Rick said, opening Gerry's passenger door.

"Not there, Rick, here," Walter said, kicking open his passenger's door. "Gerry'll understand."

Gerry glared at Rick, who froze.

"Tell 'im it's okay. This won't take long," Walter croaked.

Alarms sounded in Gerry's head. Was something wrong? He thought it best to play along, for now. "I'm sure this is important, Rick." Glancing at Walter, Gerry added, "Better be."

Walter revved the engine, waved goodbye to Gerry, who, using his thumb and forefinger, pointed a pretend pistol at him.

RICK WAS BARELY cognizant as Walter and he bumped along toward the street when a junker blocked the lot's exit. Rick recognized the jalopy first and then its driver. Chico sat admiring a Crocodile Dundee-size hunting knife that glinted in the Suburban's headlights.

Only a car's length away, now, Chico pointed his knife and shouted, "I wanna talk to you, pussy."

To Rick's surprise, Walter said, "Chico, we don't want no trouble."

"The other pussy," Chico said, before laughing hysterically.

Thinking this was *déjà vu redux*, Rick asked Walter, "How do you know these people? That guy's a crazy drug dealer." Walter's sheepish expression was no comfort.

Chico bolted from the lowrider and brandishing the knife approached Rick's door. He opened it slurring, "Where your big buddy? Your cop friend?" He grabbed Rick's shirt and thrust the knife to his throat.

Rick held his breath. Looking into Chico's face, he found no mercy. Suddenly, Chico's head snapped back and his eyes widened with surprise. Rick heard Gerry say, "¿Perdon, tu eras un puto?" Chico's head slammed against the door jamb. When Gerry released his hair, Chico slumped to the ground like a burst balloon.

Rick saw Walter point to the lowrider, still blocking the exit. Gerry turned and strode toward the jalopy.

"You fucker. I kill you!" Chico screamed, scrambling up, waving the knife.

Gerry said, "¿Quieres chupar mi verga? Entonces, vengas conmigo." He ran behind the lowrider into an adjacent alley. Chico followed in hot pursuit.

Walter poked his head out of his open window and shouted, "You'd better drive down that alley and help him. Your amigo's in some deep shit."

The center passenger slipped behind the El Camino's steering wheel. They drove away, the rust bucket wheezing and lurching as it went.

Walter shook his head and exited the lot.

Rick felt nothing, his senses dull from constant threats and agitation. He slumped against the dirty door and closed his eyes, not caring where they were going or what would befall him once they arrived.

CHAPTER 81

THE RAT-INFESTED trailer 100 meters outside of the security fence at TA-38 was Rick's newest home. Those 100 meters were the shortest infinite distance he'd ever considered. Maybe this was really semi-infinitude, something that in the past he had deemed only a mathematical construct. At least the small window of his new office, which was absent a lockable door and classified safe, looked out toward mature ponderosa pines. Unfortunately, the exterior of the window was sufficiently dirty that even after Rick cleaned the interior, the pine needles were an odd green-brown.

Rick had spent little time contemplating the previous night's unusual interactions with Gerry and Walter, not to mention Chico. Walter had related little during their brief rideabout; neither had he asked many questions. He seemed to understand Rick's circumstances: sitting on an anvil looking up at a descending sledge hammer. He hadn't even so much as mentioned Gerry's intervention in the standoff. Although Rick hadn't really feared for his life, Gerry's response made it clear that he was determined to retain control of everything.

Most bizarre was Walter's encouraging, nearly fatherly tone. Not a real father, like Rick's absentee dad, but an ideal father, caring and supportive. He could still hear Walter asking, "You making it okay?" And he was sincere when he said, "Keep your chin up, and your lip buttoned." An admonishment not to betray Gerry or the Feynman friends to the Feds, Rick assumed. At his new, old desk, doodling on a notepad, gritty from the trailer's dust-laden air, Rick was bugged by the oddest thing. Whose hide was Walter saving? His own, Rick's, or someone else's?

Days inched by. Rick sat lifeless in his office, squirming for hours at a stretch in the lumpy seat of his worn Steelcase chair. Hacking and coughing had replaced computing and jogging. The single computer occupying his desk was a vintage IBM clone without access to the classified computing partition. No one visited. His phone sat silent, until on Thursday afternoon Rick received a call from his excited real estate agent. There was an offer on his house and a fraction of its contents. A rush deal for cash. An opera diva wanted to be in during the following week to prepare for the upcoming season. He would need to decide whether to sell by the close of business.

Rick considered logging on to check his unclassified e-mail, but instead his face fell into his cupped hands. His throat was raw and his head pounded. Why bother, he thought? Just get out of here. Who of the ordained of XP-12, officing inside the fence, would know and who of my new, internet surfing trailer mates—mostly outcasts from various groups, just like me—would care. He'd decided to call the real estate agent from home and decline the offer, which was nearly $40k below loan appraisal in a neighborhood where property values had held fairly steady, even in recent years.

Outside, Rick was greeted by brilliant sunshine. His spirits rose. The first easy breath of the day filled his lungs with crisp winter air. It was bracing. Crossing the lot, he shed his aches and pains, enabled by a feeling of guarded optimism. He might make it after all. As he neared his Bimmer, a gleaming black Excursion SUV interceded, driven by Mutt, or was he Jeff? Rick's face fell when Sarkowski burst forth from the passenger's door, holding a soiled summons. The one Rick had tossed out of his window.

"Mr. Adams," he intoned, "although not required by law, I am hereby reserving you with this court order to appear in Albuquerque for questioning by the Federal Bureau of Investigation. Failure to appear could result in a warrant for your arrest and additional charges being levied against you."

Rick snatched the envelope, stared mindlessly at it, and then tossed it in the floorboard. They must really want me to show up, he thought, heading for home. If they consider me valuable enough, maybe there's a chance to strike a deal with them. Sooner or later Gerry has to be stopped. Perhaps they can do it. Rick's bronchia relaxed when he thought maybe I'm in the driver's seat now.

Entering Pojoaque, Rick slowed. He admired the cloudless sky, above the well-worn hilltops. Old country. Infertile. Flashing lights dominated his rearview. Although it was not a marked vehicle, the grill looked like a 60's muscle car. Rick pulled toward the roadside to allow it to pass. Thank God, I wasn't speeding, he thought. But surprisingly, it followed him, away from the whir of traffic. Rick cupped his hand over his nose, trying to smell his breath for traces of alcohol from the cough syrup. He took the bottle from his coat pocket and placed it prominently in the passenger's seat.

"Afternoon, Rick," R. B. said.

"Chief. Are you clearing the carbon from the cylinders of your mean machine?"

"I'm headed up to Santa Fe. But turns out, contacting you is on my to-do list."

"I'm afraid I still can't help you with the jet comparison." Rick smiled.

"Maybe there's something else that you can help me with." The Chief raised his sunglasses and locked his small, steady eyes onto Rick's. "You see, Chico ostensibly killed himself the other night."

Rick suppressed a cough. "Sorry to hear that."

"So, you were acquainted with him."

"Not really. I think Carmen knew him."

"I believe that Officer Gomez cited Chico for speeding and reckless driving, along this same stretch of road, the night you spoke at the offenders' meeting."

Rick shrugged.

"Gomez said he had seen you conversing with Chico and his posse just prior to that incident."

Rick hacked up a slimy mass and held up his hand to R. B., who regarded him through animated eyes. Rick reached toward the passenger's floorboard to retrieve a used tissue. He scooted the summons up under the seat and then spit the gunk out.

The Chief narrowed his eyes, awaiting Rick's response.

"Ah . . . well, I recall they may've tried to help Carmen. Her SUV was flooded. I ended up giving her a ride."

"How was that?" The Chief asked, grinning full-face.

Rick blushed.

"Uh-huh." The Chief continued, his face now as sober as a judge. "Well, foul play is not out of the question. The posse said that Chico was chasing somebody down the alley. Apparently fell on a big-ass knife he'd been known to carry in his vehicle. Took it right through the heart." R. B. nodded thoughtfully.

Rick erupted again. He grabbed the cough syrup bottle and took a gulp. His watery eyes itched. Rick blinked to quell his discomfort.

"Somethin' the matter?"

Rick wiped residue from his chin onto his shirt's sleeve. "Bad head cold."

"Hell of a wound," R. B. said, gazing into the distance. "Clean through the breast plate. Pierced the heart. I mean, the point literally exited his back. There was a burr on the butt of the handle where it could have hit the ground." The Chief drilled Rick's eyes again, saying, "Funny thing, the posse agreed that you were a witness. They said, Chico had it in for you. But out of nowhere this, uh, Terminator-like character showed up and saved you ass."

Rick wrinkled his forehead and nodded, trying to evince perplexity.

"He was the one Chico was chasing." R. B. hesitated before asking, "Now, what would you know about a Terminator kinda fellow?"

Rick looked down, wondering if R. B. was stringing him along, awaiting a mistake. He hedged, "Maybe they watch too much TV?"

"Usually they're not too creative. And they all couldn't be coached to tell the same lie if their lives depended on it. That's what made this story strange." R.B. eyed the ground and spit, before reengaging with Rick. "I've seen my share of knife victims. Some of them tough hombres. But I've never seen the man that could stab a thick knife blade right through you."

Rick gripped the wheel tightly, steadying his trembling hands, and said, "I was, uh, at Angel's the other night. But left early with a friend from the Lab. I can give you his contact info."

"Let me see how this sets with me next week. I may give you a call. Just to keep you clean, of course." R. B. adjusted his hat and softened his expression.

"Rick, if I was tangled up with a fictitious person like we're talking about, I'd get the hell outta Dodge before I ended up like Chico, or worse."

Rick squelched a hack, or nerves-induced tremor. "Thanks, R. B."

"You look like a guy who could use some rest. Maybe you should give Angel's and Carmen a night off."

"More good advice."

At home, Rick read the summons. He was required to appear in Albuquerque on the following Tuesday morning. So far, the Feds were playing it just like the Lee case: they gathered evidence against Rick; had off-the-record meetings with him; tried to enlist Rick to work for them; and now, the official appearance in Albuquerque. In Lee's case, that led to a lengthy incarceration—that began immediately when he was charged at the appearance— It was followed by an extraordinarily expensive legal battle. And if they didn't incarcerate Rick, what then?

Rick called the realtor and okayed the deal. Then he arranged to pick up a rental moving truck the following morning. He and a day laborer could do the heavy lifting themselves over the weekend. He had to conserve every cent of his paltry proceeds.

CHAPTER 82

S AM SAT in his home office desk chair, teacup and saucer in hand. For a while, he'd tried unsuccessfully to lose himself in Wallenberg's decades-old exploits. Rick's conspicuous absence at the MRC meeting and the sensational scuttlebutt about him were disturbing. Sam put down the drink and paced the hall toward Reba's music room. Stood in the doorway for an instant, observing her, sitting in her chair bent over a choral composition. He asked, "How's it going, dear?"

"Quite well."

Her face registered surprise at his venturing into her evening domain. Sam smiled warmly, stepping into the small room.

Reba asked, "How are things for you?"

"Ohhh, I'm a bit restless."

"I'm sorry. Is there a reason?"

"I attended an upsetting meeting today."

Reba sat up straight. "Did you say or do something wrong?"

"No, I didn't say anything, in fact."

"Well then, that's not so bad, is it? She relaxed her posture. "I'm certain that everything'll be resolved." Nonchalant, she added, "Just continue to be a noble observer."

"Rick has lost his clearance and his job," Sam blurted.

"Uh-huh. Then I suppose there are things that you haven't told me about him." She paused before adding, "And you brought him into our home. I even agreed to give Carmen vocal lessons."

"No, dear. You invited Rick and Carmen into our home."

"I stand corrected."

"I'm sorry," Sam said, waving his hands. "It's just the way he was demonized for everything from delaying the specification of a certain subsystem, for which he was primarily responsible, to the cost increase of primetime computing, in which he was uninvolved."

Silence.

Sam walked to Reba and propped himself heavily on the arm of her padded chair. His voice was solemn. "He's caught in a web. And I do not believe it was by accident."

"You've said there's much mobility at the Lab. He'll find a job in another group and probably have his clearance reinstated. You've told me how it goes for people who run afoul of procedures and protocols. The Lab is very forgiving."

Sam sat up. He stepped away from Reba. He'd never told her the particulars of the events in Cambridge decades ago, in part because of her paranoid reaction to hearing the overview. He decided to go slowly. "It won't be that easy for him. I'm convinced it was the work of you-know-who."

Reba's eyes widened. "Don't say that. Don't even think it." She faced Sam directly and asked in a tremulous voice, "Why would you jump to such an outlandish conclusion? Because Rick has struck some unusually warm chord in your too-big heart?"

"That would be incorrect."

Reba's eyes widened. "What are you not telling me?"

Sam tried to constrain his waxing emotions. Through clenched teeth he said, "I'm not telling you that I sat as dumb as a mute, which I did, while those bastards berated Rick and delighted in soiling his name, not knowing a wit of his personal risk or of the tragedy about to befall him." Sam shook his head. "Shameful *shadenfraude*."

"But you've never spoken of your colleagues as vengeful or hateful."

"It's because the project is so important. The highest national profile project the Lab has administered in decades. Bringing in an outsider to perform one of the most critical analyses, an outsider with no direct experience in the system we're building, always perplexed them. Galled them."

"Does sound strange."

"Yes. I, too, found Rick's hire strange. Now I understand the wicked selection criteria and it makes me sick."

"I'm really sorry, darling. But it's out of your hands." Reba's expression softened. She stroked Sam's hand. "There's simply nothing you can do, even though you want to help."

Sam nodded. A childhood scene scrolled through his mind. Sitting on the floor of his family's tenement, Sam pretended to play. He silently watched his father writhe under the stern gaze of Uncle George. Blameless, yet helpless to extricate himself from George's austere judgment and derision. Sam flashed forward to his father's death and George's scorn for Sam's helpless mother, who had to yield her only son to him. Sam questioned why the good at heart always seem so helpless? And why he was always incapable of helping them?

Reba rolled her hands nervously. "Sam, you know anything you do will jeopardize everything, including the lives of our family." She took Sam's hand in both of hers. Squeezed it tight. "Think of the twins."

"You're right," he said softly. And perhaps she was— "Maybe it's illogical to believe that one person can make a difference to the ill fate of another."

"Be thankful that our world is stable and has no apparent reason to change. That's all we can hope."

"I suppose I can give him a call." Sam's back ached. Enervated, he could hardly muster the strength to move. "Offer some moral support, at least." He turned to go.

"Sam," Reba said, her tone firm.

He stood still.

"Promise me that a call is all."

He gave her his back, nodding.

"I need to hear you say it."

"Yes, dear."

Alone in his office, Sam called Rick at home. No answer. No answering machine. It occurred to him that a chance meeting might be better for a casual conversation anyway. At least he'd tried. Peering down at a glossy page, Sam recoiled. His hero stared back into his eyes, disdaining and accusing.

With a shiver, Sam had a distinct vision of Hannah tumbling headlong into the blackness of the Charles River as he stood idly by.

CHAPTER 83

RICK sat at his dining table, nervously tallying his proceeds. Equity in the house—ha!, some furniture, and the Bimmer. He relived the painful hour he spent at Fa$t Buck$ earlier in the day. The fast talking, illustrated man-looking proprietor had paid him peanuts for the Bimmer. And then he'd driven Rick home in a Mercedes. All in, the money might cover a good lawyer's retainer, but there was no way that he could purchase top-notch representation for just thousands.

Nothing to do now but pack. Well, pack, clean, and store. Exhausting labor. Rick stood and was immediately doubled over with a hacking attack. Emptying his big bottle of cough syrup, he decided to go and buy more. While out, he could go into town and hire a day worker to drive the moving truck home as well as help load it. Rick pulled the All-Track's key from his pocket. Abused and tarnished, it was perfect for him.

On the way to town, Rick purchased a magnum bottle of old cough syrup at a low-down convenience store on East Palace Avenue. Dusty shelves. Dubious merchandise. A single bottle of cough suppressant was for sale. Unboxed, the bottle's bleached label was hardly readable. Its blue-black contents were smelly and gunky. He examined the expiration date and then took a big slug, thinking, just like me, expired six months ago—

A helper secured for the weekend, Rick headed straight to Blake's eatery, deluding himself that a couple of green chili cheese burgers and fries might help settle his queasy, although nearly empty, stomach. At least it'd be cheap.

As soon as he arrived home, Rick's guts rebelled against the bad medicine and spicy food. After expelling both, he assumed the fetal position on the floor and fell into tortured sleep, albeit a different fitful flavor. Absent the usual monstrous cast—Gerry alive and menacing, Renée dead and accusing—Rick was completely alone. Death lingered all about him. As he'd secretly feared since his mother's passing, during his junior year at Iowa State, he was dying without even a pet dog to mourn his passing. The fanatical fear of being alone had provoked many bad choices and hopeless romantic escapades. Truth be told, Desiree was simply the latest.

Waking early, before six a.m., was a blessing. Rick rose cold and achy. He plodded toward the kitchen, thinking he could hang meat in the house. Started a pot of coffee and then closed the mudroom door, which had been open all night. Stretching his already kinked back, he knew grueling tasks lay ahead.

AFTER DAYS of moving struggle, on Monday afternoon Rick dragged himself through the cavernous house for a final walk through. He found a small box that might hold the last of his remaining personal articles. Trudged into the bedroom and dropped the box onto the floor beside his bed. He turned to see muddy footprints on the cream color wool Berber carpeting. Everything I touch, I ruin. He wilted onto the floor and removed the soiled shoes.

Radiant heat combated the chill of the bedroom. Rick considered throwing himself chest down onto the floor to rest, but he was overheating as it was. Besides, he wouldn't have the energy to get up. Instead he opened the lower compartment of the nightstand in front of him to clear it. He found the photograph of Desiree and himself. Placed it atop the nightstand, where it had been during his first hopeful months in his new house. In the back of the drawer lay the 9 mm pistol, ammo, and his special cell phone. Rick withdrew the articles and boxed the ammo. He gripped the pistol tightly.

The gun's steel cooled his hand. Rick rubbed the barrel on his face, before examining the weapon, illuminated by shadowy moonlight entering from a partially open window. The pistol seemed to glow with a feathery bluish grey aura. A glance at his special phone caused his gut to wrench. Rick dropped the gun. Made his way to the window where he opened it fully. Arctic air filled the curtains like clipper ship sails. He exposed his congested chest with shivering relief. In a crystalline instant, Rick recognized that he was a failure; he was lost; and he was doomed. *Is my life really worth this?*

CHAPTER 84

CARMEN hastened across the pothole-laden parking lot of the El Matador apartments to her vehicle. The starter ground. Eyeing her watch, she angrily turned the key once more. The engine coughed; gas fumes filled the cabin. She must not be late for her first vocal lesson. Reba's voice rang in her ears, "five p.m., sharp." No time for obsessing, she called T'Bird at home. He seemed to be there more than ever before. She wondered if he was hiding a new live-in flame. Probably not. That would be typical of the old T'Bird. She couldn't help missing the good old T'Bird.

Moments later, the new, good old T'Bird arrived in his Thunderbird to rescue her. Driving north on 284 toward White Rock, he was quiet. Carmen realized the absence of music- or romance-related banter between them was an integral part of their transforming friendship. T'Bird's changes were momentous. She felt herself changing, too. When they were both finished growing up—or whatever this was—Carmen hoped they would still be friends.

Unwilling to sit in silence, she asked, "Okay, Big Man, what's new with you?"

"Nothing really."

"No, I mean *really* what's new with you?"

He shot her a look.

"Yeah, I know," she said. "I wouldn't understand."

Minutes later, they loped up to Sam and Reba's home. Exiting the car, Carmen said, "I'll call when I'm done." She smacked the crisp air. Blew the kiss T'Bird's way.

Carmen plodded toward the front door. She turned to wave, but the car's little round tail lights faced her. She knocked on the door, thinking that often life really was a matter of timing.

Sam opened the door. "Come in. It's freezing out there."

"Thanks." Rubbing her ungloved hands briskly, Carmen asked, "How are you?"

"Just fine. And you?"

His eyes belied his reply. Carmen hugged Sam's neck as if he were her grandfather. "I'm a bit concerned, too."

Sam patted Carmen's back and then removed her coat, asking, "How is he?"

"Really sick. Should be in bed instead of working day and night all weekend, moving out of his house." She couldn't control the twitching of her eyes, but managed not to cry.

"Why is that?" Sam asked, his eyes wide. "I'd no idea he was contemplating selling."

"It's all been a whirlwind. His trouble at the Lab. A summons of some sort."

"By whom?" Sam adjusted his glasses. "For what?" He readjusted them.

"Won't talk much to me about it. He doesn't want to *worry* me." Carmen's stomach did a flip, considering how worried she knew she ought to be.

Sam's brow creased deeply. Sotto voce, he asked, "For when?"

"In Albuquerque, tomorrow. That's why he's working himself to a pulp trying to get out of the house tonight."

"Is there a number where he can be reached? I've called his home several times without avail."

"He never carries a cell. And the house phone is probably packed away. Who knows? He calls me when he can."

"The house is number 13 on Wild Flower, isn't it?"

"Yes. Unfortunately, he's working to the exclusion of all else." She thought how much she missed the all else.

Carmen watched Sam shifting his weight from one foot to the other. He gazed at the distance; seemed to be searching for the right words. Finally, he asked, "Is he, uh, handling all of this all right?"

"On the exterior, he just seems exhausted. But I'm afraid that inside, it's worse. He needs to see a doctor. But he hates them." A tear welled in Carmen's eye. She wiped it with her shirt sleeve, like a little girl. She whispered, "I'm afraid for him."

Sam froze.

"Hello, Carmen," Reba said, entering. "Shall we begin? There's a lot of work to do this evening."

Proceeding down the hall in Reba's wake, Carmen turned to smile at Sam. She observed that he was removing a coat from the closet where he'd just stored hers.

CHAPTER 85

THE PALLID moon partially illuminated Rick's bedroom through windows and skylights that had previously charmed him. Now, he was unmoved. Life had lost its luster. He made his way to the closet where jeans and a sweater hung in the otherwise bare space. The image of a human scarecrow morbidly flashed through his mind. The clothes placed on his bed, he headed for the bathroom, determined to shave and clean himself. He would present the worthiest man he could conjure to Carmen on his first night of official moochdom at her apartment.

Once in the shower, the tepid water felt blistering. He closed the hot water tap completely. His body was an engine, running too hot. He intended to cool it down by lingering under the icy jets. Immobile, his eyes shut. His mind, dead to the world at last.

Rick's eyes popped open wide. A supernatural calm swept over him. He turned off the shower and stepped around the nautilus shape to reach for a towel. All packed. He walked easily into the bedroom and took up the Pendleton blanket from his bed. He gazed at the photo on the nightstand. In an instant of superlucidity, Rick sunk to his knees; reached for the pistol.

He huddled naked and shivering on the bedroom floor. Moonlight tinged his skin. Across the room, draperies billowed against an open window, admitting frigid air and the somber call of a coyote. The 9 mm pistol he clutched, a second-hand Ruger with a pockmarked plastic frame and blued-steel slide, both scuffed to hell, shone dully. He realized that he'd never fired a handgun. The single, chamber round had been intended for testing. Ten-round magazine, empty. He raised the pistol to his head, thinking *one is all I need*. His finger caressed the trigger. The steel soothed his febrile forehead. When I pull the trigger, he thought, the draperies will buckle with brain and bone, yet they will be neither more intelligent nor stronger. But I . . . I'll move on, possessing knowledge and experience, to explore what lies beyond.

Eyes closed, he intensified the pressure on the trigger. The world vanished; even the coyote ceased its wail. A video of his squalid life did not play in his head. A simple scene dominated his mind: on an old bridge a young man and woman lingered mid-span, entwined in a kiss. His hand trembled. The weapon fell to his thigh. It was incomprehensible that a year ago he was an assistant professor of physics, soon to be tenured, and passionately in love, soon to be wed.

He grasped the pistol and with it mastery of his fate. Married the muzzle to his head and sat for a long time. From abject silence rose the recognition or the precognition of someone calling his name. Calling him home? Looking toward the window, he slowly lowered the weapon. An instant later, BANG . . .

PART Ω
Convergence

"Ground the possession of which imports great advantage to either side, is contentious ground."

SUN TZU

THE ART OF WAR

CHAPTER 86

Bang . . . Bang. "Richard!"

. . . Bang . . . Bang . . . Bang. Sam extended his arm fully to pound on the lower margin of the open window's wooden molding. "Rick, it's Sam. Open up!"

"Granddad? That you?" Rick said, his finger still snugging the trigger.

"It's Sam. I can hardly hear you."

The pistol hit the floor. "Sam, that you?"

"Let me in, damn it! It's freezing."

"Wait a minute, will you." Rick rose and said, "Come to the front door."

Rick pulled toward him the Pendleton blanket from the bed and swathed his bare, bluing skin in it, a là a Roman Chief Joseph. The bed's sheet cascaded to the floor, nearly covering the pistol. He trudged out of the bedroom to the front door. "Sam, where are you?" He called into the yard.

A moment later, Sam appeared. "I'm here," he said, before gingerly turning Rick around and escorting him into the house. Sam removed his ski hat and shook off the cold. Quickly, he realized the interior wasn't much warmer than outside.

"Really glad you stopped by," Rick said, extending a cadaverous hand. His covering fell to the floor. He made no attempt to cover himself.

"Oh, my God," Sam said, bending down to restore Rick's toga. He gathered the blanket around him and tucked in a corner at the top. "Looks like you're moving."

"Got to do what . . . . You know."

Nodding, Sam looked around. Diamond plaster walls, custom carved corbels, nichos galore. This place was a mansion in comparison to his home. But the pale moonlight cast eerie shadows from the sparse, sheet-covered furnishings. It was like an elegant southwestern funeral parlor. "Let's go out for a warm drink," Sam said. "Hot chocolate? Maybe hot buttered rum?"

"It's too hot in here." Rick mopped his damp brow with the back of his hand. "I'll let some air in." Rick turned toward a window. Took a step; tripped on his blanket-toga.

Sam winced when Rick smacked the saltillo tile floor head first. Blood spurted from the knot that immediately bulged on his forehead. "Good God!" Sam bent to Rick. "Where are your clothes?"

"The bedroom, I think."

"Rest here," Sam said, helping Rick up to a covered chair. "I'll be right back."

SAM ENTERED the bedroom and saw the clean clothes on the bed and a photo, illuminated by moonlight and sitting on the bedside table. He bent down to recover Rick's keys from the floor. The abused Toyota key, on the fancy BMW fob, seemed emblematic of Rick's duplicitous life.

Squinting at the small photo, Sam's heart clenched at the setting: the salt and peppershaker supports of the Longfellow Bridge over the Charles River. He, himself, had photographed that site hundreds of times. From every conceivable perspective, in every season, in all types of weather. He suspected the girl in Rick's photo was his former fiancée, but for an instant she was someone else. Someone from his past.

Shaking off the reverie and glancing for other essentials to bring with him, Sam flinched observing the metallic glint of the pistol almost hidden under the sheet. The scene became clear. He shoved back the sheet with his foot. He bent to inspect the gun's marred finish, slashed barrel, and busted plastic handle, suggestive of a life badly gone awry.

"Sam, you here?" Rick leaned against the bedroom's doorjamb.

"Just getting your clothes. I'll be right there." Surreptitiously, Sam slid the gun into his coat pocket, despising its steely, deadly indifference. Sam helped Rick dress. And he put a cold compress on his forehead. What now, he wondered?

Rick abruptly said, "It was great to see you. Keep in touch."

Sam stood silent. What could he do? He'd promised Reba that he would not get mixed up with Rick. Thus, bringing him home was not an option. But how could he stand by, yet again, and do nothing? Sam shifted his weight. "Are you staying with Carmen? Let me follow you there. You're not well."

"I'm going to be just fine." Rick stepped toward Sam and swooned. Sam barely caught him. Under Rick's unsupported weight, both men slid to the floor. "Damn it, Rick. Are you crazy?" Sam glared at him. Rick looked confused. "You've got to get some help. I'm taking you to the hospital. It's . . . it's irresponsible to act this way."

"Oh, yeah?" Rick fired. "What if you were going be roasted by the FBI tomorrow. Maybe locked up and shackled just like good ol' Wen Ho because if you open your mouth you'll be killed by some monster?" Rick's eyes blazed with madness.

Sam shuddered.

"There," Rick shouted. "Tell me about being responsible when your balls are being crushed by a steamroller."

"Rick, you're not thinking clearly. You must get help. At the hospital, they—"

"Fuck the hospital. I ain't going. I'd rather die with some disease or a bullet than be caged like an animal in solitary confinement. The FBI can yank me out of the hospital. They'll ensure that my life is over next time they lay their grimy hands on me. Can't you see, I'm lost." Rick collapsed to the floor.

Sam bent to him. "Be brave," he said, reaching down for Rick's arm.

"Like you, in your isolated little world. Hiding every goddamn thing you do behind the walls of your White Rock prison. You and Reba have lived your entire lives together in self-imposed solitary confinement. Maybe that's why it doesn't sound all that bad to you."

Sam's dark eyes moistened. He knew that Rick's claim was not far from the truth. He'd known it for decades. But the sting of hearing it hurt deeply.

"Let me go," Rick said, trying to rise on his own. He fell to the hard tile floor, a puddle of a man.

Sam stood at a crossroads. It was a junction he had not been prepared to navigate before tonight. Standing tall, he said, "Rick, please come home with me. Just for tonight."

"Why bother? What can you do for me? You've no idea what I'm facing. Telling you would jeopardize your precious life."

From the beginning, Sam had watched silently as the sticky web had been woven about Rick. Now, he questioned whether he'd been powerless to save Rick from its clutch or simply refused to venture to save him. "Rick, if the truth can set a man free, then I have the key to your freedom."

"Don't get religious on me."

"Please, trust me."

"Trust? When have you ever trusted? I thought distrust was your motto."

Sam's chest sunk. He sighed, looking for words. It was one of the scariest moments of his life. Opening his hands—and his heart—he whispered, "An openhearted person like you could never understand the burdens that Reba and I bear. They were loaded upon us every day by the people who cared for us and loved us most. I know. It's incomprehensible. But they were just acting out their pain, suffering and unwittingly transferring it to us. It was all they knew to do."

Sam's respiration quickened. He felt faint. Hyperventilation? He stared in Rick's eyes; saw that his pain and anger were dissipating. It gave Sam the strength to continue. "I see now. They had no idea how much it would hurt us. But like you and me, they're only human. So please, for my sake, Rick, let me help you."

CHAPTER 87

His campfire long dead, Big John's stealthy movements were lighted by silvery moonlight. For two days and nights, he had circled his sacred plot atop Santa Fe's Sun Mountain. Alternating chant and silence, he reached upward to the vastness of the heavens and inward to his soul. He had beseeched the four principal directions, gathered a medicine bag of the elements, and recalled to himself the traditions and mysteries of his people. Interspersed with these rights, he had begged for forgiveness for his decades-old sins: the allure of social significance, the illusion of riches. Big John threw back his head and raised his clenched fists, crying aloud to the Ga'an to come forth and smite Los Alamos National Lab, the molester of sacred lands.

A great shadow swept over the summit. Then from the clear night sky, a bolt of lightning was followed by a deafening rumble of thunder. Deep, profound sound, resonating in the ether. It shook the earth, throwing him to the ground, to the flat of his back. High above, he could see the enormous creature winging northward silently over the site of his supplication, which the mountain Spirits had judged good.

Later, during his rest, Big John subdued an apparition. He wrestled *mano-a-mano* with Stillwater Begay. It was the Spirit-form of his deceased father-in-law, who had cursed him. Big John summoned superhuman strength in the battle. Even as his physical body lay catatonic, he fought violently with the Spirit, subduing its groin and demanding to know a path to redemption. Big John awoke to a clear winter's day, energized and vibrant. He sprang up from the spot where he had toiled and a bolt of fire pierced his hip joint. Through the pain, his singular thought was to travel north across the Rio Grande. Exactly where, he did not know. But at long last, The Thunderbird was guiding him.

CHAPTER 88

Two hot toddies later, Rick was amenable to getting some sleep. Sam coaxed him into the guest bedroom and soon thereafter, at Rick's request, piled an extra blanket on top of the two in which Rick was already cocooned. From outside the room, Sam heard snores. Now, it was time for Sam to face the music. Not Paganini or Rachmaninoff, but equally intense. He entered the master bedroom where Reba sat up in bed, her face a picture of fury.

"I cannot believe it," she said. "We discussed this and agreed not to get involved."

"Reba, darling, please understand that I had no idea what condition Rick was in. You saw him. He's delirious, delusional. Was about to kill himself." Sam produced Rick's pistol. Waved it to Reba, who recoiled. He dropped it to the floor; kicked it under the bed with disgust.

"Well, how about our relatives?" She asked. "Did they have people sticking their necks out for them as they were shot or worked to death? No, indeed. And if this muddle at the Lab is as bad as you say it is, will we be next? Didn't you learn anything from our families' deaths?"

Sam paused, trying to measure his reply. He searched for the right sugar-coated words—the kind he usually used when addressing his wife. But, his mind seemed to snap. This was not about saving Rick's life. It certainly was not about lives already tragically lost. It was about living life. About him. About living his own life.

He walked within inches of Reba's face. Eye-to-eye. The pace of his speech was slow and deliberate. But his tone, that was the thing. Never before had he spoken to his wife with unswerving certainty, with the authority of truth. "Yes, I learned a great deal from the horrific stories," Sam said. "Mostly how to conceal my heritage and isolate myself at all costs. How to ignore the pain and suffering of others for fear that I might attract it to myself. And that no one whosoever is worthy of my trust. I was taught it over and over again from a master, Professor George Goldschmidt, Auschwitz Survivor."

Reba's stiff-necked glare turned to a crumbling portrait of pain.

Sam adjudged that now, and only now, might she, too, be willing to face the truth. "Why, Reba, did we move out to the middle of nowhere and leave our dearest friends, just when we could've begun to enjoy them most? I'll tell you. Because we were running scared. Couldn't wait to hide out in the sunny Southwest. Why don't we go to temple or assist poor Native Americans on reservations? Why don't we offer help to anyone less fortunate? Because someone might see us. Might think of us as wealthy do-gooders. Might make us a target."

Reba squelched a whimper. He could tell that she was struggling to stand up to him, to overpower him, as usual. But he was too strong. "We have more money than we can spend," he said. "It benefits no one. Our children have moved as far from us as they can and seldom bring our grandchildren to visit. Why? Because they don't want them infected with our self-conscious disease. They don't want their kids to be confined by grief over your dead sister and my dead grandfather. Our kids have learned to enjoy life. They express themselves as they please. And, on the whole, I think they're content."

"I thought you said that you were happy," Reba stammered. "Said you have your work, books, family—"

"That's not the point. You know Robert Stroud told a reporter that he was *happy*, while incarcerated on Alcatraz Island." Sam paced the floor. "My father, now there was someone happy. Carefree, generous, too. At least when his brother was not around. He laughed and told funny stories of the old country. And he loved my mother dearly. But when Uncle George was near, father was cowed completely. And, well, knowing how George felt about my mother, father ignored her for George's sake. It was supposed to make George feel better for the love that he'd been denied. But George didn't want to feel better. He wanted revenge."

Sam threw up his hands and shook his head in dismay, disbelief. He said, "Now, this is the sick part. The Nazis were gone. George could only extract his revenge from his own blood. He was the one who instigated the gloom and despair that infected my entire family. And I know that your story isn't so different. Change a name, a gender, ditto."

Reba collapsed onto the bed. She buried her face in her hands, weeping inconsolably.

Sam knelt at the bedside and turned Reba's reddened face toward his. Gently, he dabbed at her swollen eyes with his handkerchief. "Tell me that I'm wrong. Say that not a word of what I've said is true, and I'll shut up."

"Sam, it's hard for me. Even you couldn't really understand."

He hated to oppress his wife this way. Sam never would have believed that he could go this far. But now that a fissure in her armor had been found, he wanted to smash it open. Shed the light of truth into her fettered heart. Give her an opportunity to feel what he was feeling. He was alive for the first time in . . . in . . . maybe ever.

"Reba, darling, other families who suffered and lost more than either of ours didn't act this way. They moved on. They danced and sang and recalled the old times and married new husbands or found new wives in the New World. We—George—did not."

Sam put his arms around her. He held her trembling body. Softened his tone. "I've told you innumerable times how sorry I am about your sister and her anguished death. I missed having a grandfather and had a father for too few years. I swore that I would never, ever forget the atrocities that robbed me of my family. Now, I realize that I could never forget, even if I tried. But if my Zaide were alive and saw what my life has become, he would cry a river. How would your sister feel if she knew you never sang at temple or a Seder? She was the first-born; you were the last. Your lives were bound to be different. She would chide you, saying that you are not living up to your musical gifts. You're wasting God-given talent."

There, on his knees, the very same position as when he professed his undying love for Reba and told her that he would be with her forever, Sam said, "You know what the doctor said about my heart. I may not have much time left. I don't want to waste another minute of life, hiding behind someone else's anger, pain, or fear. I want to live in the present, empowered by truth and conviction. I have proof that Burton and this Santa Fe killer are in league and have been for decades. Possibly, that proof can free Rick from his death sentence. I don't know that for sure. I don't know how. But, I want your agreement to share it with Rick and the authorities."

"I can hardly breathe," Reba said. "You know that extending yourself to someone outside your family was heresy in my family. This is something entirely new for me." She paused before adding, "We've lived good lives together. This will not split us asunder. Sleep on it and tell me how you feel in the morning."

When Reba kissed Sam's cheek and squeezed his hand, he knew that he would be with her until his dying day. Their fates were tied inextricably. Reba was his *beshert*.

CHAPTER 89

Sam awoke the following morning feeling victorious. The most hellish nightmares of his life had racked his sleep. He had fought George or an avatar of George the night through. The battle was so lifelike. Sam had refused to embrace George's claim that the only way to honor the past was to relive it daily, hourly. Ostensibly, learning the lessons of the past meant reliving them continually. Sam had vehemently disagreed. He countered his uncle's austere thesis with humanistic claims that life goes on, that the dead should bury the dead, and that but for the grace of God, any person might suffer profoundly.

Standing, Sam felt a crippling ache in his hip. He hobbled to the bathroom, ignoring the pain, believing that at last, he was guided by— He didn't want to think it.

Glancing at his watch, Sam saw that it was already a quarter after ten in New York. He accessed his old black book. Phone numbers penciled in, snail mail addresses, too. He picked up the phone and dialed.

"To what do I owe the honor of this call?"

"Ah Lenny, I'd be lying if I said it was strictly social."

"Sam, I know that."

"I have a sick friend who refuses to go to the doctor."

"I'm a doctor and I don't like going to doctors."

"But this man is under tremendous pressure. He may be ill physically and psychologically. He's febrile and goes from being flushed to shivering in an instant. And he has a congested cough. A deep hack."

"Sounds like he needs to see a GP. But, what's the mental part?"

"He, uh, might have tried to commit suicide."

"Now, how would you know that he *might* have? You see pills?"

"He's taking antidepressants." Sam bit his lip, vowing to himself not to make Rick out a maniac.

"This person needs professional help. Call the psych ward at the hospital."

"I will not do that. He's in a serious bind."

"Hmm, do you know all the medications he's taking?"

"Just the pills, and he has a huge bottle of old cough syrup, nearly finished."

"Well then, he may be suffering a psychotic reaction. Does the bottle say dextromethorphan hydrobromide?"

"I can check." Sam retrieved Rick's coat from a living room chair. Rifled through the pockets, spilling singed cornmeal. He grasped the receiver. "The label's faded. Says the active ingredient is DMX."

"People have been known to go psychotic using too much DMX alone. Add some MAOI antidepressants and John Doe could become Jeffrey Dahmer."

"You always did have a great sense of humor, Lenny."

"Sam, this is not a laughing matter. Throw the cough syrup away. For how long has he taken the antidepressants?"

"I can't say, but the bottle's fairly full. They're not even in his name. It belongs to his former fiancée, who's part of the problem, I imagine."

"My recommendation is to get him to a doctor immediately. You don't want to be liable for something this person could do to himself, or Reba, or you, for that matter."

Sam was almost ready to fold his cards. Rick was apparently really sick. Lenny was one of New York City's finest thoracic surgeons. He knew everything that was worth knowing about medicine thirty years ago. His opinion mattered. But what was news here, Sam questioned himself? He knew last night that Rick was sick and on the brink. But, wasn't that the point? Was he going to be like the bank that only lends money to people who don't need it?

"I don't care about all that," Sam said. "I'm determined to help this man. Now, will you help me or not?"

"Well, well, am I speaking to the real Sam Smith or an imposter?" Lenny jibed. "You're not exactly the contemplative, retiring Sam of old."

Sam maintained a dignified silence.

"What is it you want me to do? I'm not a magician, just a doctor. And thousands of miles away at that."

"And the best New York City has to offer, we both know that. Can you prescribe something for pneumonia or bronchitis? Maybe it would be close enough to help him. He can't go to the doctors here."

"Well, ciprofloxacin is a fairly broad spectrum antibiotic. It's like an atomic bomb for the bloodstream, killing almost everything bad floating around in it. Unfortunately, it also kills most of the good things in the GI tract. He'll have to take quality probiotics concurrently. The good news is that CIPRO, as its commonly called, works fast. A few days in most cases. Lenny paused before adding, "When my koi have infections, I deliver it to them in frozen green peas."

"How is your extended family?" Sam emphasized the final word.

"Unlike my nuclear family, they never complain."

"Ah, Lenny, you're something else," Sam enthused. "Will you call it in for me at the Gunther Pharmacy in Los Alamos. I won't forget the favor."

"I can't. But I know someone in New Mexico who can."

Afterward, Sam headed to the backyard gardening hut, as Reba referred to it. In reality, there were far fewer gardening implements than neatly stacked and sealed boxes of Sam's photographs, unclassified research papers, and memorabilia. He dove toward the bottom of a back box stack to retrieve a medium size, black metal box bearing no notation. Once in his office, Sam took a moment to center himself before lifting the rusty lid. He took a deep breath. The lid opened with a creak, exposing contents as yellowed and dusty as an ages-old burial shroud.

CHAPTER 90

ARMSTRONG paced in front of his disheveled, makeshift desk in the Albuquerque FBI offices. He groused to Agent Jackson, "I've wasted enough time. Pick him up."

"We'll need a warrant."

"Get one."

"If he resists?"

"Get him!" Armstrong raised his meaty hand, saying, "If I can't get anything from the infernal Lab management, I'll get it straight from the perp."

Armstrong reflected on Burton's having failed to provide proof of Rick's wrongdoing. Proof Armstrong was certain existed. He yanked up the antiquated desk phone and dialed Burton's office. He held the line, pinching and uncurling the cord with the thick fingers of his dry, spotted hand.

"Hello, Director Armstrong. How can I be of assistance?"

"You can decree that anyone working at the Lab who does not comply fully with my investigation into the Adams case is in violation of national security codes and will be terminated immediately and prosecuted to the fullest extent of the law, for starters."

"Is your investigation not proceeding well?"

"You know damn well it's not. And you've given me zilch."

"These things take time. But I know nothing of your investigation. That was your will, remember."

"Listen, Gavin, I'm going to require your help going forward."

"I'm delighted that we can work together to resolve this serious situation. Of course, I've never been convinced that Adams is your man. He's a mere aberration. And a potential misallocation of the Bureau's resources."

"I've decided to bring him in. I have a lot of experience getting what I want from individuals. Trying to pressure whole divisions up there on the Hill to cooperate is like trying to out-stubborn a cat."

"Let's have a strategy meeting. Remember the Lee case."

"Damn the Lee case. I'm onto something big here. And Adams is our man. If he doesn't talk, I'll throw him under the jail until he does. What I need from you is every iota of intel you have on him since his employment."

"I'm working on it. But I insist on being thorough. Haste makes—"

"I want it ASAP. We'll analyze it, sift it, comb it, cross-correlate it, eat it and shit it back out if need be in making a case against him."

AFTER LISTENING to the call, Gerry began planning Rick's immediate demise. He would not risk Rick's confinement by the Feds at this critical juncture. Nothing elaborate. He should simply disappear. The authorities would consider Rick a fugitive from justice. No reason to assume foul play. And there was still plenty of room in the freezer.

A single command entered on his keyboard summoned a detailed map of Santa Fe and its environs. A couple of numbers in multiple colors concentrated on the Hill. One blue number fewer than Gerry wanted to see. Rick's special cell phone was still off; its GPS locator had no power. Gerry realized the tradeoff for battery life and continuous monitoring had not been wise in Rick's case. But he was confident that locating Rick would not be difficult. Gerry took the opportunity to delete the red number associated with Rick's former vehicle.

CHAPTER 91

"I FEEL like I've been hit by a train," Rick said. "Thanks for sticking around here today." He added, "I think I'm going to make it." Five doses of atomic antibiotics and ten bowls of matzo ball soup, which Sam referred to as Jewish penicillin, had done the trick.

Sam formed a fighting fist with one hand.

"I don't know how to thank you and Reba," Rick said.

"Don't think about that now."

"Is she dealing with this okay?"

"We're doing well."

"I'll call Carmen and ask her to pick me up after work today. What is today, anyway?" Rick threw up his hands. "I'd be fine, if I could stop the crazy dreams. Truth is, I can't differentiate fiction from fact."

"It may not be such a good idea to call Carmen or anyone else. You're in this over your head; a pawn in a very deadly game."

"So, I spilled the beans?"

"No. I've suspected something for a while. At your house, it was clear that you had finally reached the breaking point."

"I'm damned if I don't and more damned if I do," Rick said.

"I've got something that might be helpful."

"You've done enough already." Rick managed a grin, saying, "I'll give Carmen a call. We've got one pretty good head between us."

"I'm sure that the FBI is surveilling her. Probably have been for some time now. Her phones and yours are tapped, no doubt. You were due for a formal deposition or something yesterday, weren't you?"

"Oh, yeah."

"They may have a warrant out for you. If they pick you up, you could be detained indefinitely." Sam's tone darkened. "My real concern is that they won't find you first."

Rick swallowed hard. He didn't speak.

Sam held up a large mailing envelope, from which he produced a vintage emulsion plate. It was the kind previously used by physicists for recording high resolution images of sub-atomic particle tracks. The metal border was rusty, but the image was clear, its resolution crisp. Rick recognized the central section of the Longfellow Bridge where he and Desiree had been photographed, seemingly a lifetime ago. The photo's exposure was highly unusual, demonstrating loud, unnatural colors. An emerald cast pervaded everything. Faint sparkles shown in the background and a trio, two men encompassing a girl, stood precariously on the river side of one of the massive supports, either a salt or pepper shaker. The image was time stamped 11:47:07 p.m.

Sam drew out a second plate, time stamp 11:47:19, demonstrating the two men looking downward, into the river. The girl was absent.

"Recognize anyone?"

Rick looked surprised. He took the photo and focused on the men.

Using his finger, Sam covered one man's ski hat.

"Oh, my God! The dimple. It's Gerry. When was this taken?"

"So that's what he calls himself," Sam said. "Anyone else?"

Rick covered the other man's forehead. His face was familiar, but the image's coloring and exposure were deceiving.

"Should I?"

"*Herr* security director."

Rick gasped. A younger, slimmer Burton leapt from the surface. "When were these taken? What went on there?"

"Call it thirty odd years. Gerry, or whatever alias he used then, helped Burton beat a research fraud accusation."

"By who? How?"

"By Hannah Katz, Burton's research assistant." Sam dabbed at his eyes. "How? The way he usually does. The way he did with Fred."

Rick perused the first image. Gerry's arm was around the girl's head, which was bent at an odd angle. A vision of Renée's corpse flashed into his mind. Burton's face in profile. He looked down the bridge, probably scouting for witnesses. "But, how could this happen?"

"It was my fault," Sam said, tears streaming down his stubbly cheeks.

"I don't believe that."

Sam nodded, his eyes downcast. "I developed the most sophisticated image enhancement program in the world, at the time," he admitted. "I'd always loved the honesty of photography. And so for my doctoral dissertation, I married the image enhancement code with infrared photography. The result made high-resolution photographs of heat-generating entities possible in total darkness. The DoD moved to classify it immediately. But I wanted to capture Hannah on the bridge with a Leonid meteor shower in the background, before the technology was taken away from me. Back then, I didn't have a clearance of any kind. Really didn't want one."

Rick could tell that Sam's heart was breaking. His, too. He needed to be strong for both of them. Rick lightly rested his hand on Sam's shoulder. It quivered.

Sam continued, "I had taken conventional photographs of that old bridge so many times: every season, every weather condition. That bridge was my personal symbol of freedom when I came to Cambridge from Chicago. That's a really long story. Anyway, this photo was to be my masterpiece."

"But how could you photograph them in the act? How'd you know?"

"They didn't know why we were meeting, of course. In Burton's lab, I left a note for Hannah—no cell phones back then—telling her to meet me on the bridge at midnight to see the shower. I asked her to face the Cambridge side of the River from the near saltshaker. The meteor rate was to be in excess of 100 per hour, not a storm, but a very good shower. It was a bitterly cold fall night. But I knew she would be there. She was so full of enthusiasm, and fearless. That attracted me and scared me more than anything. I was afraid of my shadow. Always had been."

"I get that," Rick said, patting Sam's shoulder.

Sam reared up. "What kind of struggling grad student would dare accuse her professor of falsifying experimental data? I was amazed." Sam added, "I mean, he held her education—and her life, it turned out—in his sooty hands."

Rick's congested chest welled with sadness and phlegm until it was too full. "Excuse me for just a minute." Rick struggled to the bathroom. Demonstrated a fist of solidarity with Sam on the way there and back.

"What happened was that I set up the bulky equipment early," Sam said, "to try to capture the bridge alone and to see if the shower could be resolved, given its weak heat signature. I was shooting by about 11:30. The camera was working perfectly, as you can see from the photos."

"There're unbelievably clear."

"Burton obviously accessed the message and altered it for an 11:45 meeting. He and this killer were waiting for her across the bridge. No one else was out. I saw the whole thing. I, uh, even heard the splash." Sam broke down completely. He wept. And his chest throbbed violently."

Rick put his arm around him. They sat together, united in the pain of the past.

Sam moaned, "She was the only woman that I ever loved with all my heart."

Rick had to ask, "What did you do? Did you try to help?"

"I couldn't move. I was petrified." Sam composed himself sufficiently to say, "I crouched and hid. I let her die alone in that black, icy water." He burst into sobs.

Rick comforted him as he mourned the death of the love of his life aloud for the first time. Sam straightened himself, preparing to speak, but grabbed at his chest.

"You okay? Let me get you some water." Rick hurried toward the kitchen. He returned to find Sam slumped to the floor. "Sam, get up. Can you hear me?" Rick took up Sam's wrist and finding no pulse, he reached for the phone.

CHAPTER 92

OVERALLS, a ball cap, and a partial facemask constituted his wardrobe. A small fumigation rig completed Gerry's disguise when he knocked on the door of Carmen's apartment. He called out, "Pest control." No response. After cracking the handle and deadbolt locks, he opened the door slowly. He feigned spraying, inspecting every inch of the place. There were traces of Rick, but it was clear that he had not slept there the previous night. Gerry placed a listening device behind the bed's headboard and exited, thinking, bug man, indeed.

Two men in dark suits rushed past Gerry. He put down his head and they ignored him. Gerry stopped and pretended to knock on an arbitrary apartment door, verifying that the men had stopped at Carmen's door. At his vehicle, Gerry observed a *clean* black SUV with blacked out windows. Except for the windows, the vehicle appeared not to be local.

Gerry removed his coveralls in his SUV, exposing his high tech, insulated biking suit. He drove to and parked at the tennis courts just short of Rick's home. Disguised by a neoprene face protector and biking helmet, he peddled his bike past number 13 and cut into an easement beyond the house. Crept up toward its rear portal and heard voices, describing window treatments to protect furniture on the residence's sun-battered western portal. Concluding that Rick was not coming back there, Gerry left the neighborhood, passing the clean SUV he had just seen at Carmen's apartments.

Back at his workshop, Gerry took his fully-charged PDA and tapped away on the screen, activating an alarm to be triggered by Rick's secure cell phone. He changed into street clothing and drove to Angel's where he parked out of sight. Carmen was a dripping little honeybee. Gerry was certain that Rick missed the hive. He'd see just how much.

CHAPTER 93

SAM sat up and waved away Rick, who knelt beside him. "I'm okay." Sam took a sip of water, before adding, "Don't get all worked up."

"You don't look okay. I'm calling 911."

"No."

"Now look who hates doctors."

"I've already been; I know my score. And frankly, I'm all right with it." Sam drank the remaining water, stood, and walked out of the room slowly. He returned shortly, stoic and less pale.

"You've done so much for me. How can I help you, Sam?"

"Just don't mention this to Reba. She's upset enough already."

Rick's face fell. "I'm really sorry about everything."

"Oh, not about you. Not entirely, anyway. It's just that life on the Hill is not what it once was. Maybe it's we who're changing."

"Does Reba know your story?"

"Not all that you know. The *Boston Globe* carried news of the investigation into what was called Hannah's suicide. Her broken neck was suspect, but a note she had presumably written was found in her apartment. She claimed to be the one who falsified the data. The affair was tied up very neatly."

"Did you demand that her handwriting be authenticated? How about the photos? I just don't get it? Why would Gerry bother to help Burton way back then?"

"All good questions, Rick, but I have no answers, except for my own cowardice." Sam plopped down into a chair. "I was too afraid to come forward immediately. After it was clear that the matter had been dropped by the police and the Institute, I felt such inner disdain. I planned to come forward, but Reba had become my confidant by then. She prevailed on me not to." Sam shook his head sorrowfully. "Reba's point that risking my life would not bring Hannah back was well taken. She's very logical and persuasive."

"I get that."

"Months later, I earned my degree, Reba and I were married, and we moved to Los Alamos. It was not until I had been at the Lab for a couple of months that I heard that Burton was here, too. We thought about moving away, but decided to keep out heads down and our eyes open."

"And you've never looked up?"

"Not until now." Sam reached for Rick's hand. He held it between both of his. "This is too important. Your life is in danger and the Lab is under assault by Burton and this killer. And God only knows who else."

"That's my take on it, too," Rick said, releasing the grip, smiling warmly.

Sam said, "Maybe you know the director is out. Soon, anyway. Probably not such a bad thing. But when GRIT blows up, O'Donnell, who'd do a better job of directing the Lab than anyone, will be a goat. He could be fired. Probably just demoted. That leaves Burton the number one candidate for the job."

"Ah, the big picture." Rick grimaced. "When Burton becomes director or even interim director, he can funnel every nuclear weapons secret the US owns to his master. Owner is probably the right word."

"There could be an even bigger picture," Sam warned. "He suddenly ascends a small pool of names in Washington from which the highest security officers in the land are chosen. Burton could conceivably become director of the CIA. Then every secret of every kind the US possesses will be for sale."

"No." Rick bit his lip.

"He's smart and patient." Sam thrust his fist downward, declaring, "And his soul belongs to the devil."

"There's got to be a way out of this."

"Burton holds all the security-related cards up there. He can fix your FBI problems. But somehow he'll have to be blocked from the directorship." Sam opened his hands wide; eyed Rick solemnly. "I just don't know how to orchestrate it."

"What does Reba say?"

"She's not in the driver's seat. I believe that you and the Lab are worth saving." Sam picked up the evidence plates and slowly extended them toward Rick.

Rick held the images. He stood silent, squelching a hand tremor. He had to be—or at least appear—brave, until he could collect himself and devise a scheme. The trick would be to free himself while minimizing the impact on Sam and Reba. Rick furrowed his brow just thinking of the word . . . *impact*.

CHAPTER 94

THE FOLLOWING morning, taking coffee with Sam at the breakfast table, a mischievous grin seized Rick's lips. He asked, "Could you do me a little favor?"

"Little in comparison to saving your neck?"

"What are the chances of Carmen coming over this afternoon for a voice lesson?" Although his life was in jeopardy, Rick felt like a different person; one especially alive. He wondered if there were a correlation.

Sam rubbed his stubbly chin.

Rick added, "Reba could call and ask Carmen to come over. Maybe in an insistent tone." He ate an emerging grin. "I think she'd know just how to do it."

"Feeling much better, I see," Sam said, smiling. "But Reba has to work. It'd look pretty strange Carmen's coming over to visit me at home from work in the afternoon."

"Give you some serious buzz in the neighborhood," Rick said, pointing a finger at Sam. "Carmen's got to be worried about me."

"Probably thinks you've jetted off to Boston again."

"Don't kid me. I'm a desperate man."

"At least your desperation's not quiet, like most men's." Sam paused. "Why not have her come over tonight? Reba can make the call."

"No good. Carmen has to work."

"She can miss one lousy night."

Sam's verve surprised Rick. He said, "Yeah, sure she can."

"Okay, I'll meet Reba for lunch. Ask her to call and set it up."

GERRY WAITED before tailing Carmen. No Feds on her back. He gunned his Bimmer and settled several car lengths behind her Cherokee. He estimated that this was the kind of diligence that often paid off big. Carmen might decide to visit Rick briefly after the little music lesson or Rick might come slinking up to the lesson itself. Gerry would stand for hours in an ice storm to catch a glimpse of Rick Adams. In reality, all he had to do was to sit in his vehicle and keep his eyes open, listening to Tchaikovsky like a balletomane, which played softly. He imagined the gracefulness of the dancers performing Swan Lake. He could almost see himself as the black swan. Ah, the *pas de deux*. Had he really done it? Been commanding yet graceful; menacing yet purposeful? For an instant, he allowed himself to recall that instead of a life of brutality and villainy, his could have been a different reality.

Gerry refocused. He drove carefully, inconspicuously, following Carmen to the undistinguished White Rock home. He observed her entry from his vehicle, parked just around the corner. Few cars passed by the home of the lesson; none stopped. Gerry was disgusted at the behemoth vehicles that populated the bedroom community. So many Suburbans and Excursions: dirty, boxy, gas guzzlers. As an old Suburban crept up and turned the corner passing him, Gerry ducked his head, wondering whether Labites understood, or cared, that the world endured an energy crisis.

From time to time, Gerry would lower his phone's MP3 player volume and ease down his passenger's side window. Each time, mello mezzo-soprano wafted from the residence's open guest bathroom window. He heard the vocal notes; saw their colors. A haven of dissociation. When Carmen emerged and drove directly to Angel's, Gerry cursed the wasted evening. His pulse banged angrily throughout his body. Temple veins bulging with anxiety and teeth grit, Gerry affirmed that Rick Adams was as good as dead.

CHAPTER 95

Sunday morning marked a watershed.

Rick had agonized over his plan for days. He decided it was the best he could do. Sam was reading *The New Mexican* in his study when Rick stepped in and began to pace in front of his desk. Sam looked up. "Yes?"

Rick nearly growled, "I've got a plan."

"All right." Sam folded the paper, looking anxious. "How can I help?"

"I'll need to borrow your car. I'm going to use my midnight credit card near GRIT's experimental area."

"You'll never get near it," Sam said. "Strictest security at the Lab."

"I need some goodies from DAHRT." Rick grinned, dangling a hand-scrawled paper scrap, a dead ringer for a grocery shopping list. "I figure the tight security at GRIT is at the expense of the security of the high explosives next door."

Sam raised his eyebrows and reached for the list. He perused it. "So you want to build a . . . bomb." He eyed Rick intently, before refocusing on the list. "A beam-splitter. They won't have that at DAHRT. You're making a laser-triggered device, I guess."

"Just a small one. I figured I could get the optics stuff from one of the unclassified labs at TA-38."

"Why build this when a prototype from OASYS Technology would be perfect?"

"Great! I'll have them overnight one to me. Okay if I order it under your name so when the Feds show up you can explain to them that you're not a terrorist?" Rick sighed. "Besides my beam is very low power. Their devices need a real laser."

"Not so fast. I happen to know there are very low power flashings available to detonate small devices called mini-pods. In case you just want to obliterate the executive floor of an office building, not the entire structure. An operative can trigger it from across the street using a pocket HeNe.

Spooks at the Lab. So, Bruno was right all along. Rick creased his brow, asking, "And how would you know that?"

"Because I'm on the scientific advisory committee at the Lab for the OASYS contract." Sam grinned. But his smile ran away when he said, "Rick, you can't just blow things or people up. That won't solve your problems; it'll create more."

Rick had underestimated what a powerful resource Sam was. But what would the personal costs of his help be? He was about to steal a bomb from the Lab for Rick's sake. Rick said, "Thanks, Sam. But I can't ask you to—"

"You're not asking me. I'm volunteering. I want to do this more than anything I've done in a long time."

"I guess your day of reckoning with Gerry has been too long coming."

Sam stiffened. "I'm not seeking revenge." He eyed the ceiling, adding, "That's not my job. And it's not yours either. This has to be a last resort. A trick left up the sleeve."

Rick sucked his teeth. Visions of the skewed heads of Renée and Hannah Katz and the charred remains of Fred tortured his brain. They stared accusingly at him in his swirling thoughts.

Sam said softly, "You can't let your encounters with evil taint you and bring you to its despicable level."

"You have my word," Rick replied. "But then, I'm going to need a low-power variable attenuator."

"That's no problem. I've got odds and ends around here that I think will work."

Rick shook his head, wondering if he and Sam were just an odd couple or a dynamic duo. He was betting his life on the latter.

When Sam returned that afternoon, bearing an unassuming cardboard box and plastic bag, filled with an OASYS Technology explosives package and a can of hair spray, respectively, Rick began to believe he might have a chance. He said, "The optical coupling won't need tight-tolerance assembly. The garage is fine. But what about Reba?"

"I can do better than the garage," Sam said. Without another word, he led Rick out the back door toward a medium-size storage shed. He opened the door and flipped a light switch. A green glow softly illuminated the crowded space. "Oops," he said, energizing a bright array of overhead lights.

Rick's lips turned upward as he recognized the Newport Corporation logo on a dust drape spread across a miniature skyline of what he knew were concealed optical components. A long, squat, flat-topped structure, evocative of a warehouse in the cityscape's environs, was located across the table from him on a back edge. It was surely a laser's housing.

Rick watched Sam carefully remove the dusty cover. Rick gawked at the display, asking, "Who keeps a precision optical bench in a tough shed?" He gently poked the table with his finger. A cacophony of hisses from each corner, suggestive of so many viper pits, sounded as the vibration isolation system damped the perturbation. "A low frequency vibration isolated optical bench, that is."

"The kind of guy who used to do real research . . . and may again some day," Sam boasted. His head sagged noticeably, adding, "Before he became an idiot cloistered away from the real action."

Rick bounced from one foot to the other, energized by Sam's participation. Interested to see if he could determine the optical setup's utility, Rick traced the laser's output through a partially mirrored beam splitter and then traced each separated beam, asking, "So, does the nuclear physicist next door have sub-critical assembly out back that he can toy with after dinner, on weekends?"

"The geologist next door has an enormous shop with every woodworking power tool known to man. He built the shop first, then spent a half-dozen years making the doors, counters, cabinets for the house."

Sam pointed to the setup. He said, "Let's get to it and tear it down."

"No way. I mean, the garage would be just—"

"This is a playpen. There's something real to put on here now."

CHAPTER 96

THE ROADS from Santa Fe to Gerry's compound were icy. The moon was blotted out by the opaque clouds of a gathering storm. Rick confined his eyes to the highway. Once exiting 285 South onto Old Spur Road, he slowed and carefully proceeded past Gerry's property. After stashing Sam's vehicle in a stand of junipers, Rick grasped Reba's flower-ornamented backpack and winced. He made for the rear of Gerry's property in a sweeping arc.

The property line achieved, Rick withdrew the hairspray and misted a cold vertical cloud. No beam. Too many wild animals about for effective perimeter control, he assumed. Video cameras were a given, but he'd just have to stay low to the ground and take his chances. He gingerly touched the barbed wire suspended on rustic, rough hewn pinion poles. No charge. He penetrated the fence and ducked, moving quickly to the rear of the workshop, collecting sodden tumbleweeds as he went.

Rick huddled near the central heating unit's housing. The motor whined a monotone. Each breath he took produced a small smoke plume that evaporated in midair. Withdrawing the hairspray and dusting a patch of the structure, he observed a faint red glow darting parallel to the foundation, about a foot off the ground and inches from the wall. The red diode laser of the intrusion system was

propagating. Rick carefully scraped away the snow from the hard ground underneath and adjacent to a section of beam. He withdrew the mini-pod which was
attached using a bungee cord to a flimsy automotive scissor jack. Eyeballing the
height of the beam splitter attached to the explosive's aperture, slowly he raised
the jack until the splitter was aligned in height with the intrusion system's laser
beam. He powered up the cell phone and checked for acceptable reception and
reinforced its connection to a bulky external battery. The power supply would
also be used to change the state of the optical attenuator that would either block
the beam or transmit it and detonate the device, in accordance with commands
received by the phone. It had worked perfectly on the bench at Sam's place.

Now for the dicey step: sliding the beam splitter into the path of the laser
beam without blowing himself to bits if he had poorly integrated his components
onsite. There was also the possibility of setting off God only knew what kind of
intrusion response. Every intrusion system was programmed differently. Most
external ones allowed for single, quick interruptions. But then, Gerry was not
most installers. Rick exhaled deeply, looking at the device. Why not crawl over
to the house and blow it to bits now? What was he waiting for, confirmation of
Gerry's maliciousness? But what of his promise to Sam? He was about to risk
his life. For what? Rick considered whether he was a liar and a cheat, just like
the Feynman friends. He demanded that he be better than them.

Tumbleweeds surrounded the device. Rick misted the air once more. The
thin red line emerged. He grasped the assembly with both hands and held his
breath. He began to move it forward, but his hands shook violently, toppling
the assembly toward the beam. Caught it before it disrupted the propagation.
He breathed heavily; sweat beaded on his forehead. This is hell, he thought. He
cupped his hands over his mouth trying to find some comfort in warm fingers.
Useless. He was perspiring and shivering cold at once. What could he do to
divert himself? Rock and roll was always the answer, but he didn't even own an
MP3 player now.

He regarded the package, thinking he hadn't checked its TNT equivalence. A
line of rock and roll lyrics pierced his thoughts: "I'm TNT; I'm dynamite. I'm TNT,
and I'll win the fight!" He began again, tapping his big toes inside soggy shoes.
By the time he sang the final word of the verse, "explode", he held the assembly
with sure hands and effortlessly thrust it into position. The beam flickered but

continued to dart parallel to the building's side and at a right angle into the variable attenuator, set to full attenuation mode. He sighed and drew his first easy breath, thinking mission accom—

Flood lights burned the landscape, bright as the fourth of July. White hot spotlights had popped up from behind the parapet; they exposed the walls and grounds for 50 meters in every direction. Video cameras wheeled to and fro, their motors buzzing with each saccade as they criss-crossed the land. If he ran, he was dead meat. Rick grabbed a sodden tumble weed and smashed himself against the heater housing. He put his head down and waited, his pounding heart marking time's agonizing passage. As quickly as it had begun the intrusion response halted. The land was once again black, contourless and vast as before. A brief response for a transient loss of beam was realistic, but was Gerry watching now? Rick waited, his breath abated. He imagined how stupid it would be to get shot because of little smoke spires emanating from tumble weeds.

After a long wait, Rick crept back to the vehicle and made his way to White Rock. Once in bed, he couldn't help but reflect on the adventure. Step one of the plan was complete. And Gerry had better watch out, because he was sitting next to a power load that only Rick could explode.

CHAPTER 97

Rick related the previous evening's events to Sam, who squirmed and nervously squinted his eyes. Rick produced his special, untraceable cell phone, Sam gasped. Rick asked, "You okay with this?" Sam balled his bony fist in support. Rick returned the gesture and energized the phone. As Burton's office line rang, Rick considered that Sam and he were in this mess together. And it was his job to extricate them.

Connie Sanders answered and tried to screen him, but Rick claimed that he had security related information of great interest to Burton. They must speak at once. Burton's voice came searing over the line. Rick could almost hear the hiss of recorder tape rolling, security S.O.P.

"Mr. Jones, this is Gavin Burton, director of Laboratory operations security. Let me make clear that any information you have relating to the security of this Laboratory must be delivered to me in person, not over an unsecure telephone line."

"This is Rick Adams. And I'm calling about your security, not the Lab's."

"Hold the line."

Rick was pretty sure the fake-sounding cough that ensued masked Burton's disengagement of the recording system.

"I do not understand your meaning," Burton replied.

"Remember Hannah Katz; how about Gerry Mueller? I'm calling to make a deal."

"I don't know what you're talking about. These names mean nothing to me." His tone grew fatherly. "Rick, you're a fugitive from justice. I understand that you're scared, grasping at straws. But this is not the way to save yourself. I can help you. I want to help you. I've been shielding your records, at my own peril, to give you time to come in."

Rick imagined Burton's pulse racing. The man was probably jerking his tie loose that instant.

"I'm glad you mentioned my records," Rick said. "And I think meeting is an excellent idea. That's the only way I'm willing to deal. I'll trade you high res images of you and Gerry killing Hannah on the Longfellow Bridge for all of my Lab records."

"What images? How could you?" Burton's voice cracked.

"I said high resolution and I mean it. In the act images, you murderous piece of shit. And you're going to get me in the clear with Gerry and the Feds. Sweep all the garbage you collected on me under the mesa. And the Lab directorship . . . forget about it—" Rick punched the air with an uppercut. He saw Sam's eyes widen.

"I, uh, still don't know what you're talking about."

"I'll call you at seven with the place and time. Just get the stuff together. And no funny business, if you want to live happily ever after." Rick ended the call with a quivering finger.

Sam clapped him on the back gently. "Good show," he said. And then he grasped his scrawny chest. His face ashen.

"Sam, you going to make it?"

"I can't let Reba see me like this. She's under so much strain already." Sam said, "Get the newspaper from the dining table, please. There's a symphonic concert tonight at Santa Fe's Lensic theatre. Call and get two of the best seats. It'll be a surprise for Reba and Carmen. Do you think Carmen will go on such short notice?"

"She's a very spontaneous lady." Rick smiled inwardly, thinking of his unexpected trip to paradise when he saw her last.

"Good. After you get the tickets, I'll call Reba and use our code phrase to put her at ease, then spring the good news. She can call Carmen and ask her."

Threatening skies loomed. Rick hoped that if a storm were approaching, it would hold off until after the exchange, planned for an isolated spot Sam had mentioned. Rick required a location without direct vehicle access in case Burton tried to double-cross him—using Gerry or the Feynman friends.

GERRY'S PDA vibrated to life. It's screen dominated by a tiny map showing a blinking beacon near the canyon in White Rock. Not taking time to congratulate himself, Gerry moved to his computer console and began a search of the phone records through the Helsinki connection, the one used by Rick's special phone. There was no need to power the phone if Rick was not going to use it. And once used, Nokia updated their records digitally, making call information available instantly.

Finding that the number was Burton's office, Gerry accessed the telecon, which the microburst transmitter in Burton's office had automatically saved to a burst transmission file. His face reddened. The scenario was perfectly clear. If Burton didn't call within the hour, informing him of the intended exchange and asking for his guidance, Gerry would insure that Burton would be terribly sorry. He needed a plan that would satisfy all conditions to maintain his safety and complete the mission if possible. Simultaneous optimization of multiple related variables was known mathematically as a variational problem. Gerry was up to the task.

CHAPTER 98

CARMEN tossed in her bed. So much for the restful afternoon nap before the gig. She could not clear her mind. And neither hot tea nor Selena had helped. Rick was the man she wanted. The singular man who could move her. And his life was in jeopardy. What was she doing about it? Napping! Or trying to. Just as she turned anxiously and eyed the clock, for the dozenth time, the phone rang.

"Hello, Carmen. This is Reba. I hope you're well."

"As well as could be expected."

"I have an invitation for you. If you're up to it."

"Really."

"Sam's been a busy bee. Purchased two tickets for tonight's performance at the Lensic Theatre. Would you care to be my guest?"

"Thanks, Reba. You two go. I've got to work."

"Oh, but that's the point, I think. Sam doesn't want to go. He wants to stay in and rest. Get me and my singing out of the house."

"Hard to believe that."

"You don't know this, but he's recently been diagnosed with a recurrent heart condition. He had a minor heart attack last year. Doctor says a bigger one—maybe the big one—is looming."

"Oh, that's so sad. Can't something be done?"

"They think he needs surgery. But he has different ideas."

"Bless him. And, I'm sorry for you, too. Maybe I could skip out. We only do two sets on weekdays."

"Tonight's is a lovely program. Beethoven's *First Piano Concerto*," Reba said.

"Probably be cathartic." Carmen poked a nail to her lips. "Okay. It's a deal."

"See you at the Lensic's lobby at 6:45."

Carmen dreaded the call to T'Bird. She'd never bailed out twice on short notice before. He would understand, but it was not the height of team play.

RAIN SHEETED the picture window of T'Bird's condo. A continual bland palate of grey-blue abstract figures painted the glass. He was considering the art of weather when Carmen called. He listened, then interrupted, "Let me get this straight. Reba's husband has a bad heart and he's surfing the WEB buying tickets for her to go out in a storm to hear a concert while he sits home?"

"Maybe a little strange," Carmen said. "But these people are different. Interestingly enough, they seem to have a reasonable relationship."

"It's okay by me. I'll just play longer leads to keep the song count down."

"Pretend it's the 60's," Carmen said.

"We'll play *In a Gadda Da Vida*."

"That's a drum solo even Diego could do."

"Maybe— Okay, have a great time. I'll drop by tomorrow."

"Thanks, T'Bird. Got to go right now. Need to be at the Lensic *pukct lisch*."

T'Bird released the call and obsessed for two minutes. Suddenly, he popped up and grabbed his buckskin coat and car keys, before dashing into the elements.

SITTING AT HIS command console, Gerry used the burst transmitter in Burton's office to eavesdrop real-time on Burton's conversation with Rick. If only he could have tapped Burton's phone line. Burton was sure to echo the meeting place. Gerry would bet on it.

Listening to Burton's side of the call, hungry, Gerry waited patiently for him to repeat the meeting location. He did not. Bristling with anger, Gerry typed an urgent message to Burton, demanding immediate contact. No reply. Gerry grabbed his PDA; powered it up; enabled GPS tracking. Jerking open his top desk drawer, he removed the Sig and a cheap throw-down piece. He speed dialed Walter, using the Hamburg connection, as he raced from the workshop to the main house, stopping only briefly to arm the explosive charge connected to the intrusion system.

CHAPTER 99

Bᴌᴀᴄᴋ ᴍᴇsᴀ's summit appeared aglow from the burgeoning moon. Rick sat in Sam's car, appraising the sacred northern New Mexican precipice he had driven by on his way to work almost every day for months. This was truly the first time he'd seen it. A web of lightning crackled. The Mesa's modest size assumed ghostly proportions in the stark illumination. Fewer than two thousand feet of elevation, maybe a couple of football fields of clear area at the summit, those were Sam's 20-year-old recollections. To Rick, it looked liked like Everest on a bad weather day.

Rain ravaged San Ildefonso Pueblo on whose land the precipice stood. The Pueblo was a few scant miles down Route 4 from White Rock, yet worlds away. In Rick's judgment, a result of White Rock's overbearing. Frozen rain hammered Sam's car. All of the trails to the summit must be muddied, eroded, and treacherous, Rick assumed. Sam had advised him to ascend the western trail: a narrow, precipitous footpath with sufficient switch backs to enable a climb. For now, he was safe and dry inside Sam's car, summoning his courage. He extended his hand to Sam and said, "It's time."

"Sure you don't want me to stay?"

"Too risky," Rick replied, as a burst of hail splattered the windshield, causing him to twitch. Rick handed Sam the special cell phone. "Keep this handy. Its convoluted routing can't be traced. It's programmed with the package's phone as speed dial button one. When it answers, press one again to change the state of the attenuator."

"But what if he's not there?"

"It's designed so he has to re-energize the system for it to detonate. The attenuator can only transmit the beam after it achieves equilibrium. So when Gerry turns off the system to enter the workshop it will settle and when he leaves the workshop and re-energizes the system . . . kaboom."

"Uh-hum."

"Hopefully after his mission is foiled, he'll be out of here never to be heard from again. You can return the mini-pod and everything'll be ducky." Rick exhaled forcefully. "In any case, don't worry. I'll use a public phone to call and tell you where to pick me up." Trying to hide his anxiety, he teased, "Maybe we'll have enchiladas in Española, at the Rio Grande Cafe."

"Got the flashlight?"

Rick waved the vintage Rayovac, saying, "Wish it was a gun. Just in case."

Sam's chin sank to his chest. Grasping Rick's hand firmly and maintaining the grip, he said, "Be safe."

"From your lips to God's ears," Rick repeated one of Sam's phrases.

Suddenly, Sam threw his arms around Rick's neck. Sam sighed. There seemed to be something he desperately wanted to say, but couldn't. Rick waited; released the embrace; looked his friend in the eyes and said, "Me, too."

Rick exited the car, cramping cold in the dreary drizzle. He stood motionless, watching the taillights disappear into the turbulent night. Turning toward the angular shards of tuff, black and shiny, Rick took a step. He nearly slipped on the mangled ground. Regained his balance and then took another. Carefully he made his way to the mesa's western side. Perilous progress. Slippery rocks and soggy soil everywhere. Pulling at outgrowths of vegetation and scrubs, Rick ascended. The drizzle ceased after a short while, but the way was hard. Poor visibility, poorer footing. Another ten minutes, he was near the summit. The climb was taking longer than Sam had assessed.

Rick reached for an overhanging juniper branch to help pull himself to terra firma. The flashlight dropped on a rock with a clank. Skittered down into a thicket. No great loss, Rick thought, glimpsing the summit, dimly illuminated by moonlight. A contentious clearing: craggy surface, dotted with coniferous trees; thick scrub vegetation; and gnarled exposed roots. Sharp projections of steely tuff abounded. Just enough visibility for tricks and shenanigans. Rick mounted the plateau. He pulled back his coat sleeve to check the time. Burton would be arriving soon. He needed to develop a position strategy fast.

"Quick trip up, given the conditions, and taking the wrong route," Burton said.

Rick froze. He saw his adversary, shrouded in pale moonlight. Burton switched a yellowish flashlight beam across the ground as he approached. How had he had time to—

"Cat got your tongue? " Burton asked.

"No. Catching my breath," Rick replied. "Not much of a night to be wasting time on the side of a mountain." Burton's black trench coat, fur felt fedora, and dark gloves came into view. Was he channeling a gangster from a bad noir film?

"I never waste time."

Rick ignored the braggadocio. Burton looked exactly like the comic character that Gerry had months ago generated and disseminated from Rick's classified computing account. Just one of the impressive array of security violations pinned on him by Gerry and the Feynman friends. Recalling the character, Rick grinned. If Burton were wearing nothing but fish net stockings under that coat, his pudd must be shriveled like an inch worm. And frozen!

"Think that's funny?" Burton snapped.

Rick ate the grin. Dread returned, quick as it had fled. Nervous and cold, Rick stuffed his hands inside his coat pockets, thrusting his fingers deep into Sunflower's warm jalapeño cornmeal.

"Don't do it," Burton shouted. He yanked an antiquated pistol from his coat.

"Hey! Use that thing and you're toast. We both want out of this, right?"

Burton extended a gloved hand. "Give me the plates. Now where'd you get 'em?"

"Put that thing away, first. Before you do something stupid with it."

"Something stupid, like blow your head off? Everyone knows you're panicked, suicidal. Now give me the stuff. And I know where you got it." Burton scowled. He narrowed his beady eyes, saying, "He'll be dealt with."

Rick got the suicide setup. So, now what? If the darkness of the night seemed both a blessing and a curse, then the rainfall that recommenced was another mixed blessing. "Of course, there's backup copies. Just to keep you honest, in case you forget."

Rick was buying time. Burton's slippery hands, good; his slippery feet, bad. If he could sprint to the mesa's edge—maybe six giant strides—and jump, the scrubs below might break his fall. Rick unobtrusively rubbed his foot against the ground assessing traction. Wet grit. Wet grass. If he didn't act fast, his ass was going to be grass. "Jump!" Rick told himself. "At least Burton will have a hell of a time finding and shooting you."

Burton stepped closer. The pistol's muzzle was now no more than a couple of feet from Rick's chest. The finger's of Burton's outstretched hand jiggled, like a kid begging candy. His grin contorted into a demonic, possessed visage.

Rick slowly pulled the envelope from inside his coat. Extended it toward Burton's wiggling fingers. Burton yanked it away and stiffened his shooting arm.

"Want these?" Rick blurted.

"What?"

Rick reached down into his coat's outer pocket and with a flick of the wrist, sprayed a handful of jalapeño cornmeal into Burton's face. Rick darted for the mesa's edge, but having gone just a few feet, he tripped on a cord-like length of exposed juniper root. Rick fell hard. His hip burned.

A shard of tuff knifed Rick's side where he lay in a puddle of mud. His hip ached as though it had splintered into a million pieces. The pain was nearly blinding, deafening. He turned and saw Burton's mouth moving. His face was flush with agitation and mottled with cornmeal. Burton stood over Rick grimacing, wiping his burning eyes.

Burton trained the revolver on Rick's head. Point-blank range. From behind Burton, from out of the blackness, an enormous being, clad in traditional Native American dress and with bizarre markings on his face, silently approached. Rick tried not to stare, to tip off Burton. His savior had appeared.

When Rick began to smile, Burton looked queerly at him. Then he pursed his lips, again stiffening his shooting arm.

The stone bashed into the back of Burton's head. Rick heard the thud. Burton fell prostrate; he lay motionless.

Rick crumpled to the ground for an instant. He regained his composure and looked up at the man-God. Sunflower's Mountain Spirits? Disbelieving, Rick asked, "Did Sunflower send you?"

"You know my wife?" the man asked.

"You're Big John!" Rick forced himself to stand. In the dimness of moonlight, he saw Burton struggling to his feet. His pistol was trained on Big John's back. "Nooo," Rick screamed, lunging. A single shot fired—

Rick felled Burton, impaling him on an exposed tuff shard. Blood pooled underneath Burton's back; a dribble of blood trickled from his mouth. Rick stood, wiping his soiled hand on his coat, staring down in disgust at Burton. He turned to Big John, hoping to find solace in his knowing eyes, but he was sprawled facedown on the mesa.

CHAPTER 100

TEPID TEA was of no interest to Sam. He released his cup in favor of caressing the big book that he had just put down. Agitated and restless, neither the triumphs of Wallenberg nor his own personal triumph of self disclosure satisfied him now. Rick's fate hung in the balance on that god-forsaken mesa. What the hell was he doing to help? Nothing. It sickened him. Sam burned to be in the fray.

How far he had come in such a short time, Sam considered. It'd been exhausting. Yet, the sea change was insufficient to satisfy his newfound desire to right wrongs, obliterate inequities. Reba's reaction had been difficult. She, more than he, had been held fast by age-old shackles. Would their relationship be unbearably strained? Sam's head and heart ached. A millstone seemed to crush his already tight chest.

A knock at the front door startled Sam. He padded over and cautiously looked through the peep hole. A strapping young Native American man stood there drenched. The man glanced furtively side-to-side. Sam backed away, sensing a blood pressure spike. He cowered. Glimpsed his frail frame in the entryway mirror. And then, Sam straightened his posture, charged the door, and flung it open. He asked, "Can I help you?"

"My name is T'Bird. I'm a friend of Carmen's and Rick's. Is he here?"

"Uh . . . well, no. He's not. Do you want to come inside?"

"You're Sam, right."

"Yes, Sam Smith." Sam extended his hand. T'Bird's shake was awkward. Sam sensed his anxiety.

"Look, Sam. I know you don't know me. I've heard good things about you from Carmen. And I know that Rick's been staying here. But something's wrong. And I may be able to help. Please tell me where he is."

"If you just come in a minute," Sam gestured, "we can talk about it."

"No time for talk. I know Rick's in danger and I feel my father is, too."

Sam stood quiet, watching the massive young man whose eyes shut as they began to water.

Sam asked, "Your father, you say?"

"He, he uh . . . ."

Sam read torture on T'Bird's face. Somehow, Sam believed he perfectly understood the feeling.

"He goes to the mountains to pray," T'Bird stammered. "I believe he and Rick are both in danger."

Sam stood silent.

"Please, tell me what you know. I have to see my father before he—"

"Black Mesa. You know the place?"

"Thanks," T'Bird said, turning and running for his car.

Sam brushed tears from his eyes as he closed the door. He had been correct. He understood exactly how T'Bird felt. Hopefully T'Bird would have that moment with his father. A moment that Sam had been denied.

RICK SAT on the ground, pelted by rain and hail. In his arms he held Big John, whose back had been drilled by Burton's shot. Big John's forehead burned. Rick applied frozen clumps to cool it. How could he get Big John down the mesa without injuring him further? Mind in overdrive, Rick heard nothing until a man stood before him in the clearing. "T'Bird!" Rick cried.

T'Bird did not speak. Swiftly he approached, and knelt beside Big John. Feeling Big John's pulse, T'Bird's furrowed brow creased deeper.

Rick watched, curious, as T'Bird darted to the edge of the clearing, pulling back branches, looking intently behind scrubs, large rocks. T'Bird bounded to Rick and said, "Over there."

"What?"

"The ceremonial site," T'Bird said. "Help me move him. I got his torso."

Big John groaned when they lifted him.

Rick winced. Drew a breath only when they had successfully laid Big John behind a large juniper at the margin of a rock ring, whose small fire had long been doused. T'Bird sat on the ground and cradled his father's head. To Rick's amazement, Big John tried to sit upright, but T'Bird restrained him. Big John pointed toward a small rock shrine in the center of the circle. A huge ebony feather shown in the moonlight. It was secured by rawhide lashing. Simple, yet majestic, Rick thought. The largest feather he had ever seen. T'Bird's face fell as he studied the plume. Rick reckoned T'Bird's expression incredulity and pain. Only then, Rick recognized that feather was much more than just a feather.

Big John shivered. Rick went back to the clearing to retrieve his coat, with which he had covered him. A sense of finality came over Rick, picking up the coat. It would be used for something else when he returned to Big John.

Rick turned toward the clearing's edge and hesitated. Rain had already erased his tracks. Where was Big John? Scanning the clearing, Rick heard a familiar voice.

"Going somewhere?"

Rick snapped around. His jaw slacked at the sight of Gerry, dressed all in black, silencer-equipped pistol in hand.

Rick's eyes darted toward Gavin's gun.

"You'll be sorry," Gerry said, glancing down at Burton.

"It was his fault," Rick said. "I didn't want to do it."

Gerry advanced to Burton's body. Stood back, extending his foot for a couple of quick kicks to the ribs. Nothing. Looking askance at the bloody pool surrounding the corpse, Gerry said, "No subtlety."

Rick quivered from cold and dread. Why put on his sodden coat? This could be his end. But how did Gerry know the meeting place. Rick blurted out, "How could you know were're here? Burton's phone is encrypted."

"So thick you never figured out who was running this show." Gerry bumped Burton's corpse once more. "He was only the face. And what's this?"

Rick watched Gerry bend down to Burton, where he recovered the envelope that Rick had brought, now rain soaked. Unbuttoning Burton's coat without a flinch and guarding Rick, Gerry slipped out Burton's, larger, blood-soaked envelope.

Gerry shook his head thoughtfully. "So fucking stupid. He actually brought the evidence." He added, "He was nothing without me."

Rick's eyes darted everywhere. This time, there was nowhere to run.

Gerry's expression turned baleful. "Burton," he said, "didn't understand that you never get all of the evidence. You can only eliminate those who have it." He focused alternately on Rick and the clearing.

Rick's dread doubled. "This won't work, Gerry. If you kill me, they'll . . . they'll hunt you down." He gestured toward the envelopes. "It's all there, I swear. All the evidence. You're free. Leave America if you hate it so much."

"Now you're getting smart," Gerry said. "But it's too late for you." He waved Rick nearer Burton's body. "See, you have so much remorse for killing this shit bag, you decided to take your own life with his gun."

Rick couldn't believe it. Everybody and their mother wanted to kill him and make it look like suicide. Gerry clutched Burton's .45. Rick wanted to yell out for T'Bird. But he had no gun. Why get both of them killed? Gerry was too sinister, too capable to be subdued, even by the strongest man without a weapon.

Gerry demanded, "Open your mouth." His evil eyes pierced their target as the .45 rose to Rick's face.

Rick sealed his lips. He widened his eyes, locking onto Gerry's in defiance.

CHAPTER 101

Reba squirmed in her plush seat in Santa Fe's Lensic Theatre. The setting was elegant, the music wonderful, yet she strained to appreciate the masterpiece being expertly performed. Of the three cadenzas Beethoven wrote for the first movement of his *First Piano Concerto*, the most ornate and difficult by far—and, of course, the one that the maestro, himself, had performed—was the third. This young pianist's deft touch engaged her for a moment. He was playing the third cadenza, and brilliantly. Half way through it, she glanced at her watch. Her thoughts were where she had decided her presence should be, at home with Sam.

Of all the trials of a lifetime, and there had been more than a few, why had this cliff presented itself now? They had raised a family together, shared more quiet-time in their modest home than most couples could stand, and in general, grown old, a bit early she had to acknowledge, together. All never having slept on bad feelings a single night. Yet she felt insecure regarding her position as Matriarch of the family. A shift of power? No. A change in the balance of influence? Definitely.

She had never attempted to overpower Sam. But he had been more than amenable to her cool-headed sense of reason. And lately, the same conservative rudder that had influenced the family's development and its low profile existence of accomplishment, humility, and religious practice had been blamed for the estrangement of their children and grandsons. An uphill battle ahead? What she wanted most was to continue her life with Sam. Secretly, Reba feared that without him, her existence would be meaningless.

Reba reached into her purse for a tissue. Carmen whispered, "Have another?"

Both women sat blotting their eyes as the orchestra and soloist achieved ethereal heights and hellish depths in the second movement. The piece's deliberate pacing and weighty musical themes produced an introspective mood throughout the hall. And during the quiet of a profound *pianissimo* passage, a woman sitting beside Reba remarked rapturously, "It's so very moving. Reminds me of a Requiem." Reba thrust her nose deeper into the tissue as a torrent ensued.

CHAPTER 102

"DROP IT, Alexei or you're dead," a man shouted from behind Gerry.

Rick remained perfectly still. He didn't need to squint through the dimness to identify that grating voice. Finally, he saw Walter training a service revolver on Gerry.

"It's over. Drop it. Now!"

To Rick's amazement, Gerry did as instructed. The dimple of satisfaction melted away. Gerry's face was calm, as blank as a sleeping child's. This was too weird. Rick shuddered from the cold. He saw Gerry's eyes panning, his head followed.

"Uh uh," Walter cautioned. "Don't turn around." Walter glanced down at Burton. "So, it was him all along. Slick operation you two had going. One for the manuals."

Rick saw Gerry's elbows move. His gloved fingers twitched. "There's another gun, Walter." Rick said.

"Probably two. And a knife, poison dart . . . what else Alexei? You told me to come prepared for the worst. I'm confident you did, too."

Walter stepped closer. No longer Walter the buffoon, he moved carefully, methodically. His revolver never wavered.

"Time's running out," Walter said. "Hands behind your back. Real slooow like."

Gerry cut his eyes right, turned slightly. Rick thought he must be trying to determine Walter's exact location. Rick's heart raced. The lump in his throat felt as big as an apple.

"My shoulder's hurt," Gerry said, his hands continuing to twitch.

"This doesn't have to be the end," Walter said. "I'm Agency. But the Bureau is on its way."

"You're bluffing," Gerry said. "You don't know shit."

"You can drop the German accent anytime. I've followed your case for five years. I know as much about you and your sick life over the past few decades as anyone could."

Rick couldn't believe his ears or eyes. Walter, a CIA agent? A few things made more sense suddenly. Who was always hanging around observing when others were actually breaking the law. Who was the single person to annoy Gerry, even to challenge him recently when fearful for Rick's safety? Who understood the stakes when he encouraged Rick to remain calm. Who knew, right from the start, that Rick was a pawn in a deadly international espionage chess game?

Rick rubbed his neck. A respite from rain, ice. No reprieve from the bone chilling cold. The good news: he was alive and apparently going to stay that way. Walter had nothing serious on him. And since Walter seemed to know everything, he knew that Rick hadn't been an assassin. Rick finally drew an easy breath.

So many questions invaded Rick's mind. If Walter cared about Rick's fate, why had he inveigled him into the Feynman friends? He knew that Rick eventually was headed for a confrontation or other deadly dilemma, just like this one. Rick's lungs began to constrict. It wasn't asthma; it was fear.

If Walter kept Rick in the game, ultimately Rick would lead him to the Lab's deep cover mole, a victory for the CIA. Walter was also clever enough to figure that Gerry's survival instincts and training would insure him a handsome trading piece in the CIA's game of *I spy*. So when Walter yanked Gerry out of the game, Rick would be left holding the bag. That son-of-a-bitch. Rick prepared to scream it to him, but Walter spoke first.

"Here's the deal," Walter croaked, approaching Gerry. He held long, plastic wire ties in his short, fat fingers. "I can guarantee you that by this time tomorrow you'll be traded to your employer in P'yongyang for one of our guys."

Gerry shifted his weight.

Walter jumped back. He cocked the revolver's hammer. "I can save you or axe you. But unless you want to end up in the chamber or spend the rest your life in the big house, you gotta cooperate. And we gotta get the hell out of here."

Rick nearly burst when Gerry nodded. And when the rasp of cinching the *cuffs* extra-tight broke the stillness, Rick's dread heightened. Walter assumed Rick was in deep enough trouble with the FBI, Walter's apparent adversaries, that no one would believe anything Rick said. Certainly the CIA would never corroborate this. Rick's blood, previously near boiling, now ran slack in his slack veins. He nearly fainted.

"Who knows your little story?" Gerry asked in a Russianesque drone.

"Just Agency. No common intel holdings with the Bureau, who are on the way."

"If they don't know, why are they here?" Gerry asked.

"Tailed your pal T'Bird."

"I could break his neck like a twig," Gerry said, eyes darting.

Hands clasped behind his back, Gerry was stoic as Walter relieved him of a throw-away piece, lodged in an ankle holster, and stiletto switchblade, shoved up his sleeve. Walter produced two black ponchos from under his coat. FBI was printed on the front and back in large yellow block letters. Dressed in the simple disguises, Walter said, "They're on the north side. Go this way." He yanked his head and Gerry lurched forward.

"Where the hell you taking him?" Rick screamed. "Walter, you son-of-a bitch, he's my alibi. He set me up. He did everything!"

"Tell the Feds," Walter sneered, vanishing with Gerry down the eastern slope.

CHAPTER 103

RICK stood bewildered. As hail began to pelt the mesa, he wondered, what now? A moment later, he saw a half-dozen potbellied men in drenched black ponchos and soft-soled wing-tipped shoes enter the clearing. They choked and gasped for breath, flashlights waving, guns drawn.

"Hands up," one of them bellowed to Rick, leveling his handgun at him. Others stole glimpses of Burton and shielded their eyes from the hail. An agent placed Burton's pistol in a plastic bag. Agent Sarkowski wheezed for breath. His face was candy-apple red again as he strode up to Rick, steel handcuffs glinting in his halogen flashlight. Sarkowski began to chant, "You have the right to remain silent . . . ." When he stopped for an instant to wipe moisture from his pudgy face, Rick darted forward and leapt off the mesa's western edge. A shot fired. He hit gnarly scrub, before rolling over roots and bashing into rocks. Rick came to rest in a shallow ravine. He jumped up, his hip burning like a brand, and ran pell-mell down hill, sloshing and skidding all the way.

QUIET ENSUED on the mesa top. With all of the agents in hot pursuit of Rick, only the occasional splatter of hail on the craggy summit disrupted the silence. T'Bird surveyed the clearing before securing the Thunderbird's feather, the symbol of his returned birthright. With near superhuman strength, he cradled his father's body in his arms. Heart to heart, they descended the treacherous southern trail. T'Bird seemed to float above the rocks and snares. Once down to his vehicle, T'Bird gently laid Big John on a worn buckskin, draped over the front seat. Lights off, they crept onto the main road.

CHAPTER 104

Step-by-step, Gerry wended his way down the precipitous eastern trail until he heard a radio squawk. He understood the word 'escape' and halted. Walter's revolver jabbed his back. Sotto voce, Gerry said, "The Feds."

"Get down," Walter whispered.

Gerry wondered how those moronic cops determined so quickly that they had escaped? There was no evidence. Certainly no footprints. He crouched low, hoping for more info to be broadcast on the old fashioned walkie talkie radios. Another squawk, unintelligible. Walter fidgeted. Cramping, Gerry thought. The terrain was steep, slick. Gerry had dug in his heels to sit steadily. His thighs burned, as if in a bike race. But much more than his masculine dominance was on the line now.

After a flurry of activity below, the squawking ceased. Walter shifted his weight again. The pistol's muzzle no longer indented Gerry's back. He knew exactly what to do. Maintaining his head and torso as still as possible, he lowered his shoulders, stretched his arms downward to the ground behind him. Raised one foot, slipped the plastic cuff underneath it. Steady. Balance. Silently he transferred his full weight back onto the lifted foot, simultaneously lifting the other. A simple maneuver—*sissonne,* without the jump— at whose conclusion, Gerry's hands rested in his lap. He relaxed his mind. The calm before the storm.

Walter grunted to proceed down. He stood and stretched. With one powerful movement, Gerry reached around and grabbed Walter's leg and slid him downhill on his back. Walter jerked to a stop. Gerry could see his face in the moonlight. He read Walter's thoughts: surprise at his fall and the loss of his pistol; horror at finding Gerry's cuffs biting into his throat, secured under his jaw bone; recognition of his imminent death.

Gerry's feet found Walter's shoulders, his thighs flexed downward as his arms, muscles angrily rippling, hauled back on the cuffs. Gerry pulled ever harder, flung back his head, neck muscles straining. He see-sawed the cuffs' serrate edges until a burst of warm blood sprayed his leg and the terrain. Steam rose through the frigid air with each blood gush. Gerry observed that the waxing moon had drifted overhead. It was tranquilizing. At that instant, he believed it radiated just for him. He hardly noticed that Walter's flailing and floundering had ceased. Paid no attention to the warmth of the blood that bathed his lower body or the gore that soiled his hands. It was an important, but messy, job. He was reassured that someone capable was executing it.

Gerry stood above Walter, appraising him: body stationary in a muck of blood, mud, and gore; throat gaped open, crimson flesh exuding; head at an impossible angle to his torso. Suicide? Hunting accident? Petty theft gone wrong? None of the above. Clearly, this was murder. Sighing, using a blade concealed in his belt buckle, Gerry severed the plastic cuffs. He cursorily massaged his wrists, noticing that Walter's thrashing had created a perfect mud—blood—angel. Gerry believed that he, himself, was an angel, of sorts. And there was more angelic work to do.

CHAPTER 105

S AM LABORED to rest himself. Exhausted from pacing the floor, he tossed in his bed. He picked from his bedside table a chronicle of Henryk Slawik's exploits in Nazi-occupied Poland. Sam was coming to identify, if ever so slightly, with these heroic men. He imagined being a real *mensch*. Liked the idea. Otherwise, everything annoyed him. The dimness of the bedside light; his cold feet.

Sam wondered what in blazes was taking Rick so long? Had T'Bird made it in time? His nerves raw, Sam heard the creak of the rain-swollen kitchen door. At least Reba was home now.

"Darling, I'm in here," Sam called out feebly. "In the bedroom." A quick glance at the bedside clock. It was too early for her to return. Had the performance been cancelled as a result of the inclement weather?

Silence.

His face smothered by the book, Sam could feel the penetration of a stare. Slowly he relaxed the volume to his lap. "So, you've come at last."

"Don't get too worked up," Gerry said, inching forward. "Remember your heart condition. Stress could trigger a massive attack."

Meeting Gerry eye-to-eye, Sam said, "You'll burn eternally."

"But not for a while yet."

"Don't be so sure." Sam jerked Rick's 9 mm from under the covers. Gerry stood at the bed's foot. He waited.

Sam leveled the pistol, saying, "I'm sending you to hell right now."

"Go on, shoot. You think what I do is so easy. Just try it."

Sam aimed the firearm at Gerry's heart. His hand quivered. He paused. It was another place, another time. A place where his guts flipped and flopped. A time when he feared peeping his head out his door, much less up into the fray. All of the programming of his past told him to run, hide. Save himself at any cost.

The dimpled chin jutted out from the cruel chiseled face. Gerry took another step toward him. His chest thrust out like some kind of goddamn superhero. It was an abomination. Sam's fingers blanched on the pistol's grip. All he had to do, he told himself, was to pull the trigger.

Gerry grabbed the bed covers and shook them toward Sam. When Gerry lunged forward, Sam squeezed the trigger. The round struck Gerry's torso, knocking him backward. He crashed to the floor.

Sam's hands quaked. His chest heaved. Had he really taken a human life? The jiggling weapon hit the bed with a poof. This was not the sweet moment of revenge of which he had dreamt. Sam felt dirty. Once again, he was bathed in shame. He bowed his head and closed his eyes.

Roaring like a demon straight from hell, bent on Sam's destruction, Gerry sprang onto the bed. Sam was stunned, horror-struck. He grabbed the gun. The barrel burned his hand. He threw it at Gerry's head. It smacked the far wall and hit the floor.

Gerry grabbed Sam's pillow from underneath his head. Sam fought hard, jabbing at Gerry's eyes, punching his armored chest. Once atop Sam, Gerry forced the pillow over his face. Crushed it down. Held Sam there, flailing and gasping.

RICK SLAMMED himself against the front door, splitting the frame as though it were balsa. Racing down the constrictive hallway, following the feeble wedge of light, he entered Sam's bedroom. Rick growled a deep, primal groan. Gerry turned. Rick shouted as he lunged headlong into Gerry, knocking him to the floor. Rick seized upon him, mauling Gerry's face and landing blow after blow to his lead-like chest.

Gerry flipped like an Olympic acrobat, expelling Rick backward to the floor. Sprang over Rick and maneuvered him into a neck-crushing headlock. Rick's eyes bulged. Gerry's teeth grit. Gerry's brawny arms applied spinal-cord-crushing force to Rick's neck. He jostled Rick's head side-to-side.

Rick saw a pistol on the floor. A gash arced across its barrel. It was his 9 mm. Sam had taken it. Rick purchased it in desperation and was now going to use it exactly as planned: to blow Gerry's head off his bulky shoulders.

Rick grabbed the pistol by its warm barrel. It definitely works, he thought, recalling loading a single chamber test round, which he never fired. And then it hit him with the energy of an exploding sun . . . the magazine was empty. But the time was now. With all his strength, Rick bashed Gerry in the back of his head, using the pistol's grip. Gerry loosened the headlock. Rick continued his mangling assault, manically crushing Gerry's skull. His blood ran warm and thick down Rick's hand and arm as a cinema of Rick's recent torments played in his brain. He gripped the barrel tighter, preparing for the final blow.

"Don't move, Adams!" Agent Sarkowski yelled. His cherubic face shone with contempt; his skin color more fire engine than candy-apple, now. His service revolver was pointed at Rick's head.

"Easy does it," Rick said, dropping the weapon and extending his arms upward, bloody hands dangling. The rage in Sarkowski's eyes suggested that he might take some pleasure in offing him.

"You are under—"

"I'm not a killer," Rick interrupted, unwedging himself from Gerry. "It's him." Rick nodded to Gerry, who lay motionless, eyes shut.

"Hands against the wall. Feet back. Spread'em, asshole." Sarkowski patted Rick down with one hand. "Hands behind your back."

When the cuff clicked on one of Rick's wrists, a deafening crash and the spray of glass shards found both men ducking for cover. Rick looked up to see Gerry's silhouette outside the house, making for the hedge. Sarkowski ran to the window and thrust out his head. He fired warning shots and screamed for Agent Jackson.

Sam groaned. Rick dived to his bedside and knelt. In his trembling hand, Sam held the special cell. He depressed the one button and fell limp. His hands gory, Rick lifted Sam's head. He felt the weakness of his pulse. Sam was almost gone.

"Hands behind your back, Adams," Sarkowski barked.

Rick could hear the faint ringing of the triggering cell phone from his special phone, now resting on the bed. He listened.

"Now, Adams!"

Rick felt a bolt of pain shoot the length of his spine as Sarkowski's boot heel dug into the soft flesh of his back. Searing pain. Still, Rick listened.

"I'm not telling you—"

The phone answered. Rick was deaf to the world. He thrust out his hand and mashed the number one. The bomb's trigger was set. Once Gerry exited his workshop, *hasta la vista*.

Rick felt a dull blow to his skull and nothing else, until regaining consciousness in the back of Agent Jackson's suv. His head resounded, watching paramedics hustle about, seeing Sam on a stretcher, and the flashing ambulance lights. As Jackson tried to pull from the driveway, Reba and Carmen blocked their egress. Rick's heart melted when Carmen flung open her door and rushed to the suv. She pressed her hand to the glass, but Rick's were shackled. He could only stare at the pained expression on her face. He felt nothing. Even his head had ceased to throb. He had become comfortably numb.

As the suv pulled onto the roadway, Carmen blew a succession of kisses to Rick, before taking her cell phone from her purse. He watched with bemusement as she dialed, wondering if she really thought that T'Bird could help him now.

CHAPTER 106

Rᴵᴄᴋ, T'Bird, Agent Jackson, and a New Mexico State Police officer made their way up the service elevator of St. Vincent's Hospital's Cardiac Care Unit. It was well before morning visiting hours. Rick's hands were manacled underneath his coat, which was draped over his shoulders like a cape. Jackson entered Sam's room alone, a sheaf of papers and his ubiquitous pad and pen in hand. For Rick and T'Bird, conversation was short, standing outside Sam's room, under the officer's watchful eye. The morbid quiet of the halls was interrupted only by intermittent squawks from the Officer's radio. Rick felt as though he'd descended to a hotter part of hell.

Down the hall, Sarkowski and a well-dressed man in his fifties carrying a briefcase, whom Rick had seen but couldn't place, strode toward them. Rick found Sarkowski's demeanor less cheery than usual. Hard to believe. The men approached and Sarkowski extended his hand, in which he held a handcuff key. A grin erupted on Rick's face as he turned around. The cuffs unlocked with a jangle. Rick held his coat under his arm and grasped his wrists.

"Mr. Adams, I'm Scott McLaughlin, your attorney." He extended his hand. Rick's head listed.

"Ms. Carmen Cdebaca contacted me and expressed your desire for my representation. I have secured your temporary release."

Rick's arched eye caught Sarkowskis's glower. It was a beautiful moment.

Jackson burst out of Sam's room. He surveyed the group and asked, "What's going on here?"

Sarkowski whined, "Lawyer McLaughlin here, got a get-out-of-jail-free card for this one," he nodded toward Rick, "from Judge Garcia."

Jackson nodded before stuffing his small notepad into his shirt pocket. In his other hand, he held the papers. "Adams, I guess it's your lucky day."

Rick glanced to T'Bird and said, "Yeah, real lucky."

"But neither of you are leaving here until you sign these non-disclosure agreements. One of you declines; we'll wait until he doesn't." Jackson jabbed paper and a pen toward Rick.

"Wait just a minute," Rick retorted.

Sarkowski dangled the cuffs gleefully.

"What's it say?" T'Bird asked.

"None of this ever happened. If you ever say it did, you could be prosecuted under the Sedition Act."

"I'd better take a look at those," McLaughlin said.

While McLaughlin perused the documents, the silence was broken by the crackle of the police radio. A gruff, harried dispatcher announced an all units alert for Santa Fe County. A devastating explosion on Old Spur Road had ruptured gas and power lines, the man said. The Officer killed the volume and eyed Jackson, who nodded. The Officer rushed down the hall toward the exit.

When Mc Laughlin and the Agents huddled together, Rick and T'Bird entered Sam's room. Rick said, "Sam, you've got enough tubes and monitoring wires to be an astronaut." He smiled. "What did you tell them?"

"The truth."

Rick rubbed his wrists again.

"It apparently set you free."

"For the moment." Rick hesitated before saying, "There's been a horrific explosion on Old Spur Road. Some kind of gas leak or something—"

He and Sam shared a solemn glance, both recognizing that winning sometimes feels like losing. But when nuclear proliferation to every terrorist group imaginable is at stake, the emptiness of taking a life must be endured.

T'Bird said, "Sam, you don't look bad for a pistol-packing physicist."

"You might consider me a bad influence in that regard," he replied.

They all laughed.

"Soon, you'll be back at the Lab," Rick said. "All of this'll be ancient history."

"We'll see about that," Sam said.

Rick believed that they both recognized the Lab was soon to be out of the nuclear weapons business. The question was what kind of meaningful business could be conducted on the Hill.

Sam said, "Clearly, the Lab's mission must evolve. There's a wealth of technical expertise and, though it may be hard to believe, viable managerial talent up there." His hands drew up, stretching out the nitro-drip tubing. "Step one is to re-brand the place."

"Not so feisty," Rick teased.

Sam relaxed his body, but continued his spiel. "The new direction must be envisioned and carried forward by the staff. DC can't legislate a better or more productive work environment. Some politicos will probably move to shutter the place after this mess breaks. Even the white-washed version they'll tell the media."

"So?" Rick asked.

"We require science that benefits mankind and the earth. And we need it now." His eyes sparkled. "I may not lead the charge, but I'll be a solid contributor." He smiled, adding, "Think green!"

"Hallelujah," Rick lampooned, cutting his eyes to T'Bird.

"So, that leaves you," Sam said. "What'll you do now, Rick?"

His halting reply was halted completely by Carmen and Reba's entry.

Carmen cried, "Oh, Ricky." She burst across the room and threw her arms around him. "We've been waiting for hours. Oh God, I've been worried sick. I love you so much." Showered his dingy face with feathery kisses.

Rick nodded to Reba, who moved quickly to Sam's bedside. She grasped his feeble hand to her lips.

Carmen interlaced her arms with Rick's and T'Bird's. Tears streamed down her cheeks. Rick's eyes welled with gladness. Carmen dashed to give Sam a quick kiss. Rick could've sworn he blushed.

"You're just in time to hear Rick's plan," Sam said, winking at her.

"He's headed on the road!" Carmen enthused. "As the drummer and chief gas dynamics guru for the best Tejano touring act since Selena."

Rick was taken aback. He flashed a nervous glance at her.

"If he's up for it," she hedged.

"Sounds like the chance of a lifetime," Sam said.

Rick threw up his hands, nodding consent. Carmen screeched and ran back to his side, fiercely hugging him.

Rick looked over to T'Bird. "We'll need a first rate guitarist."

"José Maria's your man," he replied.

"T'Bird was never into Tejano much," Carmen said. "Besides, you need a Spanish guitar for that." She batted her doe eyes at T'Bird. His expression said it all.

"Well then," Rick said. "We've got everything we need for now." He hugged Carmen. "The rest we'll just have to grow, one day at a time."

Sam looked at Reba. He said, "Amen to that."

Rick drew Carmen closer. Her soft skin and silk blouse quelled his mind just long enough for him to take an easy breath. Would it be possible for him to forget the misadventures that lay behind him? He had no doubts, given the adventures that lay ahead for them.

THE END